PRIZE STORIES 1987
The O. Henry Awards

PRIZE STORIES 1987

The O. Henry Awards

EDITED AND WITH
AN INTRODUCTION
BY WILLIAM ABRAHAMS

DOUBLEDAY & COMPANY, INC.
GARDEN CITY, NEW YORK
1987

The Library of Congress has cataloged this work
   as follows:
Prize stories. 1947–
      Garden City, N.Y., Doubleday.
         v.   22 cm.
      Annual.
      The O. Henry awards.
      None published 1952–53.
      Continues: O. Henry memorial award prize stories.
      Key title: Prize stories, ISSN 0079-5453.
      1. Short stories, American—Collected works.
PZ1.011   813'.01'08—dc19   21–9372
                                        MARC-S
Library of Congress   [8402r83]rev4

Library of Congress Catalog in Publication Data

ISBN 0-385-23594-1

CONTENTS

vi   *Contents*

PUBLISHER'S NOTE

This volume is the sixty-seventh in the O. Henry Memorial Award series.

In 1918, the Society of Arts and Sciences met to vote upon a monument to the master of the short story, O. Henry. They decided that this memorial should be in the form of two prizes for the best short stories published by American authors in American magazines during the year 1919. From this beginning, the memorial developed into an annual anthology of outstanding short stories by American authors, published, with the exception of the years 1952 and 1953, by Doubleday & Company, Inc.

Blanche Colton Williams, one of the founders of the awards, was editor from 1919 to 1932; Harry Hansen from 1933 to 1940; Herschel Brickell from 1941 to 1951. The annual collection did not appear in 1952 and 1953, when the continuity of the series was interrupted by the death of Herschel Brickell. Paul Engle was editor from 1954 to 1959 with Hanson Martin co-editor in the years 1954 to 1960; Mary Stegner in 1960; Richard Poirier from 1961 to 1966, with assistance from and co-editorship with William Abrahams from 1964 to 1966. William Abrahams became editor of the series in 1967.

In 1970 Doubleday published under Mr. Abrahams' editorship *Fifty Years of the American Short Story,* and in 1981, *Prize Stories of the Seventies.* Both are collections of stories selected from this series.

The stories chosen for this volume were published in the period from the summer of 1985 to the summer of 1986. A list of the magazines consulted appears at the back of the book. The choice of stories and the selection of prize winners are exclusively the responsibility of the editor. Biographical material is based on information provided by the contributors and obtained from standard works of reference.

INTRODUCTION

Two decades—from *Prize Stories 1967* to *Prize Stories 1987*—comprise a period of time long enough to justify one's making generalizations and taking retrospective views. Ordinarily this is just the sort of thing I have attempted to avoid in introducing each year's stories; too often the wisdom of one year contradicts the wisdom of the year before, or becomes the cliché of the next. Still, arriving at the twenty-first collection for which I have had editorial responsibility, I think it would be overly cautious not to state what I believe to be true, that the 400 stories that have appeared in the twenty-one collections represent a creative achievement of a rare order. Several of these stories, going back to the end of the 1960s and the 1970s, are on their way to classic stature, and one can predict as much for others more recent. The vitality and variety are unflagging.

Indeed, it is the variety—many forms, many voices, many attitudes and intentions—that accounts for the sense one has of an irrepressible vitality. As we know from its long history, there is no one prescribed mold for the story—that, surely, is one of its attractions to writers and readers alike. Each story written for its own sake, because its author feels it must be written *thus,* rather than in response to some condition imposed from without, becomes a kind of adventure or exploration: one listens for an individual voice, the mark of authenticity.

Fashion is something apart from this, though it is convenient and traditional to assign writers to schools, movements, and tendencies. New writers, especially, have been known to cluster together for comfort and attention. But no matter under which rubric they may write—as "new" this-that-or-the-other—in the end it is the story itself that matters, and if it is good enough, if it is its own story, it will survive the fashionable moment.

Influence, however, is something very different, and should not be confused with fashion. Consciously or not, there is no writer who has not been influenced by writers who came before. In the simple act of writing a story each new writer joins a continuum that extends from the present back to the beginnings of language and that first primitive need to tell someone about something that happened. But it is not necessary, nor especially enlightening, to establish a prehistoric lineage for the story; it is sufficient to acknowledge that the masters of this century—James, Chekhov, Joyce, Mansfield, Lawrence, Hemingway—are felt presences in the continuing story of the story. And much that is "new" is often rediscovery of an earlier discovery. Of course, one is always in search of new writers, but there is the danger that in the search one will lose sight of a significant progression, that writers will go on writing (one hopes), and bring to the story the enrichments of experience. In that sense the history of the story is of a never-ending renaissance.

It would be an exaggeration to speak of the rediscovery of "the first-person story," for its history is as long and continuous as the story itself. But in recent years there has been a dramatic increase in the numbers of such stories. Hundreds of them are being published in magazines that range from the large to the little, from the conservative to the defiantly experimental. Just under half the stories in the present collection, including the two that share First Prize, are stories in the first person. Such an outpouring can't be shrugged off as mere coincidence; it suggests a deeply felt need. The sense of truthfulness that we accord to "I" the narrator, the listener, the watcher, the witness, or to "I" the participant, bearing witness to his or her own experience, a member of the story, the explorer, the discoverer—that truthfulness exerts a powerful appeal, now especially when we are being subjected to a tyranny of facts at every level of our lives, cunningly or blatantly manipulated to keep us from the truth.

The story-memoir, or memoir-story, may seem at first glance restrictive in what it allows its author to do—after all, so much escapes the "I" and the eye. Granting, then, the limitations of a particular narrative point of view, there prove to be, on the evidence here, an astonishing variety of ways of writing such stories.

The point is perhaps best made by looking at Louise Erdrich's "Fleur" and Joyce Johnson's "The Children's Wing." Each is told in the first person; each is a distinctive achievement. Having said that, one ceases to look farther for resemblances between them. One listens instead to their very different voices.

Louise Erdrich is a poet and a writer of highly charged prose, a maker of legends and myths. She—that is, of course, her narrator, a member of the Chippewa nation who exists at the margins of the story

—like the tale she has to tell, flies high as a tornado over the real and the possible.

What are we to think of her heroine, Fleur Pillager? (The name itself is a suggestion.) When "only a girl," she is saved from drowning by two men, both of whom subsequently disappear. Is that Fleur's fault? Evidently. Here the narrator enters: "It went to show, my grandma said. It figured to her, all right. By saving Fleur Pillager, those two men had lost themselves."

When Fleur drowned again she was twenty, and we are told "though she was good-looking, nobody dared to court her because it was clear that Misshepeshu, the waterman, the monster, wanted her for himself."

The fantastication becomes dazzling in a description of the waterman:

> Our mothers warn us that we'll think he's handsome, for he appears with green eyes, copper skin, a mouth tender as a child's. But if you fall into his arms, he sprouts horns, fangs, claws, fins. His feet are joined as one and his skin, brass scales, rings to the touch. You're fascinated, cannot move. He casts a shell necklace at your feet, weeps gleaming chips that harden into mica on your breasts. He holds you under. Then he takes the body of a lion or a fat brown worm. He's made of gold. He's made of beach moss. He's a thing of dry foam, a thing of death by drowning, the death a Chippewa cannot survive.

The story to its very end remains an unanswered enigma, holding in balance the magical and the ordinary. Fleur moves from the Chippewa reservation to the town of Argus, a few miles south, and the narrator tells us she "almost destroyed that town." Are we meant to believe in what happened in Argus in the year 1920? Or is it all a gorgeous, echoing tall story, timeless as legend, brought to life again in an extraordinary retelling? The narrator comments on how old men retell the story: "It comes up different every time and has no ending, no beginning. They get the middle wrong too." One would like to believe, we are prepared to believe, that Louise Erdrich has got it right.

To go from Argus in 1920 to Manhattan in the present is a tremendous leap, but it is easily done, and in doing so one discovers yet again the vitality and the variety of the contemporary story. If the narrator in "Fleur" teases us into half-believing that the story she tells is actually true, Joyce Johnson's "The Children's Wing" presents itself as a straightforward memoir:

> The summer Nicky was so sick, I would leave work a little early and go to the Chinese takeout place on Forty-ninth Street. After a while it was my regular routine. Nicky would call me at the office and place his order. "An egg roll, of course," he'd say. "And sweet and sour shrimp. And Mom, would you bring me a Coke?" I didn't like him to have soft drinks, but he'd say, "Please, please," trying to sound pitiful, and I'd always get one for him in the end. It was hard to refuse him anything that summer. When I'd get to the hospital the other mothers would be there already with their shopping bags. Soon whole families would be gathered around the bedsides of the children, everyone eating out of foil containers or off paper plates, like an odd kind of picnic or a birthday party that had been displaced.

Simple, spare, plain, this is the language of testimony or reportage, telling us how it was. But that final word, "displaced," so precisely used, startles us with its reverberations. The story will not merely accurately recall the events of that summer when the narrator's son was "so sick," it will in its quiet, unemphatic way reveal its true meanings not only for Nicky but for the narrator too.

"Displaced" as in "displaced persons"; the D.P. camps that became familiar to us in World War II and afterward; the phrase from T. S. Eliot, "the whole world is a hospital"—symbolism abounds. But Joyce Johnson is an artist who knows how much of art lies in what is left unsaid. The narrator never raises her voice, or quavers sentimentally, or brings to the surface of her story the metaphors that lie just out of sight beneath it. The details she gives us engender a kind of urban poetry:

> The children's wing was in the oldest part of the hospital, one of those gloomy gray stone buildings put up at the turn of the century. There was a marble rotunda on the ground floor. When you took the elevator up, there was no more marble, just dim green corridors and unending linoleum and muffled fake laughter from all the television sets.

That "muffled fake laughter" is not heard in the narrator's voice. She resists the besetting temptation of the first person to tell too much about herself. We know that she is Nicky's mother, that she is divorced, that she works "at the office," that she visits him daily in the children's wing, talks sensibly to him when he telephones anxiously in the middle of the night, though she admits to a moment of private panic: "I wanted to go straight to the hospital and bring Nicky home."

In truth, we know all that we need to know, no more. The very controlled and selected way in which the story is given to us adds immeasurably to its credibility. Early on, the narrator writes, "I kept thinking Nicky's time in the children's ward would change him." And it does. That, after all, is what the story is about. Its final sentence, so brief and unadorned and inevitable, is like an epitaph carved on a gravestone. In its six words it becomes the summation of all that has gone before. Reading this story we have been displaced from conventional expectations; we are moved and enlightened.

I want to express my appreciation to Sally Arteseros, Barbara Broadhurst, and John M. Dean.

—William Abrahams

PRIZE STORIES 1987
The O. Henry Awards

FLEUR

LOUISE ERDRICH

Louise Erdrich grew up in Wahpeton, North Dakota, and now lives in
New Hampshire with her husband and collaborator Michael Dorris,
and their five children. Her first book, *Love Medicine,* won the National Book Critics Circle Award for Fiction. Her second novel, *The
Beet Queen,* was published in 1986.

The first time she drowned in the cold and glassy waters of Lake
Turcot, Fleur Pillager was only a girl. Two men saw the boat tip, saw
her struggle in the waves. They rowed over to the place she went down,
and jumped in. When they dragged her over the gunwales, she was cold
to the touch and stiff, so they slapped her face, shook her by the heels,
worked her arms back and forth, and pounded her back until she
coughed up lake water. She shivered all over like a dog, then took a
breath. But it wasn't long afterward that those two men disappeared.
The first wandered off, and the other, Jean Hat, got himself run over by
a cart.

It went to show, my grandma said. It figured to her, all right. By
saving Fleur Pillager, those two men had lost themselves.

The next time she fell in the lake, Fleur Pillager was twenty years old
and no one touched her. She washed onshore, her skin a dull dead gray,
but when George Many Women bent to look closer, he saw her chest
move. Then her eyes spun open, sharp black riprock, and she looked at
him. "You'll take my place," she hissed. Everybody scattered and left
her there, so no one knows how she dragged herself home. Soon after
that we noticed Many Women changed, grew afraid, wouldn't leave his
house, and would not be forced to go near water. For his caution, he
lived until the day that his sons brought him a new tin bathtub. Then

the first time he used the tub he slipped, got knocked out, and breathed water while his wife stood in the other room frying breakfast.

Men stayed clear of Fleur Pillager after the second drowning. Even though she was good-looking, nobody dared to court her because it was clear that Misshepeshu, the waterman, the monster, wanted her for himself. He's a devil, that one, love-hungry with desire and maddened for the touch of young girls, the strong and daring especially, the ones like Fleur.

Our mothers warn us that we'll think he's handsome, for he appears with green eyes, copper skin, a mouth tender as a child's. But if you fall into his arms, he sprouts horns, fangs, claws, fins. His feet are joined as one and his skin, brass scales, rings to the touch. You're fascinated, cannot move. He casts a shell necklace at your feet, weeps gleaming chips that harden into mica on your breasts. He holds you under. Then he takes the body of a lion or a fat brown worm. He's made of gold. He's made of beach moss. He's a thing of dry foam, a thing of death by drowning, the death a Chippewa cannot survive.

Unless you are Fleur Pillager. We all knew she couldn't swim. After the first time, we thought she'd never go back to Lake Turcot. We thought she'd keep to herself, live quiet, stop killing men off by drowning in the lake. After the first time, we thought she'd keep the good ways. But then, after the second drowning, we knew that we were dealing with something much more serious. She was haywire, out of control. She messed with evil, laughed at the old women's advice, and dressed like a man. She got herself into some half-forgotten medicine, studied ways we shouldn't talk about. Some say she kept the finger of a child in her pocket and a powder of unborn rabbits in a leather thong around her neck. She laid the heart of an owl on her tongue so she could see at night, and went out, hunting, not even in her own body. We know for sure because the next morning, in the snow or dust, we followed the tracks of her bare feet and saw where they changed, where the claws sprang out, the pad broadened and pressed into the dirt. By night we heard her chuffing cough, the bear cough. By day her silence and the wide grin she threw to bring down our guard made us frightened. Some thought that Fleur Pillager should be driven off the reservation, but not a single person who spoke like this had the nerve. And finally, when people were just about to get together and throw her out, she left on her own and didn't come back all summer. That's what this story is about.

During that summer, when she lived a few miles south in Argus, things happened. She almost destroyed that town.

When she got down to Argus in the year of 1920, it was just a small grid of six streets on either side of the railroad depot. There were two elevators, one central, the other a few miles west. Two stores competed for the trade of the three hundred citizens, and three churches quarreled with one another for their souls. There was a frame building for Lutherans, a heavy brick one for Episcopalians, and a long narrow shingled Catholic church. This last had a tall slender steeple, twice as high as any building or tree.

No doubt, across the low, flat wheat, watching from the road as she came near Argus on foot, Fleur saw that steeple rise, a shadow thin as a needle. Maybe in that raw space it drew her the way a lone tree draws lightning. Maybe, in the end, the Catholics are to blame. For if she hadn't seen that sign of pride, that slim prayer, that marker, maybe she would have kept walking.

But Fleur Pillager turned, and the first place she went once she came into town was to the back door of the priest's residence attached to the landmark church. She didn't go there for a handout, although she got that, but to ask for work. She got that too, or the town got her. It's hard to tell which came out worse, her or the men or the town, although the upshot of it all was that Fleur lived.

The four men who worked at the butcher's had carved up about a thousand carcasses between them, maybe half of that steers and the other half pigs, sheep, and game animals like deer, elk, and bear. That's not even mentioning the chickens, which were beyond counting. Pete Kozka owned the place, and employed Lily Veddar, Tor Grunewald, and my stepfather, Dutch James, who had brought my mother down from the reservation the year before she disappointed him by dying. Dutch took me out of school to take her place. I kept house half the time and worked the other in the butcher shop, sweeping floors, putting

sawdust down, running a hambone across the street to a customer's
bean pot or a package of sausage to the corner. I was a good one to have
around because until they needed me, I was invisible. I blended into the
stained brown walls, a skinny, big-nosed girl with staring eyes. Because
I could fade into a corner or squeeze beneath a shelf, I knew everything,
what the men said when no one was around, and what they did to
Fleur.

Kozka's Meats served farmers for a fifty-mile area, both to slaughter,
for it had a stock pen and chute, and to cure the meat by smoking it or
spicing it in sausage. The storage locker was a marvel, made of many
thicknesses of brick, earth insulation, and Minnesota timber, lined inside with sawdust and vast blocks of ice cut from Lake Turcot, hauled
down from home each winter by horse and sledge.

A ramshackle board building, part slaughterhouse, part store, was
fixed to the low, thick square of the lockers. That's where Fleur worked.
Kozka hired her for her strength. She could lift a haunch or carry a
pole of sausages without stumbling, and she soon learned cutting from
Pete's wife, a string-thin blonde who chain-smoked and handled the
razor-sharp knives with nerveless precision, slicing close to her stained
fingers. Fleur and Fritzie Kozka worked afternoons, wrapping their
cuts in paper, and Fleur hauled the packages to the lockers. The meat
was left outside the heavy oak doors that were only opened at 5:00 each
afternoon, before the men ate supper.

Sometimes Dutch, Tor, and Lily ate at the lockers, and when they did
I stayed too, cleaned floors, restoked the fires in the front smokehouses,
while the men sat around the squat cast-iron stove spearing slats of
herring onto hardtack bread. They played long games of poker or crib-
bage on a board made from the planed end of a salt crate. They talked
and I listened, although there wasn't much to hear since almost nothing
ever happened in Argus. Tor was married, Dutch had lost my mother,
and Lily read circulars. They mainly discussed about the auctions to
come, equipment, or women.

Every so often, Pete Kozka came out front to make a whist, leaving
Fritzie to smoke cigarettes and fry raised doughnuts in the back room.
He sat and played a few rounds but kept his thoughts to himself. Fritzie
did not tolerate him talking behind her back, and the one book he read

was the New Testament. If he said something, it concerned weather or a surplus of sheep stomachs, a ham that smoked green or the markets for corn and wheat. He had a good-luck talisman, the opal-white lens of a cow's eye. Playing cards, he rubbed it between his fingers. That soft sound and the slap of cards was about the only conversation.

Fleur finally gave them a subject.

Her cheeks were wide and flat, her hands large, chapped, muscular. Fleur's shoulders were broad as beams, her hips fishlike, slippery, narrow. An old green dress clung to her waist, worn thin where she sat. Her braids were thick like the tails of animals, and swung against her when she moved, deliberately, slowly in her work, held in and half-tamed, but only half. I could tell, but the others never saw. They never looked into her sly brown eyes or noticed her teeth, strong and curved and very white. Her legs were bare, and since she padded around in beadwork moccasins they never saw that her fifth toes were missing. They never knew she'd drowned. They were blinded, they were stupid, they only saw her in the flesh.

And yet it wasn't just that she was a Chippewa, or even that she was a woman, it wasn't that she was good-looking or even that she was alone that made their brains hum. It was how she played cards.

Women didn't usually play with men, so the evening that Fleur drew a chair up to the men's table without being so much as asked, there was a shock of surprise.

"What's this," said Lily. He was fat, with a snake's cold pale eyes and precious skin, smooth and lily-white, which is how he got his name. Lily had a dog, a stumpy mean little bull of a thing with a belly drum-tight from eating pork rinds. The dog liked to play cards just like Lily, and straddled his barrel thighs through games of stud, rum poker, vingt-un. The dog snapped at Fleur's arm that first night, but cringed back, its snarl frozen, when she took her place.

"I thought," she said, her voice soft and stroking, "you might deal me in."

There was a space between the heavy bin of spiced flour and the wall where I just fit. I hunkered down there, kept my eyes open, saw her black hair swing over the chair, her feet solid on the wood floor. I couldn't see up on the table where the cards slapped down, so after they were deep in their game I raised myself up in the shadows, and crouched on a sill of wood.

I watched Fleur's hands stack and ruffle, divide the cards, spill them to each player in a blur, rake them up and shuffle again. Tor, short and scrappy, shut one eye and squinted the other at Fleur. Dutch screwed his lips around a wet cigar.

"Gotta see a man," he mumbled, getting up to go out back to the privy. The others broke, put their cards down, and Fleur sat alone in the lamplight that glowed in a sheen across the push of her breasts. I watched her closely, then she paid me a beam of notice for the first time. She turned, looked straight at me, and grinned the white wolf grin a Pillager turns on its victims, except that she wasn't after me.

"Pauline there," she said, "how much money you got?"

We'd all been paid for the week that day. Eight cents was in my pocket.

"Stake me," she said, holding out her long fingers. I put the coins in her palm and then I melted back to nothing, part of the walls and tables. It was a long time before I understood that the men would not have seen me no matter what I did, how I moved. I wasn't anything like Fleur. My dress hung loose and my back was already curved, an old woman's. Work had roughened me, reading made my eyes sore, caring for my mother before she died had hardened my face. I was not much to look at, so they never saw me.

When the men came back and sat around the table, they had drawn together. They shot each other small glances, stuck their tongues in their cheeks, burst out laughing at odd moments, to rattle Fleur. But she never minded. They played their vingt-un, staying even as Fleur slowly gained. Those pennies I had given her drew nickels and attracted dimes until there was a small pile in front of her.

Then she hooked them with five-card draw, nothing wild. She dealt, discarded, drew, and then she sighed and her cards gave a little shiver. Tor's eye gleamed, and Dutch straightened in his seat.

"I'll pay to see that hand," said Lily Veddar.

Fleur showed, and she had nothing there, nothing at all.

Tor's thin smile cracked open, and he threw his hand in too.

"Well, we know one thing," he said, leaning back in his chair, "the squaw can't bluff."

With that I lowered myself into a mound of swept sawdust and slept. I woke up during the night, but none of them had moved yet, so I couldn't either. Still later, the men must have gone out again, or Fritzie come out to break the game, because I was lifted, soothed, cradled in a woman's arms and rocked so quiet that I kept my eyes shut while Fleur rolled me into a closet of grimy ledgers, oiled paper, balls of string, and thick files that fit beneath me like a mattress.

The game went on after work the next evening. I got my eight cents back five times over, and Fleur kept the rest of the dollar she'd won for a stake. This time they didn't play so late, but they played regular, and then kept going at it night after night. They played poker now, or variations, for one week straight, and each time Fleur won exactly one dollar, no more and no less, too consistent for luck.

By this time, Lily and the other men were so lit with suspense that they got Pete to join the game with them. They concentrated, the fat dog sitting tense in Lily Veddar's lap, Tor suspicious, Dutch stroking his huge square brow, Pete steady. It wasn't that Fleur won that hooked them in so, because she lost hands too. It was rather that she never had a freak hand or even anything above a straight. She only took on her low cards, which didn't sit right. By chance, Fleur should have gotten a full or flush by now. The irritating thing was she beat with pairs and never bluffed, because she couldn't, and still she ended up each night with exactly one dollar. Lily couldn't believe, first of all, that a woman could be smart enough to play cards, but even if she was, that she would then be stupid enough to cheat for a dollar a night. By day I watched him turn the problem over, his hard white face dull, small fingers probing at his knuckles, until he finally thought he had Fleur figured out as a bit-time player, caution her game. Raising the stakes would throw her.

More than anything now, he wanted Fleur to come away with something but a dollar. Two bits less or ten more, the sum didn't matter, just so he broke her streak.

Night after night she played, won her dollar, and left to stay in a place that just Fritzie and I knew about. Fleur bathed in the slaughtering tub, then slept in the unused brick smokehouse behind the lockers, a

windowless place tarred on the inside with scorched fats. When I
brushed against her skin I noticed that she smelled of the walls, rich
and woody, slightly burnt. Since that night she put me in the closet I
was no longer afraid of her, but followed her close, stayed with her,
became her moving shadow that the men never noticed, the shadow
that could have saved her.

August, the month that bears fruit, closed around the shop, and Pete
and Fritzie left for Minnesota to escape the heat. Night by night, running, Fleur had won thirty dollars, and only Pete's presence had kept
Lily at bay. But Pete was gone now, and one payday, with the heat so
bad no one could move but Fleur, the men sat and played and waited
while she finished work. The cards sweat, limp in their fingers, the table
was slick with grease, and even the walls were warm to the touch. The
air was motionless. Fleur was in the next room boiling heads.

Her green dress, drenched, wrapped her like a transparent sheet. A
skin of lakeweed. Black snarls of veining clung to her arms. Her braids
were loose, half-unraveled, tied behind her neck in a thick loop. She
stood in steam, turning skulls through a vat with a wooden paddle.
When scraps boiled to the surface, she bent with a round tin sieve and
scooped them out. She'd filled two dishpans.

"Ain't that enough now?" called Lily. "We're waiting." The stump of
a dog trembled in his lap, alive with rage. It never smelled me or noticed me above Fleur's smoky skin. The air was heavy in my corner, and
pressed me down. Fleur sat with them.

"Now what do you say?" Lily asked the dog. It barked. That was the
signal for the real game to start.

"Let's up the ante," said Lily, who had been stalking this night all
month. He had a roll of money in his pocket. Fleur had five bills in her
dress. The men had each saved their full pay.

"Ante a dollar then," said Fleur, and pitched hers in. She lost, but
they let her scrape along, cent by cent. And then she won some. She
played unevenly, as if chance was all she had. She reeled them in. The
game went on. The dog was stiff now, poised on Lily's knees, a ball of
vicious muscle with its yellow eyes slit in concentration. It gave advice,

seemed to sniff the lay of Fleur's cards, twitched and nudged. Fleur was up, then down, saved by a scratch. Tor dealt seven cards, three down. The pot grew, round by round, until it held all the money. Nobody folded. Then it all rode on one last card and they went silent. Fleur picked hers up and blew a long breath. The heat lowered like a bell. Her card shook, but she stayed in.

Lily smiled and took the dog's head tenderly between his palms.

"Say, Fatso," he said, crooning the words, "you reckon that girl's bluffing?"

The dog whined and Lily laughed. "Me too," he said, "let's show." He swept his bills and coins into the pot and then they turned their cards over.

Lily looked once, looked again, then he squeezed the dog up like a fist of dough and slammed it on the table.

Fleur threw her arms out and drew the money over, grinning that same wolf grin that she'd used on me, the grin that had them. She jammed the bills in her dress, scooped the coins up in waxed white paper that she tied with string.

"Let's go another round," said Lily, his voice choked with burrs. But Fleur opened her mouth and yawned, then walked out back to gather slops for the one big hog that was waiting in the stock pen to be killed.

The men sat still as rocks, their hands spread on the oiled wood table. Dutch had chewed his cigar to damp shreds, Tor's eye was dull. Lily's gaze was the only one to follow Fleur. I didn't move. I felt them gathering, saw my stepfather's veins, the ones in his forehead that stood out in anger. The dog had rolled off the table and curled in a knot below the counter, where none of the men could touch it.

Lily rose and stepped out back to the closet of ledgers where Pete kept his private stock. He brought back a bottle, uncorked and tipped it between his fingers. The lump in his throat moved, then he passed it on. They drank, quickly felt the whiskey's fire, and planned with their eyes things they couldn't say out loud.

When they left, I followed. I hid out back in the clutter of broken boards and chicken crates beside the stock pen, where they waited. Fleur could not be seen at first, and then the moon broke and showed her, slipping cautiously along the rough board chute with a bucket in her hand. Her hair fell, wild and coarse, to her waist, and her dress was a floating patch in the dark. She made a pig-calling sound, rang the tin pail lightly against the wood, froze suspiciously. But too late. In the sound of the ring Lily moved, fat and nimble, stepped right behind Fleur and put out his creamy hands. At his first touch, she whirled and doused him with the bucket of sour slops. He pushed her against the big fence and the package of coins split, went clinking and jumping, winked against the wood. Fleur rolled over once and vanished in the yard.

The moon fell behind a curtain of ragged clouds, and Lily followed into the dark muck. But he tripped, pitched over the huge flank of the pig, who lay mired to the snout, heavily snoring. I sprang out of the weeds and climbed the side of the pen, stuck like glue. I saw the sow rise to her neat, knobby knees, gain her balance, and sway, curious, as Lily stumbled forward. Fleur had backed into the angle of rough wood just beyond, and when Lily tried to jostle past, the sow tipped up on her hind legs and struck, quick and hard as a snake. She plunged her head into Lily's thick side and snatched a mouthful of his shirt. She lunged again, caught him lower, so that he grunted in pained surprise. He seemed to ponder, breathing deep. Then he launched his huge body in a swimmer's dive.

The sow screamed as his body smacked over hers. She rolled, striking out with her knife-sharp hooves, and Lily gathered himself upon her, took her foot-long face by the ears and scraped her snout and cheeks against the trestles of the pen. He hurled the sow's tight skull against an iron post, but instead of knocking her dead, he merely woke her from her dream.

She reared, shrieked, drew him with her so that they posed standing upright. They bowed jerkily to each other, as if to begin. Then his arms swung and flailed. She sank her black fangs into his shoulder, clasping him, dancing him forward and backward through the pen. Their steps picked up pace, went wild. The two dipped as one, box-stepped, tripped each other. She ran her split foot through his hair. He grabbed her kinked tail. They went down and came up, the same shape and then the same color, until the men couldn't tell one from the other in that light and Fleur was able to launch herself over the gates, swing down, hit gravel.

The men saw, yelled, and chased her at a dead run to the smoke-house. And Lily too, once the sow gave up in disgust and freed him. That is where I should have gone to Fleur, saved her, thrown myself on Dutch. But I went stiff with fear and couldn't unlatch myself from the trestles or move at all. I closed my eyes and put my head in my arms, tried to hide, so there is nothing to describe but what I couldn't block out, Fleur's hoarse breath, so loud it filled me, her cry in the old language, and my name repeated over and over among the words.

The heat was still dense the next morning when I came back to work. Fleur was gone but the men were there, slack-faced, hung over. Lily was paler and softer than ever, as if his flesh had steamed on his bones. They smoked, took pulls off a bottle. It wasn't noon yet. I worked awhile, waiting shop and sharpening steel. But I was sick, I was smothered, I was sweating so hard that my hands slipped on the knives, and I wiped my fingers clean of the greasy touch of the customers' coins. Lily opened his mouth and roared once, not in anger. There was no meaning to the sound. His boxer dog, sprawled limp beside his foot, never lifted its head. Nor did the other men.

They didn't notice when I stepped outside, hoping for a clear breath. And then I forgot them because I knew that we were all balanced, ready to tip, to fly, to be crushed as soon as the weather broke. The sky was so low that I felt the weight of it like a yoke. Clouds hung down, witch teats, a tornado's green-brown cones, and as I watched one flicked out and became a delicate probing thumb. Even as I picked up my heels and ran back inside, the wind blew suddenly, cold, and then came rain.

Inside, the men had disappeared already and the whole place was trembling as if a huge hand was pinched at the rafters, shaking it. I ran straight through, screaming for Dutch or for any of them, and then I stopped at the heavy doors of the lockers, where they had surely taken shelter. I stood there a moment. Everything went still. Then I heard a cry building in the wind, faint at first, a whistle and then a shrill scream that tore through the walls and gathered around me, spoke plain so I understood that I should move, put my arms out, and slam down the great iron bar that fit across the hasp and lock.

Outside, the wind was stronger, like a hand held against me. I struggled forward. The bushes tossed, the awnings flapped off storefronts, the rails of porches rattled. The odd cloud became a fat snout that nosed along the earth and sniffled, jabbed, picked at things, sucked them up, blew them apart, rooted around as if it was following a certain scent, then stopped behind me at the butcher shop and bored down like a drill.

I went flying, landed somewhere in a ball. When I opened my eyes and looked, stranger things were happening.

A herd of cattle flew through the air like giant birds, dropping dung, their mouths opened in stunned bellows. A candle, still lighted, blew past, and tables, napkins, garden tools, a whole school of drifting eyeglasses, jackets on hangers, hams, a checkerboard, a lampshade, and at last the sow from behind the lockers, on the run, her hooves a blur, set free, swooping, diving, screaming as everything in Argus fell apart and got turned upside down, smashed, and thoroughly wrecked.

Days passed before the town went looking for the men. They were bachelors, after all, except for Tor, whose wife had suffered a blow to the head that made her forgetful. Everyone was occupied with digging out, in high relief because even though the Catholic steeple had been torn off like a peaked cap and sent across five fields, those huddled in the cellar were unhurt. Walls had fallen, windows were demolished, but the stores were intact and so were the bankers and shop owners who had taken refuge in their safes or beneath their cash registers. It was a fair-minded disaster, no one could be said to have suffered much more than the next, at least not until Fritzie and Pete came home.

Of all the businesses in Argus, Kozka's Meats had suffered worst. The boards of the front building had been split to kindling, piled in a huge pyramid, and the shop equipment was blasted far and wide. Pete paced off the distance the iron bathtub had been flung—a hundred feet. The glass candy case went fifty, and landed without so much as a cracked pane. There were other surprises as well, for the back rooms where Fritzie and Pete lived were undisturbed. Fritzie said the dust still coated her china figures, and upon her kitchen table, in the ashtray, perched the last cigarette she'd put out in haste. She lit it up and finished it, looking through the window. From there, she could see that the old smokehouse Fleur had slept in was crushed to a reddish sand and the stockpens were completely torn apart, the rails stacked helter-skelter. Fritzie asked for Fleur. People shrugged. Then she asked about the others and, suddenly, the town understood that three men were missing.

There was a rally of help, a gathering of shovels and volunteers. We passed boards from hand to hand, stacked them, uncovered what lay beneath the pile of jagged splinters. The lockers, full of the meat that was Pete and Fritzie's investment, slowly came into sight, still intact. When enough room was made for a man to stand on the roof, there were calls, a general urge to hack through and see what lay below. But Fritzie shouted that she wouldn't allow it because the meat would spoil. And so the work continued, board by board, until at last the heavy oak doors of the freezer were revealed and people pressed to the entry. Everyone wanted to be the first, but since it was my stepfather lost, I was let go in when Pete and Fritzie wedged through into the sudden icy air.

Pete scraped a match on his boot, lit the lamp Fritzie held, and then the three of us stood still in its circle. Light glared off the skinned and hanging carcasses, the crates of wrapped sausages, the bright and cloudy blocks of lake ice, pure as winter. The cold bit into us, pleasant at first, then numbing. We must have stood there a couple of minutes before we saw the men, or more rightly, the humps of fur, the iced and shaggy hides they wore, the bearskins they had taken down and wrapped around themselves. We stepped closer and tilted the lantern beneath the flaps of fur into their faces. The dog was there, perched among them, heavy as a doorstop. The three had hunched around a barrel where the game was still laid out, and a dead lantern and an empty bottle, too. But they had thrown down their last hands and hunkered tight, clutching one another, knuckles raw from beating at the door they had also attacked with hooks. Frost stars gleamed off their eyelashes and the stubble of their beards. Their faces were set in concentration, mouths open as if to speak some careful thought, some agreement they'd come to in each other's arms.

* * *

Power travels in the bloodlines, handed out before birth. It comes down through the hands, which in the Pillagers were strong and knotted, big, spidery, and rough, with sensitive fingertips good at dealing cards. It comes through the eyes, too, belligerent, darkest brown, the eyes of those in the bear clan, impolite as they gaze directly at a person.

In my dreams, I look straight back at Fleur, at the men. I am no longer the watcher on the dark sill, the skinny girl.

The blood draws us back, as if it runs through a vein of earth. I've come home and, except for talking to my cousins, live a quiet life. Fleur lives quiet too, down on Lake Turcot with her boat. Some say she's married to the waterman, Misshepeshu, or that she's living in shame with white men or windigos, or that she's killed them all. I'm about the only one here who ever goes to visit her. Last winter, I went to help out in her cabin when she bore the child, whose green eyes and skin the color of an old penny made more talk, as no one could decide if the child was mixed blood or what, fathered in a smokehouse, or by a man with brass scales, or by the lake. The girl is bold, smiling in her sleep, as if she knows what people wonder, as if she hears the old men talk, turning the story over. It comes up different every time and has no ending, no beginning. They get the middle wrong too. They only know that they don't know anything.

THE CHILDREN'S
WING

JOYCE JOHNSON

Joyce Johnson is a native New Yorker. She is the author of two novels,
Come and Join the Dance and *Bad Connections,* and of a memoir,
Minor Characters, which won the 1983 National Book Critics Circle
Award for Autobiography. Her fiction has been published in *The New
Yorker, Harper's, Ms.,* and *Fiction.* Her forthcoming novel is *In the
Night Café.*

The summer Nicky was so sick, I would leave work a little early and go
to the Chinese takeout place on Forty-ninth Street. After a while it was
my regular routine. Nicky would call me at the office and place his
order. "An egg roll, of course," he'd say. "And sweet and sour shrimp.
And Mom, would you bring me a Coke?" I didn't like him to have soft
drinks, but he'd say, "Please, please," trying to sound pitiful, and I'd
always get one for him in the end. It was hard to refuse him anything
that summer. When I'd get to the hospital the other mothers would be
there already with their shopping bags. Soon whole families would be
gathered around the bedsides of the children, everyone eating out of foil
containers or off paper plates, like an odd kind of picnic or a birthday
party that had been displaced.

The children's wing was in the oldest part of the hospital, one of
those gloomy gray stone buildings put up at the turn of the century.
There was a marble rotunda on the ground floor. When you took the
elevator up, there was no more marble, just dim green corridors and
unending linoleum and muffled fake laughter from all the television
sets.

I was never in the ward when the television wasn't on. The kids must have pressed the switches the moment they woke up. If you came in the afternoon, it would be soap operas or game shows; in the evening it would be reruns of *M*A*S*H* or *The Odd Couple.* There was a volunteer who called herself The Teacher and came around with little workbooks. She told me once she was going to bring Nicky some literature to explain what a biopsy was. In a stern voice I said, "I'd much rather you didn't."

I kept thinking Nicky's time in the children's ward would irrevocably change him. A shadow was falling across his vision of life and there was nothing I could do. Once I went to talk to a psychiatrist. He said, "What can I tell you? Either this will do damage to your son, or he will rise to the occasion and be a hero." This immediately comforted me, though it's hard to say why. Somehow I could accept the logic of that answer.

Nicky had seniority in Room K by August. New little boys kept coming and going, accident cases mostly. They lay beached on those high white beds, bewildered to find themselves in arrested motion. Each had been felled by some miscalculation—running out too fast in front of a car, jumping off a fence the wrong way. They'd go home with an arm or leg in a cast and sit out the summer, listening for the bell of the ice-cream truck, driving their mothers crazy. "Hey man, what you break?" they'd ask Nicky, looking at the plaster around his torso with respect. "You break your back or something?"

He could explain his condition as if he were a junior scientist laying out an interesting problem, using the language he'd picked up from the doctors—"left lumbar vertebra . . . unknown organism." He'd say, "You see, in the X-ray there's a white swelling on the left lumbar vertebra." There were men in a laboratory hunting the unknown organism. He made it sound like a movie—you could imagine the men in their white coats bent over their test tubes. All they had to do was find it, he'd say in a confident voice, and then they could cure him.

Sometimes I'd look around the room and stare at all those simple broken limbs in envy. I wondered if Nicky did that, too. Why had it been necessary for him to learn the awful possibilities, how your own body could suddenly turn against you, become the enemy?

He was the little scientist and he was the birthday boy. When the pain would come, he'd hold on to my hand the way he had at home on those nights I'd sat up with him. "Do you see that?" he'd say, pointing to the decal of a yellow duckling on the wall near his bed. "Isn't that ridiculous to have that here, that stupid duck?"

I agreed with him about the duck and Room K's other decorations—brown Disneyesque bunnies in various poses, a fat-cheeked Mary and her little lamb, all of them scratched and violently scribbled over. I could see how they threatened the dignity of a ten-year-old. The hospital would turn you into a baby if you didn't watch out.

I kept buying Nicky things; so did his father. With a sick child, you're always trying to bring different pieces of the outside in, as if to say, *That's* the reality, not this. There was a game called Boggle that he was interested in for a week, and his own tape recorder, which fell off the bed one day and broke, and incredibly intricate miniature robots from Japan. All this stuff piled up around him. The fruit my mother brought him turned brown in unopened plastic bags.

Nicky liked only one thing, really; he could have done without all the rest. A fantasy war game called D&D that was all the rage among the fifth graders. I never even tried to understand it. I just kept buying the strange-looking dice he asked for and the small lead figures that he'd have to paint himself—dragons and wizards and goblins—and new strategy books with ever more complicated rules. "I want to live in a fantasy world," he told me. I remember it shocked me a little that he knew so explicitly what he was doing.

He refused to come back from that world very much. There were nights he'd hardly stop playing to talk to me. He'd look up only when I was leaving to tell me the colors he needed. When I'd encourage Nicky to get to know the other kids, he'd look at me wearily. "They don't have the same interests," he'd say.

"Maybe you could interest them in what you're doing."

"Mom . . . I can't. I'd have to start them from the beginning."

Still, I was grateful to the makers of D&D, grateful he had a way to lose himself. There were things happening in the children's wing I didn't want him to find out about, things I didn't want to know. If you walked those corridors you passed certain quiet, darkened rooms where there were children who weren't ever going to get well; there were parents on the elevator with swollen faces who'd never look you in the eye. A little girl in Room G died during visiting hours. I could hear her as soon as I got off on the fifth floor, a terrible high-pitched, rattling moan that I'll never forget. It went on and on and there were doctors running down the hall with machinery.

I walked into Nicky's room with my shopping bag from the Chinese takeout place. He was staring at all his figures lined up in battle formation; he didn't say hello. The other kids weren't saying much either. Their parents hadn't come yet. One little boy, looking scared, asked me, "What's that noise out there?" "Oh, someone's very sick tonight," I said, and I closed the door. I just shut the sound out. I suppose any other parent would have done the same. The strange thing was, I felt I'd done something wrong, that we all should have acknowledged it somehow, wept for the child who was dying.

I used to try to get Nicky out of bed for some exercise. We'd walk up and down outside his room very slowly, the IV apparatus trailing along on its clumsy, spindly stand like a dog on a leash. Some nights we'd sit on the brown plastic couch in the visitors' lounge, and Nicky would drink his Coke and go over his strategy books.

A mentally disturbed boy appeared there one night. He was tall and had a man's build already, muscled arms and shoulders, though I later found out he was only fifteen. He had a face that could have been beautiful, but you didn't want to see his eyes. They were red and inflamed, emptier than a statue's. I thought of the word *baleful* when I saw them. The boy with the baleful eyes. He was wearing dirty jeans and an old gray T-shirt. I thought he might have come in off the street.

Nicky and I were alone. This boy walked right over and stared down at us. I spoke to him softly, trying to sound calm. "Are you looking for someone?" I said.

He shook his head, grinning. "Who? Looking for Mr. Who. Have you seen Who?"

I said I hadn't seen him.

"Are you a nurse? You're not a nurse."

"The nurses are outside," I said. "Just down the hall."

He sat down next to Nicky. He rapped on Nicky's cast with his knuckles. "Hello Mr. Who. Want a cigarette?"

Nicky was sitting very still. "No thanks. I don't smoke," he said in a small voice.

The boy laughed and stood up. He took out a pack of cigarettes and some matches. He lit a match and held it up close to Nicky's face for a moment. Then he lit his cigarette with it and stared down at us a while longer. "My name is Joseph," he said. "Do you like me?"

"I like you very much," I said.

He studied me a long time, almost as if I were someone he remembered. Then he threw the cigarette on the floor and drifted out.

Earlier that day, a boy from Nicky's room had gone home. When we got back there, we saw that the empty bed had been taken. A small suitcase stood beside it and a nurse was tucking in the blanket, making hospital corners. A little while later an intern led Joseph in, dressed in pajamas. "Mom," Nicky whispered. "They're putting him in *here.*"

"Don't worry about it, honey," I told him.

I went out to the nurse on duty at the desk and made a complaint. They had no right to put a boy like that in with sick children. The children would be frightened, they had enough to contend with.

"It's the only bed available," the nurse said. "There's no private room for him now. Try to understand—he's sick, too, he needs care. We're going to watch the situation very carefully." I told her about the cigarettes and the matches. She said, "My God. We'll take care of that."

"Where does he come from, anyway?" I asked, and she told me the name of some institution upstate.

My telephone rang in the middle of the night. A nurse said, "Hold on. Your son insists on speaking to you."

Nicky got on the phone, all keyed up and out of breath. "Mom, you have to give me some advice. You know that guy Joseph?"

"What's the matter, Nick?" I said.

"Well, guess who he's picked to be his friend? He keeps getting off his bed and coming over to talk to me. It's too weird. I don't know what to say to him, so I just listen."

I wanted to go straight to the hospital and bring Nicky home. I said, "I guess you're doing the right thing, honey." I asked him if he was scared.

"Not so much. But it's hard, Mom."

"The next time he bothers you, just pretend you're asleep. Maybe he'll go to sleep, too."

"O.K.," Nicky said. "Can I call you again if I have to?"

I turned on the lights and sat up and read so I'd be sure to hear the phone. I called him back early in the morning. Joseph was sleeping, Nicky told me. The nurse had finally given him some kind of pill.

I went to the office as usual but I couldn't get much accomplished. Around three I gave up and went to the hospital. They were mopping the corridors and a game show was on in Room K. A housewife from Baltimore had just won a walk-in refrigerator and a trip for two to Bermuda. "Yay! It's the fat lady! I knew it!" a kid was yelling. I found Nicky propped up in bed painting a dragon, making each scale of its wing a different color. I looked around for Joseph, but I didn't see him.

"I'm concentrating, Mom," Nicky said.

"Is everything O.K.?" I whispered.

With a sigh he put down his brush. "Joseph is taking a walk. That's what Joseph does. But don't worry—he'll be back." Then he said, "Mom, sometimes Joseph seems almost all right. I ask him questions and he tells me very sad things."

"What kinds of things?"

"Stuff about his life. He doesn't go to school, you know. He lives in a hospital with grown-ups. He thinks he's going to live there a long time —maybe always."

When Nicky was little, I used to take him to nursery school on the way to work. It wasn't convenient, but I never minded. The place, as I recall it, was always yellow with sunlight. Green sweet potato vines climbed up the windows and there were hamsters dozing in a cage. In the morning the teacher would put up the paintings the children had done the day before. You could smell crayons, soap, chalk dust. And all the little perfect children pulling off their coats had a shine about them, a newness. I was getting my divorce then. Sometimes the thought of that bright place would get me through the day, the idea that it was there and that Nicky was in it—as if I'd been allowed a small vision of harmony.

I thought of it again that afternoon at the hospital. I couldn't get back to it; it was lost, out of reach.

In the institution Joseph came from, they must have kept him very confined. In the children's wing he roamed the corridors. One day a nurse found him standing in a room he shouldn't have been in and had to bring him back to Room K. "Joseph, you stay in here," she admonished him. He walked up and down, banging his fists against the beds. He poked at little kids and chanted at the top of his voice, "Hey! Hey! What do you say today!"—which might have been a form of greeting.

He stopped by Nicky's bed and watched him paint the dragon. He pressed down on it with his thumb. "Hey, the mad monster game!"

"Wet paint, Joseph," warned Nicky.

Joseph took the dragon right off the night table. "Joseph, you creep!" Nicky yelled, his eyes filling with tears.

I went over to him and held out my hand. "I'm sorry. Nicky needs his dragon." It was odd how Joseph inspired politeness.

He stared down at my open palm as if puzzling over its significance. "That wasn't Nick's," he said.

Joseph stood by the door in the evening when the families came, when the bags of food were opened and the paper plates passed around. I went out to get Nicky a hamburger and a chocolate milkshake. When I came back, the room smelled of fried chicken and everyone was watching *The Odd Couple.* Joseph lay on his bed. He had put his arm over those red eyes, as if the light were hurting him.

Nicky tapped my arm. "Do you see that, Mom? No one came for him."

I said, "Maybe there's no one to come, Nicky."

"Someone should."

I handed him his milkshake. He peeled the paper off the straw and stuck it through the hole in the lid of the container. For a while he twirled it around. "Mom, I think you should get him something. Can you?"

I went down to the machines in the basement and got Joseph an ice-cream sandwich. I put it on his dinner tray. I said, "Joseph, this is for you." His arm stayed where it was. I touched his shoulder. "Do you like ice cream?" I said loudly.

Mrs. Rodriguez, who was sitting beside the next bed, talking to her son Emilio, whispered to me fiercely. *"Loco. Muy loco.* You understand? No good here. No good."

She wasn't wrong. I couldn't argue. The ice-cream sandwich was melting, oozing through its paper wrapping. I went back to Nicky and took him for his walk.

Later, out in the corridor, we saw Joseph. He took a swipe at Nicky's cast as we passed him and yelled after us, "Dragon Man and the Mom!" There was chocolate smeared all over his mouth.

The next day I bought an extra egg roll at the takeout place. It seemed I'd have to keep on with what I'd started, though I had no idea how much Joseph would remember. I kept thinking of him during visiting hours, lying there alone. What I really wanted was to walk into Room K and find him gone, some other arrangement made, so I could remove him from the list of everything that troubled me.

When I got to the hospital, some of the other parents were there, earlier than usual. They were standing in the corridor near the head nurse's desk. One of the mothers had her arm around Mrs. Rodriguez, who was wiping her eyes with some Kleenex. They gestured to me to join them. "The supervisor is coming to talk to us about our problem," someone said.

"What happened?" I asked Mrs. Rodriguez.

She blew her nose; it seemed hard for her to speak. "Joseph! Joseph! Who do you think?"

Joseph had somehow gotten hold of some cigarettes and matches. He had held a lighted match near Emilio's eyes. "To burn my son!" cried Mrs. Rodriguez. Emilio was only eight, a frail little boy with a broken collarbone.

I put down my shopping bag and waited with the others. When the supervisor came, I spoke up, too. Irresponsibility, negligence, lack of consideration—the words came so fluently, as if from the mouth of the kind of person I'd always distrusted, some person with very sure opinions about rightness and wrongness and what was good for society.

The supervisor already had his computer working on the situation. "Just give us an hour," he said.

In Room K an orderly had been posted to keep an eye on Joseph. He'd made Joseph lie down on his bed. The children were subdued; they talked in murmurs. Even the television was on low, until a parent turned up the volume. There was an effort to create the atmosphere of the usual picnic.

Nicky looked wide-eyed, pale. "Did you hear what Joseph did to Emilio?"

I leaned over him and pushed the wet hair off his forehead. "Nicky, don't worry about Joseph anymore. They're going to move him in a little while to a room by himself."

I started opening containers from the Chinese takeout place, and there was the egg roll I'd meant to give Joseph. I angled my chair so that I wouldn't have to see him. It was as though life were full of nothing but intolerable choices.

"Eat something," I said to Nicky.

In a loud, dazed voice, a kid in the room was talking on the phone. "Hey, Grandma, guess who this is? I'm gonna see you soon, you bet. I'm gonna get on a plane and fly. Yeah, I'll bring my little bathing suit. Gonna see you, Grandma. Gonna see you."

"Mom," Nicky whispered. "Can you hear him?"

We were there when he left, everyone was there. Two nurses came in and walked over to him. "Joseph, it's time to get moving now," one of them said. "Let's get your personal things together."

They got him out of bed very quickly. One took his suitcase; the other had him by the arm. The orderly positioned himself in front of them. Nicky turned his face into the pillow when they started walking between the rows of beds. I was holding his hand and he kept squeezing my fingers, not letting go.

As he passed by us, Joseph broke away from the nurse. For a moment he loomed over Nicky and me. He kissed me on the top of the head. Then they took him out into the long, dim corridors.

When Nicky was thirteen, he said he couldn't remember much about his childhood. He wanted to, but he couldn't. The whole subject made him very angry. "What I remember," he said, "is Joseph."

Nicky got well but he got old.

THE DARKNESS OF LOVE

ROBERT BOSWELL

Robert Boswell's collection of stories, *Dancing in the Movies,* was the
1985 winner of the Iowa School of Letters Award for Short Fiction.
His first novel, *Crooked Hearts,* will be published in May 1987 by
Knopf. He lives with his wife in Evanston, Illinois, where he teaches
creative writing for Northwestern University.

> *the darkness of love,*
> *in whose sweating memory all error is forced.*
>
> —*Amiri Baraka*

DAY I

When Handle woke at ten in the morning, he got up and walked to
the far window. Hungover, he half expected the sound of traffic or the
fading drone of an airliner as he lifted the window. He had lived in the
city for so long that even after two weeks in Tennessee, he found the
quiet of the green countryside severe and foreign. Trees just appeared
outside his window, new, each morning. He had come to escape the
city, but his dreams returned him each night to New York, sometimes
in a patrol car, but most often on his feet, in an alley, running after a
bone-skinny black boy who would suddenly turn, knife in his hand, and
Handle would wake, startled that the boy's face was his, a younger face,
but essentially his.

Handle dressed in the corduroy jeans he'd bought for the trip and
pulled a blue t-shirt with white lettering over his head. His wife had

given him the shirt which read, *HANDLE WITH CARE.* He walked back to look at the trees again. Wind through the leaves sounded like people speaking, and the sound of voices made him feel more at home. He closed the window quietly, as if the noise would disturb the trees, the grass, or his in-laws, who, he was sure, had been awake for hours.

As he turned from the window to his unmade bed, he pictured his wife stealing a few minutes extra sleep, waiting for him to kiss her neck and shake her awake. The image of her brown body against the white sheets sparked a memory—a night before they were married. He had promised to meet her in the lobby of an auditorium and was running late. In the dim lights of the smoke-filled lobby, he'd had trouble finding her. Finally he spotted her across the room, leaning against the wall opposite him. That was the memory; Marilyn, tall, thin, dark against the white stucco wall, wearing a thick beige coat fringed with fur, staring into the crowd with an expression of anticipation and melancholy. At that moment, she looked as beautiful as anyone he'd ever seen. But that whole evening, as Handle saw it, revolved around that one frozen image of his future wife leaning against a wall looking sad, beautiful, eager.

Handle had spent the past two weeks with Marilyn's parents, trying to relax, with mixed results. He'd enjoyed the time, but couldn't escape the nagging discontent that had driven him away from the city, his home, his wife. Louise, Marilyn's sister, had arrived from Los Angeles two days ago, giving him someone else to talk to. She'd just completed her second year of law school. Marilyn would finish her finals today and by tomorrow she would be in Tennessee as well.

"You sleep later every day," his sister-in-law said, smiling at him as he walked down the stairs. Louise's eyes had always fascinated him, the same light brown as her skin, but luminous.

He grinned at her. "I might have had a little too much to drink last night."

"That's safe to say." She waited for him to say something more, then moved her hands from her hips to her shoulders, crossing her arms. In one hand she held a book of Emily Dickinson. "You've missed breakfast, but if you talk really sweet, I *might* be persuaded to warm up the biscuits and make some gravy."

"Too early for me to think about food," Handle said, thinking of how tired he was of milk gravy and flat biscuits. He thought he'd like a steak, a New York cut, but he smiled at his lovely sister-in-law. "Maybe later, Louise."

"Later will be too late." She laughed and walked out of the room. Handle watched the swish of her hips and knew he'd been away from his wife too long. But he had to admit that the way Louise walked had always interested him. Her hips rolled like the shoulders of a swimmer.

He and Marilyn had been married six months when he first met Louise. The two sisters walked in the front door of the apartment, each carrying suitcases and laughing. Louise's beauty had shocked him: her eyes, her walk, the trace of Tennessee in her voice that seemed to come and go as she wished. He thought of his wife again, her handsome face and long, angular body. He knew being away from her made Louise seem more appealing. Her presence always kept his interest in Louise in perspective.

Handle walked into the kitchen, took a bottle of orange juice from the refrigerator, and brought the bottle to his mouth. Orange juice and aspirin were key ingredients in his favorite hangover cure.

"Wayne Handle, we have glasses in this house, and I'd be beholding if you'd use one."

Handle looked at his mother-in-law standing with her hands on her hips just as Louise had stood earlier. That posture must run in the family, he thought. "Good morning, Annalee," he said and took another swig of orange juice. He noticed the flyswat in her hand. "Kill anything yet?"

Her face lost its sternness. "I ought to kill you, drinking all night, telling foolish stories, sleeping the lifelong day away. What am I going to tell Marilyn when she gets here? That her husband's been acting like some teenage boy?" She giggled and the sound reminded Handle of his wife. "If you'd told that story about the alligator one more time, we'd all shot you." She laughed out loud.

"They made me do it."

"Louise and Marvin are gluttons for punishment." Annalee laughed again and walked out the screen door into the sunlight. Another inherited trait, he thought: wandering off to end a conversation. He looked out the screen door just as Annalee brought her flyswat down the leg of her husband who had been dozing in the porch swing. Marvin never lifted his head, but raised his huge left arm and swatted Annalee on her behind. Who's the teenager? Handle wondered.

Before he'd met his in-laws, Handle had heard a story that had shaped his opinion of Annalee and Marvin. Their old dog Hoot had gone blind. Marvin speculated it stemmed from eating inky cap mushrooms, but Annalee insisted age had blinded the yellow dog. Too old to adjust, Hoot would become confused in the big yard, howling until someone came after him. He began shitting in the living room and lifting his leg on the furniture. But Marvin couldn't bear the thought of putting Hoot to sleep. He'd found the dog as a pup cradled in the boughs of the purple magnolia that marked the northeast corner of their property. Who put the dog there or why, they never discovered, but Marvin attached real significance to finding a puppy in a tree. Annalee finally solved the problem. She made a trail with bacon grease from the front porch to the old barn where he liked to pee, to the thick grass near the purple magnolia where he liked to shit, and back to the porch. The old dog ran this circle the last two months of his life. When he finally died, Marvin insisted they bury him under the purple magnolia. Annalee dug the hole and buried the dog. The tree promptly died, leaving Marvin to speculate on the connectedness of all living things. Annalee argued that she may have severed the taproot while digging the grave, but Marvin ignored her explanation.

Just as Handle turned away from the screen door, Marvin's thick voice boomed across the porch. "Handle, come quick. This woman's getting feisty. I need you to tell her that alligator story again." He paused as Annalee started laughing. "That ought to calm her down."

Handle yelled back through the screen, "I was on patrol, first year on the force . . ."

"Aggh." Annalee swatted Marvin one last time and ran with her hands over her head into the yard. Handle's laughter hurt his head, and he decided to go to the bathroom to search for aspirin.

Four aspirin were left in the bottle. Cupping his hand under the running faucet, he swallowed all four. As he lifted his head from the sink, his face rose in the mirror on the medicine cabinet, a dun-brown face several shades drabber than when he'd left the city. His eyes appeared yellow. He cupped his hands again and slapped his face with cold water. Running his fingers through his hair, he parted it at just the spot his teeth parted, in the middle. Twice during his stay, Annalee and Marvin had cut off arguments when they heard him approach. He realized they were acting especially cheerful for his benefit, going out of their way to make him feel comfortable, knowing he must be in some kind of trouble to have come to Tennessee alone. He wanted to give them something in return, the thing they needed—an explanation.

He wanted to tell them that his job had become too much, that the ugliness and violence of being a cop had become overwhelming. He believed that would be adequate. They could nod their heads knowingly or shake their heads sadly, then relax, even quarrel with him if they wanted. Better yet, if he could give them an incident—perhaps he'd killed a man in self-defense—they could forgive and console him. However, the incident he had to tell was neither violent nor vulgar, but he had been unable to deal with it and unable still to discuss it.

It had happened in a bar. Off duty, he'd waited for a friend who had tickets for the Mets. As he drank a beer and looked over the bar, he noticed a kid in the booth directly behind his barstool, a black kid, fairly young, who he recognized as some kind of offender. He couldn't place the kid, but he'd seen the face connected with something serious. Across the booth from him, another boy, white and very young, squirmed in his seat. He could tell something was going on under the table, probably passing drugs.

Handle tried to watch them without being seen. He didn't know exactly what was going on or where he'd seen the black kid, but he had no doubt the kid was a bad seed. He could just tell. The bartender brought him another beer. As he looked up to pay for it, he noticed a mirror with a Budweiser ad, and in it, the kid, his lap, and a white hand groping his crotch. Even then, knowing they weren't dealing in anything but each other, Handle couldn't shake the feeling that the kid was no good.

His friend finally arrived, another cop, white, mumbling that there was enough time for another beer. "Turn around slow," Handle said. "The black kid in the booth, who is he?"

His friend looked, then turned back, shaking his head. "Don't know him, but he looks something like that Jenkins kid was shot last week. You remember," he said, "that shit who stabbed women through the ribs as he raped them."

Handle became frightened, turning around so quickly he knocked over his beer and startled the kid. The boy looked him straight in the face, and Handle could see he resembled the Jenkins boy some. He had the same high cheekbones, the same uplifted upper lip, the same empty stare, and he was black, most of all, he was black.

Handle tried to ignore the incident, go on with his life, but he'd lost his edge, questioned too many decisions and motivations, discovering that he looked at black men a little harder than whites. He knew the term for it: *He had an eye out for bad niggers.* Finally, he'd told Marilyn he needed to get away, even though she had two weeks of school left. She'd seen his uneasiness and seemed relieved that he could point to his job as the problem. Handle, however, couldn't tell her that he thought of himself as a racist.

Handle rinsed his face again with cold water and walked out of the bathroom. Across the hall, in the walk-in closet under the stairs, Louise tried to pull sheets from the top shelf. As she stretched for the sheets, her white muslin dress rose to her thighs, revealing her white underwear and the curves of her bottom. Handle thought of the summers she'd spent with them in New York. Once that first summer he had come home early, a little shaken from a scuffle with an afternoon drunk, and found her and Marilyn naked on the patio playing cards. "Expecting someone else?" he'd asked. Marilyn had been startled, but Louise laughed and reached behind her for her dress. Then she had been a year away from completing college. Now she was just a year away from becoming a lawyer. Always something about her was just unresolved.

Louise turned with the sheets in her hands and caught him staring. "You scoundrel," she said with a hint of accent. She threw the sheets at him. "You could have helped me out."

"It was more fun watching." He caught the sheets and threw them back. The top sheet inflated as it flew.

She laughed and stumbled as the sheets caught her full in the face. "Wayne Handle, you're the most worthless man I know."

He waited for her to pull the sheets from her face so he could see if that stern look was there, to see if that was an inherited trait as well as the habit of using his full name. But before he could see her face, she lunged at him, pushing the sheets over his head, laughing as she knocked him off balance, and they both fell to the hardwood floor.

He pulled the sheets off his head, looked at Louise sprawled face down at his feet, her dress up to her waist. Her body bounced with its own laughter. The throb of his headache quickened as he laughed. She sat up quickly and straightened her dress. "Worthless," she said, smiling. "Worthless."

A drizzle began in the afternoon and became a full fledged rain before dark. At dusk, with stomachs full of mashed potatoes and mutton, the family sat in separate chairs on the porch and watched the rain fall. Handle thought the rain looked like pencil lines on cheap paper. For a moment he pictured himself in the first grade, his fat, red pencil in his hand, copying the alphabet from the cards over the blackboard. He remembered Mrs. Hayes, his first grade teacher, stalking the aisles with her ruler to swat the back of the head of anyone caught talking. Handle realized he was smiling. The image of that old woman, her white hair hovering around her black head like a cloud, seemed comical. But she had taught him how to read. In her class he had decided to become a teacher. He wondered when he'd lost track of that.

"There's nothing like rain, except maybe fire, that can hold a body for hours, just watching it," Marvin said. Marvin was so large that any chair he sat in was too small. Handle remembered his own father sitting in one of the first grade desks, waiting to have a word with Mrs. Hayes, wanting to see if she could teach him to read the way she'd taught his son. The image of his father faded. Both Marvin and Annalee had taught in rural Tennessee schools. Handle had wanted to talk with them about teaching, but he'd never told anyone he'd wanted to be a teacher and couldn't bring himself to share the secret with them.

He looked back at the rain and picked up his bottle of beer. "The ocean," he said, feeling the cold bottle in his hands. "I could stare at the

ocean all day." Handle pictured a wave coming toward him looking like
a cupped hand which would flatten just before reaching him.

"I've heard people say that," Marvin said.

"I can look at stars that way," Annalee said. "Nights without a
moon."

Each of them turned toward Louise, waiting for her to complete the
circle of conversation. She said nothing, sitting with her legs tucked
under her body, staring at the rain.

"Darling," Annalee said, looking at her daughter, "I've seen you
staring at a man's bottom so long and hard, I'd have sworn it was going
to fall off."

Marvin smiled, Annalee and Handle laughed. Louise forced a smile,
then let it fade. "Words," she said. "I can look at words on a page until
they seem to glow." Handle could see the shine in her eyes.

"You always loved books," Marvin said. "I've never seen a child take
to books so young."

Handle's eyes hadn't left Louise. Something about her sitting there,
staring off into the darkening sky, her hair with drops of rain like jewels
—Handle became afraid he was falling in love, or that he had been in
love since that first summer and never admitted it, that he might scoop
her up in his arms, here in front of her parents, and carry her to the
room where he slept and make love with her. He tried to shrug off the
feeling, staring out into the rain and reminding himself that Marilyn
would be back by tomorrow night, and such thoughts would seem silly
to him. But he couldn't resist looking back to her again.

"Louise," Annalee said, rising from her chair, "you want to help with
the dishes?"

Handle didn't want Louise to move. "I'll help you, Annalee," he said.
As he stood, he heard Louise's voice, as if coming from the distance,
"Thank you."

Handle washed and Annalee dried. The window over the sink covered with steam, and the sound of rain filled the room. Annalee
hummed a tune Handle recognized but could not remember. He liked
the feel of the hot water on his arms and hands, but Louise's eyes, her
voice, hung in his mind.

"Will Marilyn need four years to get her degree?" Annalee ran a towel in circles over a dish.

"She could make it in three if her old classes transfer. Why?"

"Just wondering," she said and began humming again.

"What's that you're humming?"

She stopped, thought for a minute, then laughed. "Why I don't know. I was just humming away, but soon as you asked it left me. What did it sound like?"

Handle laughed. "Something like a cat in heat."

Annalee slapped his shoulder with the dish towel. "Now you shouldn't be mean to your mother-in-law. You don't talk that way to Marvin, and you're sure not mean to Louise."

Handle handed her another dish. He smiled, but felt suddenly uneasy, wondering if his feelings toward Louise might be more obvious than he'd thought. He tried to discard the notion and concentrate on the dirty pot in his hands. They worked for a few moments to the sound of rain before Annalee started humming again.

She stopped abruptly. *Georgia on my Mind.*"

"Ray Charles," Handle said.

"Now that's out of the way, I'm going to ask you straight out, Wayne Handle."

Handle felt his stomach tense, afraid she might say something about Louise.

"Are you and my daughter going to have children?"

His stomach relaxed, but he didn't really know how to answer the question. "Marilyn's got to finish school."

Annalee stared at him for a second, then nodded. "School's a wonderful thing. Between Louise and Marilyn, I'm going to have the most educated daughters in Tennessee—if they were in Tennessee." She put the dish in the cupboard and took the pot from Handle. "The only thing I'd worry about is if Marilyn *did* get pregnant, Louise might run out and do the same, married or not." The screen door opened and Marvin walked through the kitchen to the living room smiling at them as he passed. Annalee watched her husband, then turned back to the cupboard. "At least there'd be a few little ones around."

"While I'm in town tomorrow, I ought to buy you a puppy," Handle said. "Maybe two." He smiled at her, but she wasn't really amused. "Annalee, that's your dream, not ours."

She smiled weakly and patted his arm. "I know, sweetheart."

Handle put his arm around her in a half hug, but a new question formed for him: what was their dream? He finished the few remaining dishes, and Annalee shooed him out of the kitchen. The rain still fell steadily and Louise hadn't moved, feet tucked under her body, watching the darkness of evening fall with the rain. Talking with Annalee about his wife had diffused the charge that Louise had carried, so Handle took the chair next to her and looked off into the sky just as a flash of lightning painted a crooked path between dark clouds, then vanished.

"Daddy's gone to bed," Louise said.

Handle nodded, but looked past her to the rain. A thin stream of water dripping from the corner of the roof caught the light and looked like a long strand of twisting tinsel.

"We're all a little worried about you," Louise said.

Finally someone had said it, Handle thought, but he didn't know what he could say in return. He might tell her that their worry showed in the kindness they extended him, but that sounded patronizing and avoided the question. Besides, he considered that the generosity of the family made it even more difficult to talk. When he'd first met Marvin and Annalee, he'd resented their marriage, believing it made Marilyn expect too much. Now, they'd been so careful to create an atmosphere of goodwill, that to introduce his problems into the household seemed ugly and ungracious. Looking at Louise's patient face, he gave the most honest answer he could. "I don't think I can talk about it."

"Have you talked with Marilyn?"

"I wanted to." He folded his arms and looked back into the rain. "I thought once or twice this past week I might talk with Marvin or Annalee, but I can't seem to do it."

"Is your marriage in trouble, Handle?"

He looked at her again, the soft curves of her cheek, the deep brown of her eyes, then shook his head from side to side. "Sometimes I get this feeling. Riding in a patrol car with some white jackass, I get this queasy feeling, and I wonder who I'm trying to fool. But I always convince myself it's better there's one cop who doesn't want to bust black heads, even when he has to. Now I believe that's just what they want me to think."

Louise still stared at him, waiting. He knew she wouldn't settle for an answer so general, but he couldn't tell her more. So he stared back at her and found himself watching the minute changes in her face, how her eyebrows lifted and curved back to their normal shape as she moved from waiting for a response to a different attitude. Her eyes became slightly moist. Her lips moved almost imperceptibly as if mouthing a whisper. They sat quietly on the porch for several moments, just looking at one another while the rain fell.

"Oh Handle," Louise said very softly. "What are you doing here without Marilyn?"

Handle felt something collapse inside him. Handle told her about the bar and the boy, the white groping hand, and that face, that blank brown face; he told her about the realization he'd come to about himself and how it had affected his work and his life. He spoke quickly, anxiously, watching her face, wondering what she would think of him. She listened patiently, but without giving away her thoughts. When Handle finished the story, he paused, but Louise said nothing and he didn't feel comfortable with the silence. "The department was all right. They know cops get crazy sometimes if they can't get away. And Marilyn understood, or said she did. She believed I needed to get away from dealing with rapists and pimps and junkies. I let her believe that. I didn't know how to tell her the truth."

"Why can't you tell her what you just told me?"

He tried to think of the real answer. Why had he been able to tell Louise what he couldn't tell his wife or her parents? What quality had he invested in her he hadn't in the others. Perhaps it was just the moment, he thought. But looking at her again, he couldn't believe that was true. "I always wanted to be a teacher. Can you imagine that? I never told anyone. I wanted to teach kids to read."

Louise reached over and put her hand on his arm. "That first summer I met you, I don't know if you remember this, but Marilyn's friend was pregnant. She was your neighbor, but I can't remember her name."

Handle nodded.

"When she miscarried, it was so awful. We thought she might die, the bleeding was so bad, and she was hysterical."

"I remember," Handle said.

"By the time you got home from work, she was hospitalized, but Marilyn and I were wrecks—we were scared. You were so good that night, Handle. You were so strong. I . . ." She stopped and stared at his face as if what she was about to say were written there. Then she closed her eyes. "You'll get over this," she said flatly.

Handle waited for her to open her eyes again. He heard the screen door open, turned, and saw Annalee looking back at them. Only then did he realize Louise's hand was still on his arm.

"Still raining, I see," Annalee said in a voice barely above a whisper.

Handle nodded. The hand on his arm felt like an iron. Annalee walked by them to the porch swing. As she walked by, Louise lifted her hand and opened her eyes. The three of them sat without speaking for a long time. The rain fell and Annalee hummed another unrecognizable song.

Handle woke at two a.m. from another dream of the city, of running down an alley after a scared kid and realizing someone was running after him. The quietness of the country dark wakened him further. He pulled on his pants, then sat on the bed another moment, letting his eyes adjust to the dark and his ears to the quiet. He decided to have a beer, sit on the porch, and just listen to the still darkness.

The light from the refrigerator was so stark that the beer didn't look good to him, but he took one anyway and started toward the porch. A light shone in the living room and he walked in to turn it off. In the corner of the room, under a light, Louise sat in a chair, reading a book. She was wrapped in a gray-blue comforter.

Handle stood in the doorway. "What are you reading?"

She didn't look up at first, finishing something, clearly aware of his presence before he spoke. "Emily Dickinson," she said, then reached out her hand for the beer.

Handle walked over and gave her the bottle, looking at the thin straps that held her white cotton nightshirt in place. "Why are you always reading that woman?"

"Because she wrote like I think, because she loved words for themselves."

Handle squatted to be eye level with her and took back the beer. "You ought to read black writers," he said. "Richard Wright, Ellison, Baldwin."

"Those are all men. What makes you think I'm more black than I am woman?" She sat up straighter in the chair and turned the light toward the wall so she could see his face without the glare of the light.

Handle looked into her eyes and started to smile, but he could see she was serious. "Because of your past. Because of your parents."

"One of my parents *is* a woman." She spoke without a trace of accent.

"But they're both black." He smiled, hoping the conversation would become less serious.

"Mostly," she said.

Handle lost his smile and moved closer to her. "What's got you talking this way?"

"We've got plenty of white in us, like it or not."

"All right, but who loves you? Who accepts you?"

"Women. The men, black men, white men, they want me, but they don't accept me. You'd be surprised how many men will make fools of themselves trying to get me to go out with them, sleep with them." She looked him in the eyes. "Even you, Handle. You're just like any other man. You look at me and picture me writhing under you, singing out your name."

Handle's first impulse was to deny it, but he stifled the urge, knowing she would just laugh. He felt curiously hurt yet moved, realizing he was seeing Louise clearly for the first time. He'd known her studious side and her playful side, but he'd never seen this part of her before, the part that tries to make the others converge into some meaningful whole.

Louise finally spoke again, looking away. "Besides, I've read all those men, and let me tell you they're more men than black."

Handle said nothing.

"And you, you're more man than you'll ever be black."

Handle straightened his back and furrowed his brows. "I'm a black man."

Louise giggled but stopped; her voice was without laughter. "You're a cop. They pay you to put niggers in jail."

Handle felt a heavy twist in his throat and an urge to slap her, but he held off. Her face still seemed hard, not phony sternness, but a real hard glare. "Where'd you get this anger, Louise? I've never seen it in you before."

"It's been here," she said, looking down at the book in her lap. "You think men have a corner on anger? All those angry black men you've read got you thinking a woman can't feel anger?"

"But what's made *you* angry?"

"Goddamn you, Handle. Don't you see what it is? You can be so damned stupid."

He waited for her to continue, not knowing what to say, recognizing in himself a familiar, uneasy feeling. An uncomfortable excitement began to build in his chest.

Louise stared down at her hands. "I want to sleep with my sister's husband," she whispered.

Handle put his hand on her cheek and turned her to face him.

"Christ, I hate this," Louise said. "I never wanted this to happen."

Handle moved his thumb across her cheek to catch a tear, then pulled her close. Her arms slowly moved around his body. Handle became aware suddenly of the quietness of the country. Both fear and desire filled him so that his chest shook to contain them. He clung to her and they sat in the dark several minutes.

Louise lifted her head and kissed Handle lightly on the lips, and Handle found himself kissing her back. "If you weren't Marilyn's husband, I'd make love with you right here, right now. Or if I could just be sure."

Handle stared into her brown eyes and realized the luminous quality was a trace of green that floated in and out of the brown. He pressed his lips against hers and felt her tongue moving across his teeth. He pulled back and saw more tears running down her face.

"If I could be sure," Louise said. She shook her head from side to side. "Handle, I don't know whether I want you in spite of the fact you're Marilyn's husband, or *because* you're her husband. If I could be sure, I don't think anything would matter." She put her hand behind his head and pulled him to her. They kissed, and she let her head fall against his chest.

The warmth of her face against his chest both saddened and excited him. He wondered if part of his desire was because she was Marilyn's sister, but he didn't want to believe it was that ugly. They sat in darkness for several minutes. Handle took a deep breath and held it, trying to calm himself. He didn't want to act without thinking, without trying to make sense of what he was feeling. It had been an emotional night, he told himself. Without his wife, he had turned to her sister. But tomorrow Marilyn would be back, he thought, and his feelings toward Louise would return to what they had been before.

He wanted to tell her this, tell her that what they were feeling was loneliness and a shared pain brought into focus by their friendship, that this, and not love, motivated them. Looking at her in his arms, he wavered, wondering what love was, if not this. But he resolved to tell her that as much as they longed for each other, they shouldn't make love, that her sister would be here tomorrow and change what they believed they were feeling.

Before he could tell her, she lifted her head, brushed her lips across his cheek, stood slowly, and walked out of the room to her bed. Handle listened to her feet on the stairs and her bedroom door opening and closing. He waited a few moments, then walked into his room.

DAY 2

Handle slept late again. When he woke, he lay in bed listening. On the porch, Marvin sang to himself, a song Handle couldn't quite make out. He heard the noise of water running through the pipes and pictured Annalee washing the dishes after breakfast. He wondered about Louise. Was she still sleeping? Was she reading? He wondered if words sometimes appeared before her face, in bold print, independent even of paper.

He walked to the window and looked out at the trees, suddenly becoming aware of a memory he'd long forgotten. He believed it was his oldest memory, yet he visualized it clearly, as if it were happening: He stands on his mother's huge bed, his hands on the oak headboard, looking out the window, beyond the salt cedar's branches. A hen blown into the pond flaps its wings, claws on the water, as thick, misting rain shadows the yard and forms large, clear drops on the boughs of the tree.

Handle wondered about the memory, its significance, because it seemed important, although he believed the event itself was unimportant. He couldn't even bring himself to believe something important about his life was tied up in the image or his memory of it. It was the thing itself, its clarity. He remembered it as if, for just an instant, time had puddled, and a moment passed before its flow resumed. He held on to the picture a few more moments, then let it go.

He showered and dressed, paying special attention to his hair. He shaved and covered his neck with sweet smelling aftershave lotion, unsure whether this care was for his wife whom he hadn't seen in two weeks or her sister.

He loved his wife, but there had been times when he felt the need of another woman, when he found it inconceivable to think that he'd never make love to any woman but Marilyn. During such times women inevitably seemed available and desirable, but Handle had never had an affair. The conflict had nothing to do with his love for Marilyn. He needed the security of their relationship. But he also wanted to throw himself into relationships, to be consumed by the many and various women he desired. For years it had been Louise who had held these pulls in balance by siphoning off those desires harmlessly. Their flirtatious friendship had stabilized his marriage.

Down the stairs, he heard Marvin still singing. "On the run all night, on the run all day . . ." Handle laughed.

Annalee's voice came through the open kitchen door. "Is that finally you, Handle?"

"I'm finally me." He stepped into the living room and looked into the corner where Louise sat with a book in her hands. "What is it today?" he asked softly.

She looked up at him solemnly, then smiled. "Gwendolyn Brooks, have you read her?"

Handle shook his head. "Never heard of her." Louise turned back to the book, and Handle tried for a moment to picture her as she had been last night, resting in his arms. Instead, he saw her once again on the porch with drops of water glistening in her hair. Their flirtatious friendship was over, he realized. The confessions of the past night had ended it. They would have to find a new way to deal with one another.

Handle walked out onto the porch. Clouds obscured much of the sky, but the sun still shone brightly. Perspiration formed along Handle's forehead as soon as he stepped outside. Marvin stopped singing as Handle closed the screen door.

"Trains," Marvin said. His shirt had damp splotches at the armpits and center of his chest.

"What about them?"

"My father could sit in the Chicago switching yard and watch trains come and go all night." Marvin smiled but his eyes were distant. "They meant something more to him than they ever did to me. I don't know exactly what. Freedom maybe. Adventure."

"Direction," Handle said, surprised at the sound of his voice. He pictured the tracks, the black ties and heavy rails. He liked the image, its solidity. And the train, he pictured the train moving down the tracks with its remarkable conviction. The image became so strong that he barely heard Marvin reply.

"Maybe. Direction's a hard thing to come by."

Handle intended to walk in the woods. The afternoon rains had kept him inside too much and the anticipation of Marilyn's arrival made him restless, so he decided to explore the woods before the sky darkened. A long field of new corn separated the woods from the house. The knee high stalks had been recently thinned and weeded, hoed-out as Marvin called it, creating an appealing symmetry to the plants and rows.

Handle walked through the corn, inhaling the fragile odor of the green stalks and looking ahead at the woods. Perhaps the mud discouraged him, accumulating around the edges of his tennis shoes so that he had to stomp it off or lift his feet high and walk like a man in snowshoes. But the woods would be less muddy than the plowed rows and his shoes were already too muddy to wear into town to pick up Marilyn, so something else caused him to stop just before the perfect rows ended. He considered the question, but couldn't say why.

Handle straddled a corn stalk, stared into the woods, and tried to think of the names of the trees. Maples he knew, the leaves like stars with winged pairs of seeds that pirouette to earth, but he didn't see any maples. The trees that marked the end of the field might have been sycamores or oaks, beeches or hickories. As long as he didn't know their names, they were just trees, blocking the sun and engendering darkness. Handle turned away from the woods.

As he began his walk back to the house, he spotted Louise leaning against the concrete birdbath behind the barn. She waved as if washing a window pane. The birdbath was the gray of concrete and the barn, the gray of rotting lumber, but Louise's shirt was blood red, conspicuous in the landscape, making her appear closer than she actually was. She straightened as he walked to her and put her hands in the pockets of her blue denim cut-offs.

"Why don't you go in?" She twisted slightly from the waist as she spoke. The tail of her red shirt looped over her wrists.

Handle felt she'd read his thoughts. "Was it that obvious?"

"Marilyn and I used to play in the woods when we were kids." Her eyes left Handle for the woods. "If you go back far enough, there's a hollow. It was our secret place."

She smelled of cigarettes. On the ground next to the birdbath, white cigarette butts lay scattered like a mutilated alphabet. Handle realized he'd never seen her smoke in her parents' house although she smoked often when she visited New York. The barn hid this spot from view of the house, and Handle realized that this too was a secret place for her. "I never had a secret place."

"All kids do," Louise said. "You've just forgotten."

A wasp flew by Handle's head. He followed its flight to the eave of the barn. "My father kept a pretty short leash." He looked back to Louise. She still stared out at the woods, and Handle suddenly became uneasy. Sweat gathered at his temples and the base of his jaw. The sheer greenness of the trees, the grass at his feet, became suffocating. Only the corn, the green stalks separated by rich, brown earth, soothed him. They had room to breathe.

Louise began giggling and turned toward Handle. She rested her hands against the birdbath and leaned against it again. "The day after Marilyn got caught in the barn with Bobby Dill—Oh, they weren't doing anything. She was only in the eighth grade. But the day after, I took a boy out to our secret spot, the hollow. I couldn't let Marilyn get one up on me." She laughed. "Neither of us knew what to do when we got there, so I acted mad and screamed terrible, mean things at him, hoping Marilyn or somebody would hear. But the hollow is too far out, no one could hear."

Louise laughed again and dipped her head. Handle laughed with her, but still felt edgy. Louise shook her head. "I always had to outdo Marilyn. I thought I was over that."

Her head was still cast down, but Handle could see her face reflected in the rainwater in the birdbath, coppery and clear. Above them wasps hummed at the openings of their finger-shaped nests. "When Marilyn gets here," Handle said, "I'm going to tell her . . ."

"I wouldn't." Louise looked up quickly from the bath.

"No, about my job, why I had to leave."

"I was afraid you meant . . ." She shook her head violently. "Last night on the porch, when you told me about that boy in the bar, I thought about the men I know, so sure of themselves they're blind, or just the opposite, like puppies—I think of what I want in a man and I see it in you, but maybe that's not it. Maybe whatever I see in you I make myself want." She turned away from him, rested again against the birdbath, but faced the dense trees. "What it really is—I see you and Marilyn happy and I want that. I guess I want to take it from her. It's awful, but it must be the truth."

Handle wanted to tell her she was being too hard on herself, but he didn't want to encourage her to believe she really loved him. At least he didn't think he wanted to. At the same time, he didn't want to believe her desire for him was just rivalry with her sister. In some dark corner of his heart, he wanted her to want *him*. But he also wanted it to be over. Handle said nothing. For several moments they stared at the fields. Above them, wasps fanned their mud nests, their whine as electric as the surge of blood.

Louise turned toward Handle, reached into the birdbath, and withdrew a penny. Waves rippled in circles from the point her hand entered and left the water, and pennies sparkled beneath them like jewels. She placed one damp penny in his mouth, on his tongue, and put another in her mouth. Handle tasted the tart metal and watched Louise. He remembered the taste from childhood, and suddenly he remembered crawling on top of the bookcase in his parents' living room, pulling open the door to the linen closet that was above the clothes closet, and hoisting himself up. The closet was so high it was never used, except by him, his secret place, where, with the door just cracked open, he could watch the world from a safe distance. He remembered the narrow view afforded by the cracked door and the thrill of the jump down onto the couch. For a moment, Handle felt the thrill of the secret fall. He started to tell Louise, but decided not to, even though she was the first person ever to find her way there. Instead, he tasted the penny and watched her watch him.

Louise finally took the penny from her mouth and dropped it back into the water. "Pennies," she said and smiled, then walked away from him, around the corner of the barn.

The temperature in Monroe, Tennessee was close to ninety degrees. Handle sat on the bench outside the tiny bus depot. He had been unable to convince himself that the twenty minute drive to the city would only take twenty minutes. In New York, he would have run into heavy traffic or an accident blocking the road and would have arrived just in time. But he wasn't in New York, so he sat on the bench to wait twenty minutes for the bus.

He looked up and down the city's main street. The air in Monroe didn't seem real to him. He was more comfortable with the sky the color of primer paint. A weimaraner sniffed at his shoes, then walked a few yards away and shat on the concrete sidewalk. A man and a woman, holding hands, crossed the intersection of Manhattan and Magnolia against the traffic light. The man had his shirt off. Tufts of black hair on his shoulders and back made Handle think of haircuts, of having clipped hair down the back of his shirt. The woman watched her feet as she walked, as if they began walking on their own and she just followed, curious and somehow saddened by the asphalt under them.

Ten minutes before the bus was due, an unshaven man wearing a checkered coat a full size too large walked on the sidewalk next to the bench where Handle sat. He held his arm stiffly behind his back as if he were twisting his own arm to force himself to speak. He was talking to himself as he walked by Handle. "You never take into consideration the whole heart," he said as he passed the bench.

Handle thought of Amy Hansen, a past neighbor and former friend of Marilyn's. He remembered Amy, pregnant and excited about being a mother, spending Saturdays with them while her husband was working driving a bus. Marilyn had wanted a child badly during that period. They discussed it almost every night. After the miscarriage, Amy lost her mind. She feared that one day her head would just fall off her shoulders. At that moment, a red-headed woman with a beehive hair-do passed Handle's bench. She placed one spiked heel in the dog shit as she walked away. In a way Handle couldn't explain, the woman legitimized Amy's fear. Anything is possible, he thought.

The bus was on time. Marilyn stepped off looking softer and younger than he'd remembered. As he hugged her and kissed her, the constancy of his love for her returned instantly. Only after the feeling returned did he realize it had been gone at all. She was full of conversation about her final exams, her last minute essay, her longing for him, but as they drove through the thick Tennessee countryside, Handle began thinking of the night before. He questioned whether he could talk with Marilyn but decided to try.

"I don't like being a cop," he said and looked at her. For an instant she had the same look he'd remembered her having in the lobby years ago: sad, eager, beautiful. "Most of all, I don't like thinking like a cop."

"I've never known you to think like anyone but Wayne Handle," she said.

"Well, Wayne Handle is a cop."

"So how do cops think?" She took hold of his arm with both hands.

"There are certain types we've got to keep on a short leash," Handle said.

"For instance?"

"For instance: blacks."

Marilyn nodded and looked off down the road. Her parents' farm became visible in the distance. "Sometimes you can feel things you don't really believe."

"But how do you tell?"

Handle watched as her gaze left the approaching farm and found him. He loved her gentle face, her unlined forehead and smooth cheeks, her dark and relentless eyes, the perfect ellipse of her mouth. "I love you, Wayne. Everything else I guess at." She lay her head against his shoulder as he guided the car off the main road toward the white farmhouse. He could see Marvin sitting on the porch, watching them approach.

"I thought for sure you'd be fat by now," Marvin said, stepping down the porch steps to greet his daughter. "But you get prettier everytime I see you."

She had to jump to throw her arms around the neck of her father. She laughed as she said, "Hi Daddy." Handle could hear the drawl beginning to return with her first words.

Annalee came out of the screen door with Louise just behind her. "Oh Marilyn, we were about to fall apart, waiting for you," her mother said, opening her arms.

Marilyn took a few steps to her mother and wrapped her arms around her. "Hi Mama." Even as she hugged her mother, Handle could see his wife's eyes looking toward Louise. He watched as she burst into Louise's arms, saying, "Loosie, Loosie." Handle had forgotten how much taller Marilyn was, how Louise always looked childlike next to her.

The warmth cut loose in the yard was more than even the sky could bear, and large drops of rain began to fall. "Would you look at that," Marvin said. "These northern women always seem to bring the rain with them."

* * *

The rain continued through the afternoon and dinner. It was still raining when the table had been cleared, the dishes done, and Marilyn, Louise, Annalee, and Handle joined Marvin on the porch. Handle and Marilyn sat together, arms around each other.

"I can hardly believe we have the whole family together," Annalee said. "Of course, with daughters at either end of the country, I guess we shouldn't expect it too often, but it's nice we're all here."

"I had a dream about being here," Marilyn said. "I dreamt I was up in my room getting ready for bed. I was grown up, but the room was just like it was when I was little. The bed even had that frilly green bedspread Grandma made for me."

"I still have that bedspread," Annalee said.

"I heard a noise outside and I went to the window. All the stars were falling out of the sky into the yard. I ran down the stairs and out to the yard. When I got close, I could see that the stars were ceramic dolls with blue eyes and clothes of silver. They were beautiful."

Handle kissed Marilyn on the cheek.

"That's a lovely dream," Louise said.

Marvin and Annalee exchanged a long look. "Darling," Annalee began. "How well do you remember Grandmother Perkins?

"You were only four or five when she died. She was silly about you. I guess because you were the only grandchild she lived to see. Anyway, she was always making you things, like that bedspread."

"I never did like that thing," Marvin said.

"And giving you things, spoiling you every chance she got. One of the things she gave you was a doll, a white porcelain doll with blue eyes, and she may have been wearing silver clothes. I don't remember."

"I remember her," Marvin said. "That doll had a frilly silver dress on."

"Daddy, I never knew you took an interest in dolls," Louise said.

"I remember because I broke the damn thing. It wasn't a doll made for children anyway, made to look at."

"She'd had it since she was a little girl," Annalee said. "But it had never been played with because her father hated the thing because it was so white and had blue eyes. So she saved it for her kids, but since Marvin was her only child, she just hung on to it. I guess she knew she was dying and wanted you to have the doll even though you weren't old enough to take care of it."

"I wasn't old enough either. I dropped the damn thing and Mother was ready to take my head clean off." Marvin laughed. Annalee smiled and patted him on the shoulder. The sound of the rain returned as though it had been quiet while the story was being told.

"It's funny you'd remember that. You were so tiny," Annalee said.

"I didn't remember it," Marilyn said. "I dreamt it."

Marvin grunted. "I wonder why your mind stored that doll away all these years, just to bring it out now?"

Handle looked out into the rain and thought of the recurring dreams he had of being chased down the streets of the city. He envied Marilyn for her dream. He thought of Marvin's grandfather telling his daughter to put the doll away. He respected the man for that gesture, however cruel it must have seemed to the little girl who would become Marvin's mother. He looked at his wife and wondered how many white dolls were locked within her, waiting to present themselves unexpectedly. He decided he didn't envy her dream. It was, after all, just a beautiful nightmare.

The family talked and listened to the rain. They talked about Louise finishing school and Marilyn finally going back to school. They talked about the conversation of two nights ago, how they kept making Handle tell his alligator story over and over while Annalee complained. Marvin's thick voice shook the porch as he imitated Handle finishing the story. "There I was standing on a table in the corner of that rundown dive, with a damn alligator staring at me, looking hungry, and before my partner will call for help he wants to know if it's an alligator or a crocodile." Everybody laughed and drank wine or beer. "An alligator or crocodile," Marvin repeated and laughed again. Handle wondered if they liked the story because the fool asking the question was white.

"Marvin Perkins, if I hear that story one more time, you'll be wondering whether what hit you was a pot or pan," Annalee said. "Then you and Handle both'll be sleeping in the woods."

It was nearly eleven when the rain began to dissipate and the family moved inside and to bed.

Who can say why a man full of good food and just enough beer, tired from laughing with people he loves and making love with his wife, cannot sleep? And who can be sure that light is not sometimes detectable even through solid walls? At 3 a.m. in the doorway of his in-laws' family room, Handle stared across the room into the far corner. Louise sat in the arm chair, bare shouldered, wrapped in the gray-blue comforter, hands in her lap with a book of poetry. The low reading lamp shone directly on the book, her brown hands, the folds in the comforter. "Louise," Handle said, his voice a hoarse whisper, almost inaudible. She didn't hear. In the indirect light, her face was like the reflection of a face in a dark window—rounded, softened by the night. Her eyes, cast down, gave her a sleepy look, but visible below their hoods, they lit like tiny candles.

She either hadn't seen him, or chose to ignore him, waiting for him to step forward. He had been sure that Marilyn's arrival would stop his thoughts of Louise. When that didn't happen, he believed that after making love with his wife his feelings toward Louise would dissipate. But here he was, confident of his love for his wife, unable to sleep thinking about her sister. He could still stop. He could walk back up the stairs, crawl across his sleeping wife, and return to the familiar, sleepless dark. Handle stepped backwards, out of the room. He pivoted out of the doorway and leaned against the wall. His heart rattled around in his chest like tennis shoes in a clothes dryer. He closed his eyes, but the figure of her in the chair, wrapped in the comforter, took shape, as if imprinted on his retina.

Handle slid silently down the wall into a squat. Moonlight shone through the window on the dining table, coating the polished mahogany with white light. On the floor, beyond the lip of the table, a half-circle of light, scattered at the edges, approached Handle slowly. He pulled his feet back unconsciously, but then he heard a page turn in the next room and dropped to his knees in the puddle of light. Crooking his head into the opening, he stared again at Louise, dark ovals shadowing the base of her neck, a black splinter separating her lips. He pulled back, settled flat on the floor, his back against the wall. Moonlight reached the middle of his thighs. He tried to sort out his thoughts, but they came too fast and he couldn't make sense of them. He felt suspended in mid-jump, the instant before reaching one side or the other or beginning the fall.

Moonlight reached his lap, lit half the doorway. The polished table glowed white, like the surface of a calm lake. He tried to picture just such a lake to calm himself, but the pull of Louise in the next room permitted him no tranquility. He gripped the doorjamb backhanded to pull himself up, the throb of blood in his hand so strong, he thought the hand might pulse red. He stood in the half-lit doorway, moonlight scattering at his feet.

Louise closed her book and looked up at him. His doubts fell away almost instantly, his thoughts slowed, and he became calm and sure. For a second, he thought of the conversation of the night before and wondered whether he came to her as a black man or just as a man. He couldn't answer the question or even consider it, not that the differences were indistinct, but unimportant. Something larger was present, something he'd hoped to contain in a secret place hopelessly small. This time he couldn't tell himself Marilyn's arrival would make it retreat. It wasn't the flickering of lust or the simple glow of desire that led him to her, but the total darkness of love.

Handle walked toward her but stopped before he reached her chair. She leaned forward when he stopped. "Does it surprise you I'm here?" she asked.

"No," Handle said. "It surprises me *I'm* here."

"This was always my favorite place to read, wrapped in a blanket after everyone had gone to sleep. It was always my part of the house." She ran her hand down the comforter, smoothing the wrinkles.

The room was silent. Handle and Louise stared at each other bravely. Louise lifted her hand to the reading lamp and shut the light. Handle took another step forward, feeling a sudden urge to kneel before her. He squatted, eye level with her, gripped the arm of the chair. Her hair smelled like cinnamon. A shuddering in his chest threatened to topple him, so he went to one knee to balance himself.

"When Marilyn arrived," Louise said, "I knew immediately how I felt about her. And about you." She put her hand to his temple, the tips of her fingers resting there so lightly, Handle couldn't be sure she touched him at all. He became afraid again, afraid she might reject him, afraid she might not. "I love my sister." Her fingers brushed across his cheek and jaw. "I could never do anything *just* to hurt her. When I realized that, I knew I loved you as well, Handle."

Handle took her hand from his face, cupped it in his hands as if it were a liquid he was about to drink.

"Mamma and Daddy are old. They sleep like children," Louise said. "Marilyn was so tired. She won't wake." She opened the comforter and Handle looked at her body, the shapes and angles, the turns and shadows. He worried that Marilyn might wake and find him missing, or that Marvin or Annalee might want a glass of milk or a breath of air and discover them. But the time for worry had passed and he was helpless to stop. "Just for tonight," Louise said, coming into his arms.

He kissed her lips, her breasts. He ran his lips down her neck. As their bodies touched, the world stepped back and they entered a private realm. Handle spread the comforter on the floor and they lay together, holding each other, running their hands lightly over their bodies.

They made love slowly. And as they made love, Handle thought of the boy in the bar with another boy's white hand in his lap, he thought of Annalee and Marvin making love at just this pace, this slow pace. He thought of his wife, exhausted from the bus ride, wine, and lovemaking, sleeping in the dark quiet, and he thought of the dark itself, of his dark skin, of Louise's eyes with their flash of green, of rain falling straight to the earth, of pennies sparkling under rainwater, of Marvin as a little boy watching his father watch the trains in the Chicago switching yard, of a train charging ahead, full speed into the darkness, absolutely confident that the rails will take it home into the light, of Louise, here, with him, right now, making love with him, of this night, this instant.

They made love, and the evening seemed to condense into one moment. Handle held Louise close and kissed her dark lips, feeling as though the moment had a life of its own, and that life beat within them both, independent of the dark world around them. And that, perhaps, was enough, he thought, an interval of clarity, one clear, resonant note that stops momentarily the daily march of events. Handle dressed slowly. He kissed Louise again and returned to sleep with his wife, confident he had witnessed the movement from now to then tremble, where love was as visible and tangible as the rain.

DAY 3

Although he'd lain awake much of the night, Handle woke feeling strong and refreshed, but when he looked at his wife dressing, a haze separated them. She caught him staring. "How did you sleep?" she asked.

He smiled, thought he should tell her fine, then thought that was silly, he should tell her the truth, that he'd been awake most of the night. But the real truth was that he'd made love with her sister. He felt awkward, so he shrugged his shoulders and rolled onto his side. His face burned with embarrassment.

"I slept like a child," Marilyn said. She sat on the edge of the bed and laid her hand on his back. "It's so peaceful here."

He didn't want to look at her, so he rooted his head into the pillow. Then he felt ridiculous, making the situation worse by acting guilty. He started to roll over to face her, but decided that might be too bold, that if she got a good look at his face she would know. He worked his head into the pillow again, his eyes closed. "Uh huh, peaceful," he said, but his voice didn't sound right to him.

Marilyn slapped him on the butt. "Wayne Handle, are you going back to sleep?"

What had come over him? He felt panicky with every question. He should turn to her, he thought. No, he should be still. He should be natural as if nothing had happened. Handle tried to think of a natural thing to do. After a moment of deliberation, he scratched his jaw.

Marilyn resumed dressing. "You're going to sleep your life away."

He felt the slight tip of the bed for each leg as she pulled on her jeans. He heard her stand and the zipper, then she was back on the bed again, shifting her weight as she slipped on her socks and shoes. She seemed to be dressing very slowly.

"Should I save you any breakfast?"

He could feel her right above him, but he kept his eyes closed. "No," he said. Then she was breathing down his neck. Her lips pressed against his cheek, liquid and hot. He waited for the sound of the door opening and closing, then opened his eyes a crack to be sure she was gone.

Handle sat up in the bed. He had never been unfaithful to Marilyn and up to now hadn't thought of the past night in those terms. It had seemed different, separate from his life with Marilyn. He'd believed he'd tried to do what was right in order to be true to Louise, to himself, to love. He closed his eyes and thought of Louise. He remembered the softness of her cheek against his chest, the smell of her body, the rhythm of her breathing, the cinnamon smell of her hair. No, he thought, making love with Louise was as genuine as taking a breath.

But when he opened his eyes he saw Marilyn's negligé draped across the dresser and lost his surety. He stood and walked to the window. The sky had cleared, and the unobscured sun shone so brightly that it seemed to be an answer to a question he could not formulate. Low limbs of the trees were calm, but wind whipped through the high branches.

Handle took a long shower and shaved slowly. He thought of Marilyn and their marriage. For an instant, he thought he should take her aside and suggest they have children, but he knew the idea grew out of fear and guilt. He wondered whether he was afraid of losing Marilyn or just afraid of her knowing how he'd betrayed her. He'd believed that his lovemaking with Louise had a certain purity, a clarity that transcended convention. But he knew he couldn't explain that to Marilyn and knew that although he'd been honest with himself and Louise, he'd betrayed Marilyn nonetheless. He cupped his hands under the faucet and took a drink. The swallow of water felt like a stone in his throat.

He dressed slowly, then sat on the bed trying to sort out his feelings when he heard steps on the stairs. Sure it was Marilyn, he jumped from the bed and walked to the door, hoping to be moving, to appear to have direction when he met her. He stepped into the hall with his head down. The figure near the top of the stairs froze. Louise held a book in one hand, the other clutched her skirt. She looked like a school girl caught in the hallway without a pass.

Handle looked past her. The stairs and room below were empty. She crossed her arms in front of her chest and smiled weakly. He wanted to grab her by the shoulders and shake her, but he knew immediately that was dishonest. He nodded at Louise and hurried down the stairs.

Handle sat in the porch swing with his head tilted back and eyes closed. The sun on his face felt good and gave him an excuse to be still. For the whole of the morning he'd tried to deal with the gnawing at his stomach that made him feel like a criminal. Then, lying in the sun, pretending to relax, it occurred to him that he was a criminal. He thought of all the punks he'd arrested who'd said it'd seemed right at the time.

"Handle."

He recognized Marvin's deep voice, but didn't want to open his eyes. "Yes," he said.

"Taking the women shopping. Might have a couple of beers if you're interested."

"Think I'll stay here."

Marvin laughed. "I dreamt about alligators last night." He laughed again. "I was raising them like cows."

Handle offered a smile and opened his eyes, shading them from the sun with his right hand. Marvin and Annalee stood just in front of him, their backs to the sun, two dark shapes, but connected like amoeba in the last stages of splitting. Handle realized they were holding hands. They looked somehow comic and he laughed.

Marvin and Annalee smiled back at him, then turned and walked to their car. Handle watched them walk. The screen door opened and his wife stepped on the porch. "You want some magazines or anything, Wayne?"

Handle looked at her for a long time before answering by shaking his head. She smiled at him then hurried to catch her parents. Handle watched her go, feeling she might be gone a long time. He closed his eyes and listened to the car as it drove away. He took a deep breath and tried to relax.

He decided not to think about Marilyn or Louise or anything, but to just relax. Wind pushed through the leaves and birds played out a tune he could almost imagine as a saxophone solo. He tried to picture himself as a teacher in a crowded classroom. But the screen door opened then the swing swayed with the weight of another. He kept his eyes closed.

Louise's voice came out of the darkness. "We should talk, Handle."

Handle nodded but kept his eyes closed. "I feel terrible."

"I know."

"Everytime I see Marilyn, I think I'm going to cry," he said. It wasn't exactly the truth, but the truth was worse.

"Maybe you just need to cry."

Her voice sounded thick and low, then he heard vibration in her breathing and knew she'd begun to cry. Until his eyes became accustomed to the light, she was a blur of color. But her shape settled, and Handle saw Louise clearly; a woman, eyes red from crying, arms folded across her chest to stop herself from shaking. He saw her separate from his vision of her, as a person absolutely apart from him. A new part of her was naked, and Handle might have recognized the same in himself, but he was unable to resist touching her.

Louise shrugged his arms off her. "Someone could see," she said.

Handle looked out over the empty fields and still trees, then followed Louise inside. "It seemed right," he said when they reached the living room.

She turned and held him. They sat in the couch and held one another. Handle tried to make sense of what he felt. He closed his eyes and thought of his wife and how afraid he was of losing her. Already, he knew, he had created a distance between them. Then he thought of arriving with Marilyn at the farm, how she had burst into Louise's arms. Handle began to cry, knowing how much Louise had lost as well. He held her tighter, feeling closer to her than ever because of the loss they shared.

When they quit crying, Handle found he could not let her go. His arms felt solid, like cement. He knew he had to let her go, but he couldn't move. His heart pounded so vigorously, he recognized it as a muscle working inside him. He kissed her. She began crying again but kissed him back. Everytime he lifted a hand it returned to her. He could pull back, but he could not pull away.

Handle followed Louise up the stairs to her room where they made love again, without the clarity of emotion or the genuine belief in its honesty they'd had the night before, but with the sincerest of necessity. While they made love, they listened for sounds of the car returning. They hurried, wondering how they had kept from worrying about being caught the night before. They dressed quickly afterwards.

"We can never let this happen again," Louise said.

Handle had his hand on the door. "I know," he said.

They left the room separately without kissing or saying goodbye.

Handle could not stay in the house with Louise. He walked through the long, straight rows of corn quickly. He walked directly to the woods and into the thick brush that bordered the fields. High weeds licked the insides of his legs. The woods were dense and quiet, the trees still. Sunlight through the trees speckled Handle and the ground with moving patterns, like an active disease magnified to become visible. Handle walked quickly, head down, leading with his arms like a swimmer, through the woods. Louise and Marilyn played here as children, he thought as he ducked under a low limb and pushed himself through a narrow space between two trees. He was flooded with smells, the sharp green smell of the trees with new leaves, the dusty odor of bark, the mildly bitter smell of certain weeds when they broke under his step. The boy in the bar, his blank brown face, flashed in his vision, as if the boy were behind a tree watching him. Handle ignored the image and kept walking. A fallen trunk blocked his way, lying at a diagonal between trees, its white guts open, soft and spongy from rain and decay. Handle carefully placed his foot in a white pocket and lifted himself over. He pushed on, breathing heavy, his heart thudding against his chest. He lifted a thin limb and stepped under it into a narrow path. Turning immediately, he followed the path, increasing his speed. The path widened and Handle began to run, hands flailing at limbs and leaves. It struck him how much this was like his dream, how the path seemed like an alley, but he didn't slow down to think. His heart labored again like a muscle. The splotches of sunlight became larger. Then the forest opened up. The trees fell away. He'd reached the hollow.

Chest nodding, lungs aching, muscles in his legs twitching, Handle

stood straight and looked over the hollow. Milkweed and morning glo-
ries rimmed the clearing, muddled with tall grass and jimson weed. In
the middle, about fifteen yards from Handle, a clump of cattails grew
out of the high grass. Handle leaned against a tree to catch his breath.
This had been their secret place, he thought. He tried to picture them as
little girls in short ruffled dresses and corn rows, but his mind wouldn't
cooperate, giving instead himself as a little boy with his father, and not
in the country but in the city, a sidewalk. A policeman tells his father
that colored men do not look directly at white women and anyone his
age shouldn't have to be told. His father's face, blank and brown, his
head nodding, as he assures the policeman he wasn't doing anything
and he certainly won't do it again. Handle walked into the weeds and
high grass to the center. Water sloshed against his shoes and he smelled
the acrid, stagnant pool of shallow water at the heart of the hollow.

As he stood among the cattails, he heard his father's voice calling
someone *a coal black son of a bitch.* The sound of his father's voice
stopped Handle, fixed him among the cattails, stationary as a tree
stump. Was it that simple? Handle felt he'd just remembered a secret as
pictures of his father flashed relentlessly in his mind—his father proud
his skin was lighter than his brother-in-law's, his father, consumed by
self-hatred, nodding politely to the policeman then cursing about some
niggers making it hard on the rest. Handle grabbed a handful of cattails
and broke off their heads. He dropped all but one, threw it, and
watched it spin like a propeller. Handle closed his eyes and there in his
personal darkness were Louise and Marilyn.

Handle walked back to the edge of the hollow, but he couldn't find
the path. He circled the clearing, but he'd become disoriented and had
no idea which way to turn. He circled the hollow in the opposite direction, but it did no good. Finally, he just set out into the woods. Already,
clouds thickened the sky. The randomness of the trees, the irregular
angles of the branches, oppressed him. He hesitated under a thorn tree,
wanting to make some kind of sense of his direction, wishing he could
create a reasonable order. But the woods relinquished none of their
confusion. Handle decided to simplify the world. He would think of
Marilyn. He would concentrate solely on his wife and wander the

woods with her image casting out the others. He decided his love for her would prevail.

With this resolution, he began walking again. He pushed through the dense woods for over an hour before he found the trail again, and with each step he'd pledged his love for Marilyn, Marilyn, Marilyn. By the time he emerged from the woods, he felt renewed, confident his love for his wife would defeat the darkness that threatened them.

Handle insisted that he and Marilyn prepare supper. Marvin had bought a country ham while he'd been in town. They began by slicing the ham into thick steaks. Then Marilyn tore off leaves of lettuce while Handle sliced tomatoes into crescents. Handle found himself full of enthusiasm for the work and for his wife, kissing her on the cheek or the back of the neck after each detail of the meal was completed.

Marilyn had set out several potatoes. Handle rummaged through the silverware drawer for a potato peeler, then began peeling them, working very quickly.

Marilyn laughed. "Those were going to be baked potatoes."

Handle smiled and shrugged. "How about mashed potatoes?" Marilyn just laughed again, so he began peeling them once more. The peels went quickly. He chopped them into smaller pieces to boil. Handle liked the appearance of the pieces of potatoes with cut edges and straight sides. He chopped them rapidly and tossed them into a pan, working with so much enthusiasm that Marilyn began to laugh. Handle smiled at her, then began laughing himself, pressing the pan of chopped potatoes into his side. That they were together doing something and laughing over it, delighted Handle and he laughed harder. He laughed until he had tears in his eyes and still laughed. He dropped the pan of potatoes and doubled over laughing. He sank to the floor and sat flat, back against a cupboard, legs straight out in front of him and laughed. He laughed until Marilyn began to cry. He could see she was crying, but he couldn't stop laughing until she held him so tightly against her chest that she suffocated the laughter.

"You're scaring me, Wayne," she whispered. They helped each other up the stairs to the bed, where they lay holding one another until Handle fell asleep.

By suppertime, rain fell like strands of hair perfectly combed. Annalee and Louise finished preparing the meal Handle and Marilyn had abandoned. They set the table, then Annalee took the dishes away and set the table again with her best china, a blue willow design passed down to her from Marvin's mother. Since Handle and Marilyn still had not come down to eat, Annalee decided to bathe and change clothes. She chose a yellow summer dress with a large ruffled collar. The dress was a gift from Marvin. She'd worn it only once, the day he'd given it to her more than a year ago. Designed for a younger woman, the dress made Annalee look old and lean. Marvin always bought her clothes meant for younger women, not so much due to his incomprehension of fashion, although he knew nothing about it, but due to his blindness to his wife's aging. Annalee knew the dress was unattractive on her and incongruent with the rainy weather, but she wanted to wear something cheerful.

Marvin sat at the head of the table. Annalee and Louise sat to his right, Handle and Marilyn to his left. He lay ham steaks on each of the plates passed to him, smelling each one and licking his lips. He still wore the overalls and work shirt he'd worn into town. Having carefully cultivated the image of a country farmer, Marvin always wore overalls when he went into town. Everyone knew he leased out his farm land, and his spotless, pressed overalls would fool no one who didn't know, but Marvin enjoyed the masquerade and his friends played along as unwittingly as he did.

Louise hadn't bathed or changed clothes. The heat of the kitchen combined with the general humidity caused her white blouse to stick and wrinkle against her skin. A gravy stain ran from her first button across her heart and disappeared under her arm. Her hair, greasy with sweat, formed wet arrows across her forehead. It matted flat on one side of her head and puffed out on the other, giving her head a lopsidedness associated with anger, with defiant carelessness. Her face had the flat, dissatisfied look of a child being punished.

As Marvin passed out the ham steaks, he told Handle about his dream of raising alligators. "Milking them was the worst," he said. "They're set so close to the ground."

Afraid to laugh after his laughing fit, Handle smiled and nodded. He kept his eyes on Marvin serving the ham or Annalee, garish as a sunflower in the yellow dress. He didn't want to look at Louise or Marilyn. Sitting at the table with both of them overtaxed his circuits. But as he accepted his plate from Marvin, he couldn't help but look at Louise. She looked haggard and angry. Marvin still looked to him, and Handle felt obligated to say something. He didn't want the supper to be one of those long, silent meals where people eat slowly and chew quietly. He had hoped they would talk around him, but now he felt he had to offer something. His collar felt tight around his throat, but it was unbuttoned almost half way down his chest. "I was thinking about Amy Hansen," he offered, unsure where the words had come from.

Marilyn placed her hand over his and gently squeezed. She smiled at him. Her hand was unusually warm.

"She was your neighbor, wasn't she?" Annalee asked, a question she and everyone at the table knew the answer to.

Handle didn't know what to say. Words were too treacherous. He shook his head. "What ever happened to her?" he asked faintly. It was understood that the question was not to be answered.

Handle suddenly remembered a little boy who'd killed his brother during an argument. He remembered the boy sitting in the back of the patrol car while they waited for the juvenile officers. The boy kept asking about his brother, "What's going to happen to him now?" Handle shook his head as if to shake the memory out. As quickly as it left, his father entered, on the sidewalk, hearing the white cop tell him colored men did not look directly at white women. Self-hatred washed over him for a moment, a sensation Handle recognized but had never before named, a legacy from his father.

Annalee had begun telling a story about a student she'd had the last year she'd taught, a little boy, half the size of his classmates, who gave her a poem the last day of class. She had committed the poem to memory.

Boys have bubbles when they talk too fast
Girls scrape their knees worse for dresses
Dogs eat shoes in the closet
Teachers give everything names.

Handle filled with sadness. It became obvious to him that his life had taken a wrong turn, that he should have been a teacher. It struck him that Louise looked like a troubled child. Then he realized why she looked so bad. She'd made herself unattractive so he would have less trouble ignoring her. The realization came so suddenly he gasped for air and stared at Louise, knowing her matted hair and dirty shirt were emblems of love. She looked back at him and Handle could believe the space between them was illuminated by a field of intense yellow light. By the time Louise looked down, Handle felt panicky, sure they'd given themselves away. But Marilyn ate undisturbed and Marvin drank milk. Annalee's face, however, was vacant with fear and recognition.

"The rain seems so odd to me," Marilyn said, looking up from her plate. "I guess because it had been so clear in New York." She picked up her napkin and wiped Handle's forehead of sweat. "It's so humid," she said.

No one picked up the conversation. Annalee just stared straight ahead. Handle could no longer look at her. He couldn't look at Louise, her love for him disfiguring her. He couldn't look at his wife, caring for him while she sat directly across from his lover, her sister. He looked at Marvin, but had to look away from him, so oblivious to the destruction going on around him. He looked down to his plate and realized he hadn't eaten a bite.

"I was just thinking about old Hoot," Marvin said. "Blind as a stump from eating those inky cap mushrooms. Used to chew a whole mouthful up at once." He looked to Annalee, but she wasn't listening, so he looked away from her. "Annalee still claims he was just too old to see, but I know better."

"Remember when he sniffed Reverend Lee's leg, then peed on him right in the living room?" Marilyn laughed as she spoke.

Handle knew how this story was told. Annalee was ignoring her parts.

"He shit in my bed," Louise said flatly without looking up.

Annalee turned and stared at Louise as if she'd spoken in a foreign language.

"Would have died as a pup but I run out in the freezing cold after he'd been attacked by whatever bird it was had hatched him in the first place." Marvin chewed ham as he spoke.

Annalee was supposed to say there wasn't any such bird, so Marilyn could talk about the perfect white ground and the little dog, head up in the snow, steam rising from his exposed intestines, the snow next to him soiled by blood and shit. But Annalee wasn't speaking. She stared at Louise and Louise stared back now. Finally Louise spoke, still looking at her mother. "Mama saved the dog. She took him to the vet."

"You women always stick together." Marvin looked to Handle. "We never get credit for a thing in this household. Fact is, I practically gave the dog mouth to mouth."

"But Mama got his sight back," Marilyn said.

They looked at Annalee again. She finally turned away from Louise and back to her plate. "The dog's been dead for years," she said.

Handle wanted her to finish the story. She was supposed to tell about the bacon grease, making the path for the dog, so Marilyn could say, "to the old barn where he liked to pee," and Louise could say, "to the purple magnolia where the grass was thick and soft where he liked to shit," then Marvin would jump in saying how he'd found the dog in the branches, *in the branches,* then Annalee would say that was no reason to bury him there and kill the tree. Handle could hear it all in his mind, the way it was supposed to go. "Just goes to show," Marvin would say, "that all living things are joined one way or another, everything touches everything else." Then Annalee would scoff and say she'd probably cut the taproot while digging the grave. But the story had been killed and hovered over them.

Louise had begun to cry silently, catching the tears with her fingers before they even left her eyes. Handle could not bear to be at the table any longer. "Excuse me," he said, but he wasn't sure he said it loud enough for anyone to hear.

He stepped into the hall, thinking he would wash his face in the bathroom sink and compose himself. He opened the door and stepped into the room quickly, pulling the door closed behind him. The room was pitch dark. He felt for the wall switch, but couldn't find it. He slapped the wall high and low, but the light switch was gone. He felt the other side, but the wall was gone, the room had changed. He stepped forward. Something lit on his face. He ducked, swatted at it, but when he stood again it was back on his face. He grabbed it, a string. Pulling it, the room lit—the walk-in closet. Handle had turned the wrong way. He pulled the light cord again, stepped out of the closet, and crossed the hall into the bathroom.

Handle and Marilyn went to bed shortly after supper, but Handle couldn't sleep. He lay next to his wife in the dark and began to shiver as if with a fever. He sat up in bed with his back to his wife.

"Wayne."

He looked over his shoulder at her.

"Talk with me, Wayne." She switched on the light next to the bed.

"I love you," Handle said, still with his back to her. "You've got to believe that."

She placed her hand on his back. "You're just confused."

He could only stare at her.

"When we get back to New York, if you can't go back to work, then we'll find something else. Sometimes people get trapped into doing things they don't believe, and they don't even realize they're trapped. But you realize it, Wayne, that's why it's so hard for you." She put an arm around him and pressed her face against his back. "But now that you've realized what's happened, it may be easier to deal with."

Handle lay back in the bed beside her. He needed to be in their bedroom. This room was too clean, too large. He needed the dark wood dresser they'd found together and began refinishing and never finished, the closet so stuffed with clothes the door was always open. He needed the clutter of married life to remind him who he was.

"It's just the police," Marilyn said. "You meet so many desperate people." She took his chin, turned him to face her. "You're not racist, Wayne. You know you love me. How could you love me if you were racist? How could you love yourself?" She kissed his forehead. "You love me, you just told me so. And you love Mama and Daddy. You love . . ."

Handle cupped his palm over her mouth to stop her. He pulled her close and kissed her. She turned out the light and they kissed once more.

It was still dark. Handle had slept twice during the night, once for almost an hour. He let his eyes adjust to the darkness and looked at the shape his wife made in the bed as he slipped on his pants.

He walked down the stairs quietly, carefully and stepped into the living room. Louise was in the corner. She had no book. There was no light. The comforter was wrapped tightly around her. When she saw him, she began shaking her head from side to side. She covered her face with her hands.

"I've been here all night," she whispered. "I was hoping you wouldn't come."

She stood. They held each other, afraid to talk. Louise led him out of the living room into the hall. She opened the door to the walk-in closet and spread the comforter. With the door closed, the closet was absolutely dark. They positioned themselves carefully away from the walls which might creak if pressed against. They made love, controlling their breathing as much as they could, pausing if they heard a noise. When they finished, they kissed once, but neither could say that what they'd done was right or that it was over or that there was any escape.

TIDE POOLS

ALICE ADAMS

Alice Adams grew up in Chapel Hill, North Carolina, and graduated from Radcliffe; since then she has lived mostly in San Francisco. Her most recent novel, *Superior Women,* was published by Knopf in 1984, and a collection of short stories, *Return Trips,* appeared in 1985.

For some years I lived alone in a small white clapboard house, up on a high wooded bluff above the Mississippi River, which I could hardly see —so far down, glimpsed through thick vines and trees, and so narrow just there.

This was near Minneapolis, where I was an assistant professor at a local college. Teaching marine biology. And I thought quite a lot about the irony of my situation—a sea specialty in the landlocked Midwest. (I am from Santa Barbara, California, originally, which may explain quite a bit.)

During those Minnesota years, despite professional busyness, a heavy teaching load, labs, conferences, friends, and a few sporadic love affairs, I was often lonely, an embarrassing condition to which I would never have admitted. Still, and despite my relative isolation, at that time I regarded the telephone as an enemy, its shrill, imperative sound an interruption even to loneliness. When my phone rang I did not anticipate a friendly chat. For one thing, most of my friends and lovers were also hardworking professionals, not much given to minor social exchange.

Thus, on a summer night about a year ago, a rare warm clear twilight, reminding me of Southern California, I was far from pleased at the sound of the telephone. I had just taken a bath and finished dressing; I was going out to dinner with a man I had met recently, whom I thought I liked. (Was he calling to break the date? Native distrust has not helped my relationships with men, nor with women.) We were going out to celebrate my birthday, actually, but I did not imagine that the ringing phone meant someone calling with congratulations, my birthday not being something that I generally talk about.

What I first heard on picking up that alien instrument was the hollow, whirring sound that meant a long-distance call, and I thought, How odd, what a strange hour for business. Then, as I said hello, and hello again, I heard silence. At last a female voice came on, very slurred. But then words formed. "Judith? Have I got Miss Judith Mallory? *Doctor* Mallory?"

"Yes—"

"Judy, is that you, truly? Truly Jude? Judy, do you know who this is?" An excited, drunken voice, its cadence ineradicably familiar to me —and only one person has ever called me Jude. It was Jennifer Cartwright, my closest early-childhood friend, my almost inseparable pal— whom I had not heard from or about for more than twenty years, not since we both left Santa Barbara, where we grew up together, or tried to.

I asked her, "Jennifer, how are you? Where are you? What are you doing now?"

"Well, I'm back in our house, you know. I've come back home. I've been here since Mother died, and I guess I'm doing O.K. Oh Judy, it's really you! I'm so happy . . ."

Happy was the last thing that Jennifer sounded, though; her voice was almost tearful.

"Oh, Jennifer." I was assailed by an overwhelming affection for my friend, mixed with sadness over whatever ailed her just now, including being so drunk. I had not even known that her mother was dead. Nicola —Nickie Cartwright, whom I had also cared about a lot.

My own parents had both been dead for some time, which is one reason I had had no news from Santa Barbara. Also, since they died of so-called alcohol-related ailments, I was perhaps unreasonably alarmed at Jennifer's condition. A nervous stomach, which is no stomach at all for booze, had kept me, if unwillingly, abstemious.

"And oh!" Jennifer's voice sounded indeed much happier now. "I forgot to say happy birthday. Judy, Jude, happy happy birthday! Every year I think of you today, even if I haven't ever called you."

"You're so good to remember," I told her. "But really, tell me how you are."

"Oh, you tell me! First off, you tell me just what you have on." Such a perfect Jennifer question—or Nickie: Nickie, too, would have asked me what I was wearing, in order to see me, and to check on how I was.

To please Jennifer I should have described a beautiful, colorful dress, but a lack of imagination, I believe, has kept me honest; I tend to tell the truth. My former (only) husband observed that I had a very literal mind, and he might have been right, as he was with a few other accurate accusations. In any case, I told Jennifer, "Just a sweater and some pants. My uniform, I guess. But they're both new. Black. Actually, I'm going out to dinner. This man I met—"

Jennifer began to laugh, her old prolonged, slow, appreciative laugh, and I thought, Well, maybe she's not so drunk. Just a little tipsy, maybe, and overexcited.

"Oh, Jude." Jennifer was laughing still. "You're going out on a date, and we're so old. But you sound like you're about sixteen, and wearing something pink and gauzy."

Rational, sober person that I am, I could have cried.

But Jennifer went on in a conversational, much less drunken way. "I think about you so much," she said. "And everything back then. All the fun we had. Of course, since I've moved back here it's all easier to remember."

"I'm really sorry to hear about Nickie," I told her.

"Well, just one more terrible thing. Everyone gets cancer, it seems like to me. Honestly, Jude, sometimes I think being grown up really sucks, don't you? To use a word I truly hate."

"Well, I guess."

"Your parents die, and your husbands turn out bad. And your kids—oh, don't even talk to me about kids."

Her voice trailed off into a total silence, and I thought, Oh dear, she's fallen asleep at the telephone, out there in California, in that house I know so very well. The house right next door to the house where my parents and I used to live—in fact, its architectural twin—on what was

called the Santa Barbara Gold Coast, up above the sea. I wondered
what room Jennifer was in—her own room, in bed, I hoped. I called out
"Jennifer!" over all that space, Minnesota to California. Calling out
over time, too, over many years.

Her laugh came on again. "Oh, Jude, you thought I'd gone to sleep.
But I hadn't, I was just lying here thinking. In Mother and Dad's big
old bed. You remember?"

"Oh, of course I do." And with a rush I remembered the Sunday
morning when Jennifer and I had run into the Cartwrights' bedroom, I
guess looking for the Sunday papers, and there were blond Scott and
blonder Nickie in their tousled nightclothes, lying back among a pale-
blue tangle of sheets. Not making love, although I think we must have
caught them soon after love. They may have moved apart as we came
in; Scott's hand still lingered in Nickie's bright, heavy uncombed hair.
At the time, I was mostly struck by their sleepy affection for each other,
so clearly present. I can see it now, those particular smiles, all over their
pale morning faces.

The room, with its seascape view, was almost identical to my parents'
bedroom, and their view. My parents slept in narrow, separate beds.
They were silent at home except when they drank, which loosened them
up a little, though it never made them anywhere near affectionate with
each other.

In any case, I surely remembered the Cartwrights' broad, blue-
sheeted carved-mahogany bed.

I asked Jennifer, "Your father—Scott died too?" Although I think I
knew that he must have. But I used to see Scott Cartwright as the
strongest man I ever knew, as well as the most glamorous, with his
golfer's tan, and his stride.

"Just after your mother died. They were all so young, weren't they?
Dad had a stroke on the golf course, but maybe that's the best way to
go. Poor Mother was sick for years. Oh, Judy, it's all so scary. I hate to
think about it."

She had begun to trail off again, and partly to keep her awake, in
contact, I asked her if she had married more than once; I thought I had
heard her say "husbands," plural, but it was hard to tell, with her
vagueness, slurring.

But "Oh, three times!" Jennifer told me. "Each one worse. I never seem to learn." But she sounded cheerful, and next she began to laugh. "You will not believe what their names were," she said. "Tom, Dick, and Harry. That's the truth. Well, not actually the whole truth—I can't lie to my best old favorite friend. The whole truth is, the first two were Tom and Dick, and so when I went and got married the third time I had to call him Harry, even if his name was Jack."

I laughed—I had always laughed a lot with Jennifer—but at the same time I was thinking that people from single, happy marriages are supposed to marry happily themselves. They are not supposed to make lonely, drunken phone calls to old, almost forgotten friends.

Mostly, though, I was extremely pleased—elated, even—to have heard from Jennifer at all, despite the bad signs, the clear evidence that she was not in very good shape. As we hung up a few minutes later I was aware of smiling to myself, the happy recipient of a happy birthday present. And like most especially welcome, sensitive presents, this gift from Jennifer was something that I had not known I needed, but that now I could no longer do without: a friend for talking to.

I went out for dinner with my new beau in a rare lighthearted mood, but I may have seemed more than a little abstracted: I was thinking of Jennifer, her parents, and California.

When Jennifer and I were friends, all that time ago, I truly loved her, but I also coveted almost everything about her: her golden curls, small plump hands, her famously sunny disposition, but most especially and most secretly I envied her her parents. I wanted them to be mine.

I have since learned (hasn't everyone?) that this is a common fantasy; Freud tells us that many children believe they have somehow ended up with the wrong set of parents. But at the time I naturally did not know this; guiltily I felt that only I had such an evil wish, to be rid of my own parents and moved in with another set. If it could somehow be proved, I thought, that I had been stolen by this dark and sombre couple with whom I lived, while all along I was really a Cartwright child—then I would be perfectly happy. And if Jennifer's parents were mine, then of

course Jennifer and I would be truly sisters, as so often we spoke of
wishing that we were.

From the moment I saw them, even before seeing Jennifer, I was
drawn to Scott and Nickie Cartwright, a tanned couple getting out of a
new wood-panelled station wagon to look at a house for sale, the house
next door to our house. I liked their bright splashy clothes, and the
easy, careless way they walked and laughed; I wanted them to be the
people to buy that house.

I thought that they looked too young to be parents; that they turned
out to have a little girl just my age was a marvellous surprise, a bonus,
as it were.

My own parents did not like the look of the Cartwrights, at first.
"Lots of flash" was my Vermont mother's succinct summation; and my
father's: "That garden they're buying needs plenty of solid work. I hope
they know it." But fairly soon the four grownups took to dropping in on
each other for a cup of coffee or a Coke, maybe, during the day; and at
night they all got together for drinks. The Cartwrights, from St. Louis,
had a sort of loose-style hospitality to which even my fairly stiff-man-
nered parents responded.

What must initially have won my stern parents' approval, though,
was the Cartwrights' total dedication to their garden. Even before actually moving in they began to spend their weekends digging among the
dahlias, pruning hibiscus, trimming orange blossoms, and probing the
roots of ivy. And once they lived there, all during the week beautiful
Nickie in her short red shorts could be observed out clipping boxwoods,
often mowing the lawn. And watering everything.

On weekends, around dusk if not sooner, the four of them would
start in on their Tom Collinses, Gin Rickeys, or fruity concoctions with
rum. Eventually one of the grownups (usually Nickie Cartwright)
would remember that Jennifer and I should have some supper, and the
two men (probably) would go out for some fried clams or pizza. Later
on they would pretty much forget all about us, which was fine with
Jennifer and me; we could stay up as long as we liked, giggling and
whispering.

All the grownups that I knew at that time drank; it was what I
assumed grownups did when they got together. Jennifer and I never

discussed this adult habit, and "drunk" is not a word we would have used to describe our parents, ever. "Drunk" meant a sort of clownish, TV-cartoon behavior.

My parents as they drank simply talked too much; they told what seemed to me very long dull stories having to do with Santa Barbara history, early architects, all that. The Cartwrights, being younger, listened politely; Nickie laughed a lot, and they sat very close together.

Certainly my parents were never clownish or even loud; God knows they were not. In a bitter, tight-mouthed way they might argue at breakfast; a few times (this was the worst of all) I could hear my mother crying late at night, all by herself.

Because I had never heard them do so, I believed that the Cartwrights never argued, and I was sure that beautiful happy Nickie Cartwright never cried, and maybe she did not.

In the days that succeeded that first phone call from Jennifer, I thought considerably about her, about her parents, and mine. With terrible vividness I remembered the strength of my yearning for the Cartwrights, and I was assailed—again!—by the sheer intensity of all that childhood emotion, my earliest passions and guilts and despairs.

Quite as vividly, though, I also remembered the simple fun that we used to have, Jennifer and I, as children, especially on the beach. Since I had always lived there in Santa Barbara, on the California coast, and the Cartwrights were originally from inland Missouri, I was Jennifer's guide to the seashore. Bravely kicking our sneakers into tide pools, Jennifer and I uncovered marvels: tiny hermit crabs, long swaying seaweed, all purple. Anemones. Jennifer would squeal at dead fish, in a high, squeamish way, as I pretended not to mind them.

I also showed Jennifer the more sophisticated pleasures of State Street, the ice-cream parlors and the hot-dog stands. As we both grew up a little I pointed out the stores. Tweeds & Weeds, my mother's favorite, was always too conservative for the Cartwright ladies, though. Nickie loved frills and lots of colors; she dressed herself and Jennifer in every shade of pink to tangerine. My mother ordered almost all of my clothes from the Liliputian Bazaar, at Best & Co.

* * *

Undoubtedly the tide pools and my happy fascination with them to a great extent determined my later choice of a career, although a desire to displease and/or shock my parents must have figured largely also. Biology to them connoted sex, which in a general way they were against.

And possibly in some way of my own I made the same connection. In any case, I am forced to say that so far I have shone neither professionally nor in a romantic way. I did achieve a doctorate, and some years later an assistant professorship, at relatively early ages, but I do not feel that I will ever be truly distinguished.

As one of my more kindly professors put it, my interest in marine biology could be called aesthetic rather than scientific. I excel at drawing—urchins, starfish, snails.

As to my romantic history, it got off to a shaky start, so to speak, with my marriage to a fellow-biologist, a man who after two years of me announced that colleagues should not be married to each other. (This could be true, but it had been his idea, originally.) He left me for a kindergarten teacher in Chicago, where his next teaching job happened to be. I became involved with an elderly musicologist, who was married; later with a graduate student in Speech and Drama, who, I came to believe, used coke, a lot of it.

Three men, then—my husband and two subsequent lovers—who presented certain problems. However, surely I do, too? I am hardly "problem-free" or even especially easy to get along with. I am moody, hypersensitive, demanding.

In any case, these days as far as men are concerned I am running scared.

After that first birthday call, Jennifer telephoned again, and again. She seemed to have an unerring instinct for the right time to call, not an easy feat with me. (I once knew a man who always called me when I was brushing my teeth; I used to think that if I really wanted to hear from him I had only to get out my toothbrush.) In Jennifer's case, though, it may have been that I was simply so glad to hear from her.

I gathered that her present life was quite reclusive; she did not seem to know where anyone else whom we had known was now. I gathered, too, that she was quite "comfortably off," to use an old phrase of my mother's. My mother thought "rich" a vulgar word, and perhaps it is. Anyway, I was very glad that Jennifer was comfortable.

As I got used to talking to Jennifer again, sometimes I would find myself scolding her. You should get out more, take walks, get exercise, I would say. Go swimming—there must be a pool around. And what about vitamins? Do you eat enough? And Jennifer would laugh in her amiable way, and say she was sure I was absolutely right.

Jennifer's memory for long-gone days was extraordinary, though. She reminded me of the day we decided that to be kidnapped would be a thrilling adventure. We put on our best dresses and paraded slowly up and down State Street, conversing in loud voices about how rich (we liked the word) our parents were. Yachts, Spanish castles, trips on the Queen Mary, penthouses in New York—we mentioned all the things the movies had informed us rich people had, and did.

"You had on your striped linen," Jennifer perfectly recalled, "and I was wearing my lavender dotted swiss." She laughed her prolonged, slow chuckle. "We just couldn't understand why no one picked us up. Rich and adorable as we were. You remember, Jude?"

Well, I would not have remembered, but Jennifer brought it all back to me, along with our beach walks, the beautiful tide pools, the white sand, the rocks.

I began to look forward to those phone calls. I felt more and more that my connection with Jennifer was something that I had badly missed for years.

I believe I would have enjoyed talking to Jennifer under almost any circumstances, probably, but that particular fall and winter were bad times for me—and seemingly the rest of the world: Ethiopia, Nicaragua. In the American Midwest, where I was, unemployment was rife, and terrible. And to make everything worse the snows came early that year—heavy, paralyzing.

In a personal way, that snowed-in, difficult winter, things were especially bad: I was not getting along at all with my latest beau, the man who came to take me out to dinner on the night of Jennifer's first phone call. This was particularly depressing since we had got off to a very, very good start—not fireworks, not some spectacular blaze that I would have known to distrust, but many quiet tastes in common, including cats (he had five, an intensely charming fact, I thought, and they all were beautiful tabbies). The truth was that we were quite a lot alike, he and I. Not only our tastes but our defects were quite similar: we were both wary, nervy, shy. Very likely we both needed more by way of contrasting personality—although his former wife had been a successful actress, flamboyant, a great beauty, and that had not worked out too well, either. In any case, we further had in common the fact of being veterans of several mid-life love affairs, both knowing all too well the litany of the condition of not getting along. We exhibited a lessening of interest in each other in identical ways: an increase in our courtesy level. We pretended surprise and pleasure at the sound of each other's voice on the phone; with excruciating politeness we made excuses not to see each other. (At times it occurred to me that in some awful way I was becoming my parents—those super-polite role models.) And then we stopped talking altogether, my lover and I.

The next year was to be my sabbatical from the college, and none of my plans seemed to be working out in that direction, either. Nothing available at Woods Hole, nothing in San Diego. Or Berkeley, or Stanford.

Around March, with everything still going bad and no signs of spring, I realized that I had not heard from Jennifer for several weeks. Some instinct had all along advised me that I should wait to be called, I should not call Jennifer. Now, however, I did; I dialled the number in Santa Barbara. (Easy enough to come by: Jennifer, an unlikely feminist, had returned to her maiden name.)

It was not a good conversation. Jennifer was very drunk, although it was only about six at night, California time. She was drunk and sad and apologetic, over everything. She was extremely polite, but I felt that she was not even certain who I was; I could have been almost anyone. Any stranger, even, who happened to call, selling magazine subscriptions or offering chances to buy tax-free municipal bonds.

I was seriously worried, and after a little time I came to certain serious decisions.

I did the following things, in more or less this order:

I made an appointment and went to see the head of my department, and after some conversation, some argument, we struck up a bargain, of sorts: I would be granted a year's leave of absence (this involved less pay than a sabbatical, which was one of my selling points), and in return for this great favor I would teach an extra section of the general-science course for freshmen on my return.

I put up a notice on the bookstore bulletin board about renting out my house; from a great many applicants (probably I should have asked for more money) I selected a nice young couple from the music department. The only problem was that two people in the house would need all my small space; I would have to store everything but the furniture.

Through a national real-estate outfit I located a real-estate agent in Santa Barbara, who (this seemed an omen, a sure sign that I was on the right track) had a listing just a couple of houses down from Jennifer's—a garage apartment, mercifully cheap.

I called Jennifer, and as though it were a joke I said that I was coming out for a year, to take care of her.

And that is where I am now, and what I am doing. My apartment is in an alley half a block from Jennifer's house, the Cartwright house—and of course from my parents' house, too, the house that I sold when they died: my money for graduate school. My apartment is tiny, but since I am not there much, no matter. I have room for my drawing board, shelves of books and stacked papers; and outside there is a tiny scrap of a yard, where a neighbor cat comes to visit occasionally (he is beautiful—a pale-gray, long-eared, most delicate-footed creature).

I am beginning to run into a problem with space for clothes, though. When I first got here Jennifer was so depressed, she said, by the darkness of my wardrobe ("Judy, you can't go around like that, not out here, in those professor clothes") that we have done a lot of State Street shopping, by way of brightening up my look. "But you're wonderful in that red silk," Jennifer insisted.

Jennifer herself, for a person who drinks or who has drunk that much, looks remarkably well. Needless to say, I was more than a little nervous about seeing her again: how would she look? I was so scared, in fact, that I gave very little thought to how I would look to her, and I think actually I am the one who has aged more. Jennifer is thin, a little frail and shaky on her feet, that is true, but her skin is still good, fine and pink, and her eyes are blue and clear. She just looks like a very, very pretty woman, of a certain age.

The first few weeks of my stay I made all the obvious suggestions having to do with drink: the Betty Ford place, or A.A., or just a plain good doctor. Well, Jennifer refused to go to anything, as I might have known she would—she has always been extremely stubborn. She even says that her doctor says she is perfectly all right. Two explanations for that last occur to me: (1) she does not tell her doctor, or did not, how much she really drinks, or (2) the doctor himself is an alcoholic; I've heard that a lot of them are.

I have made a couple of strong advances, though. One is in terms of nutrition. I have instituted a heavy regimen of vitamins, and also I do most of the shopping and cooking. I go down to the docks for fresh fish, and on Saturday mornings there is a Farmers' Market, with lovely California vegetables and fruits. We eat very well, and I am sure that Jennifer eats a lot more with me around.

Another considerable advance is that Jennifer has entirely given up hard liquor, and now only drinks wine, white wine. In her big blue Ford station wagon we drive down to the new liquor store just off State Street. A handsome, bright-brassy, airy space. We walk around among the wooden crates and bins and shelves of bottles. This particular store deals mostly in California wines, and there are always some interesting new labels. New wineries keep turning up all over the state, even in very unlikely places, like San Luis Obispo or San Diego. We laugh at some of the names, which are often a little outlandish: Witches' Wish? And we admire the designs of the labels. We have even come to conclude that there is a definite correlation between beautiful labels and first-rate wines. Vichon, for example, one of our favorites, has an especially pretty picture on its bottle.

One of the best aspects of this whole venture for me is my discovery that after all I really can drink wine, with no ill effects. When I first came out I would have one glass of wine at dinner, to keep Jennifer company, as it were. Then sometimes two, then sometimes another at home.

And now, in the late afternoons, though still too early to start over to the Cartwrights'—to Jennifer's house—I begin to think how nice a cool dry glass of wine would taste, and then I think, Well, why not? This is, after all, a sort of vacation for me. And so I pour myself one. I take the wine outside. I sit in one of the half-collapsed but still quite comfortable rattan chairs, in my tiny yard with its minute view of the evening sea, the sky, the burning sun. I sip, and in a peaceful way I contemplate my return to Santa Barbara.

I almost never think about my parents, or those old unhappy days spent here with them, growing up. Our family house has been remodelled almost beyond recognition, for which I am grateful. Only very infrequently do I feel its presence as that of a ghost, looming there just next to the Cartwright house.

I do not worry in the way that I used to about my career—that career, teaching at Minnesota. Marine biology. Sometimes I think I could stay right here forever (someone else could take on the freshman sections), and maybe get into something entirely new. I could walk on the beach and make sketches. (I do that already, of course; I mean I could do it in a more programmatic way.) Maybe someday I would be good enough to have a show, and maybe sell some. Or I could give drawing lessons at some local school. I might even, as we say, *meet someone.* Some nice young bearded man, with leftist views and a fondness for cats. A farmer, maybe; he might wander into the market some Saturday morning, with some lovely artichokes.

Jennifer and I have agreed that I should be the one to keep our store of wine, despite my small quarters. The bottles are stacked in silly places all over my rooms, some under the bed, for example. When I start over to Jennifer's house at dinnertime I just bring along one bottle; in that way I can keep a check on Jennifer's intake. Which is now down to a couple of glasses a day, I believe.

It is interesting and to me a little spooky to see how entirely un-changed the Cartwright house is. Everything is just the same, but since it all looks, as always, brightly new—the fabrics on the upholstered furniture, for instance, the cushions and draperies—everything must in fact *be* new. Jennifer must have gone out and found duplicates to re-place all the worn-out stuff—and with such precision. What trouble she must have gone to, getting everything just right, getting Nickie's look! Including the flourishing garden, now tended by a nice Japanese couple.

All I said was that it looked really great, what a relief it was to see so little changed—which I know must have pleased Jennifer. She would not have wanted the extreme nature of her pursuit to be mentioned.

As I thought in Minneapolis about coming out here, one of my many conscious or semiconscious fears (worries about Jennifer's looks and her general health naturally being foremost) was a nagging, shadowy worry that as Jennifer and I talked it would somehow come out that Nickie and Scott had been less than the happy, fair, affectionate couple I used to see, and to long for. Heaven knows we would talk a lot, endless talk, and without (probably) coming out and saying so (Jennifer is unusually discreet) she might let me know that sometimes they, like my own parents, used to have recriminatory breakfasts, silences, bitterness. Maybe, even, handsome Scott had affairs, and Nickie cried. That would be a more usual, contemporary ending to their story—and in some circles it would "explain" Jennifer.

But from what Jennifer did say, that sad version would seem not to have taken place; according to her, the sadness was of quite another sort. "My mother was so upset when Dad died she just never got over it, never at all" is what Jennifer said. "Never even looked at anyone else, and you know how pretty she always was."

Well, I do remember how pretty Nickie was, and I can accept that version of her life, I guess. In fact, I would rather: it is what I thought I saw.

"I sometimes wonder if I got married so many times to be just the opposite," Jennifer once mused. "Not to depend on any one person in that way."

"Well, maybe" was all I could contribute. But then I added, "And my parents didn't get along, so I only dared try it once?"

"Lord, who knows?" Jennifer laughed.

Often, as we talked, new memories would assail one or the other of us.

"Do you remember the surprise you planned for Scott one time, on his birthday? The *real* surprise?" I asked Jennifer one night.

She seemed not to, and so I told her: "You led him on into the house when he got home from work, and you told him that you'd found what he'd like better than anything in the world. You brought him to the door of the back-hall closet, and when he opened it up there was Nickie, laughing and jumping out to hug and kiss you both."

"Oh, *yes!*" cried Jennifer. "I'd forgotten that, and how could I forget? But you see what I mean, Judy, Jude? Who could ever come up with a relationship like that?"

Who indeed? Most surely not I, I reflected.

But mostly Jennifer and I are not so serious. Our dinners are fun. We remember school friends, boys, our teachers; we go over and over the people we knew and the times we had back then, just remembering and laughing. Not deeply, intellectually scrutinizing, as I might have with other friends, at another time.

Jennifer subscribes to all the fashion magazines, and sometimes sitting there at dinner we may just leaf through a couple. Most of the newest styles are quite ugly, if not downright ludicrous, we are agreed. But every now and then there will be something really pretty; we will make a note to check it out in the downtown stores.

Jennifer has not taken a newspaper for years, and since I have been out here I have not really read one, either. I find it a great relief, in fact, not to know just how awful things have become. How entirely out of control the whole terrifying world is.

We did at first go over some of the unfortunate events of both our marriages, and in a discreet way I told her about my love affairs. I found that, recounting them to Jennifer, I could make them really funny. She liked the story about the man who always called when I was brushing my teeth, and she appreciated my version of my most recent relationship, the man and I becoming more and more polite as we liked each other less. She told me a couple of funny stories about her husbands, though I think their names are what she most likes to remember.

Jennifer does not talk about her children, except to say that she has three of them, all moved East. Three girls. Two work in New York, one lives on a farm in Vermont—no grandchildren that she has mentioned —and since she never seems to hear from her daughters I would guess that they don't get along. But I never ask.

By the time we have finished our dinner, our bottle of wine, we are both rather sleepy. We get up from the table, and together we walk out to the front hall. Jennifer opens the door, we say good night; we kiss, and I go outside and listen for the sound of the lock behind me.

I walk the short, safe distance down the road to my apartment.

If the weather is nice, a warm night, I may sit outside for a while, something I could almost never have done in Minnesota. Maybe I will have one more glass of wine. Maybe red, a good zinfandel, for sleep.

Just sitting there, sipping my wine, I think a lot, and one of my conclusions has been that, all things considered, even living alone, I really feel better and better out here, and I think I have never been so happy in my life.

The visitor cat must by now be on to my habits, for sometimes at these moments I will feel the sudden warm brush of his arching back against my leg. I reach to stroke him. He allows this, responding with a loud purr—and then, as suddenly as he appeared, with a quick leap out into the dark he is gone.

while still

hey were
atomic
pennant.
hich he
of St.

fungo
th of
eeing
ous
e in
us.
an
ed
or

BLIGHT

TUART DYBEK

For Ed and Al

collection of stories, *Childhood and Other Neighbor-*
ntly been reissued in paper by Ecco Press. This is his
ce in the O. Henry Collection. Stuart Dybek currently
g at Western Michigan University.

years between Korea and Vietnam, when rock and roll
erfected, our neighborhood was proclaimed an Official

J. Daley was mayor then. It seemed as if he had always been,
always be, the mayor. Ziggy Zilinsky claimed to have seen
or himself riding down 23rd Place in a black limousine flying
hose little purple pennants from funerals, except his said WHITE
it. The Mayor sat in the back seat sorrowfully shaking his head
o say "Jeez!" as he stared out the bulletproof window at the winos
king on the corner by the boarded-up grocery.

Of course, nobody believed that Zig had actually seen the Mayor.
ggy had been unreliable even before Pepper Rosado had accidentally
eaned him during a game of It-with-the-Bat. People still remembered
as far back as third grade when Ziggy had jumped up in the middle of
mass yelling, "Didja see her? She nodded! I asked the Blessed Virgin
would my cat come home and she nodded yes!"

All through grade school the statues of saints winked at Ziggy. He
was in constant communication with angels and the dead. And Ziggy
sleepwalked. The cops had picked him up once in the middle of the

night for running around the bases in Washtenaw Playground
asleep.

When he'd wake up, Ziggy would recount his dreams as if t
prophecies. He had a terrible recurring nightmare in whic
bombs dropped on the city the night the White Sox won the
But he had wonderful dreams, too. My favorite was the one in w
and I and Little Richard were in a band playing in the cente
Sabina's roller rink.

After Pepper brained him out on the boulevard with a bat—a
bat that Pepper whipped like a tomahawk across a 20-yard wid
tulip garden that Ziggy was trying to hide behind—Zig stopped s
visions of the saints. Instead, he began catching glimpses of fai
people, not movie stars so much as big shots in the news. Every on
a while Zig would spot somebody like Bo Diddley going by on a
Mainly, though, it would be some guy in a homburg who looked
awful lot like Eisenhower, or he'd notice a reappearing little gray-hai
fat guy who could turn out to be either Nikita Khrushchev or May
Daley. It didn't surprise us. Zig was the kind of kid who read newsp
pers. We'd all go to Potok's to buy comics and Zig would walk out wit
the *Daily News.* Zig always worried about things no one else care
about, like the population explosion, people starving in India, the world
blowing up. We'd be walking along down 22nd and pass an alley and
Ziggy would say, "See that?"

"See what?"

"Mayor Daley scrounging through garbage."

We'd all turn back and look, but only see a bag lady picking through
cans.

Still, in a way, I could see it from Ziggy's point of view. Mayor Daley
was everywhere. The city was tearing down buildings for urban renewal
and tearing up streets for a new expressway, and everywhere one looked
there were signs in front of the rubble reading:

SORRY FOR THE INCONVENIENCE
ANOTHER IMPROVEMENT
FOR A GREATER CHICAGO
RICHARD J. DALEY, MAYOR

Not only were there signs everywhere, but a few blocks away a steady stream of fat, older, bossy-looking guys emanated from the courthouse on 26th. They looked like a corps of Mayor Daley doubles and sometimes, especially on election days, they'd march into the neighborhood chewing cigars and position themselves in front of the flag-draped barbershops that served as polling places.

But back to blight.

That was an expression we used a lot. We'd say it after going downtown, or after spending the day at the Oak Street Beach, which we regarded as the beach of choice for sophisticates. We'd pack our towels and, wearing our swimsuits under our jeans, take the subway north.

"North to freedom," one of us would always say.

Those were days of longing without cares, of nothing to do but lie out on the sand inspecting the world from behind our sunglasses. At the Oak Street Beach the city seemed to realize our dreams of it. We gazed out nonchalantly at the white-sailed yachts on the watercolor-blue horizon, or back across the Outer Drive at the lake-reflecting glass walls of high-rises as if we took it all for granted. The blue, absorbing shadow would deepen to azure, and a fiery orange sun would dip behind the glittering buildings. The crowded beach would gradually empty, and a pitted moon would hover over sand scalloped with a million footprints. It would be time to go.

"Back to blight," one of us would always joke.

I remember a day shortly after blight first became official. We were walking down Rockwell, cutting through the truck docks, Zig, Pepper, and I, on our way to the viaduct near Douglas Park. Pepper was doing his Fats Domino impression, complete with opening piano riff: *Bum-pah-da bum-pah-da dummmmm . . .*

> Ah foun' mah thrill
> Ahn Blueberry Hill . . .

It was the route we usually walked to the viaduct, but since blight had been declared we were trying to see our surroundings from a new perspective, to determine if anything had been changed, or at least appeared different. Blight sounded serious, Biblical in a way, like something locusts might be responsible for.

"Or a plague of gigantic, radioactive cockroaches," Zig said, "climbing out of the sewers."

"Blight, my kabotch," Pepper said, grabbing his kabotch and shaking it at the world. "They call this blight? Hey, man, there's weeds and trees and everything, man. You shoulda seen it on 18th Street."

We passed a Buick somebody had dumped near the railroad tracks. It had been sitting there for months and was still crusted with salt-streaked winter grime. Someone had scraped WASH ME across its dirty trunk, and someone else had scrawled WHIP ME across its hood. Pepper snapped off the aerial and whipped it back and forth so that the air whined, then slammed it down on a fender and began rapping out a Latin beat. We watched him smacking the hell out of it, then Zig and I picked up sticks and broken hunks of bricks and started clanking the headlights and bumpers as if they were bongos and congas, all of us chanting out the melody to *Tequila.* Each time we grunted out the word "tequila," Pepper, who was dancing on the hood, stomped out more windshield.

We were revving up for the viaduct, a natural echo chamber where we'd been going for blues-shout contests ever since we'd become infatuated with Screamin' Jay Hawkins's *I Put a Spell on You.* In fact, it was practicing blues shouts together that had led to the formation of our band, the No Names. We practiced in the basement of the apartment building I lived in: Zig on bass, me on sax, Pepper on drums, and a guy named Deejo who played accordion, though he promised us he was saving up to buy an electric guitar.

Pepper could play. He was a natural.

"I go crazy," was how he described it.

His real name was Stanley Rosado. His mother sometimes called him Stashu, which he hated. She was Polish and his father was Mexican—the two main nationalities in the neighborhood together in one house. It wasn't always an easy alliance, especially inside Pepper. When he got pissed he was a wild man. Things suffered, sometimes people, but always things. Smashing stuff seemed to fill him with peace. Sometimes he didn't even realize he was doing it, like the time he took flowers to

Linda Molina, a girl he'd been nuts about since grade school. Linda lived in one of the well-kept two-flats along Marshall Boulevard, right across from Assumption Church. Maybe it was just that proximity to the church, but there had always been a special aura about her. Pepper referred to her as "the unadulterated one." He finally worked up the nerve to call her, and when she actually invited him over, he walked down the boulevard to her house in a trance. It was late spring, almost summer, and the green boulevard stretched like an enormous lawn before Linda Molina's house. At its center was a blazing garden of tulips. The city had planted them. Their stalks sprouted tall, more like corn than flowers, and their colors seemed to vibrate in the air. The tulips were the most beautiful thing in the neighborhood. Mothers wheeled babies by them; old folks hobbled for blocks and stood before them as if they were sacred.

Linda answered the door and Pepper stood there holding a huge bouquet.

"For you," Pepper said.

Linda, smiling with astonishment, accepted the flowers; then her eyes suddenly widened in horror. "You didn't—?" she asked.

Pepper shrugged.

"*¡Lechón!*" the Unadulterated One screamed, pitching a shower of tulips into his face and slamming the door.

That had happened over a year before and Linda still refused to talk to him. It had given Pepper's blues shouts a particularly soulful quality, especially since he continued to preface them, in the style of Screamin' Jay Hawkins, with the words "I love you." *I love you! Aiiiyyaaaaaaa!!!*

Pepper even had Screamin' Jay's blues snork down.

We'd stand at the shadowy mouth of the viaduct, peering at the greenish gleam of light at the other end of the tunnel. The green was the grass and trees of Douglas Park. Pepper would begin slamming an aerial or board or chain off the girders, making the echoes collide and ring, while Ziggy and I clonked empty bottles and beer cans, and all three of us would be shouting and screaming like Screamin' Jay or Howlin' Wolf, like those choirs of unleashed voices we'd hear on *Jam with Sam*'s late-night blues show. Sometimes a train streamed by, booming overhead like part of the song, and we'd shout louder yet, and

I'd remember my father telling me how he could have been an opera singer if he hadn't ruined his voice as a kid imitating trains. Once, a gang of black kids appeared on the Douglas Park end of the viaduct and stood harmonizing from bass through falsetto just like the Coasters, so sweetly that though at first we tried outshouting them, we finally shut up and listened, except for Pepper keeping the beat.

We applauded from our side, but stayed where we were, and they stayed on theirs. Douglas Park had become the new boundary after the riots the summer before.

"How can a place with such good viaducts have blight, man?" Pepper asked, still rapping his aerial as we walked back.

"Frankly, man," Ziggy said, "I always suspected it was a little fucked up around here."

"Well, that's different," Pepper said. "Then let them call it an Official Fucked-Up Neighborhood."

Nobody pointed out that you'd never hear a term like that from a public official, at least not in public, and especially not from the office of the mayor who had once promised, "We shall reach new platitudes of success."

Nor did anyone need to explain that Official Blight was the language of revenue, forms in quintuplet, grants, and Federal aid channeled through the Machine and processed with the help of grafters, skimmers, wheeler-dealers, an army of aldermen, precinct captains, patronage workers, their relatives and friends. No one said it, but instinctively we knew we'd never see a nickel.

Not that we cared. They couldn't touch us if we didn't. Besides, we weren't blamers. Blight was just something that happened, like acne or old age. Maybe declaring it official mattered in that mystical world of property values, but it wasn't radical, like condemning buildings or labeling a place a slum. Slums were on the other side of the viaduct.

Blight, in fact, could be considered a kind of official recognition, a grudging admission that among blocks of factories, railroad tracks, truck docks, industrial dumps, scrapyards, expressways, and the drainage canal, people had managed to wedge in their everyday lives.

Deep down we believed what Pepper had been getting at: Blight had nothing to do with ecstasy. They could send in the building inspectors and social workers, the Mayor could drive through in his black limo, but they'd never know about the music of viaducts, or churches where saints winked and nodded, or how right next door to me our guitar player, Joey "Deejo" DeCampo, had finally found his title, and inspired by it had begun the Great American Novel, *Blight*, which opened: "The dawn rises like sick old men playing on the rooftops in their underwear."

We had him read that to us again and again.

Ecstatic, Deejo rushed home and wrote all night. I could always tell when he was writing. It wasn't just the wild, dreamy look that overcame him. Deejo wrote to music, usually the *1812* Overture, and since only a narrow gangway between buildings separated his window from mine, when I heard bells and cannon blasts at two in the morning I knew he was creating.

Next morning, bleary-eyed, sucking a pinched Lucky, Deejo read us the second sentence. It ran 20 ball-point scribbled loose-leaf pages and had nothing to do with the old men on the rooftops in their underwear. It seemed as though Deejo had launched into a digression before the novel had even begun. His second sentence described an epic battle between a spider and a caterpillar. The battle took place in the gangway between our apartment buildings and that's where Deej insisted on reading it to us. The gangway lent his voice an echoey ring. He read with his eyes glued to the page, his free hand gesticulating wildly, pouncing spiderlike, fingers jabbing like a beak tearing into green caterpillar guts, fist opening like a jaw emitting shrieks. His voice rose as the caterpillar reared, howling like a damned soul, its poisonous hairs bristling. Pepper, Ziggy, and I listened, occasionally exchanging looks.

It wasn't Deejo's digressing that bothered us. That was how we all told stories. But we could see that Deejo's inordinate fascination with bugs was surfacing again. Not that he was alone in that, either. Of all our indigenous wildlife—sparrows, pigeons, mice, rats, dogs, cats—it was only bugs that suggested the grotesque richness of nature. A lot of kids had, at one time or another, expressed their wonder by torturing them a little. But Deejo had been obsessed. He'd become diabolically adept as a destroyer, the kind of kid who would observe an ant hole for hours, even bait it with a Holloway Bar, before blowing it up with a cherry bomb. Then one day his grandpa Tony said, "Hey, Joey, pretty soon they're gonna invent little microphones and you'll be able to hear them screaming."

He was kidding, but the remark altered Deejo's entire way of looking at things. The world suddenly became one of an infinite number of infinitesimal voices, and Deejo equated voices with souls. If one only listened, it was possible to hear tiny choirs that hummed at all hours as on a summer night, voices speaking a language of terror and beauty that, for the first time, Deejo understood.

It was that vision that turned him into a poet, and it was really for his poetry, more than his guitar playing, that we'd recruited him for the No Names. None of us could write lyrics, though I'd tried a few takeoffs, like the one on Jerry Lee Lewis's *Great Balls of Fire:*

> My BVDs were made of thatch,
> You came along and lit the match,
> I screamed in pain, my screams grew
> higher,
> Goodness gracious! My balls were on fire!

We were looking for a little more soul, words that would suggest Pepper's rages, Ziggy's prophetic dreams. And we might have had that if Deejo could have written a bridge. He'd get in a groove like *Lonely Is the Falling Rain:*

> Lonely is the falling rain,
> Every taste
> Seems the same,
>
> Lonely is the willow tree,
> Green dress draped
> Across her knee,
>
> Lonely is the boat at sea . . .

Deejo could go on listing lonely things for pages, but he'd never arrive at a bridge. His songs refused to circle back on themselves. They'd just go on and were impossible to memorize.

He couldn't spell, either, which never bothered us but created a real problem when Pepper asked him to write something that Pepper could

send to Linda Molina. Deejo came up with *I Dream,* which ended with
the lines:

I dream of my arms
Around your waste.

Linda mailed it back to Pepper with those lines circled and in angry
slashes of eyebrow pencil the exclamations: ¡LECHON! ¡¡ESTUPIDO!!
PERVERT!!!

Pepper kept it folded in his wallet like a love letter.

But back to Blight.

We stood in the gangway listening to Deejo read. His seemingly nonstop sentence was reaching a climax. Just when the spider and caterpillar realized their battle was futile, that neither could win, a sparrow
swooped down and gobbled them both up.

It was a parable. Who knows how many insect lives had been sacri-
ficed in order for Deejo to have finally scribbled those pages?

We hung our heads and muttered, "Yeah, great stuff, Deej, that was
good, man, no shit, keep it up, be a best seller."

He folded his loose-leaf papers, stuffed them into his back pocket,
and walked away without saying anything.

Later, whenever someone would bring up his novel, *Blight,* and its
great opening line, Deejo would always say, "Yeah, and it's been all
downhill from there."

As long as it didn't look like Deejo would be using his title in the near
future we decided to appropriate it for the band. We considered several
variations—Boys from Blight, Blights Out, The Blight Brigade. We
wanted to call ourselves Pepper and the Blighters, but Pepper said no
way, so we settled on just plain Blighters. That had a lot better ring to it
than calling ourselves the No Names. We had liked being the No Names
at first, but it had started to seem like an advertisement for an identity
crisis. The No Names sounded too much like one of the tavern-spon-
sored softball teams the guys back from Korea had formed. Those guys
had been our heroes when we were little kids. They had seemed like
legends to us as they gunned around the block on Indians and Harleys

while we walked home from grade school. Now they hung out at corner taverns, working on beer bellies, and played softball a couple of nights a week on teams that lacked both uniforms and names. Some of their teams had jerseys with the name of the bar that sponsored them across the back, but the bars themselves were mainly named after beers—the Fox Head 500 on 25th Street, or the Edelweiss Tap on 26th, or down from that the Carta Blanca. Sometimes, in the evenings, we'd walk over to Lawndale Park and watch one of the tavern teams play softball under the lights. Invariably some team calling itself the Damon Demons or the Latin Cobras, decked out in gold-and-black uniforms, would beat their butts.

There seemed to be some unspoken relationship between being nameless and being a loser. Watching the guys from Korea after their ball games as they hung around under the buzzing neon signs of their taverns, guzzling beers and flipping the softball, I got the strange feeling that they had actually chosen anonymity and the loserhood that went with it. It was something they looked for in one another, that held them together. It was as if Korea had confirmed the choice in them, but it had been there before they'd been drafted. I could still remember how they once organized a motorcycle club. They called it the Motorcycle Club. Actually, nobody even called it that. It was the only nameless motorcycle gang I'd ever heard of.

A lot of those guys had grown up in the housing project that Pepper and Ziggy lived in, sprawling blocks of row houses known simply as "the projects," rather than something ominous-sounding like Cabrini-Green. Generations of nameless gangs had roamed the projects, then disappeared, leaving behind odd, anonymous graffiti—unsigned warnings, threats, and imprecations without the authority of a gang name behind them.

It wasn't until we became Blighters that we began to recognize the obscurity that surrounded us. Other neighborhoods at least had identities, like Back of the Yards, Marquette Park, Logan Square, Greektown. There were places named after famous intersections like Halsted and Taylor. Everyone knew the Mayor still lived in Bridgeport, the neighborhood he was born in. We heard our area referred to sometimes as Zone 8, after its postal code, but that never caught on. Nobody said,

"Back to Zone 8." For a while Deejo had considered *Zone 8* as a possible title for his novel, but he finally rejected it as sounding too much like science fiction.

As Blighters, just walking the streets we became suddenly aware of familiar things we didn't have names for, like the trees we'd grown up walking past, or the flowers we'd always admired that bloomed around the blue plastic shrine of the Virgin in the front yard of the Old Widow. Even the street names were mainly numbers, something I'd never have noticed if Debbie Weiss, a girl I'd met downtown, hadn't pointed it out.

Debbie played sax, too, in the band at her all-girls' high school. I met her in the sheet-music department of Lyon & Healy's music store. We were both flipping through the same Little Richard song books. His songs had great sax breaks, the kind where you roll onto your back and kick your feet in the air while playing.

"Tenor or alto?" she asked without looking up from the music.

I glanced around to make sure she was talking to me. She was humming *Tutti Frutti* under her breath.

"Tenor," I answered, amazed we were talking.

"That's what I want for my birthday. I've got an alto, an old Martin. It was my Uncle Seymour's. He played with Chick Webb."

"Oh, yeah," I said, impressed, though I didn't know exactly who Chick Webb was. "How'd you know I played sax?" I asked her, secretly pleased that I obviously looked like someone who did.

"It was either that or you've got weird taste in ties. You always walk around wearing your neck strap?"

"No, I just forgot to take it off after practicing," I explained, effortlessly slipping into my first lie to her. Actually, I had taken to wearing the neck strap for my saxophone sort of in the same way that the Mexican guys in the neighborhood wore gold chains dangling outside their T-shirts, except that instead of a cross at the end of my strap I had a little hook from which the horn was meant to hang.

We went to a juice bar Debbie knew around the corner from the music store. I had a Coco-Nana and she had something with mango, papaya, and passion fruit.

"So how'd you think I knew you played sax? By your thumb callus?" she laughed.

We compared the thumb calluses we had from holding our horns. She was funny. I'd never met a girl so easy to talk to. We talked about music and saxophone reeds and school. The only thing wrong was that I kept telling her lies. I told her that I played in a band in Cicero in a club that was run by the Mafia. She said she'd never been to Cicero, but it sounded like really the pits. "Really the pits" was one of her favorite phrases. She lived on the North Side and invited me to visit. When she wrote her address down on a napkin and asked if I knew how to get there I said, "Sure, I know where that is."

North to Freedom, I kept thinking on my way to her house the first time, trying to remember all the bull I'd told her. It took over an hour and two transfers to get there. I ended up totally lost. I was used to streets that were numbers, streets that told you exactly where you were and what was coming up next. "Like knowing the latitude," I told her.

She argued that the North Side had more class because the streets had names.

"A number lacks character, David. How can you have a feeling for a street called 22nd?" she asked.

She'd never been on the South Side except for a trip to the museum. I'd ride the Douglas Park "B" train home from her house and pretend she was sitting next to me, and as my stop approached I'd look down at the tarpaper roofs, back porches, alleys, and back yards crammed between factories, and try to imagine how it would look to someone seeing it for the first time.

At night, 22nd was a streak of colored lights, electric winks of neon glancing off plate glass and sidewalks as headlights surged by. The air smelled of restaurants—frying burgers, pizza parlors, the cornmeal and hot-oil blast of *taquerías*. Music collided out of open bars. And when it rained and the lights on the oily street shimmered, Deejo would start whistling *Harlem Nocturne* in the back seat.

I'd inherited a '53 Chevy from my father. He hadn't died, but he figured the car had. It was a real Blightmobile, a kind of mustardy, baby-shit yellow where it wasn't rusting out, but built like a tank, and rumbling like one, too. That car would not lay rubber, not even when I'd floor it in neutral, then throw it into drive.

Some nights there would be drag races on 25th Place, a dead-end street lined with abandoned factories and junkers that winos dumped along the curb. It was suggested to me more than once that my Chevy should take its rightful place along the curb with the junkers. The dragsters would line up, their machines gleaming, customized, bull-nosed, raked, and chopped, oversize engines revving through chrome pipes; then someone would wave a shirt and they'd explode off, burning rubber down an aisle of wrecks. We'd hang around watching till the cops showed up, then scrape together some gas money and go riding ourselves, me behind the wheel, and Ziggy fiddling with the radio, tuning in on the White Sox while everyone else shouted for music.

The Chevy had one customized feature: a wooden bumper. It was something I was forced to add after I almost ruined my life forever on Canal Street. When I first inherited the car all I had was my driver's permit, so Ziggy, who already had his license, rode with me to take the driving test. On the way there, wheeling a corner for practice, I jumped the curb on Canal Street and rumbled down the sidewalk until I hit a NO PARKING sign and sent it flying over the bridge. Shattered headlights showered the windshield and Ziggy was choking on a scream caught in his throat. I swung a U and fled back to the neighborhood. It took blocks before Ziggy was able to breathe again. I felt shaky, too, and started to laugh. Zig stared at me as if I were crazy and had purposely driven down the sidewalk in order to knock off a NO PARKING sign.

"Holy Christ! Dave, you could have ruined your life back there forever," Zig told me. It sounded like something my father would have said. Worries were making Ziggy more nervous that summer than ever before. The Sox had come from nowhere to lead the league, triggering Zig's old nightmare about atom bombs falling on the night the White Sox won the pennant.

Besides the busted headlights, the sign pole had left a perfect indentation in my bumper. It was Pepper's idea to wind chains around the bumper at the point of indentation, attach the chains to the bars of a basement window, and floor the car in reverse to pull out the dent. When we tried it the bumper tore off. So Pepper, who saw himself as mechanically inclined, wired on a massive wooden bumper. He'd developed a weird affection for the Chevy. I'd let him drive and he'd tool down alleys clipping garbage cans with the wooden front end in a kind of steady bass-drum beat: BOOM BOOM BOOM.

Pepper reached the point where he wanted to drive all the time. I understood why. There's a certain feeling of freedom you can get only with a beater, that comes from being able to wreck it without remorse. In a way it's like being indestructible, impervious to pain. We'd cruise the neighborhood on Saturdays, and everywhere we looked guys would be waxing their cars or tinkering under the hoods.

I'd honk at them out the window on my sax and yell, "You're wasting a beautiful day on that hunk of scrap."

They'd glance up from their swirls of Simonize and flip me the finger. "Poor, foolish assholes," Pepper would scoff.

He'd drive with one hand on the wheel and the other smacking the roof in time to whatever was blaring on the radio. The Chevy was like a drum-set accessory to him. He'd jump out at lights and start bopping on the hood. Since he was driving, I started toting along my sax. We'd pull up to a bus stop where people stood waiting in a trance and Pepper would beat on a fender while I wailed a chorus of *Hand Jive;* then we'd jump back in the Chevy and grind off, as if making our getaway.

Finally, I sold Pepper the Chevy for $25. He said he wanted to fix it up. Instead, he used it as a battering ram. He drove it at night around the construction sites of the new expressway, mowing down the blinking yellow barricades and signs that read: SORRY FOR THE INCONVENIENCE . . .

Ziggy, who had developed an eye twitch and had started to stutter, refused to ride with him any more.

The Sox kept winning.

One night, as Pepper gunned the engine at a red light on 39th, the entire transmission dropped out into the street. He, Deejo, and I pushed the car for blocks and never saw a cop. There was a slight decline to the street and once we got it moving the Chevy rolled along on its own momentum. Pepper sat inside steering. With the key in the ignition the radio still played.

"Anybody have any idea where we're rolling to?" Deejo wanted to know.

"To the end of the line," Pepper said.

We rattled across a bridge that spanned the drainage canal, and just beyond it Pepper cut the wheel and we turned off onto an oiled, unlighted cinder road that ran past a foundry and continued along the river. The road angled downhill, but it was potholed and rutted and it took all three of us grunting and struggling to keep the car moving.

"It would have been a lot easier to just dump it on 25th Place," Deejo panted.

"No way, man," Pepper said, "we ain't winos."

"We got class," I said.

The road was intersected by railroad tracks. After half an hour of rocking and heaving we got the Chevy onto the tracks and from there it was downhill again to the railroad bridge. We stopped halfway across the bridge. Pepper climbed onto the roof of the car and looked out over the black river. The moon shined on the oily surface like a single, intense spotlight. Frankie Avalon was singing on the radio.

"Turn that simp off. I hate him," Pepper yelled. He was peeing down onto the hood in a final benediction.

I switched the radio dial over the late-night mush music station— Sinatra singing *These Foolish Things*—and turned the volume on full. Pepper jumped down, flicked the headlights on, and we shoved the car over the bridge.

The splash shook the girders. Pigeons crashed out from under the bridge and swept around confusedly in the dark. We stared over the side half expecting to see the Chevy bob back up through the heavy grease of the river and float off in the moonlight. But except for the bubbles on the surface, it was gone. Then I remembered that my sax had been in the trunk.

A week later, Pepper had a new car, a red Fury convertible. His older cousin Carmen had co-signed. Pepper had made the first payment, the only one he figured on making, by selling his massive red sparkle drum set—bass, snare, tom-tom, cymbals, high-hat, bongos, conga, cowbell, wood block, tambourine, gong—pieces he'd been accumulating on birthdays, Christmases, confirmation, graduation, since fourth grade, the way girls add pearls to a necklace. When he climbed behind those drums he looked like a mad king beating his throne, and at first we refused to believe he had sold it all, or that he was dropping out of school to join the marines.

He drove the Fury as gently as a chauffeur. It was as if some of the craziness had drained out of him when the Chevy went over the bridge. Ziggy even started riding with us again, though every time he'd see a car pass with a GO GO SOX sign he'd get twitchy and depressed.

Pennant fever was in the air. The city long accustomed to losers was poised for a celebration. Driving with the top down brought the excitement of the streets closer. We were part of it. From Pepper's Fury the pace of life around us seemed different, slower than it had from the Chevy. It was as if we were in a speedboat gliding through.

Pepper would glide repeatedly past Linda Molina's house, but she was never out as she'd been the summer before, sunning on a towel on the boulevard grass. There was a rumor that she'd gotten knocked up and had gone to stay with relatives in Texas. Pepper refused to believe it, but the rest of us got the feeling that he had joined the marines for the same reason Frenchmen supposedly joined the Foreign Legion.

"Dave, man, you wanna go by that broad you know's house on the North Side, man?" he would always offer.

"Nah," I'd say, as if that would be boring.

We'd just drive, usually farther south, sometimes almost to Indiana, where the air smelled singed, and towering foundry smokestacks erupted shooting sparks like gigantic Roman candles. Then, skirting the worst slums, we'd head back through dark neighborhoods broken by strips of neon, the shops grated and padlocked, but bands of kids still out splashing in open hydrants, and guys standing in the light of bar signs, staring hard as we passed.

We toured places we'd always heard about—the Fulton produce mart with its tailgate-high sidewalks, Midway Airport, skid row—stopped for carry-out ribs, or at shrimp houses along the river, and always ended up speeding down the Outer Drive, along the skyline-glazed lake, as if some force had spun us to the inner rim of the city. That was the

summer Deejo let his hair get long. He was growing a beard, too, a
Vandyke, he called it, though Pepper insisted it was really trimmings
from other parts of Deejo's body pasted on with Elmer's glue.

Wind raking his shaggy hair, Deejo would shout passages from his
dog-eared copy of *On the Road,* which he walked around reading like a
breviary ever since seeing Jack Kerouac on *The Steve Allen Show.* I
retaliated in a spooky Vincent Price voice, reciting poems off an album
called *Word Jazz* that Deej and I had nearly memorized. My favorite
was "The Junkman," which began:

> In a dream I dreamt that was no dream,
> In a sleep I slept that was no sleep,
> I saw the junkman in his scattered yard. . . .

Ziggy dug that one, too.

By the time we hit downtown and passed Buckingham Fountain with
its spraying, multicolored plumes of light, Deejo would be rhapsodic.
One night, standing up in the back seat and extending his arms toward
the skyscraper we called God's House because of its glowing blue dome
—a blue the romantic, lonely shade of runway lights—Deejo blurted
out, "I dig beauty!"

Even at the time, it sounded a little extreme. All we'd had were a
couple of six-packs. Pepper started swerving, he was laughing so hard,
and beating the side of the car with his fist, and for a while it was like he
was back behind the wheel of the Chevy. It even brought Ziggy out of
his despair. We rode around the rest of the night gaping and pointing
and yelling, "Beauty ahead! Dig it!"

"Beauty to the starboard!"

"Coming up on it fast!"

"Can you dig it?"

"Oh, wow! I am digging it! I'm digging beauty!"

Deejo got pimped pretty bad about it in the neighborhood. A long
time after that night, guys would still be asking him, "Digging any
beauty lately?" Or introducing him: "This is Deejo. He digs beauty." Or
he'd be walking down the street and from a passing car someone would
wave, and yell, "Hey, Beauty-Digger!"

The last week before the Fury was repoed, when Pepper would come
by to pick us up, he'd always say, "Hey, man, let's go dig some beauty."

A couple of weeks later, on a warm Wednesday night in Cleveland,
Gerry Staley came on in relief with the bases loaded in the bottom of
the ninth, threw one pitch, a double-play ball, Aparicio to Kluszewski,
and the White Sox clinched their first pennant in 40 years. Pepper had
already left on the bus for Parris Island. He would have liked the celebration. Around 11 p.m. the air-raid sirens all over the city began to
howl. People ran out into the streets in their bathrobes crying and
praying, staring up past the roofs as if trying to catch a glimpse of the
mushroom cloud before it blew the neighborhood to smithereens. It
turned out that Mayor Daley, a lifelong Sox fan, had ordered the sirens
as part of the festivities.

Ziggy wasn't the same after that. He could hardly get a word out
without stammering. He said he didn't feel reprieved, but as if he had
died. When the sirens started to wail, he had climbed into bed clutching
his rosary which he still had from grade-school days, when the Blessed
Mother used to smile at him. He'd wet the bed that night and had
continued having accidents every night since. Deej and I tried to cheer
him up, but what kept him going was a book by Thomas Merton called
Seven Storey Mountain, which one of the priests at the parish church
had given him. It meant more to Zig than *On the Road* did to Deejo.
Finally, Ziggy decided that since he could hardly talk anyway, he might
be better off in the Trappists like Thomas Merton. He figured if he just
showed up with the book at the monastery in Gethsemani, Kentucky,
they'd have to take him in.

"I'll be taking the vow of silence," he stammered, "so don't worry if
you don't hear much from me."

"Silence isn't the vow I'd be worrying about," I said, still trying to
joke him out of it, but he was past laughing and I was sorry I'd kidded
him.

He, Deejo, and I walked past the truck docks and railroad tracks,
over to the river. We stopped on the California Avenue Bridge, from
which we could see a succession of bridges spanning the river, including

the black railroad bridge we had pushed the Chevy over. We'd been walking most of the night, past churches, under viaducts, along the boulevard, as if visiting the landmarks of our childhoods. Without a car to ride around in, I felt like a little kid again. It was Zig's last night and he wanted to walk. In the morning he intended to leave home and hitchhike to Kentucky. I had an image of him standing along the shoulder holding up a sign that read GETHSEMANI to the oncoming traffic. I didn't want him to go. I kept remembering things as we walked along and then not mentioning them, like that dream he'd had about him and me and Little Richard. Little Richard had found religion and been ordained a preacher, I'd read, but I didn't think he had taken the vow of silence. I had a fantasy of all the monks with their hoods up, meditating in total silence, and suddenly Ziggy letting go with an ear-splitting, wild, howling banshee blues shout.

The next morning he really was gone.

Deejo and I waited for a letter, but neither of us heard anything.

"He must have taken the vow of silence as far as writing, too," Deejo figured.

I did get a post card from Pepper sometime during the winter, a scene of a tropical sunset over the ocean, and scrawled on the back the message: *Not digging much beauty lately.* There was no return address, and since Pepper's parents had divorced and moved out of the projects I couldn't track him down.

There was a lot of moving going on. Deejo moved out after a huge fight with his old man. Deej's father had lined up a production-line job for Deejo at the factory where he'd worked for 23 years. When Deej didn't show up for work the first day his father came home in a rage and tried to tear Deejo's beard off. So Deejo moved in with his older brother, Sal, who'd just gotten out of the navy and had a bachelor pad near Old Town. The only trouble for Deejo was that he had to move back home on weekends, when Sal needed more privacy.

Deejo was the last of the Blighters still playing. He actually bought a guitar, though not an electric one. He spent a lot of time listening to scratchy old 78s of black singers whose first names all seemed to begin with either Blind or Sonny. Deejo even cut his own record, a paper-thin 45 smelling of acetate, with one side blank. He took copies of it around

to all the bars that the guys from Korea used to rule, and talked the
bartenders into putting his record on the juke box. Those bars had
quieted down. There weren't enough guys from the Korean days still
drinking to field the corner softball teams any more. The guys who had
become regulars were in pretty sad shape. They sat around, endlessly
discussing baseball and throwing dice for drinks. The juke boxes that
had once blasted The Platters and Buddy Holly had filled up with
polkas again and with Mexican songs that sounded suspiciously like
polkas. Deejo's record was usually stuck between Frank Sinatra and
Ray Charles. Deej would insert a little card hand printed in ball-point
pen: HARD HEARTED WOMAN BY JOEY DeCAMPO.

It was a song he'd written. Deejo's hair was longer than ever, his
Vandyke had filled in, and he'd taken to wearing sunglasses and huara-
ches. Sometimes he would show up with one of the girls from Loop
Junior College, which was where he was going to school. He'd bring her
into the Edelweiss or the Carta Blanca, usually a wispy blonde with
scared eyes, and order a couple of drafts. The bartender or one of us at
the bar would pick up Deejo's cue and say, "Hey, how about playing
that R5?" and feed the juke box. *Hard Hearted Woman* would come
thumping out as loud as the *She's Too Fat Polka,* scratchy as an old 78,
Deejo whining through his nose, strumming his three chords.

> Hard hearted woman,
> Oh yeah, Lord,
> She's a hard hearted woman,
> Uuuhhh . . .

Suddenly, despite the Delta accent, it would dawn on the girl that it
was Deejo's voice. He'd kind of grin, shyly admitting that it was, his
fingers on the bar tapping along in time with the song, and I wondered
what she would think if she could have heard the one I wished he had
recorded, the one that opened:

> The dawn rises,
> Uuuhhh,
> Like sick old men,
> Oh Lord,
> Playing in their underwear on the rooftops,
> Yeah . . .

* * *

Back to blight.

It was a saying that faded from my vocabulary, especially after my parents moved to Berwyn. Then, some years later, after I quit my job at UPS in order to hide out from the draft in college, the word resurfaced in an English lit survey class. Maybe I was just more attuned to it than most people ordinarily would be. There seemed to be blight all through Dickens and Blake. The class was taught by a professor nicknamed "the Spitter." He loved to read aloud and after the first time, nobody sat in the front rows. He had acquired an Oxford accent, but the more excitedly he read and spit, the more I could detect the South Side of Chicago underneath the veneer, as if his *th*'s had been worked over with a drill press. When he read us Shelley's "Hail to thee, blithe spirit," I thought he was talking about blight again until I looked it up.

One afternoon in spring I cut class and rode the Douglas Park "B" back. It wasn't anything I planned. I just wanted to go somewhere and think. The draft board was getting ready to reclassify me and I needed to figure out why I felt like telling them to get rammed rather than just saying the hell with it and doing what they told me to do. But instead of thinking, I ended up remembering my early trips back from the North Side, when I used to pretend that Debbie Weiss was riding with me, and when I came to my stop this time it was easier to imagine how it would have looked to her—small, surprisingly small in the way one is surprised returning to an old grade-school classroom.

I hadn't been back for a couple of years. The neighborhood was mostly Mexican now, with many of the signs over the stores in Spanish, but the bars were still called the Edelweiss Tap and the Budweiser Lounge. Deejo and I had lost touch, but I heard that he'd been drafted. I made the rounds of some of the bars looking for his song on the juke boxes, but when I couldn't find it even in the Carta Blanca, where nothing else had changed, I gave up. I was sitting in the Carta Blanca having a last, cold *cerveza* before heading back, listening to *CuCuRuCuCu Paloma* on the juke box and watching the sunlight streak in through the dusty wooden blinds. Then the juke box stopped playing, and through the open door I could hear the bells from three

different churches tolling the hour. They didn't quite agree on the precise moment. Their rings overlapped and echoed one another. The
streets were empty, no one home from work or school yet, and something about the overlapping of those bells made me remember how
many times I'd had dreams, not prophetic ones like Ziggy's but terrifying all the same, in which I was back in my neighborhood, but lost,
everything at once familiar and strange, and I knew if I tried to run, my
feet would be like lead, and if I stepped off a curb, I'd drop through
space, and then in the dream I would come to a corner that would feel
so timeless and peaceful, like the Carta Blanca with the bells fading and
the sunlight streaking through, that for a moment it would feel as if I'd
wandered into an Official Blithe Area.

THE JANEITES

JAMES LOTT

> James Lott is Dean of the College at Mary Baldwin College in
> Staunton, Virginia. He graduated from the University of Tennessee,
> received a Master's from Vanderbilt and a Ph.D. from the University
> of Wisconsin. He has published fiction in the *Southern Review, South-
> ern Humanities Review, Emrys Journal, South Carolina Review,* and
> *Virginia Quarterly Review.*

Mr. Owen is reading *Emma,* his favorite book. He has, in fact, been
reviewing it for several days so that the details will be fresh in his mind
for this afternoon's meeting. He has laid the book open on the kitchen
table, and when he runs across a passage he thinks his wife would like,
he reads it aloud.

" 'Human nature is so well disposed toward those who are in interesting situations,' " he says, " 'that a young person, who either marries or
dies, is sure to be kindly spoken of.' You remember this now, don't you,
Alma? Mr. Elton is going to marry Augusta Hawkins, and she'll become Mrs. Elton. I know you'll remember her—the odious Mrs. Elton?"

Alma looks at him for a moment, sets her mouth in a tiny O, then
looks away.

"She's the one like Mrs. Salesby," Mr. Owen says. "Remember Mrs.
Salesby?"

Mrs. Salesby was a neighbor of theirs years ago, whom Alma one day
had decided was Mrs. Elton in the flesh. A vulgar woman, contemptuous of everyone except her family, she possessed a wealthy sister, whom
no one ever saw but about whom she talked constantly. "The people she
has working for her," she would say. "Why, I really *don't* think she
knows how many there *are,* exactly: oh, not that they're numberless, of

course. You shouldn't think *that"* (with a laugh) "but there are some—
in the *nether* regions, so to speak—whom she has never seen. 'They also
serve who only stand' as *Shakes*peare said." And Alma's eyes would
widen with amusement as she listened, standing there on the front steps
of the house and pulling her sweater tightly around her, and in the
evenings—after their daughters were asleep and they had finished the
dishes and done whatever reading they had—she would sometimes imi-
tate Mrs. Salesby: "But my *dear,* so much *mon*ey, and all in*her*ited, of
course. Her husband's never earned a *pen*ny of it, not *he!"* The odious
Mrs. Salesby.

Mr. Owen looks at his wife: her eyes appear dilated, and there is no
clear separation between the blue and the white. Her eyes are the colors
of the Dutch tiles lined up on the shelf behind her head, and her white
hair—chopped short and in straight bangs—makes her look like a little
Dutch girl grown suddenly old.

Mrs. Armstrong, who has been putting dishes in the cabinet, comes
and stands at the table and holds out three pills: one round and white,
one white with a red band, one orange (shaped, Dr. Sandys observed,
like a tiny football). Mr. Owen takes the white pill and holds it to
Alma's mouth, which opens instantly in a way which reminds him of
the games they played when their daughters were children. *(Here comes
the airplane,* he or Alma would say. *Zoom, zoom! Where is the airport?
Where is the hangar?* And Randall, or Eleanor, would open her mouth
and receive the Cream of Wheat, or the single green bean stuck to the
prongs of a tiny fork.) He places the pill on Alma's tongue and holds
the glass of water to her lips, and before she drinks, her eyes almost
focus on him, but then her face goes blank again and she swallows. He
gives her the red and white pill and, as Mrs. Armstrong turns away,
puts the orange one in his shirt pocket. When he touches his wife, she
seems to understand who he is.

"Good girl," Mrs. Armstrong says when she turns back to them.
("So well named," Mr. Owen told Alma when they hired Mrs. Armstrong and Alma could still appreciate some of what he said. "I imagine
her in front of mirrors, grimace and groan, admiring her own biceps.")
Now she is a necessary third in their household and no longer anyone to
laugh at.

" 'The charming Augusta Hawkins,' " he continues, " 'in addition to all the usual advantages of perfect beauty and merit, was in possession of an independent fortune, of so many thousands as would always be called ten.' 'The *usual* advantages,' " he repeats. "A wonderful touch. I've never noticed it before."

Later that morning, Mr. Owen sits at the desk in the living room, writing a letter to Randall and Eleanor. He writes the same message to both, copying each paragraph, as he finishes it, from one sheet of stationery to another. "I think your mother still enjoys the reading at breakfast: I'm not so sure about Mrs. Armstrong. I thought she would leave us over Proust, such clearing of throat and heaving of shoulders. I *do* skip passages until I find something your mother might enjoy. Perhaps that disturbs Mrs. Armstrong's natural sense of continuity, or perhaps it's just impatience. She is truly wonderful for us, though. She cooks, cleans, even handles your mother's medicine to make certain I don't forget. Dr. Sandys insisted on that when she came to us. She hoards it up and parcels it out like candy."

He wants to avoid writing about their mother's condition. He wants Randall and Eleanor to feel cheered by everything he has to say, as if he were telling them an interesting story.

"We are thriving," he writes. "Your mother and I have lived together for 40 years with very little to vex or disturb us." He knows Eleanor will hear the echo from *Emma*—Randall will merely think the words sound old-fashioned—but he doesn't write it just to give his younger daughter the pleasure of recognition. He always tries to think of his life that way. He and Alma *have* had no serious problems—minor illnesses, both theirs and their daughters', financial problems in the early 1950's when he decided to return to college—but nothing until now has been more than temporarily perturbing. "I can still manage," he writes. "I have a firm grip on everything. I manage to keep myself occupied."

He hesitates to mention the Society. To his daughters and their husbands—Randall in California, Eleanor north and east of there near Helena, Montana—the Society seems like very little. "I wish you hadn't given up golf," Randall said recently. "There are people in Richmond who golf, I know." Her voice over the phone is always strident, as if she can't accept the 3000 miles between her father and herself and wants the fervor of her words to pull him closer. And even Eleanor, witty like her mother and yet mild and preoccupied, wrote in a letter recently that she was happy he enjoyed the Society but didn't he think he should get away more? "Once every other month," she said, and he could feel her attention wandering even on the blue note paper. "Only six times a year. That's hardly enough to say it's anything."

He can't think how to tell them that the Society is all he wants now, how to confide in them at all, to tell them how the diminishing of everything seems right to him. Whenever he thinks of his daughters, in fact, he is reminded how distant, how unreal, *their* lives are to *him,* how much more vivid the two of them are in photographs. Randall behind a huge bouquet of roses at the Academy graduation, Eleanor posed over the piano keyboard in the den of the house they sold 15 years ago.

He looks at the two pieces of stationery on the desk top. He has written less than half a page, but he can think of nothing more to say. He decides that he will have more to tell them in the evening, and he folds both sheets of paper and slips them into one of the pigeon holes at the back of the desk.

After lunch, when he is sure Alma is safely in bed, he leaves the apartment and walks the three blocks to the bus stop. The last block lies beyond the area he is familiar with, but he has the bus schedule in his pocket and knows exactly when he can board and where he will get off, so he is not anxious. Once he gets to the Club, he will again be on familiar ground. He thinks of himself as moving from island to island, the bus like a benign ship over which he has to exercise no control.

At the stop a large unpleasant-looking woman is already sitting on the bench. Mr. Owen prepares to speak to her, but she glances at him and then shuts her eyes. She is wearing a black straw hat and a purple dress with a slip strap white against her arm, and she is apparently living out an interior scene of some consequence to herself, even of some violence, for she occasionally bites her lip and sits forward as if she wants to say something. Once she speaks—"And I'd just like him to *try!"*—but catches herself before saying more, then turns her massive back to Mr. Owen.

When the bus pulls to the curb, he isn't surprised that the woman shoves ahead, grabs both metal bars, and then heaves herself up the steps as if no one else is waiting to board. He tries to think of the name of the woman in *Persuasion* whose substantial size (he can almost quote the description) makes her comic even when she is weeping for her scapegrace son, but the name will not come to him.

There are two black boys on the bus, young men really. One is wearing a cap, and the other is wearing a felt hat with the front brim turned up. They are sitting on the back seat with their radio, a large silver and grey box with two round speakers like saucers, between them. The volume is so high that the bus seems to have room for nothing besides the sound. Mr. Owen can tell by the stiff set of the driver's back that *he* will not do anything about the noise. The other people on the bus—the fat woman, two younger women, a man who looks disreputable despite his coat and tie (an unsuccessful salesman, Mr. Owen guesses)—cluster near the front. Everyone seems determined to pretend the music isn't there.

Seated, Mr. Owen unfolds the notice of today's meeting: it is printed on heavy cream paper with Anna Lefroy's drawing of Chawton Cottage at the top. "At October's meeting," he reads, "we'll enjoy something different, a general discussion of *Emma.* Come prepared to speak about any of the characters. We want a lively discussion." The notice says that Professor Mary Sturm from the University will read a paper. He has never heard of Professor Mary Sturm, but he has hopes despite her name. Her paper is entitled "A Defense of Mrs. Elton." Mr. Owen enjoys irony, and he looks forward to Professor Sturm's brand.

He himself has thought of some interesting things to say about Mrs. Elton. She has long been a favorite villainess of his. When he tries to imagine her now, he sees Mrs. Salesby again, and he remembers when Alma first saw the resemblance: "I think she must have read the book," Alma said. "I think she models herself after Mrs. Elton on purpose. She has some devious purpose in mind we can't begin to *guess* at." Mr. Owen decides the other members of the Society would like to hear about Mrs. Salesby.

As the bus gets closer to the University, several more people get on, but no one gets off. Outside, through the windows, the houses grow larger and statelier, and he sees people walking, singly or in twos or threes, along the sidewalks, in a way they never do around his apartment building. Because of the loud music in the bus, he imagines the people outside walking in silence, or whispering to one another. The bus passes the Museum, and he begins to look for the Civil War monuments which tell him he is near the University. After that, he will be at the Club. He thinks of how quiet it will be there.

When the two boys exit, suddenly and jerkily, disturbing the old men and the pigeons in the tiny park which stretches out from the bus door, the bus seems empty and hollow. The boys were not so bad, he decides —silly and thoughtless, but not bad. He watches them, shoving at each other and laughing, until the bus moves forward and leaves them behind.

As he expected, the Club meeting room is quiet. He takes a seat on the second row. Only a few members are here before him, and he recognizes them all. The only other man is Mr. Asquith, whose wife leads him into and out of every meeting like a sad, obedient dog. Mr. Owen has never heard him speak—though *Mrs.* Asquith is quite vocal—but there is always in his face a look of resigned disagreement with everything anyone says. Mr. Owen nods to Mrs. Beatty, tightly done up today in brown wool with what looks like a cameo at her throat, and to Mrs. McAteer, who wiggles her fingers beside her cheek in response. He remembers that the fat woman in *Persuasion* is Mrs. Musgrove.

At the front of the paneled room are a long table and a lectern, from the top of which an empty microphone holder hooks meaninglessly into the air. Mrs. Arnold, the day's moderator, comes in a side door with a thin woman in red, obviously Professor Mary Sturm, and the two of them stand talking at the table while Mrs. Arnold eyes the flexible microphone neck with disapproval and Professor Sturm glances down at the notebook she has placed on the table top.

As he looks at Professor Sturm, his enthusiasm for the discussion wanes. She is a tall woman with a protruding chin. Her dress looks too big for her, and her black hair is already falling from the loose twist on the back of her head. She looks like someone who wouldn't enjoy reading Jane Austen, let alone talking about her.

Most of the other people who begin to fill up the room are familiar to him, the sort of people who relish the novels they're here to discuss. He wonders what Alma would say about Professor Sturm: *We should really give her a chance, don't you think? Still.* . . . For the first few months of his membership he brought Alma to the meetings and she was able to understand some of what was said. There followed several months when, although Alma stayed home, he took notes to share with her in the evening. Now he doesn't do that.

Mrs. Arnold introduces Professor Sturm. "A wonderful opportunity," she says, "to hear a true scholar share with us her interesting—and I think you will find 'provocative'—ideas about Miss Austen." Mrs. Arnold clears her throat, as if she wants to say more, then pulls the offending neck of the microphone stand down and forward. "I know you'll listen eagerly to what she has to say." Mr. Owen is reminded of a teacher telling her children to be polite.

When she begins to speak, Professor Sturm pitches her voice so low that Mr. Owen has to lean forward and cup his hand behind his ear to make out the words. She is so clearly uncomfortable that Mr. Owen begins to feel sorry for her. He tries to catch her eye so that he can nod reassuringly, but she fixes her gaze on the paper she is reading.

As she reads, though, she grows calmer. After some introductory comments—how critics have responded to *Emma*—she begins summarizing the plot, and Mr. Owen sits back. The material is so familiar to him that he needn't pay close attention; he enjoys the sensation of being reminded of what he already knows, and he begins to feel grateful to the speaker and sorry for his first reaction to her. Then, however, without any warning, she begins speaking nonsense: "And it is this Mrs. Elton who has been universally despised by Austen's critics. But is there really any difference in the final analysis between Mrs. Elton and any other character in the novel? Is she really worse than the heroine, in fact? If she violates the norms of the society depicted in the novel, isn't it possible that the norms, indeed the society, are corrupt and her violence against them—despite her own lack of self-knowledge—is justified?"

Mr. Owen thinks he has misunderstood, for no one else looks disturbed. Mrs. Arnold has her eyes fixed on something in the back of the room which she seems to find mildly hypnotic. To the left of him Mrs. Beatty plays absentmindedly with her cameo; to his right Mrs. McAteer is looking at her hands folded in her lap.

Professor Sturm talks about each character in the novel. Everyone, according to her, is caught in a vile world whose standards of order and taste corrupt and dehumanize. The things she says seem so wrong to Mr. Owen that he tries not to listen: he tries to think of something else instead. But her voice, which has grown louder, is as insistent as the music on the bus.

"And so Mrs. Elton only *seems* vulgar to a reader who identifies him/herself with a landed gentry—and perhaps to that part of Austen attached through rudimentary longing to such a world. But Mrs. Elton's vulgarity is, in fact, the energetic challenge to the complacency which lulls, which in fact deadens, the other characters. She is Austen's clearer self attacking a world Austen herself could no longer embrace: a world smug and decadent, ripe for change or death, no longer attached to any reality outside the minds of snobs." Mr. Owen feels as if the woman has walked directly up to him and spat in his face.

When she sits down, there is applause, but when Mrs. Arnold asks for questions, no one responds. "No questions?" she says. "I can't believe it." She turns to Professor Sturm. "They're usually very talkative," she says, as if she were discussing a classroom of children. "You've given us a lot to think about." Professor Sturm smiles in a way which shows she agrees.

Because someone has to reply, Mr. Owen stands up. "I have a question," he says, but he cannot think yet exactly what it is. Everyone watches him, and Mr. Asquith, still the only other man in the room, smiles—surprisingly—as if something pleasant has happened.

"I don't see how you can believe any of that," Mr. Owen thinks at last to say. "We knew someone just like Mrs. Elton, and she was rude and loud-mouthed. A braggart, that's what she really was. She always had to tell us how much better she was than anyone else, when all along we knew we were—I know it sounds wrong to say this—better than she. I can't describe her manners." He pauses, and everyone in the room looks at him. He knows they expect a question, but he cannot attach his indignation to any idea. His mind will not connect anything. "I just wish my wife could be here to show you how vulgar she was and how. . . . The point is she was just like Mrs. Elton and it *matters* that she not be. . . ." But what should she not be? Accepted? Defended? He hasn't said what he wants to say. It is something else that matters, something entirely different.

"I'm not sure what your question is," Professor Sturm says, "but I *am* sure that vulgarity isn't as bad as it's cracked up to be." She pauses for the laughter her remark calls forth, and Mr. Owen realizes everyone is grateful to her for relieving the embarrassment he has caused. "I'm also sure a life spent merely avoiding vulgarity isn't good enough. I think Austen would agree with me."

When he fails to sit down, Mrs. Arnold tells him that she has asked for questions and if he has one, she's certain Professor Sturm will be happy to respond. She adds that Professor Sturm has to leave in a few minutes and then the Society members will have a general discussion. "Perhaps," she says, "you could save your own comments for then."

"You don't know, do you?" he says. He is speaking to Professor Sturm. "You don't know how anything you say touches something else, do you? In what other people care about? That's my question." Professor Sturm's face has grown blank, as if he has committed a blunder she chooses to ignore, and, when he looks all around him, the faces of the people he knows grow blank also. Their expressions erased, they hold their heads still in the neutral air, waiting.

The bus ride home is uneventful, and he thinks, not about the Society meeting, but about something else, like a page from a novel:

"There's nothing we can do," Dr. Sandys told him. "I could send you somewhere, to a neurosurgeon or the University hospital, but there's nothing anyone can do. She'll get worse, more and more confused. There's just nothing. Look," he said. He held a book open and showed Mr. Owen a picture. "It's what happens in the brain. Here, the synapses allow connections: little electrical impulses jump back and forth and carry signals. Here they can't do that. You can see why."

To Mr. Owen both pictures looked like nothing which could be important to him or Alma. They were black and white and they depicted what looked like coral or fungus, nothing that either he or Alma could care about. He could not imagine the picture having anything to do with Alma's brain. He could not understand how the shredded fungus in the picture could mean anything.

"Here," Dr. Sandys continued. "I'm giving her three prescriptions and some samples. First, a tranquilizer, very mild. This second one is mostly phenobarbitol, to prevent seizures. And this is amitriptyline. It's an anti-depressant. Make certain she only has one each day: they're very powerful!" He held his palm open so that Mr. Owen could look at the oddly shaped pill. "Doesn't it remind you of a little orange football?"

Mr. Owen drove Alma into the city. There was a drugstore which had been there when they were children and which had been restored to look the way it had then. They sat in wirebacked chairs at a small marble topped table and ate ice cream. The smell of the drugstore was disinfectant and alcohol, like the doctor's office.

"I'm sorry," Alma said. "I feel as if I'm moving in and out of the sunlight. It's hard sometimes to remember what things are and what I should do with them."

She held up her spoon. "Fork," she said. And they both laughed as if she had never in her life said anything more clever.

"She had a restless afternoon," Mrs. Armstrong says. "I think she knew you were gone." She puts Alma to bed at 8:00 and then goes to her own room, and Mr. Owen can hear the sound of her television set through the wall.

When he thinks it is safe, he opens the drawer of the sideboard. Under the linen tablecloths, which they no longer use, is a small mahogany box, divided into two sections, for two decks of cards. Only one side, however, contains cards: in the other are several orange pills—he counts 22. He has averaged keeping one out of every three Mrs. Armstrong has given him, and he has been building the collection for two months, ever since he decided what to do. He drops in the 23rd pill: in less than two more months, before Christmas, he will have 40, 20 for Alma and 20 for himself.

He is tired but wants to finish his letter before he goes to bed.

"I had an interesting day," he writes. "I rode the bus to the Society meeting: that always makes me feel like someone on a boat being taken somewhere nice. There was a woman—a large woman, all wrapped up in purple like Lent—who reminded me of Mrs. Musgrove in *Persuasion:* I suppose I had Jane Austen on my mind. There were two boys on the bus who were more active than the rest of us could live up to. They reminded me of you girls as children, full of noise and mischief. At the meeting a woman from the University said some outrageous things, but I think I set her straight (not as well as your mother would have done, of course). I told her about Mrs. Salesby—do you remember our old neighbor?—and I explained how she was like the characters Jane Austen clearly despises. I think the University woman saw my point, though maybe *she* was too much like Mrs. Salesby herself. Both *very* vulgar women."

He hears the footsteps before Alma appears at the entrance to the living room. He watches her as she goes to the mirror and looks at herself. Then he gets up and walks to her side. The two of them in the mirror, with the single lamp burning, look very old, older than they are. Alma's face is puzzled, and she starts making little whimpering noises as she stares at her reflection.

He takes her arm and, when she tries to pull away from him, grasps her by the elbow and begins to guide her around the room. In a few minutes, he knows, she will grow calm and he can take her back to her bed.

He imagines they are strolling along a sidewalk, passing other couples. The sun is shining, but there is a cool breeze. Something significant has happened which they do not yet understand, and the two of them are enjoying a well-deserved rest. They lean towards each other and whisper. Their conversation probes the meaning of whatever it is they have experienced, and through their talk they begin to see the pattern in what has occurred. When they tire of walking, they will go into one of the stately houses set back from the street on green lawns. He imagines that the rooms will be white with high ceilings: he cannot imagine any furniture, or any sound. The rooms will be very quiet, empty like the pages at the ends of all the books they have ever read. He realizes that he yearns for the emptiness.

As Alma's restlessness subsides, she begins touching everything they pass—the roll-top desk, the back of the wing chair, the arms of the sofa. Then, as he leads her out of the room, she opens and closes her hand along the smooth wall, as if there might be something there to clutch.

BASIL FROM HER GARDEN

DONALD BARTHELME

Donald Barthelme is the author of thirteen novels, the most recent, *Paradise,* was published by Putnam. He is a member of the American Academy and Institute of Arts and Letters. He lives in New York City.

A—In the dream, my father was playing the piano, a Beethoven something, in a large concert hall that was filled with people. I was in the audience and I was reading a book. I suddenly realized that this was the wrong thing to do when my father was performing, so I sat up and paid attention. He was playing very well, I thought. Suddenly the conductor stopped the performance and began to sing a passage for my father, a passage that my father had evidently botched. My father listened attentively, smiling at the conductor.

Q—Does your father play? In actuality?

A—Not a note.

Q—Did the conductor resemble anyone you know?

A—He looked a bit like Althea. The same cheekbones and the same chin.

Q—Who is Althea?

A—Someone I know.

Q—What do you do, after work, in the evenings or on weekends?

A—Just ordinary things.

Q—No special interests?

A—I'm very interested in bow-hunting. These new bows they have now, what they call a compound bow. Also, I'm a member of the Galapagos Society, we work for the environment, it's really a very effective—

Q—And what else?

A—Well, adultery. I would say that that's how I spend most of my free time. In adultery.

Q—You mean regular adultery.

A—Yes. Sleeping with people to whom one is not legally bound.

Q—These are women.

A—Invariably.

Q—And so that's what you do, in the evenings or on weekends.

A—I had this kind of strange experience. Today is Saturday, right? I called up this haircutter that I go to, her name is Ruth, and asked for an appointment. I needed a haircut. So she says she has openings at ten, ten-thirty, eleven, eleven-thirty, twelve, twelve-thirty— On a Saturday. Do you think the world knows something I don't know?

Q—It's possible.

A—What if she stabs me in the ear with the scissors?

Q—Unlikely, I would think.

A—Well, she's a good soul. She's had several husbands. They've all been master sergeants, in the Army. She seems to gravitate toward N.C.O. Clubs. Have you noticed all these little black bugs flying around here? I don't know where they come from.

Q—They're very small, they're like gnats.

A—They come in clouds, then they go away.

A—I sometimes think of myself as a person who, you know what I mean, could have done something else, it doesn't matter what particularly. Just something else. I saw an ad in the Sunday paper for the C.I.A., a recruiting ad, maybe a quarter of a page, and I suddenly thought, It might be interesting to do that. Even though I've always been opposed to the C.I.A., when they were trying to bring Cuba down, the stuff with Lumumba in Africa, the stuff in Central America. . . . Then here is this ad, perfectly straightforward, "where your career is America's strength" or something like that, "aptitude for learning a foreign language is a plus" or something like that. I've always been good at languages, and I'm sitting there thinking about how my résumé might look to them, starting completely over in something completely new, changing the very sort of person I am, and there was an attraction, a definite attraction. Of course the maximum age was thirty-five. I guess they want them more malleable.

Q—So, in the evenings or on weekends—

A—Not every night or every weekend. I mean, this depends on the circumstances. Sometimes my wife and I go to dinner with people, or watch television—

Q—But in the main—

A—It's not that often. It's once in a while.

Q—Adultery is a sin.

A—It is classified as a sin, yes. Absolutely.

Q—The Seventh Commandment says—

A—I know what it says. I was raised on the Seventh Commandment. But.

Q—But what?

A—The Seventh Commandment is wrong.

Q—It's wrong?

A—Some outfits call it the Sixth and others the Seventh. It's wrong.

Q—The whole Commandment?

A—I don't know how it happened, whether it's a mistranslation from the Aramaic or whatever, it may not even have been Aramaic, I don't know, I certainly do not pretend to scholarship in this area, but my sense of the matter is that the Seventh Commandment is an error.

Q—Well if that was true it would change quite a lot of things, wouldn't it?

A—Take the pressure off, a bit.

Q—Have you told your wife?

A—Yes, Grete knows.

Q—How'd she take it?

A—Well, she *liked* the Seventh Commandment. You could reason that it was in her interest to support the Seventh Commandment for the preservation of the family unit and this sort of thing but to reason that way is, I would say, to take an extremely narrow view of Grete, of what she thinks. She's not predictable. She once told me that she didn't want me, she wanted a suite of husbands, ten or twenty—

Q—What did you say?

A—I said, Go to it.

Q—Well, how does it make you feel? Adultery.

A—There's a certain amount of guilt attached. I feel guilty. But I feel guilty even without adultery. I exist in a morass of guilt. There's maybe a little additional wallop of guilt but I already feel so guilty that I hardly notice it.

Q—Where does all this guilt come from? The extra-adulterous guilt?

A—I keep wondering if, say, there is intelligent life on other planets, the scientists argue that something like two per cent of the other planets have the conditions, the physical conditions, to support life in the way it happened here, did Christ visit each and every planet, go through the same routine, the Agony in the Garden, the Crucifixion, and so on. . . . And these guys on these other planets, these lifeforms, maybe they look like boll weevils or something, on a much larger scale of course, were they told that they shouldn't go to bed with other attractive six-foot boll weevils arrayed in silver and gold and with little squirts of Opium behind the ears? Doesn't make sense. But of course our human understanding is imperfect.

Q—You haven't answered me. This general guilt—

A—Yes, that's the interesting thing. I hazard that it is not guilt so much as it is inadequacy. I feel that everything is being nibbled away, because I can't *get it right*—

Q—Would you like to be able to fly?

A—It's crossed my mind.

Q—Myself, I think about being just sort of a regular person, one who worries about cancer a lot, every little thing a prediction of cancer, no I don't want to go for my every-two-years checkup because what if they find something? I wonder what will kill me and when it will happen and how it will happen, and I wonder about my parents, who are still alive, and what will happen to them. This seems to me to be a proper set of things to worry about. Last things.

A—I don't think God gives a snap about adultery. This is just an opinion, of course.

Q—So how do you, how shall I put it, pursue—

A—You think about this staggering concept, the mind of God, and then you think He's sitting around worrying about this guy and this woman at the Beechnut TraveLodge? I think not.

Q—Well He doesn't have to think about every particular instance, He just sort of laid out the general principles—

A—He also created creatures who, with a single powerful glance—

Q—The eyes burn.

A—They do.

Q—The heart leaps.

A—Like a terrapin.

Q—Stupid youth returns.

A—Like hockey sticks falling out of a long-shut closet.

Q—Do you play?

A—I did. Many years ago.

Q—Who is Althea?

A—Someone I know.

Q—We're basically talking about Althea.

A—Yes. I thought you understood that.

Q—We're not talking about wholesale—

A—Oh Lord no. Who has the strength?

Q—What's she like?

A—She's I guess you'd say a little on the boring side. To the innocent eye.

Q—She appears to be a contained, controlled person, free of raging internal fires.

A—But my eye is not innocent. To the already corrupted eye, she's—

Q—I don't want to question you too closely on this. I don't want to strain your powers of—

A—Well, no, I don't mind talking about it. It fell on me like a ton of bricks. I was walking in the park one day.

Q—Which park?

A—That big park over by—

Q—Yeah, I know the one.

A—This woman was sitting there.

Q—They sit in parks a lot, I've noticed that. Especially when they're angry. The solitary bench. Shoulders raised, legs kicking—

* * *

A—I've crossed both major oceans by ship—the Pacific twice, on troopships, the Atlantic once, on a passenger liner. You stand out there, at the rail, at dusk, and the sea is limitless, water in every direction, never-ending, you think *water forever,* the movement of the ship seems slow but also seems inexorable, you feel you will be moving this way forever, the Pacific is about seventy million square miles, about one-third of the earth's surface, the ship might be making twenty knots, I'm eating oranges because that's all I can keep down, twelve days of it with thousands of young soldiers all around, half of them seasick— On the Queen Mary, in tourist class, we got rather good food, there was a guy assigned to our table who had known Paderewski, the great pianist who was also Prime Minister of Poland, he talked about Paderewski for four days, an ocean of anecdotes—

Q—When I was first married, when I was twenty, I didn't know where the clitoris was. I didn't know there was such a thing. Shouldn't somebody have told me?

A—Perhaps your wife?

Q—Of course, she was too shy. In those days people didn't go around saying, This is the clitoris and this is what its proper function is and this is what you can do to help out. I finally found it. In a book.

A—German?

Q—Dutch.

A—A dead bear in a blue dress, face down on the kitchen floor. I trip over it, in the dark, when I get up at 2 A.M. to see if there's anything to eat in the refrigerator. It's an architectural problem, marriage. If we could live in separate houses, and visit each other when we felt particularly gay— It would be expensive, yes. But as it is she has to endure me in all my worst manifestations, early in the morning and late at night and in the nutsy obsessed noontimes. When I wake up from my nap you don't *get* the laughing cavalier, you get a rank pigfooted belching blunderer. I knew this one guy who built a wall down the middle of his apartment. An impenetrable wall. He had a very big apartment. It worked out very well. Concrete block, basically, with fibre-glass insulation on top of that and sheetrock on top of that—

Q—What about coveting your neighbor's wife?

A—Well on one side there are no wives, strictly speaking, there are two floors and two male couples, all very nice people. On the other side, Bill and Rachel have the whole house. I like Rachel but I don't covet her. I could covet her, she's covetable, quite lovely and spirited, but in point of fact our relationship is that of neighborliness. I jump-start her car when her battery is dead, she gives me basil from her garden, she's got acres of basil, not literally acres but— Anyhow, I don't think that's much of a problem, coveting your neighbor's wife. Just speaking administratively, I don't see why there's an entire Commandment devoted to it. It's a mental exercise, coveting. To covet is not necessarily to take action.

Q—I covet my neighbor's leaf blower. It has this neat Vari-Flo deal that lets you—

A—I can see that.

Q—I am feverishly interested in these questions.

Q—Ethics has always been where my heart is.

Q—Moral precepting stings the dull mind into attentiveness.

Q—I'm only a bit depressed, only a bit.

Q—A new arrangement of ideas, based upon the best thinking, would produce a more humane moral order, which we need.

Q—Apple honey, disposed upon the sexual parts, is not an index of decadence. Decadence itself is not as bad as it's been painted.

Q—That he watched his father play the piano when his father could not play the piano and that he was reading a book while his father played the piano in a very large hall before a very large audience only means that he finds his roots, as it were, untrustworthy. The father imagined as a root. That's not unusual.

Q—As for myself, I am content with too little, I know this about myself and I do not commend myself for it and perhaps one day I shall be able to change myself into a hungrier being. Probably not.

Q—The leaf blower, for example.

* * *

A—I see Althea now and then, not often enough. We sigh together in a particular bar, it's almost always empty. She tells me about her kids and I tell her about my kids. I obey the Commandments, the sensible ones. Where they don't know what they're talking about I ignore them. I keep thinking about the story of the two old women in church listening to the priest discoursing on the dynamics of the married state. At the end of the sermon one turns to the other and says, "I wish I knew as little about it as he does."

Q—He critiques us, we critique Him. Does Grete also engage in dalliance?

A—How quaint you are. I think she has friends whom she sees now and then.

Q—How does that make you feel?

A—I wish her well.

Q—What's in your wallet?

A—The usual. Credit cards, pictures of the children, driver's license, forty dollars in cash, Amex receipts—

Q—I sometimes imagine that I am in Pest Control. I have a small white truck with a red diamond-shaped emblem on the door and a white jumpsuit with the same emblem on the breast pocket. I park the truck in front of a subscriber's neat three-hundred-thousand-dollar home, extract the silver cannister of deadly pest killer from the back of the truck, and walk up the brick sidewalk to the house's front door. Chimes ring, the door swings open, a young wife in jeans and a pink flannel shirt worn outside the jeans is standing there. "Pest Control," I say. She smiles at me, I smile back and move past her into the house, into the handsomely appointed kitchen. The cannister is suspended by a sling from my right shoulder, and, pumping the mechanism occasionally with my right hand, I point the nozzle of the hose at the baseboards and begin to spray. I spray alongside the refrigerator, alongside the gas range, under the sink, and behind the kitchen table. Next, I move to the bathrooms, pumping and spraying. The young wife is in another room, waiting for me to finish. I walk into the main sitting room and spray discreetly behind the largest pieces of furniture, an oak sideboard, a red plush Victorian couch, and along the inside of the fireplace. I do the study, spraying the Columbia Encyclopedia, he's been looking up the Seven Years' War, 1756–63, yellow highlighting there, and behind the forty-five-inch RCA television. The master bedroom requires just touches, short bursts in her closet which must avoid the two dozen pairs of shoes there and in his closet which contains six to eight long guns in canvas cases. Finally I spray the laundry room with its big white washer and dryer, and behind the folding table stacked with sheets and towels already folded. Who folds? I surmise that she folds. Unless one of the older children, pressed into service, folds. In my experience they are unlikely to fold. Maybe the au pair. Finished, I tear a properly made out receipt from my receipt book and present it to the young wife. She scribbles her name in the appropriate space and hands it back to me. The house now stinks quite palpably but I know and she knows that the stench will dissipate in two to four hours. The young wife escorts me to the door, and, in parting, pins a silver medal on my chest and kisses me on both cheeks. Pest Control!

A—Yes, one could fit in in that way. It's finally a matter, perhaps, of fit. Appropriateness. Fit in a stately or sometimes hectic dance with nonfit. What we have to worry about.

Q—It seems to me that we have quite a great deal to worry about. Does the radish worry about itself in this way? Yet the radish is a living thing. Until it's cooked.

A—Grete is mad for radishes, can't get enough. I like frozen Mexican dinners, Patio, I have them for breakfast, the freezer is stacked with them—

Q—Transcendence is possible.

A—Yes.

Q—Is it possible?

A—Not out of the question.

Q—Is it really possible?

A—Yes. Believe me.

THE ISLAND OF VEN

GINA BERRIAULT

Gina Berriault's latest short story collection, *The Infinite Passion of Expectation* was published by North Point Press, as was her latest novel *The Lights of Earth*. A film, for which she wrote the screenplay, was based upon her story "The Stone Boy," and starred Robert Duvall and Glenn Close. She lives in Mill Valley, California.

"Ellie, listen to this: *In the evening after sunset, when according to my habit I was contemplating the stars in a clear sky, I noticed that a new and unusual star, surpassing all others in brilliancy, was shining almost directly above my head, and since I had, almost from boyhood, known all the stars in the heavens perfectly, it was quite evident to me that there had never before been any star in that place in the sky. I was so astonished at this sight that I was not ashamed to doubt the trustworthiness of my own eyes. A miracle indeed!* Ellie, you know what it was? A colossal stellar explosion, a supernova. But back then they thought the heavens were changeless, and so there's young Brahe gazing up at the new star one calm evening and he figures it's a miracle. No telescopes yet and he didn't need one. Even when the sun came up he could see it."

Noel read quietly, a lodger respectful of the hour of midnight in this foreign city and of the little family who had rented out a room on this night of the tourist season when all hotels were filled and who were asleep somewhere in the dark apartment. Like a tour guide whose memory isn't equal to the task and who reads over salient points each night before sleep, he was sitting up in bed, reading from the concise but colorful book on early European astronomers. A tour guide, but hers alone.

The beds were single, and he had pushed them together so he could take her in his arms and comfort her in the night, though she never asked for comforting. She lay with her hands under her cheek, palms together, watching his profile and loving him almost reverently, yet at an errant distance from him, as if she loved him only in memory; and at a distance from their son beyond the actual miles, wherever he was on his own journey; and at the farthest distance from their daughter, *Nana*, a distance never to be comprehended, even as the child's sixteen years of life had become only a mystification of the mother.

"Listen, sounds like he went around the bend: *The star was at first like Venus and Jupiter, giving pleasing effects, but as it then became like Mars, there will next come a period of wars, seditions, captivity and death of princes, and destruction of cities, together with dryness and fiery meteors in the air, pestilence and venomous snakes. Lastly, the star became like Saturn, and there will finally come a time of want, death, imprisonment and all sorts of sad things.* Sounds like he freaked out. Imagine Einstein writing that in his journal?"

She saw him as he must have been when he was a boy—six, seven— adjusting the telescope an uncle had given him, bringing a star down close to his backyard for the first time, convinced then, he had told her, that the silvery music of crickets all around in the summer night was really the sound the stars were making. On so many nights of their years together, when he sat late over his work and she heard him go out into the garden to gaze at the stars, she wondered if he were seeing all things again as indivisible, or trying to, or not trying. The measuring of vast distances, incredible velocities—it was this that enthralled him. At parties, when the other guests wandered out into a patio, a garden, lifting their faces to a placid moon, he would gently remind them of something they may have neglected to remember, that those far lights and all the galaxies were racing away from the earth and from one another. *The farther the distance from us, the faster they're leaving us behind. Imagine four hundred million miles an hour?* And they would smile obligingly as over a joke on them all.

His face was softened by the lamplight, and she saw again how Nana had resembled him, and felt again the same mute alarm that, back home, drew her up from the bed in the middle of the night, alone as if she had no husband, nor ever had children, nor even parents to begin.

She closed her eyes. This journey was his offering of love, a ritual of healing. By visiting together the places where the early astronomers had lived, the narrow Golden Street in Prague where they had strolled, a castle in Italy from where one had viewed the heavens, he hoped to humanize them for her. They, too, had suffered afflictions of the soul, yet despite their earthly trials they had never turned their eyes away from all that marvelous beckoning up there.

The lamp was switched off. Darkness now in this room in a stranger's house. This night and one more night when they returned from their day's trip to the Island. Noel bent over her and kissed her face imperceptibly as you kiss a sleeping person lost in the self. She said "I'm awake" and he took her in his arms. A street of trees. Branches stirred close to the small, high window, and distant sounds from the Tivoli Gardens—fireworks and music—trembled against the glass. She lay very still. Any movement, no matter how small, might wake the little family like incoherent words spoken out from her sleep.

By boat from Copenhagen to the town of Landskrona on the Swedish Coast. Old brick buildings with corby steps, factories blowing out sulphurous smoke. And now by a tough little boat, its yellow smokestack the only touch of color on the heavy gray Baltic Sea or a slender finger of that sea but so wide both shores were lost to view. A sea she had never thought about or ever wished to cross. They had climbed up from the hold to stand on deck. She had felt confined, deprived of the sight of the wind-driven swells the boat was striking against. The other passengers, Swedes, Danes, seemed content down there on hard benches in company of their bicycles and cases of beer and fruit. Like a compliant patient wanting to believe in a cure, she kept her gaze straight ahead to see the island the moment it came in sight. She must have glanced away. The island had risen the moment her head was turned.

The iron, stark look of it gave her an imagined view of immense rocks under the water. An island so precariously small, leveled down eons ago by fierce winds and sweeping torrents and monstrous waves, until water and wind calmed down and lay back. The inhabitants now, how did they feel about it? Stay calm. They must tell themselves to stay calm, and if the waters begin to rise again and the winds to stir again, some exquisite instrument, designed by a mind like Noel's, will detect the slightest threat in the depths of the sea, in the atmosphere, and everyone will be warned in ample time to hop onto their bicycles and peddle away to the nearest church, which, since it was four, five hundred years old, was to last forever.

A harbor town for those who trusted in fair weather always. Houses, gardens, low fences, trees, all on the very edge of deep gray water, little sailboats pleasantly rocking as if upon a transparent azure sea. The boat was moored, the passengers walked their bicycles up the rise and rode off past an approaching wagon drawn by two tawny horses and followed by two men walking leisurely. The horses stopped, the passengers climbed down. Except a little boy and his mother, the boy asleep on the blue wooden bench, his head in his mother's lap. The visor of his cap was tipped back, baring his face to the sky. Tiny purple flowers clung to the edge of his jacket pocket. The boy opened his eyes and, surprised by the sky, closed them again, and Ellie, watching, pictured his face growing older, his eyes less surprised day by day, night by night. Carefully the mother and child climbed down.

"Tycho Brahe's museum?" Noel's voice always sharply friendly in a foreign land. The driver, up on his high seat, appeared to nod.

The wagon joggled along the road that must be in the very center of the island, like a spine, and Noel sat very erect. The pale sun was turning his light hair to silver, a swift aging he didn't know about. Some of the gray of the sea was taken up and spread in a high, flat film over the sky, and the shadow of it, or the reflection, crept over the land, over the fields the tawny color of the horses and over the green meadows and the black cattle and over the thatched roofs of barns and cottages. Roofs thick as those in pictures she had painted for a children's book. Nana in her small chair by her mother's chair had watched everything come to life, sooner for her than for all the other children in the world: Squat cottages under an indigo sky dotted with white stars, and in the nightgreen stalks of grass, a cricket. Unlike those cozy roofs, unlike that painting years ago, these thatched roofs they were passing could be overrun by rivers of fire.

The horses were halted, the driver waited for somebody to climb down. Nobody did. "Tycho Brahe," he said to the air.

Noel leaped down, helped her down, and the horses clopped on. No bicycle, no wagon appeared along the road from either horizon. The silence must be the presence of the sea, unseen but all around, a silence not to be trusted. Across the road—a Turistgarden, deserted, white slat tables and chairs under trees, and far back a yellow-brick hotel strung with colored lightbulbs. On their side of the road—a church, red-brick with slate roof, pink roses in the yard; the Tycho Brahe Museet, closed, so small it must contain only a few precious books, a few drawings. Far back, a row of giant mulberry trees, and by the trees a tall stone statue. The Astronomer.

"It's him!"

Noel hurried toward it, as if the statue were the man himself about to flee, and, following, she found him roaming around the statue, gazing up with scholarly respect, gazing down at the indecipherable inscription carved along the sides of the base. Twice as tall as any man on earth, the astronomer wore a cloak that hung down to the soles of his boots, knickers of many stony folds, a ruff around his neck. His head thrown back, he scanned the heavens, his goatee pointing at the great shallow bowl of earth where his observatory had stood. Out in the fields behind him a farmer was burning chaff and the smoke passed close to the ground, a long, long, ribbon, and farther away a tractor started up and a rabbit bounded along before it. A lone seagull was soaring high over all, just under the layer of gray clouds.

They stepped down the slope of the wide grassy bowl, so shallow it was almost imperceivable, and stood within the lost observatory, within the Castle of the Heavens, as fancifully, as airily beautiful as castles that are only imagined. Every stone gone, carted away by the peasants, and all its coveted carvings taken away by a king's mistress to decorate her own small castle. Nothing left, and where the foundation had been now filled with five centuries of earth. A toad at their feet stayed where it was, unafraid of large, slow animals. Up there at the top of his castle in the night, how did the astronomer look to a boy straining his neck to see from a highest branch? Was he plotting an invasion of the heavens? Was he a nocturnal predator on the trail of a celestial creature? The peasants must have lain awake, afraid that each night was the night the avenging angels would swoop down to destroy the island in an unearthly fire.

"Ellie, are you hungry? Are you thirsty?"

They sat down by the toad, and Noel brought up from his knapsack a bottle of mineral water, raisins, cheese, sweet crackers.

"If you eat this raisin, all my wishes will come true." He kissed her temple.

She took the raisin on her lip, swallowed it. All his wishes, she knew, were for her recovery, and hers were not. The tricks, the jokes, the conundrums—he hoped to take them back to that spirited time at the beginning of their future together, a young couple again, picnicking on the spot from where a universe had flowered.

Along the road now in search of the astronomer's underground observatory, Noel consulting a map given him by the tourist office in Copenhagen. His light boots stirred up puffs of dust, her sandals stirred up none. She had got so thin, her legs, though bare and tan, were a warning to her. The winds—Noel was saying—buffeted the castle, interfering with the precision of observations, and so the astronomer had taken his instruments underground. What did they think *then?* she wondered. Up so high and then so deep? What did they think when they saw him walking along this same road at night, wrapped in his cloak, his gleamy, gloomy eyes always upward, at his side a servant with a lantern, cautioning him about his step. That he was hiding from the wrath of God? That everyone else would perish? That when he poked his silver nose out from his underground refuge, the silver nose affixed with wax to replace his own lost in a duel, it would not melt, it would only turn gold, reflecting that unearthly fire.

By the side of the road, a girl and two boys were running about within a fantasy place no larger than their own yard. Strange copper shapes rose up from a carpet of short dry grass. Geometrical shapes, like a dome, a tent, a cone. The little girl slid down the slanting copper roof of the closed-up entrance, like the entrance to a cellar, and the boys followed, all shouting dares, their voices ringing back on the still air to the church and the mulberry trees. Skylights—they were the astronomer's skylights that segment by segment were opened to the night's panorama. Scales of green-blue patina covered them, and hinges hung loose.

"Come look."

Noel opened a section of the dome, and the children came up beside them, the little girl pressing close to her. Almost twelve feet down to rocks and bottles, earth and rainwater. While Noel and the children looked down into the lost interior, waiting for something to come into view, while the children shuffled their black leather sabots and a rooster crowed close by, she gazed down at the girl's blond hair—how silky, how shiningly new under the sun. The little girl was the first to laugh, a mocking titter, and the boys took it up, roughly. They already knew there was nothing down there.

Out on the sea again, the waters darker, films of rain in the distance, the harbor shrinking, its cottages, low walls, trees, masts, all sliding under the sea. It was night when the boat slowed into the harbor at Landskrons. From far in the heavy dusk, she had mistaken the trees of the town for piles of iron ore or coal. They sat in the dimly-lit small waiting station, on a bench against the wall, until yellow lights, white lights moved through the murky night with the hushing presence of a large boat bound for Copenhagen.

Noel led her down into the salon, into the rousing noise of drinkers at every table and the portable organ's music, pounded out by a young man in suit and tie. Glasses everywhere on red tablecloths, gliding on spilled beer. An elderly woman danced alone among the few dancing couples, eyes closed, the flesh of her lifted arms swaying. Next to Ellie at the table, a handsome old man in a dark suit. Noel, leaning across her, asked him where the boat was from. An excursion boat, leaving Copenhagen in the morning and returning at night—and the whole day's pleasure was evident on his rosy face, a look that might have been there the first day of his life.

"American?"

"Yes," said Noel.

"Did you come by flying machine?"

Ellie nodded, looking into his face, seeing a boy out in the night, his eyes lifted to a moving light lower than the stars, an amazing machine that flew and filled the dome of the sky with an echoing roar. As much of a miracle, as much of a portent as Brahe's star.

"We went to Tycho Brahe's island," she said.

"Ah. A tourist garden is there. My sister was there for the honeymoon."

"One night," she said, "he saw an immense star that wasn't there before. He said it meant the death of princes, all sorts of sad things. He believed our destiny is in the stars. Yourself, do you believe that?"

She could see he was amused by her. He must hear this kind of talk from strangers in taverns, fellow passengers on excursion boats out for a day of revelry, their need to be intimately serious rising fast like the foam on their beers.

"Ah yes." Agreeable. A kind man, strongly old, how many faces had he gazed into as he was gazing into hers? Beloved faces, the others, each one gone while he lived on and on. A time to be born and a time to die. It was the only way to accept their going, the only way to ease the alarm.

Spaced green lights in the night, out there: the shore of somewhere moving slowly past. In the taxi to their tranquil street of trees, Noel was silent, wondering, she knew, if she had gone over the edge, if she had given up her mind to the astronomer's superstitious one. A lamp was on in the hall, for them. The little family was asleep.

When he lay down in his separate bed he leaned over her and brushed the wisps of hair from her brow, hoping, she knew, to clear her mind by clearing her brow. She lifted her arms and brought his head down upon her breasts, an embrace alive again, and, holding him, a picture of the astronomer composed itself for her mind's eye, for her hand someday. Out in his garden, the young Brahe, his face lifted to that strange brilliance, to that inescapable portent, its reflection floating in his eyes and in the gems on his plump fingers and on every leaf turned toward the heavens and in the dark waters of the fountain.

THE VILLAGE

JIM PITZEN

Jim Pitzen is a former bricklayer who returned to college in 1981 and earned a B.A. in English. He is currently attending the University of Montana, working toward an M.F.A. in Creative Writing. An infantry veteran of Vietnam, he served with the First Cavalry in the Central Highlands. He is from Walker, Minnesota.

The village was ancient. It lay nestled in a peaceful valley in the Central Highlands, midway between Hanoi and Saigon and just forty kilometers from the South China Sea.

The first houses built upon these same sites had been houses of mud walls mixed with rice-straw binder and thatched rice-straw roofs (as were these houses).

The first time that the village was destroyed in war (it had been destroyed many times before that by flood) was during the War of the Two Villages, or the War Between the North and the South. The village had been destroyed by war many other times by the Chinese, the Cambodians, the Chinese, the Thailanders, the Huns, the Chinese, the French, and the Japanese.

The people of the village had become so good at having their village destroyed by war that they knew exactly how to go about it. First they would hide all the food and plows and scythes. They would drive all the water buffalo into the jungle. Then, gathering all the people of the village except for one old and worthless grandmother who was too weak to travel, they would disappear into the jungle. The village had been destroyed so many times and the people of the village had become so good at having it destroyed that the village actually did not exist any more; in fact it had never existed, and neither had the people who were so good at disappearing. It was all an illusion, but it did not matter because the soldiers who were coming to destroy it and who had always come to destroy it were an illusion also; and all the wars, and all their causes that had ever destroyed the village were also illusions. In fact everything was an illusion except for the jungle, which was an orderly place where things existed to be killed and eaten. All humankind and all the possessions and passions of humankind (including war) were illusions. Human beings had created themselves in their own minds (they were fabrications of their own imaginations) and their minds were such disorderly places that they had forgotten how or why they had created themselves so they were doomed to wander about trying to uncreate themselves.

The jungle and the mosquitoes and the leeches were orderly because they had not been created but had always been and always would be, and they fit in their natural place and knew it and did not try to be anything else. The jungle and the mosquitoes and the leeches watched with amusement the imaginary soldiers destroying the illusory village over and over and over again, and they sucked the imaginary blood of the imaginary soldiers just to keep up the illusion.

"Cheechee, cheechee," the monkey called.

The slightly built, blond soldier jumped awake, at first frightened, then guilty. He'd been sleeping on guard again. At dawn, too, the worst time. He squirmed around. The soaked jungle fatigues had given him a swimming-suit itch all over except on his bare brown arms where the mosquitoes feasted. He wiped them off, killing fifteen or twenty on each arm.

Fucking mosquitoes, he thought, fucking monsoon. The mosquitoes buzzed and the rain dripped from the huge-leafed banana tree above him. His jungle boot reached out and nudged Hardje's foot.

Hardje awoke instantly. His thumb checked the safety on his M-16. He wiped the mosquitoes from his bare brown arms. He whispered, "What?"

Tyler whispered back, "Almost dawn."

Hardje sat up, shivered; his wet jungle fatigues clung to him.

Light began to grow in the east and spread slowly. Tyler whispered, "You need a shave."

"So fucking what," Hardje said.

They sat and listened to the elephant grass grow; green, six feet tall, taller, and still growing. The rain hissed. Monkeys called. Parrots began to quarrel.

Hardje grunted and said, "They're not going to hit us. They'd of done it by now."

Tyler wiped at the mosquitoes and nodded. "Listen to the parrots."

Hardje wiped the mosquitoes from his arms and stood up slowly, groaning at the stiffness in his muscles. "Son of a bitch," he said.

Tyler grinned and said, "I fell asleep again. Just at dawn. Dammit. I can't stay awake at dawn."

Hardje shrugged. "Neither can anyone else."

The parrots and monkeys called.

Hardje started to wipe the mosquitoes from his arm, changed his mind, and scratched his neck instead. He said, "Well, leech time."

He pulled down his pants (nobody wore underwear anymore because of jock itch) and removed his shirt. His rear end and legs glowed white next to his mahogany arms and chest and back. The leeches, black and two inches long, clung to him, one on each inner thigh, two more at the beltline, one on his back just beneath the shoulder blade. Red pockmarks scattered over his skin traced the leeches that had gone before.

"Mosquito dope?" Tyler asked.

The mosquito dope, G.I. Gin, made the leeches curl up, writhing, and let go, but the alcohol made the bites burn like fire.

"Fuck it," Hardje answered. He began slowly pulling off a leech, one of the two at his beltline. The reddened, irritated skin lifted with the leech, its suction-cup mouth clinging. Then the leech let go suddenly. Bright blood trickled down Hardje's lower stomach and disappeared into the reddish-brown pubic hair. He threw the leech down and stamped it into the ground.

"Fucking things," Hardje said. "Fucking valley."

With a steady hand he pulled off three more leeches, tossing them into the tall grass. "How in hell do they get in your pants?" he said. "I had my pants tucked into my boots, and my belt was so fucking tight I couldn't breathe."

Tyler shrugged and wiped the mosquitoes from his arms.

Hardje looked over his shoulder. "Get that bastard, will you?" Tyler stood and pulled the leech from Hardje's back.

"Rain's letting up," Hardje said.

Tyler nodded.

"You leech yourself yet?" Hardje asked.

Tyler shook his head no.

"Talkative bastard, ain't you," Hardje said.

Tyler nodded and began to strip as Hardje started to dress.

The rain had stopped but would continue to fall from the canopy of trees covering them like a tent.

"Sun's gonna shine," Hardje said. "Gonna get hotter than hell."

He took his entrenching tool and scraped the rotting vegetation from a small spot on the ground. As the leaves turned over, an exposed leech curled and uncurled. "Rotten bastard," Hardje said. He ground it into the mud beneath his heel. "It ain't natural. We're half a mile from the river, and these bastards are all over."

Tyler plucked a blood-engorged leech from near his groin and looked around. He impaled the leech on one of the bright green, three-inch-long thorns that covered the trunk of a nearby tree. He grinned as the leech squirmed and bled.

"What are you grinning about?" Hardje said. "It's your blood."

"I only had one," Tyler said. He pulled his pants up, trapping several mosquitoes.

"Of course," Hardje said. "You ain't as sweet as I am."

Tyler dug into a side pocket of his backpack and retrieved an empty C-ration can with holes punched in the bottom. He set it on the small patch of ground Hardje had cleared. He reached into another pocket of his backpack and brought out a small wad of C.4, a plastic explosive for blowing bunkers and tunnels. He rolled it into a tight wad the size of a walnut and dropped it into the C-ration-can stove. He opened a can of beans and franks almost all the way around with his P-38 can opener, pried the lid back and, using it as a handle, set the can carefully on the stove. He pulled a plastic bag from his shirt pocket, unrolled it, and took out a book of matches. The C.4 flared wildly and burned out in five seconds; the beans and franks bubbled. Tyler lifted the can off the stove, sat down on the wet ground, and began eating with a plastic spoon. He watched Hardje open a can of ham and lima beans and shuddered as he set them on the stove.

"You ever seen wood ticks?" he asked Hardje.

Hardje nodded. "I'm from Minnesota."

"Lima beans look like big gray wood ticks on a dog's neck."

Hardje grinned. "Next time you get a can of wood ticks, give 'em to me. I'll eat 'em." He took a big bite, chewed, swallowed, and belched.

Tyler shook his head sadly and said, "No couth. That's your problem. You ain't got no couth."

Swenson, coming up from the next position to the south, parted the elephant grass. "Saddle up," he said. "We're moving out in fifteen. Pass the word."

He turned and disappeared as Hardje began to move toward Cadwell's position to the north. Tyler chopped a hole in the ground and threw the empty cans in it. He put away his stove and lit a Camel, sitting down alongside his pack. He wiped the mosquitoes from his arms. The thin material of his jungle fatigues was already dry except for the seat of the pants and the spots where the trees had dripped. He couldn't see the sun but knew it must be out. Steam was rising from the ground in pillars. He flicked the ember from his cigarette, sliced the paper with his thumbnail, scattered the tobacco, and rolled the paper into a tiny ball that he ground beneath his heel. He checked the safety on his M-16, thought about another cigarette, changed his mind, and sat.

Hardje appeared out of the steam, his uniform soaked from the wet grass. He dropped to one knee, wiped the mosquitoes from his arms, and said, "Guess who got point?"

Tyler stared at him in disbelief. "Christ. You just had it last week."

Hardje nodded and sat down. They sat not talking. Finally Tyler said, "Bastards."

Hardje nodded again. They sat. Swenson shouted, "Everyone pull back to the trail."

The trail was not on any map. It was, possibly, just a game trail, but it wandered more or less in the right direction, following the monsoon-swollen river, crossing and recrossing it, down out of the highlands toward the east and the An Loa Valley twenty kilometers away, toward the South China Sea.

The yellow clay floor of the trail was slippery and sticky. The clay built up on the cleats of Hardje's canvas jungle boots, making him three inches taller. With every step, his feet slid and skidded. The sweat poured out. He wiped the mosquitoes off his arms and checked the safety on his M-16.

Point position. The first man in the company. The lead man. The first man to hit the shit. Point position. Life-expectancy: three days.

Hardje moved slowly down the trail. The jungle was quiet. He watched the ground, the trail, the trees. Watched for trip wires, slender threads attached to booby-trapped mortar rounds, to grenades. Watched for punji stakes, splinters of bamboo smeared in human feces, guaranteed infection if one scratched your skin. Watched for snipers who tied themselves to the tree tops. Watched for ambush. Watched for pit vipers, for cobras. Watched. Sweat burned his eyes. His stomach felt tight, wanted to vomit. The trail wound through the jungle. Hardje stopped, looked back, caught Swenson's attention. He pointed at the punji stakes hidden in the tall grass. Swenson nodded. Hardje wiped the mosquitoes from his arms, moved on. Up a slight rise, then down to the yellow river that tore at its banks. He hesitated, watched the other bank, sick with fear. A perfect ambush spot. He watched, sweat burning his eyes. He checked the safety on his M-16 and plunged into the water. Waist-high water deepened to his armpits near the tall, curved bank on the far side. Then he was across, scrambling up the slippery bank, holding his breath, into the jungle. Nothing. No Charlie. He went back to the bank and waved the company across.

Hardje moved down the trail and sat on a rotting log. The training manual said that an infantry company should be able to march four miles an hour. It had taken him half an hour to go half a mile, yet he felt that he was moving too fast.

The company gathered on the trail behind him. He saw Tyler and waved. The company commander signaled him to move out. He groaned and cursed under his breath but stood up and began the cautious movement once more, watching.

Tyler wiped the mosquitoes from his arms and watched Hardje move out of sight around a bend in the trail. Tyler felt guilty that he wasn't on point. It had been three weeks. He also felt angry about his guilt. He knew Hardje was the best point man in the company. But still, it was past his turn. On and on the argument went as he moved with the company.

The saturated ground steamed in the 120-degree heat. This week's marching song, the song Tyler used to blot out all thought, started to run through his mind. "When Johnnie Comes Marching Home Again." Last week it had been "Up, Up and Away."

The company moved down the trail, one hundred men, eighteen to twenty years old, one hundred thousand thoughts about dying and being paralyzed and having arms and legs blown away and being bitten by snakes and spiders and centipedes and being stung by scorpions. Thinking of people back home. Thinking how glad they were that Hardje was on point. One hundred men with sweat-soaked uniforms, with huge backpacks that occasionally clinked and clunked.

Hardje paused to watch a dark purple butterfly on a black flower, and the company slowed and stopped behind him. He moved on down the trail and they followed.

Hardje paused as a mottled green and yellow, eighteen-foot constrictor slithered across the trail. He grinned as he thought about Tyler's snake phobia. He'd tell Tyler about this one tonight. He wiped the mosquitoes from his arms. Sweat washed the blood away. He checked the safety on his M-16 and moved on. The company followed.

The steaming trail dropped abruptly back down to another river crossing. Hardje stopped, checked his watch. Ten o'clock. He remembered a deer-hunting trip in the snow, how the buck's bloody entrails steamed as he plunged his stinging hands in the body cavity to remove them. He stared at the opposite bank. Stared. Sliding down the bank into the river, up to his waist, to his armpits, then across and scrambling up the other bank and back into the jungle. The company followed, cursing and grumbling and clinking and clanking.

Down the yellow trail. A trail that grew wider as other foot trails joined it from the hills (or took off from it into the hills). Hardje knew these small trails meant that Charlie used the path for disbursing the weapons and food that came in by sea. He moved down the trail watching each step, watching ahead. He stopped on the edge of a small clearing. Rice paddies and dikes, half a mile across, and on the far side, a small village. He signaled for the company to halt, watched as the company commander worked his way through the men who had collapsed alongside the trail. Hardje wiped the mosquitoes from his arms. He saw a huge, hairy tarantula the size of his hand walk across the trail, lifting high two or three legs at a time and planting them carefully, as if it didn't like the mud. Hardje shuddered.

The C.O. said from ten feet away, "What's up, Norway?"

Hardje pointed with his chin.

The C.O. looked around the rice paddy, at the village. He cursed softly. "Son of a bitch. This isn't on the map. How many houses?"

Hardje replied, "Fifteen. Maybe more."

The C.O. nodded. "Well, move out to the first dike and wait for the company to catch up. We'll have to search and destroy the vil. I'll try and get battalion headquarters on the horn."

Hardje waded up to his waist in the shitty-smelling water. He fingered the safety of his M-16, crouched, and waded toward the dike. He heard the company entering the water behind him but kept his eyes glued on the houses and the trees, expecting to die at any time. When the men all reached the dike and crouched down, the word came down the line: "Take it."

As one man, the company rose, clambered over the dike, slid into the next lower paddy, waded, and clambered over the next dike, slid into the next lower rice paddy, and waded.

Hardje and Tyler flicked the safeties off their M-16s and leaped into the first house and halfway across the dirt floor. They stood, holding their breath. Nothing happened. Quiet. There were only two more rooms. Two black, open doorways. They stood staring, waiting for the other to choose a door. Then from the door on the left came the most unearthly wail that either man had ever heard. Their knees sagged. They wanted to vomit, to run, but hadn't the strength to do either. They looked at each other and, rifles ready, entered the room.

When their eyes adjusted to the dark, they saw on a bed of rice-straw mats an incredibly old woman. (They couldn't tell if she was man, woman, or monkey, but they somehow knew.)

She was not much larger than a two-year-old child, shriveled, shrunken, sightless, toothless, nearly hairless, her feet and hands curled up like claws. As they stood, staring, she once again emitted the hideous, shrieking moan. Tyler turned to run but Hardje grabbed him, steadied him. They stared at each other, at her.

The two men stretched Hardje's poncho out alongside the old woman, slid her onto it, and carried her out of the cryptlike blackness of the room, through the main room of the house and into the sunlight. They called for a medic and told the radio operator to call in a Med-Evac chopper because the woman was in pain.

Actually she had been moaning not in pain but because the other people who did not live in the village and who did not disappear when the soldiers did not come out of the jungle had taken from her finger the brass ring that had belonged to her great-great-great-grandmother. The people who did not disappear took the ring because they felt that the soldiers who were not coming to the village that wasn't there would think it was gold and would steal it. So the grandmother was really moaning about her missing ring, and she never moaned again because she died when the sunlight hit her, though the men in the company never knew it because the medic refused even to look at her because she was so ugly. They loaded the old woman on the helicopter and she was never again seen in the village by the people who didn't live there nor by the nonexistent soldiers.

The knot of men watched the chopper pound away toward the south and Landing Zone Linda. The C.O. said, "All right, break it up. One grenade would get you all. Let's finish searching the vil. When you're done we'll burn what will burn and blow the walls with C.4."

The men carried all military-looking items to the hard-packed yard of the house that had been cleared by Hardje and Tyler. The most danger-ous-looking items were a crossbow; an old curve-bladed sword; a long-barreled French muzzle-loader; and a small bronze statue of a gargoyle-faced dog with a dragon's tail, which had a star at the end.

Tyler leaned back in the shade of a coconut palm. He checked the safety on his M-16 and laid it across his lap. He opened a can of C-ration beef stew. Hardje wiped the mosquitoes from his arms and leaned back against the wall of the house and began eating his canned scrambled eggs, white bread, and peanut butter.

Each man swallowed a pink salt tablet, a large orange malaria tablet, and a small white malaria tablet and began to eat, more with resignation than with relish.

"I hate this shit," Hardje said conversationally.

Tyler shrugged. "It doesn't matter," he said. He belched. He looked to the west, at the bank of clouds that was crowding the mountains. "Be raining in an hour. This place'll never burn. We'll have to blow it all."

Hardje nodded. He finished the cold eggs and tossed the can over his shoulder, through the glassless window and into the house, where it clunked across the hard floor. Hardje lit a cigarette with a Zippo lighter, sighed. "Well," he said, "I suppose we might as well start."

Tyler nodded and pitched his garbage after Hardje's. He lit a cigarette and stood up. Grabbing his entrenching tool from his pack, he stepped to the house and began chopping the soil away from the foundation. When he judged the area was large enough, he packed C.4 against the foundation, stuck a blasting cap in it, and packed the mud back around the C.4. He strung electrical wire, which was connected to the blasting cap, over to the front yard where the others were waiting with other wires. Hardje wired them all to one main wire and began wading across the rice paddy to the closest dike, unrolling wire as he went.

When all the charges were set and all the wires strung and all the men down behind the rice paddy dike, the C.O. ordered, "Fire the hole!"

Hardje turned back once to look at the village. The cloud of dust still hung in the air. Just then, as if someone had turned on a switch, the rain started again and Hardje turned and plunged once more down the trail, under the dark canopy of leaves, looking carefully for booby traps and snipers and ambushes, and the company behind him followed with clinking, clunking packs.

Down the muddy trail under the dripping trees. Measuring time not in hours or minutes but in aching, weary steps. Shoulders slumping beneath the straps of heavy packs. Step by step, one step at a time, pick up a heavy foot and swing it forward, slog it down into the mud, a few thousand steps and a mile and a few muddy miles and a few more muddy miles and it was nearly dark and the C.O. signaled to set up a perimeter.

Hardje and Tyler readied their position without a word. Hardje chopped the tall grass, clearing firing lanes. Tyler set out trip flares and Claymore mines. Tyler pulled his stove from his pack and asked Hardje if he had any C.4 left. Hardje, standing in the gathering darkness, wiped the mosquitoes from his arms and nodded. "In the side pocket," he said.

As Tyler reached for the pack, his hand brushed Hardje's M-16. It tipped, falling. Tyler grabbed for it. His finger touched the trigger. Hardje had forgotten to check the safety back in the village because the old woman had unnerved him. The shell exploded. Hardje bent over. Looked at Tyler. Sat down.

Tyler said, "No."

He jumped to Hardje's side, asked, "Where?"

He saw Hardje's hands clutching his lower stomach. He unbuckled Hardje's belt, pulled his pants down, his shirt up. There was a tiny hole, not much larger than a leech scar. A stream of blood trickled down and lost itself in reddish-brown pubic hair.

"It doesn't look bad," Tyler said. "It really doesn't."

Hardje's eyes glazed over.

Tyler frantically rolled him over on his stomach. Steaming red entrails with globs of yellow fat poured out a hole the size of his fist in the middle of Hardje's back. The blood burned Tyler's hands as he tried to stuff the guts back in.

Mosquitoes drawn by the blood swarmed.

A leech slowly, sinuously slithered beneath Tyler's belt and snuggled up in the wet warmth of his groin. Tyler wiped the mosquitoes from his unfeeling arms as he cried.

The people who did not live in the village that wasn't there heard the steel blades of the phantom helicopter chopping through the monsoon with Hardje's imaginary corpse. They looked up and saw its spectral shape slipping through the shadows of the clouds, and they stirred their rice.

WHAT FEELS LIKE THE WORLD

RICHARD BAUSCH

Richard Bausch is the author of three novels, *Real Presence, Take Me Back,* and *The Last Good Time.* A collection of his stories, *Spirits and Other Stories,* will appear in May 1987. He has published short fiction in *The Atlantic, Ploughshares,* and *The New Virginia Review,* and he is a recipient of both National Endowment for the Arts and Guggenheim Fellowships in Fiction. He is currently on the faculty of the writing program at George Mason University in Fairfax, Virginia, where he lives with his wife, Karen, and their three children.

Very early in the morning, too early, he hears her trying to jump rope out on the sidewalk below his bedroom window. He wakes to the sound of her shoes on the concrete, her breathless counting as she jumps—never more than three times in succession—and fails again to find the right rhythm, the proper spring in her legs to achieve the thing, to be a girl jumping rope. He gets up and moves to the window and, parting the curtain only slightly, peers out at her. For some reason he feels he must be stealthy, must not let her see him gazing at her from this window. He thinks about the heartless way children tease the imperfect among them, and then he closes the curtain.

She is his only granddaughter, the unfortunate inheritor of his big-boned genes, his tendency toward bulk, and she is on a self-induced program of exercise and dieting, to lose weight. This is in preparation for the last meeting of the PTA, during which children from the fifth and sixth grades will put on a gymnastics demonstration. There will be a vaulting horse and a mini-trampoline, and everyone is to participate. She wants to be able to do at least as well as the other children in her class, and so she has been trying exercises to improve her coordination and lose the weight that keeps her rooted to the ground. For the past two weeks she has been eating only one meal a day, usually lunch, since that's the meal she eats at school, and swallowing cans of juice at other mealtimes. He's afraid of anorexia but trusts her calm determination to get ready for the event. There seems no desperation, none of the classic symptoms of the disease. Indeed, this project she has set for herself seems quite sane: to lose ten pounds, and to be able to get over the vaulting horse—in fact, she hopes that she will be able to do a handstand on it and, curling her head and shoulders, flip over to stand upright on the other side. This, she has told him, is the outside hope. And in two weeks of very grown-up discipline and single-minded effort, that hope has mostly disappeared; she is still the only child in the fifth grade who has not even been able to propel herself over the horse, and this is the day of the event. She will have one last chance to practice at school today, and so she is up this early, out on the lawn, straining, pushing herself.

He dresses quickly and heads downstairs. The ritual in the mornings is simplified by the fact that neither of them is eating breakfast. He makes orange juice, puts vitamins on a saucer for them both. When he glances out the living-room window, he sees that she is now doing somersaults in the dewy grass. She does three of them while he watches, and he is not stealthy this time but stands in the window with what he hopes is an approving, unworried look on his face. After each somersault she pulls her sweat shirt down, takes a deep breath, and begins again, the arms coming down slowly, the head ducking slowly under: it is as if she falls on her back, sits up, and then stands up. Her cheeks are ruddy with effort. The moistness of the grass is on the sweat suit, and in the ends of her hair. It will rain this morning—there's thunder beyond the trees at the end of the street. He taps on the window, gestures, smiling, for her to come in. She waves at him, indicates that she wants him to watch her, so he watches her. He applauds when she's finished—three hard, slow tumbles. She claps her hands together as if to remove dust from them and comes trotting to the door. As she moves by him, he tells her she's asking for a bad cold, letting herself get wet so early in the morning. It's his place to nag. Her glance at him acknowledges this.

"I can't get the rest of me to follow my head," she says about the somersaults.

They go into the kitchen, and she sits down, pops a vitamin into her mouth, and takes a swallow of the orange juice. "I guess I'm not going to make it over that vaulting horse after all," she says suddenly.

"Sure you will."

"I don't care." She seems to pout. This is the first sign of true discouragement she's shown.

He's been waiting for it. "Brenda—honey, sometimes people aren't good at these things. I mean, I was never any good at it."

"I bet you were," she says. "I bet you're just saying that to make me feel better."

"No," he says, "really."

He's been keeping to the diet with her, though there have been times during the day when he has cheated. He no longer has a job, and the days are long: he's hungry all the time. He pretends to her that he's still going on to work in the mornings after he walks her to school, because he wants to keep her sense of the daily balance of things, of a predictable and orderly routine, intact. He believes this is the best way to deal with grief—simply to go on with things, to keep them as much as possible as they have always been. Being out of work doesn't worry him, really: he has enough money in savings to last a while. At sixty-one, he's almost eligible for Social Security, and he gets monthly checks from the girl's father, who lives with another woman and other children, in Oregon. The father has been very good about keeping up with the payments, though he never visits or calls. Probably he thinks the money buys him the privilege of remaining aloof, now that Brenda's mother is gone. Brenda's mother used to say he was the type of man who learned early that there was nothing of substance anywhere in his soul, and spent the rest of his life trying to hide this fact from himself. No one was more upright, she would say, no one more honorable, and God help you if you ever had to live with him. Brenda's father was the subject of bitter sarcasm and scorn, and yet, perhaps not so surprisingly, Brenda's mother would call him in those months just after the divorce, when Brenda was still only a toddler, and she would try to get the baby to say things to him over the phone; she would sit there with Brenda on her lap and cry after she had hung up.

"I had a doughnut yesterday at school," Brenda says now.

"That's lunch. You're supposed to eat lunch."

"I had spaghetti, too. And three pieces of garlic bread. And pie. And a big salad."

"What's one doughnut."

"Well, and I didn't eat anything the rest of the day."

"I know," her grandfather says. "See?"

They sit quiet for a little while. Sometimes they're shy with each other—more so lately. They're used to the absence of her mother by now—it's been more than a year—but they still find themselves missing a beat now and then, like a heart with a valve almost closed. She swallows the last of her juice and then gets up and moves to the living room, to stand gazing out at the yard. Big drops have begun to fall. It's a storm, with rising wind and, now, very loud thunder. Lightning branches across the sky, and the trees in the yard disappear in sheets of rain. He has come to her side, and he pretends an interest in the details of the weather, remarking on the heaviness of the rain, the strength of the wind. "Some storm," he says finally. "I'm glad we're not out in it." He wishes he could tell what she's thinking, where the pain is; he wishes he could be certain of the harmlessness of his every word. "Honey," he ventures, "we could play hooky today. If you want to."

"Don't you think I can do it?" she says.

"I know you can."

She stares at him a moment and then looks away, out at the storm.

"It's terrible out there, isn't it?" he says. "Look at that lightning."

"You don't think I can do it," she says.

"No, I know you can. Really."

"Well, I probably can't."

"Even if you can't. Lots of people—lots of people never do anything like that."

"I'm the only one who can't that *I* know."

"Well, there's lots of people. The whole thing is silly, Brenda. A year from now it won't mean anything at all—you'll see."

She says nothing.

"Is there some pressure at school to do it?"

"No." She answers simply, looking directly at him.

"You're sure."

She's sure. And of course, he realizes, there *is* pressure: there's the pressure of being one among other children, and being the only one among them who can't do a thing.

"Honey," he says lamely, "it's not that important."

When she looks at him this time, he sees something scarily unchild-like in her expression, some perplexity that she seems to pull down into herself. "It is too important," she says.

He drives her to school. The rain is still being blown along the street and above the low roofs of the houses. By the time they arrive, no more than five minutes from the house, it has begun to let up.

"If it's completely stopped after school," she says, "can we walk home?"

"Of course," he says. "Why wouldn't we?"

She gives him a quick wet kiss on the cheek. "Bye, Pops."

He knows she doesn't like it when he waits for her to get inside, and still he hesitates. There's always the apprehension that he'll turn away or drive off just as she thinks of something she needs from him, or that she'll turn to wave and he won't see her. So he sits here with the car engine idling, and she walks quickly up the sidewalk and into the building. In the few seconds before the door swings shut, she turns and gives him a wave, and he waves back. The door is closed now. Slowly he lets the car glide forward, still watching the door. Then he's down the driveway, and he heads back to the house.

It's hard to decide what to do with his time. Mostly he stays in the house, watches television, reads the newspapers. There are household tasks, but he can't do anything she might notice, since he's supposed to be at work during these hours. Sometimes, just to please himself, he drives over to the bank and visits with his old co-workers, though there doesn't seem to be much to talk about anymore and he senses that he makes them all uneasy. Today he lies down on the sofa in the living room and rests a while. At the windows the sun begins to show, and he thinks of driving into town, perhaps stopping somewhere to eat a light breakfast. He accuses himself with the thought and then gets up and turns the television on. There isn't anything of interest to watch, but he watches anyway. The sun is bright now out on the lawn, and the wind is the same, gusting now and again and shaking the window frames. On the television he sees feasts of incredible sumptuousness, almost nauseating in the impossible brightness and succulence of the food: advertisements from cheese companies, dairy associations, the makers of cookies and pizza, the sellers of seafood and steaks. He's angry with himself for wanting to cheat on the diet. He thinks of Brenda at school, thinks of crowds of children, and it comes to him more painfully than ever that he can't protect her. Not any more than he could ever protect her mother.

He goes outside and walks up the drying sidewalk to the end of the block. The sun has already dried most of the morning's rain, and the wind is warm. In the sky are great stormy Matterhorns of cumulus and wide patches of the deepest blue. It's a beautiful day, and he decides to walk over to the school. Nothing in him voices this decision: he simply begins to walk. He knows without having to think about it that he can't allow her to see him, yet he feels compelled to take the risk that she might; he feels a helpless wish to watch over her, and, beyond this, he entertains the vague notion that by seeing her in her world he might be better able to be what she needs in his.

So he walks the four blocks to the school and stands just beyond the playground, in a group of shading maples that whisper and sigh in the wind. The playground is empty. A bell rings somewhere in the building, but no one comes out. It's not even eleven o'clock in the morning. He's too late for morning recess and too early for the afternoon one. He feels as though she watches him make his way back down the street.

His neighbor, Mrs. Eberhard, comes over for lunch. It's a thing they planned, and he's forgotten about it. She knocks on the door, and when he opens it she smiles and says, "I knew you'd forget." She's on a diet too, and is carrying what they'll eat: two apples, some celery and carrots. It's all in a clear plastic bag, and she holds it toward him in the palms of her hands as though it were piping hot from an oven. Jane

Eberhard is relatively new in the neighborhood. When Brenda's mother died, Jane offered to cook meals and regulate things, and for a while she was like another member of the family. She's moved into their lives now, and sometimes they all forget the circumstances under which the friendship began. She's a solid, large-hipped woman of fifty-two, with bright young green eyes and a wide, expressive mouth. The thing she's good at is sympathy; there's something oddly unspecific about it, as if it's a beam she simply radiates.

"You look so worried," she says now. "I think you should be proud of her."

They're sitting in the living room, with the plastic bag on the coffee table before them. She's eating a stick of celery.

"I've never seen a child that age put such demands on herself," she says.

"I don't know what it's going to do to her if she doesn't make it over the damn thing," he says.

"It'll disappoint her. But she'll get over it."

"I don't guess you can make it tonight."

"Can't," she says. "Really. I promised my mother I'd take her to the ocean this weekend."

"I walked over to the school a little while ago."

"Are you sure you're not putting more into this than she is?"

"She was up before dawn this morning, Jane. Didn't you see her?"

Mrs. Eberhard nods. "I saw her."

"Well?" he says.

She pats his wrist. "I'm sure it won't matter a month from now."

"No," he says, "that's not true. I mean, I wish I could believe you. But I've never seen a kid work so hard."

"Maybe she'll make it."

"Yes," he says. "Maybe."

Mrs. Eberhard sits considering for a moment, tapping the stick of celery against her lower lip. "You think it's tied to the accident in some way, don't you?"

"I don't know," he says, standing, moving across the room. "I can't get through somehow. It's been all this time and I still don't know. She keeps it all to herself—all of it. All I can do is try to be there when she wants me to be there. I don't know—I don't even know what to say to her."

"You're doing all you can do, then."

"Her mother and I . . ." he begins. "She—we never got along that well."

"You can't worry about that now."

Mrs. Eberhard's advice is always the kind of practical good advice that's impossible to follow.

He comes back to the sofa and tries to eat one of the apples, but his appetite is gone. This seems ironic to him. "I'm not hungry now," he says.

"Sometimes worry is the best thing for a diet."

"I've always worried. It never did me any good, but I worried."

"I'll tell you," Mrs. Eberhard says. "It's a terrific misfortune to have to be raised by a human being."

He doesn't feel like listening to this sort of thing, so he asks her about her husband, who is with the government in some capacity that requires him to be both secretive and mobile. He's always off to one country or another, and this week he's in India. It's strange to think of someone traveling as much as he does without getting hurt or killed. Mrs. Eberhard says that she's so used to his being gone all the time that next year, when he retires, it will take a while to get used to having him underfoot. In fact, he's not a very likable man; there's something murky and unpleasant about him. The one time Mrs. Eberhard brought him to visit, he sat in the living room and seemed to regard everyone with detached curiosity, as if they were all specimens on a dish under a lens. When he spoke, his voice was cultivated and quiet, full of self-satisfaction and haughtiness. They had been speaking in low tones about how Jane Eberhard had moved in to take over after the accident, and Mrs. Eberhard's husband cleared his throat, held his fist gingerly to his mouth, pursed his lips, and began a soft-spoken, lecture-like monologue about his belief that there's no such thing as an accident. His considered opinion was that there are subconscious explanations for everything. Apparently, he thought he was entertaining everyone. He sat with one leg crossed over the other and held forth in his calm, magisterial voice, explaining how everything can be reduced to a matter of conscious or subconscious will. Finally, his wife asked him to let it alone, please, drop the subject.

"For example," he went on, "there are many collisions on the highway in which no one appears to have applied brakes before impact, as if something in the victims had decided on death. And of course there are the well-known cases of people stopped on railroad tracks, with plenty of time to get off, who simply do not move. Perhaps it isn't being frozen by the perception of one's fate but a matter of decision-making, of will. The victim decides on his fate."

"I think we've had enough now," Jane Eberhard said.

The inappropriateness of what he had said seemed to dawn on him then. He shifted in his seat and grew very quiet, and when the evening was over he took Brenda's grandfather by the elbow and apologized. But even in the apology there seemed to be a species of condescension, as if he were really only sorry for the harsh truth of what he had wrongly deemed it necessary to say. When they were gone, Brenda said, "I don't like that man."

"Is it because of what he said about accidents?" her grandfather asked.

She shook her head. "I just don't like him."

"It's not true, what he said, honey. An accident is an accident."

She said, "I know." But she would not return his gaze.

"Your mother wasn't very happy here, but she didn't want to leave us. Not even—you know, without . . . without knowing it or anything."

"He wears perfume," she said, still not looking at him.

"It's cologne. Yes, he does—too much of it."

"It smells," she said.

In the afternoon he walks over to the school. The sidewalks are crowded with children, and they all seem to recognize him. They carry their books and papers and their hair is windblown and they run and wrestle with each other in the yards. The sun's high and very hot, and most of the clouds have broken apart and scattered. There's still a fairly steady wind, but it's gentler now, and there's no coolness in it.

Brenda is standing at the first crossing street down the hill from the school; she's surrounded by other children yet seems separate from them somehow. She sees him and smiles. He waits on his side of the intersection for her to cross, and when she reaches him he's careful not to show any obvious affection, knowing it embarrasses her.

"How was your day?" he begins.

"Mr. Clayton tried to get me to quit today."

He waits.

"I didn't get over," she says. "I didn't even get close."

"What did Mr. Clayton say?"

"Oh—you know. That it's not important. That kind of stuff."

"Well," he says gently, "is it so important?"

"I don't know." She kicks at something in the grass along the edge of the sidewalk—a piece of a pencil someone else has discarded. She bends, picks it up, examines it, and then drops it. They walk on. She's concentrating on the sidewalk before them, and they walk almost in step.

"I'm sure I never could do a thing like that when I was in school," he says.

"Did they have that when you were in school?"

He smiles. "It was hard getting everything into the caves. But sure, we had that sort of thing. We were an advanced tribe. We had fire, too."

"Okay," she says. "Okay."

"Actually, with me, it was pull-ups. We all had to do pull-ups. And I just couldn't do them. I don't think I ever accomplished a single one in my life."

"I can't do pull-ups," she says.

"They're hard to do."

"Everybody in the fifth and sixth grades can get over the vaulting horse," she says.

How much she reminds him of her mother: there's a certain mobility in her face, a certain willingness to assert herself in the smallest gesture of the eyes and mouth. She has her mother's green eyes, and now he tells her this. He's decided to try this. He's standing, quite shy, in her doorway, feeling like an intruder. She's sitting on the floor, one leg outstretched, the other bent at the knee. She tries to touch her forehead to the knee of the outstretched leg, straining, and he looks away.

"You know?" he says. "They're just the same color—just that shade of green."

"What was my grandmother like?" she asks, still straining.

"She was a lot like your mother."

"I'm never going to get married."

"Of course you will. Well, I mean—if you want to, you will."

"How come you didn't ever get married again?"

"Oh," he says, "I had a daughter to raise, you know."

She changes position, tries to touch her forehead to the other knee.

"I'll tell you, that mother of yours was enough to keep me busy. I mean, I called her double trouble, you know, because I always said she was double the trouble a son would have been. That was a regular joke between us."

"Am I double trouble?"

"No," he says, smiling at her.

"Is that really why you didn't get married again?"

"Well, no one would have me, either."

"Mom said you liked it."

"Liked what?"

"Being a widow."

"Yes, well," he says.

"Did you?"

"All these questions," he says.

"Do you think about Grandmom a lot?"

"Yes," he says. "That's—you know, we remember our loved ones."

She stands and tries to touch her toes without bending her legs. "Sometimes I dream that Mom's yelling at me."

"Oh, well," he says, hearing himself say it, feeling himself back down from something. "That's—that's just a dream. You know, it's nothing to think about at all. And I'll bet these exercises are going to do the trick."

"I'm very smart, aren't I?"

He feels sick, very deep down. "You're the smartest little girl I ever saw."

"You don't have to come tonight if you don't want to," she says. "You can drop me off if you want, and come get me when it's over."

"Why would I do that?"

She mutters, *"I would."*

"Then why don't we skip it?"

"Lot of good *that* would do," she says.

For dinner they drink apple juice, and he gets her to eat two slices of dry toast. The apple juice is for energy. She drinks it slowly and then goes into her room to lie down, to conserve her strength. She uses the word *conserve,* and he tells her he's so proud of her vocabulary. She thanks him. While she rests, he does a few household chores, trying really just to keep busy. The week's newspapers have been piling up on the coffee table in the living room, the carpets need to be vacuumed, and the whole house needs dusting. None of it takes long enough; none of it quite distracts him. For a while he sits in the living room with a newspaper in his lap and pretends to be reading it. She's restless too. She comes back through to the kitchen, drinks another glass of apple juice, and then joins him in the living room, turns the television on. The news is full of traffic deaths, and she turns to one of the local stations that shows reruns of old situation comedies. They both watch *M*A*S*H* without really taking it in. She bites the cuticles of her nails, and her eyes wander around the room. He knows he could speak to her now, could make his way through to her grief—and he knows, too, that he will do no such thing; he can't even bring himself to speak at all. There are regions of his own sorrow that he simply lacks the strength to explore. And so he sits there watching her restlessness, and at last it's time to go over to the school. Jane Eberhard makes a surprise visit, bearing a handsome good-luck card she's fashioned herself. She kisses Brenda, behaves exactly as if Brenda is going off to some dangerous, faraway place. She stands in the street and waves at them as they pull away, and Brenda leans out the window to shout good-bye. A moment later, sitting back and staring out at the dusky light, she says she feels a surge of energy, and he tells her she's way ahead of all the others in her class, knowing words like *conserve* and *surge*.

"I've always known them," she says.

It's beginning to rain again. Clouds have been rolling in from the east, and the wind shakes the trees. Lightning flickers on the other side of the clouds. Everything seems threatening, relentless. He slows down. There are many cars parked along both sides of the street. "Quite a turnout," he manages.

"Don't worry," she tells him brightly. "I still feel my surge of energy."

It begins to rain as they get out of the car, and he holds his sport coat like a cape to shield her from it. By the time they get to the open front doors, it's raining very hard. People are crowding into the cafeteria, which has been transformed into an arena for the event—chairs set up on four sides of the room as though for a wrestling match. In the center, at the end of the long, bright-red mat, are the vaulting horse and the mini-trampoline. The physical-education teacher, Mr. Clayton, stands at the entrance. He's tall, thin, scraggly looking, a boy really, no older than twenty-five.

"There's Mr. Clayton," Brenda says.

"I see him."

"Hello, Mr. Clayton."

Mr. Clayton is quite distracted, and he nods quickly, leans toward Brenda, and points to a doorway across the hall. "Go on ahead," he says. Then he nods at her grandfather.

"This is it," Brenda says.

Her grandfather squeezes her shoulder, means to find the best thing to tell her, but in the next confusing minute he's lost her; she's gone among the others and he's being swept along with the crowd entering the cafeteria. He makes his way along the walls behind the chairs, where a few other people have already gathered and are standing. At the other end of the room a man is speaking from a lectern about old business, new officers for the fall. Brenda's grandfather recognizes some of the people in the crowd. A woman looks at him and nods, a familiar face he can't quite place. She is holding a baby; the baby is staring at him over her small shoulder. She turns to him now and steps back a little to stand next to him.

"What a crowd," she says.

He nods.

The baby protests, and he touches the miniature fingers of one hand.

"How is—Brenda?" she says.

"Oh," he says, "fine." And he remembers that she was Brenda's first-grade teacher. She's heavier than she was then, and her hair is darker. She has a baby now.

"I don't remember all my students," she says, shifting the baby to the other shoulder. "I've been home now for eighteen months, and I'll tell you, being at the PTA meeting makes me see how much I don't miss it."

He smiles at her and nods. He's beginning to feel awkward. The man is still speaking from the lectern, a meeting is going on, and this woman's voice is carrying beyond them, though she speaks out of the side of her mouth.

"I remember the way you used to walk Brenda to school every morning. Do you still walk her to school?"

"Yes."

"I always thought that was so nice to see." She turns and seems to watch the speaker for a moment, and then speaks to him again, this time in a near whisper. "I hope you won't take this the wrong way or anything, but I just wanted to say how sorry I was about your daughter. I saw it in the paper when Brenda's mother . . . You know. I just wanted to tell you how sorry. When I saw it in the paper, I thought of Brenda, and how you used to walk her to school. I lost my sister in an automobile accident. I know how you feel—it's a terrible thing to have happen. I mean it's much too sudden a thing. I'm afraid now every time I get into a car."

"You're very kind," he says.

"It seems so senseless," she murmurs. "There's something so senseless about it when it happens. My sister went through a stop sign. She just didn't see it, I guess. But it wasn't a busy road or anything. If she'd come along one second later or sooner nothing would've happened. So senseless. Two drivers coming along two roads on a sunny day and they come together like that. I mean—what're the chances, really?"

He says nothing.

"How's Brenda handling it?"

"She's strong," he says.

"I remember when she first came into my class. She told everyone in the first minute that she'd come from Oregon. That she was living with her grandfather, and her mother was divorced."

"She was a baby when the divorce—when she moved here from Oregon."

This seems to surprise the woman. "Really," she says, low. "I got the impression it was recent for her. I mean, you know, that she had just come from it all. It was all very vivid for her, I remember that."

"She was a baby," he says. It's almost as if he's insisting on it. He's heard this in his voice, and he wonders if she has too.

"Well," she says, "I always had a special place for Brenda. I always thought she was very special. A very special little girl."

The PTA meeting is over, and Mr. Clayton is now standing at the far door with the first of his charges. They're all lining up outside the door, and Mr. Clayton walks to the microphone to announce the program. The demonstration will commence with the mini-trampoline and the vaulting horse: a performance by the fifth and sixth graders. There will also be a break-dancing demonstration by the fourth-grade classes.

"Here we go," the woman says. "My nephew's afraid of the mini-tramp."

"They shouldn't make them do these things," Brenda's grandfather says, with a passion that surprises him. He draws in a breath. "It's too hard," he says, loudly. He can't believe himself. "They shouldn't have to go through a thing like this."

"I don't know," she says vaguely, turning from him a little. He has drawn attention to himself. Others in the crowd are regarding him now —one, a man with a scraggly beard and a V-necked shirt, looking at him with something he takes for agreement.

"It's too much," he says, still louder. "Too much to put on a child. There's just so much a child can take."

Someone asks gently for quiet.

The first child is running down the long mat to the mini-trampoline; it's a girl, and she times her jump perfectly, soars over the horse. One by one, other children follow. Mr. Clayton and another man stand on either side of the horse and help those who go over on their hands. Two or three go over without any assistance at all, with remarkable effortlessness and grace.

"Well," Brenda's first-grade teacher says, "there's my nephew."

The boy hits the mini-tramp and does a perfect forward flip in the air over the horse, landing upright and then rolling forward in a somersault.

"Yea, Jack," she cheers. "No sweat. Yea, Jackie boy."

The boy trots to the other end of the room and stands with the others; the crowd is applauding. The last of the sixth graders goes over the horse, and Mr. Clayton says into the microphone that the fifth graders are next. It's Brenda who's next. She stands in the doorway, her cheeks flushed, her legs looking too heavy in the tights. She's rocking back and forth on the balls of her feet, getting ready. It grows quiet. Her arms swing slightly, back and forth, and now, just for a moment, she is looking at the crowd, her face hiding whatever she's feeling. It's as if she's merely curious as to who is out there, but he knows she's looking for him, searching the crowd for her grandfather, who stands on his toes, unseen against the far wall, stands there thinking his heart might break, lifting his hand to wave.

MONITOR

MILLICENT DILLON

Millicent Dillon is the author of *Baby Perpetua and Other Stories, The One in the Back Is Medea* (a novel), and *A Little Original Sin,* a biography of Jane Bowles. She lives in San Francisco.

When I was a child in the sixth grade in Manhattan, many years ago, I was made Monitor of the Bells. Four times during the school day I would go to the principal's office and get the key. Then I would mount the three steps to the raised landing on the second floor. Behind me were the classrooms, enclosed by high wooden walls on rollers. I crossed in front of the flag, and there, set in the wall, covered by a glass door, was the bell case.

To ring the bells at the precise moment of nine, of twelve, of one, and of three was my public responsibility. This obligation to absolute accuracy before others lifted me to a plane of intense excitement. It was as if I were the one who set and gave the time for school to begin and end. I knew, of course, that this was only a mechanical function that I performed, but that did not stop me from feeling the urgency of the power that flowed through me.

I opened the glass door with the key, waited for the exact moment for the minute hand to reach twelve, and then pressed the main bell. The sound reverberated through the school. Immediately thereafter I pressed each bell in a row of bells that corresponded to the individual classrooms. I can still recall (my thumb's memory?) the feeling of a metal disk exerting its back pressure upon the pad of my thumb, the slight inner concavity where it would rest.

The school had no name, only a number, P.S. 46. As I have aged I have grown far less exact, particularly about numbers, but I remember the number of the school because during the entire sixth grade we practiced the song to be sung at graduation. To the tune of the Cornell anthem, it went:

> Forty-Six, oh, Forty-Six
> You we love so well.
> We will ever sing your praises,
> Forty-Six, farewell.

A few of the children, the more daring, if not the more radical, amended the last word to "Go to Hell." I was pleased and pleasantly shocked by their words. But the true sense of what was radical lay inert in me, buried along with the recognition of mysteries far more terrifying in the punishment they would bring than the simple utterance of "Hell." This I say now, though then I fought off—successfully—the slightest awareness of what was mysterious. It was replaced—covered over—by my intense struggle to prove myself the best, to win out in competition over the others, whether boy or girl, though I was small and thin, the smallest in the class by far. Having been awarded the Monitorship of the Bells was in itself a recognition and a promise of further reward to come. Winning out seemed a road that beckoned straight ahead as long as I would be careful to follow tenaciously and not be diverted into side paths.

It was Dr. Arnold, the principal of the school, who had appointed me to the Monitorship out of all the others. He was a large, red-faced, red-haired man, who sweated profusely even—especially—in winter. He had a voice so loud, it could shake the wooden walls. He smiled on me benignly. At times I have thought of that smile as evidence of his sly pleasure at confounding the others by appointing me, the smallest in the sixth grade and a girl. At other times I have thought of that smile as proof of a compassionate gesture to something not beefy in himself, something separate and unrecognized.

Being Monitor separated me from the others, bestowed upon me a freedom of movement out of time, though I set the time. I did not have to line up with the other children in the yard downstairs. I walked freely into the principal's outer office, where I would occasionally see Dr. Arnold and he would smile and pat me on the arm. I was free to come into class later than the others. Even as I sat at my desk there was the knowledge that I could leave my seat earlier than they. I sat, intense as ever, working to do better than the others, alert to competition and at the same time excited by the prospect of my appointed duty.

Our teacher was Mr. Polonski, a dapper man, cocky in his walk, but soft-spoken. He was quite short, shorter in fact than the biggest boys in the class. The pupils were seated by size, so of course I was in the front row. The larger children, who were in the back, seemed by definition to be the slower ones. They were the ones, the boys in particular, who would challenge Mr. Polonski in a way that would now seem relatively inoffensive. But when crossed, Mr. Polonski would amplify his voice to thunderous proportions and would yell obscenities. Once, I remember, he smacked a boy taller than he. (Did the boy scuffle with him? No, I think he just stood there and did nothing.)

I cannot really be sure about size in absolute terms. I think Mr. Polonski was small and I think Dr. Arnold was large. But whatever the actual volumetric space they occupied, we invested their beings with such power that they inhabited an enormous "virtual" space for us. As principal Dr. Arnold was monumental; Mr. Polonski, as teacher, was only slightly less so. But if we magnified, we also denigrated—reduced—mocked. The butt of our jokes was Mrs. Russell, who taught Music Appreciation and Sewing. She had been in a terrible fire—so the story went—and all her hair had been burnt off. That was why she wore a red wig that would now and then slip suddenly and dangerously to one side. Pity for elders was not in our vocabulary. There were few enough occasions for the small malice that eroded their huge images.

When Mrs. Russell taught Music Appreciation during Assembly, the temptation to mockery became irresistible. It was like a flame that went from one student to the other, the reflection of that flame, false or true, that had singed the hair off her head.

One snowy morning—for some reason it seems to me now that all school mornings were snowy—I ran through the school yard, the long narrow space between the iron-spiked fence and the dark brick facade, up the steps and into the front door. The others were already on line in the open area where the students gathered, waiting for the bell to be rung. The teacher on patrol kept yawning and shaking his head, then turning and checking the clock, then turning again to see that no one spoke. The smell of the damp clothes in the dark enclosed space was a familiar, even elating smell to me. It reminded me that I was on my own battleground, ready to show that I could beat out the others, to be first.

I ran up to the second floor and entered the principal's office. The outer room, lined with metal cabinets, dark wooden cabinets, and bookcases, was empty. The door to Dr. Arnold's inner office was shut. I heard the sound of low voices and then a thundering voice, "Son of a bitch—I don't need—" descending into a squabble of words. The door opened and Mr. Polonski emerged, head down. He did not see me, I was in the corner getting the key. He went to his mail slot and stood before it, his back to me. He did not look dapper, he did not look cocky, he did not look large. I did not know what he looked like. I could not see around him to see.

Furtively I slipped out of the office, mounted the podium, unlocked the glass case, and at the precise moment of nine, rang the main bell and the successive bells, pushing each disk hard with my thumb. I shut the glass door and locked it, returned the key to the office—Dr. Arnold's door was shut again—hung my coat in the cloakroom, and went to my seat.

His voice soft as ever, Mr. Polonski announced that today there would be a Music Assembly. At his signal the two biggest boys in the back row got up to roll the walls out of the way. Our class, one of the two front rooms, was now completely exposed to view. Before us was the raised landing. It was strange to turn and see the other classes behind us, robbed of their walls. In my mind, the classes seem now to have stretched on infinitely into the distance, though of course that could not have been so.

After the Pledge of Allegiance and the singing of "America the Beautiful," Mrs. Russell mounted the podium and turned to face us. To one side of her was the flag, to the other side a record player and a few records. Behind her the door of the bell case reflected the overhead lights. Blowing on her pitch pipe, Mrs. Russell began the session of Music Appreciation. To help us recognize each piece and its composer, we were taught a ditty, to be sung to the beginning of the melody. The one for "Humoresque" went:

> Come away into the wildwood
> Dream the dream of happy childhood
> Dvorak's "Humoresque" will show the way.

In the air, around me, behind me, I could feel the stirring of resistance to Mrs. Russell. Soon the laughter would begin, soon the necessity would be to hold back the laughter, particularly if one sat near the ringleader, Joseph Sbunsky, who was adept at mimicry.

Joseph Sbunsky was a curly-haired boy with fair blue eyes. Often he held his hands folded across his breastbone in a gesture that made him seem angelic. He sat one row behind me in the next aisle and I could sense him readying himself to mock Mrs. Russell. I looked down, biting my lips, and when I looked up, at the edge of my vision I saw Mr. Polonski and behind him, sweating, in his shirt sleeves, Dr. Arnold.

Mrs. Russell put on the record of "Humoresque." The needle kept jumping to the wrong groove, to "Dream the dream of happy childhood." As she leaned over to see what the trouble was, her wig began to slip to one side. I heard a muffled laugh. I did not want to laugh. I knew Mr. Polonski and Dr. Arnold were standing where they could see me. I tried not to laugh. I tried to make Mrs. Russell not funny. I made myself think of her in a fire, to force the sense of tragedy to overcome the contagion of laughter. But it did not work. I dug my fingernails into my palms. I tried to look at Mrs. Russell as if through other eyes. I pretended I was in her sewing class, where, in fact, I felt inept, all thumbs. Sewing was a skill I could not master, though I always told myself I did not want to master it. I hated its tidiness and its constraint.

At the end of each sewing lesson Mrs. Russell gave a short lecture on behavior—"Deportment," it was called. One of her most frequently repeated admonitions was, "The most important thing for young girls to remember is to go to the bathroom when you have to. It is very bad for young girls to hold it." I was puzzled by this warning, I could not understand the point of it, but now even this seemed funny to me. Everything I could think of was tainted by the irresistible impulse to explode into laughter. I felt it shaking me. I struggled to make it unnoticeable by moving, by frowning, by looking up as if I were concentrating with enormous intensity. As the shaking started in me again, threatening to go into spasm, I made myself sing, "Come away into the wildwood," as instructed.

When the doors had been rolled back around us, Mr. Polonski began to yell. "What way is that to behave?"

We all sat and said nothing.

"Don't think for a minute that I'm going to put up with that kind of behavior. It's bad enough to act up in the classroom, but out there in front of everybody. You, Joseph, tell me, what was so funny? What was everyone laughing about?"

"I wasn't laughing," Joseph Sbunsky said, the pale half-moons under his eyes seeming darker.

"Don't tell me what you were or weren't doing. That isn't what I asked you. I saw everyone around you giggling. What were they giggling about?"

Joseph shook his head. "I don't know." His hands fluttered to his chest.

"Howard!" Mr. Polonski yelled. "What are you doing?"

Howard Morris, an awkward abstracted boy, who sat next to me, jumped up in confusion. "I wasn't doing anything. I was doing my arithmetic."

"When I'm talking, you pay attention, you can do your arithmetic later."

Head hanging, Howard sat at his desk. "But Mr. Polonski—"

"What now?"

"But—I think there's an error in the book."

"Where?" said Mr. Polonski.

"The fifth problem on page sixty-three. I'm sure it's the wrong answer in back."

Mr. Polonski took out his arithmetic book. He turned the pages, then he looked up. "Don't think I've forgotten what I was saying. We'll come back to that later, but for now we're going to do our arithmetic." Suddenly he thundered, "And you'd all better pay attention or else—"

Now that we were shut in again, all the giggling past, all the yelling past (would Mr. Polonski remember and come back to it?), there was a staleness in the room which I tried to overcome by throwing myself into doing the arithmetic, better and faster than the others. (At the A & P on Broadway there was a clerk who wrote the prices of the grocery items on a brown paper bag and in one move of his pencil, flying up the double column, would instantaneously have an answer. When I went to the store with my mother for the weekly shopping, did I feel—I must have felt—the tension in my mother as the grocery items were gathered before the final sum? Was she spending too much? There was only so much money—too little money. It had to be used for food, for shoes to be repaired, for rent. Was she going beyond what was allotted?

No, I did not feel that in her. I only waited for the moment of lightning calculation and each time marveled at the clerk's skill.)

The door opened and Dr. Arnold stood upon the threshold. He beckoned to Mr. Polonski with one finger and Mr. Polonski flushed. He went out and shut the door behind him. In an instant he returned. "I will be back shortly. You have all the problems on page sixty-three to finish and if you get those done you can go to sixty-four. I do not want to hear one sound from this room while I'm gone. Not one, do you understand me?"

Suddenly he said, "Celia, come up here to my desk and be Monitor while I'm away. I want you to write down the name of anyone who doesn't behave. If she has any trouble with any of you," he threatened, "she'll mark you down and that demerit will go on your report card."

I sat at Mr. Polonski's desk after he had shut the door. The desk was larger than I thought, the chair was larger too. The class looked strange from the front. Everything usually to the left was now to the right. Before me—clearly—were all those whom I could not see when my back was to them. I had my arithmetic book with me and continued to work on the problems at Mr. Polonski's desk. Now and then I looked at the class. They were working quietly. I felt I wanted to grin, but to grin was not right. Outside the snow was falling again.

A noise, the slightest of stirring, began, then stopped. I looked up. There was nothing. Everyone was working busily. No one looked at me. The radiator was hissing. I returned to my own work.

The noise recurred, louder this time. I looked up and saw that Howard Morris was scrabbling on his hands and knees in the aisle.

"What are you doing?" I asked.

He waited until he was in his seat to answer me. "I was getting my paper." He put his paper on the desk and smoothed it with his arm. "It's all wrinkled. He did it," he said, pointing to Joseph Sbunsky. "He took it and crumpled it up. He threw my paper on the floor."

"I did not. He's a liar." Joseph Sbunsky didn't even look up from his work.

"You did too."

"I did not." Now Joseph Sbunsky took his right hand and passed it over the top of his head to behind his left ear and began to scratch it. It was a gesture Howard Morris often used when he was concentrating on an arithmetic problem. Someone giggled. Frances Joel, a tall heavy girl, the only girl in the back, got up and came forward with a whitened eraser in her hand and began to powder Howard Morris's black hair.

"Quit it," he said, trying to fend her off.

"Quit it," I said.

"Make me," she said. She kept on powdering Howard Morris's hair as he flailed at her.

The flame of giggling was back again in the room, but now I had to stop it in them, not in myself. I stood up, conscious of my smallness behind that desk. My voice trembling, I said, "If you don't stop, I'm going to give you a demerit." I did not want to mark her down, I felt that it would be wrong to do that. Somewhere or other I had learned or come to believe that the only fight worthwhile was when you were fighting with the odds against you. But the odds were not against me at that desk. I was leaning on a power that was not mine. "You'd better not try," she warned, "or I'll get you."

I felt a sudden rush of rage engulf me. It seized upon the power that was there at that desk as its own—and I wrote her name down.

There was a noise outside the door. Frances Joel ran back to her seat, surprisingly fast for such a heavy girl. Everyone else became absorbed in their work as Mr. Polonski opened the door.

"All right, Celia. You can go back to your seat now." He went to his desk. As I sat down, I knew everybody was waiting for him to say something about the demerit I had marked. But since he said nothing, they were sure that I had not marked her name down, that I had only pretended to do so.

Joseph Sbunsky raised one hand from his chest, where it lay folded upon the other.

"Yes?"

"Will you go over the fifth problem again, please?"

Perhaps, I thought, he did not see where I marked her name down. Then I thought, it's just as well if he doesn't see it. Then I felt a coward for feeling that. But he must have seen it, I told myself.

When it was time for the bells to be rung for noon I got up and went to the office and got the key. The door to Dr. Arnold's inner office was open but he was not there. I climbed the landing and opened the glass case and, at the exact moment of twelve, pushed the main bell, then all the other disks. I felt as if that were all I was doing, just pushing a row of disks. The pushing itself had changed, everything about being a Monitor of the Bells had changed, as if I'd usurped a place that was not mine in the classroom and I was still usurping what did not belong to me.

I went home, I had lunch, I started back to school.

Instead of taking the direct route to school, I chose to go the long way around, up Riverside, then turning and going east along the cemetery. Through the iron gates, I saw the grey oblongs of the graves humped by snow. The impulse to go slow, to do a radical thing, not to be at school on time, came upon me like an unwanted thing and I began to run towards Broadway, away from the grey stones and the enclosing gates.

At Broadway I ran across to the middle island, then had to wait as the light had changed. Standing there, waiting, I remembered another day when ice had covered the streets. A large truck was waiting at the intersection, its engine idling, as I had begun to cross with the light. As I ran, I slipped on the ice. From the ground I looked up at the huge engine beside me and I had had the terror that it might not wait, that if the light changed it would go ahead and roll right over me.

* * *

In the narrow yard between the iron spikes and the old brick facade, the students who had not gone home for lunch were milling about. So there was still time left. Sweating with relief, I decided to go upstairs and put my coat in the cloak room first. As I shoved my coat in among the others—there were so many and they were so heavy—I smelled that familiar damp smell and I was almost back in my own territory. I was the Bell Monitor and soon I would ring the bells.

I heard a noise and turned. Frances Joel was coming at me. I knew the instant I saw her that Mr. Polonski had seen the mark against her (had held her after class? had yelled at her?) I felt a sense of gratefulness that, after all, I had not been betrayed by him, but that gratefulness put me off. I waited, in a kind of paralysis, for her to reach me.

She came up to me and she hit me across the face with her hand. Yet one more instant I was paralyzed, stunned by the blow and even more by the thought that she would hit me. She was hitting me and she was bigger than I was. Now it changed, now it was my fight. The rage I had felt at Mr. Polonski's desk, that rage in a silent rush came upon me. I became a swinging, lunging thing. I did not know if I was hurt, I did not know if others were watching. I only knew I had to hit her back. A look of surprise came upon Frances Joel's wide face. She held out her arm, a long arm, to ward me off.

Backed against the damp overcoats and jackets, held away from her by her arm, I kept swinging and hitting. I am going to be late, the bells are going to be late, the thought came to me.

But engulfed by the smell of those damp coats and jackets, I kept swinging at what was not there, at what I could not reach.

BIG DOG

NORMAN LAVERS

Norman Lavers has published a novel, *The Northwest Passage,* a collection of short stories, and two books of criticism. He has held an Iowa Writers Workshop writing fellowship and an NEA fellowship. He teaches creative writing at Arkansas State University.

She of course wanted the old villa about five miles out of town, surrounded by lantana and bougainvillea, with its quaint patio and tile roof through which, in places, you could see the metallic blue Mediterranean sky. He looked at the plumbing, the improvised electric wiring, the inconvenient distance from the shops—"We'll have our bikes," she said. "Winter, wet and rainy, is coming even here," he said—and gave a decisive negative. He wanted the brand new apartment on the fourth floor in the middle of town, everything working, right in the center of things. She saw the sterile functionalism, the cool anonymous neighbors, the lack of anything alive and growing, and in her own passive way dug in her heels. She apologetically asked, he abruptly demanded, that the real estate agent show them something else, and they compromised on an older, more lived-in apartment on the edge of town with fields and a lagoon to look at off their balcony, which was only one floor up from the ground. Also, they were childless, and she had noticed a frail elderly couple in the little house next door. Her curiously inverted maternal instinct always needed old people to protect and preserve.

He for his part—well—he didn't know what he was going to do, only that, when he found it, he would rush at it head first, and it would not long resist him. Some people in this world are dreamers, sleeping light and dreaming through the night, half awake by day, their dreams rushing in at every odd moment. For such people—she was a bit like this—

the place is only partly important, because so much of their life goes on independently from place. He was the other way, constantly fully alert, taking in everything, obsessively seeing and learning every process around him at the top of his speed, putting all of himself into it. But it had to be the *it* that was objectively out there, and when it was not there for him, and his interest flagged, he was deeply asleep in a moment, his face sagging, his mouth drooped open. In this way he was like those sharks who must swim constantly their whole life, because if they pause, the oxygen is no longer carried past their breathing apparatus, and they die.

But the doctor had ordered him to rest, and he had taken the long overdue sabbatical. He meant to rest, however, one hundred percent. He laid out the campaign in his head. He had first of all quit smoking cold turkey, and after reading every book, had set up a balanced diet for himself that would work off his extra sixty pounds. He would go down to the beach and do distance swimming in the morning as long as the weather stayed warm—it was already the end of September—and he had bought a knife-thin racing bike for distance biking in the afternoon till he had lost his extra weight, at which time the doctor told him he could begin running. Right now the weight would be too much strain on his knees.

On the day they looked at their apartment, clouds covered the distant view. But on the day they moved into it from their hotel it was clear. They did their grocery shopping, haltingly in the unfamiliar language— and she made them their first pot of tea, and they sat out on their balcony, and at that point for the first time realized that it was the mountain that would dominate their view. It was Puig Major, rising 6000 feet straight up out of the sea. In the local island dialect Puig was pronounced like Pooch, so he dubbed the mountain Big Dog. It was a bare pinnacle of rock. She decided it was a volcanic spewing, magma pressing up from the dark middle of the world. He saw in it another—to him even more dramatic—orogenetic force, the great African plate pressing north into the Eurasian plate, pushing and squeezing up the land between this wrinkle which went from the Atlas mountains in Morocco the length of the western Mediterranean at last curving north-ward and culminating in the Alps.

"What are you going to do?" he said.

"For the rest of my life?" she said. "For this year? Or just this morning?"

"Those three in that order."

"I'm just going to go on puttering for my life. For this year I want to do some different kind of painting, but I don't know what yet. And for this morning I'm going to lie on the beach with my new bikini. I'll be the one you don't notice because I'll still have my top on. And you're coming too. This is vacation, rest, change. You're going to lie on the beach and take it easy on your heart."

"My heart is okay."

"Now. But you're in the number one risk category."

"Yeah, well there's another side to that equation. More and more evidence is coming in that there is also a number one risk cancer personality, and that's marked by people who are too passive."

"I'm not too passive."

"Only because I keep agitating you."

"Well, if I keep pulling you back, it's for your own good."

"Hey, stop pushing me around," he said, smiling and she smiled too, both because it was so unusual for her to be assertive in anything, and because on the face of it the idea was so ludicrous. She had never weighed over ninety pounds. He wasn't tall, but he was broad as a door, and had gone to university on football scholarships till he got a head injury and began passing out. Then to the amazement of his jock friends, he went on and made it through academically, even through the PhD, and taught in a university with surprising brilliance. He took his first chance to move to a department chairmanship, and then to a Dean of Arts and Sciences position. No matter where he was, he systematically set about learning his and everyone else's job, then began working on ways to improve them, and by the time he had made himself indispensable, was beginning to get bored.

They were funny to see together on the beach. She was like his child with her tiny perfect body. When he put suntan lotion on her, one of his hands could cover her whole back. His stomach was big, but his chest was massive.

"I'm going for a swim."

"I'm going to lie here and soak up the sun."

He marched out into the sea up to his knees. At the farthest end of the harbor, two or three miles away, was the last out ship channel marker. He dove in with an immense splash and struck out towards it. He was so buoyant he seemed to wallow at the surface, rolling from side to side with his formless but powerful crawl stroke. He did not let up his pace till he reached the marker. There, he held on for a few minutes, breathing hard, and waited, but nothing struck his heart. He swam back at a somewhat more leisurely pace, and walked out onto the beach, water streaming off his shaggy body, his muscles pumped up to even more herculean proportions.

He lay down next to her and watched the topless bathers for a while, then watched all the people on the beach one after the other, trying to guess about their lives from what they looked like. He watched the windsurfers for a while, but that didn't seem very challenging.

"I can't stand lying here doing nothing," he said.

They went back to the apartment and had lunch and she went on sunbathing on the balcony, this time with no bikini. He liked that and watched her for a while, and then they made love. Once when they were staying with friends they had been making love in the guest bedroom when they realized there was a long mirror beside the bed. They looked over and saw the huge hairy monster with the tiny fragile child engulfed under him, and they both laughed so hard they had to stop what they were doing. But luckily for the most part they made love with their eyes closed, and it was the one thing he did gently, and she did fiercely.

When he stood up, the mountain was there in his view. He rode his bike up as high as the road went, chained it to a tree, and climbed to the top of the mountain. He looked around and saw water on all sides. "So much for that," he said, and was back at the flat in time to fix a drink before dinner.

"This island might start getting a bit small," he said. And while she watched him, his attention lapsed, and his eyes lost focus, and his face sagged in the direction of gravity. It was the end of their first day in the apartment.

* * *

However, he threw himself into his study of the language. He was fascinated to see how logical it was, how efficient. How by merely changing *a* to *e* in the verb paradigms they could be made to reflect action from a different perspective. He would study a particular point of grammar all morning, wandering around the house muttering, then in the afternoon he would walk downtown and try to talk to a newsagent, to a shopkeeper, working everything they said around so that he could use that particular point of grammar. He bought a tiny tape recorder which he kept in his pocket where it couldn't be seen, and recorded conversations, then played them over and over again when he got back to the apartment, analyzing them. He saw the ad, taped to a shop window, for a group of language tutors, and hired one to come by every morning for an hour class.

She in the meantime in her very quiet way slowly put her stamp on their living space. She filled the balcony and every empty spot with pots of growing plants. The rather standardized furnishings in their furnished apartment seemed as if they would resist personalization, but with the tiniest shifts—the equivalent of changing *a* to *e*—she turned each area into something recognizably her own. Each meal she fixed was individual and beautiful to look at, the local food and dishes given a slightly oriental quality. She had gone to Japan one summer to study painting and was delighted to find a whole country just her size, and designed and organized the way she designed and organized a meal or a room. She had studied Japanese for several months before going over, and he told her it was the perfect language for her, as it seemed to consist of dozens of ways of apologizing for your presence.

He was not by any means blind to the small and perfect beauty always surrounding her, and that he himself sat in somewhat jarringly, but no longer uneasily. He liked it. Maybe she could extend her subtle power to him, and make him, within her magic circle, somewhat less gross and incongruous. She seemed to think it was no problem.

"You mean strength matters too, not just beauty."

"Not exactly," she said. "I mean they're not different. My painting master showed me a very old painting. There were three figures. Quite intentionally, I'm sure, there was no attempt to make the composition interesting. It was just three forms, all the same size, placed equidistant across the board they were painted on. One was a peony, traditionally epitomizing beauty, but that only lasts for a day. The next was a lion, incredible strength and fearlessness and vitality. The third was a rock, perdurable, resistless, eternal."

"And they all belonged in the same painting."

"More than that. They were all the same shape. If you squinted your eyes slightly—"

"So you would see them as an oriental would."

"Yes, I hadn't thought of that—you would see that the stone really looked very much like the peony, the peony like the lion, and so on. That what was perfect in the flower was enduring, that what was beautiful in the stone was transitory, that the lion's strength was as fragile, his courage as perfect—you could probably say this all better than I can."

"No. I think I understand," he said. It was her he couldn't fathom. She was the one process he couldn't analyze, had given up trying to, which is why perhaps he never grew bored with her.

He thought he had dismissed the mountain after the first day, and yet as he paced through the apartment muttering hypothetical conversations, at the end of his pace he was always on the balcony looking at Big Dog.

"It's never the same twice," he said.

"Have you just noticed that?" she said.

Now he also noticed what she was doing. She had taken out a large sheet of water-color paper and with a pencil and a straight-edge was lightly platting it out in 2½ inch squares. He sat and watched her. She fumbled hestitatingly through her life, but when she worked she was almost grimly efficient. Now she took an ordinary sheet of paper and cut a 2½ inch square out of the middle of it and held it at arm's length before her, and looked at the mountain through it. With her other hand she did drawings of the mountain, and when she had one that pleased her, she traced it on her tracing paper. Then she turned her tracing paper over and blacked the backside with a soft pencil. She turned the paper face up again and placed it over the first of the squares on her big sheet of water-color paper, and with a hard pencil went over the lines of her original drawing, so that the carbon underneath transferred the line to the water-color paper. Slowly and carefully she repeated this over each square.

He began taking an interest in the process. "You know there is such a thing as carbon paper, that would do the job a lot quicker and easier."

She ignored him.

"What you're going to do now is paint it every time it changes, right?"

"Mm-hmm."

"Now's the time to start," he said, beginning to take over. "There's a neat lenticular cloud forming over the peak. Here, I'll set up a chair and table for you."

"I have to fix your lunch right at the moment."

"That can wait. This is more important. It's already shifting."

But she went in and began preparing lunch. Partly, she was resisting having him take over. She could be as stubborn as he was. More so. In her soft but persistent way she could wear him down as water does stone. He knew this and felt helpless now, wishing he had not said anything. He had not meant to take over her idea, it's just that it had seemed like such a good idea to him, and he was already anticipating the pleasure he would have in seeing the mountain captured in each new view. He told himself not to say another word, otherwise she would not do it at all. Even as he looked, the lens cloud was lifting and losing its shape, and before he sat down to lunch it was gone forever.

In the morning when he opened his eyes, it immediately came to mind, and though he would like to have lain there holding her small intensely warm body, he got up and rushed to the balcony. After a night of high winds—the stormy season was fast approaching—the air was absolutely clear. The mountain seemed much closer, and the slant light gouged a deep black shadow across part of the front. The hard rock glowed in the sun.

"You should see it now," he said eagerly, going back to the bed. "It's the absolutely primal rock right now, no atmospheric effects, simply what is there, the bare bones." He said it as temptingly as possible, barely restraining himself from saying, "This is the time to start." She was not buying, however. She wanted something else for the moment and reached her arms up to him.

When he got up the second time a bank of cloud as solid as whipped cream was pushing up against one side of the mountain, and puffy clouds were appearing in a line above the horizon. He stopped himself from remarking on it, but she read his eyes perhaps. She went into the kitchen and began preparing their breakfast.

While they ate breakfast, the space between Big Dog and two smaller closer mountains filled in with solid cloud or fog, and a high overcast crept over the sky subduing the light, except for a point of sun still illuminating the peak, as if at the end of a gloomy tunnel. Then the overcast thickened, and the light on the mountain failed, and it was only a dull gray outline. The cloud system moved rapidly, clearing from behind them, and soon the sky was clear overhead, and sun covered the land, leaving only the mountain in a swirling gloom. He was in agony watching the changes, each ideally illustrative of a new facet of the mountain's personality, and each quickly lost. In the meantime she had gone out to do the shopping.

In the evening it went through all the same or similar changes in reverse, only this time everything bathed in fire, until at last the mountain, clear again, was stark and black against a sky like a thin sheet of molten steel slowly cooling and darkening. They sat long over their after-dinner coffees watching until the last spark was extinguished.

In the middle of the night he got up and came to look at it. The clouds had built up again and all outside was intensely purple black, except where reddish lightning flickered about the peak as if around the head of some monster about to be brought to life. He went back to the bed, aching to tell her, to get her to see it, but she was breathing easily, fast asleep.

* * *

The next day, she packed him lunch and a thermos, which he put in his backpack, and he took off on his bike heading for a town 25 miles down the coast, on the other side of the mountain, where he would have a different view of it. The wind had shifted direction and was coming from the mountain, and thunderheads were building behind it. He didn't bother to take a raincoat. He only had on a tee-shirt, shorts, and sneakers, so it didn't matter if he got wet. He headed down the coast road, his huge legs pumping into the wind, his eyes squinted against the dust. When he reached the other town, it was windy, but clear and warm, tourists heading for the beaches. He could see the tremendous clouds over the mountain and what looked like a dense curtain of rain heading towards the apartment. The whole storm system seemed to be generated directly out of the mountain itself. He thought of her alone in the apartment with the storm approaching. She would be worrying about him, not realizing he was clear out of it, sitting against a tree and having a cup of coffee. He looked at the apartment in his mind room by room and thought what ought to be done. They had had strong winds before, so she knew to latch the shutters and not leave a door or window open in such a way that the wind could slam it shut and shatter the glass. But they had not up to now had rain. He remembered a stupid design flaw. The flat roof of the apartment complex drained down a large pipe which idiotically emptied onto their black-walled balcony and thence out a small hole in the floor of the balcony. In a real torrential downpour, he estimated, that hole might be just fast enough to empty the balcony and keep it from backing up and flooding the kitchen. But, and here was a problem, there was a complicated grate fitted into the hole, which he should have removed as soon as he saw it, but had not. It created enough of an obstruction that it would stop the balcony from draining fast enough. He had not bothered to tell her to remove it in case of a storm, imagining that he would be there himself to do it. He thought of her coping with the flood, putting up towels against the door to dam the flood, bailing into the sink, and then he saw clearly the refrigerator with its electric motor on the bottom. Two inches of water in the kitchen—which she would be standing in—would reach the motor and short it out, electrocuting her.

Now he rode the bike with the wind and like the wind, his half-full thermos lying beside the road where he dropped it. Ahead of him the clouds thickened. Then he was over wet ground and deep puddles where the storm had passed, plowing through six inches of flood water in low parts of the road. The black wall of rain beyond which all was obscured was still ahead of him. Then he heard and felt the first big splats of water and in moments the rain was so thick he could barely see. To make things worse, as he crossed the edge of the cyclone, the wind shifted around until it was driving straight against him again, blinding him and now stinging him with hail, like shrapnel from the lightning bursting all around him. His broad body worked like a negative sail, an air anchor, holding him back as in a dream of running underwater. His massive thighs were nonetheless equal to any temporal wind and he pumped grimly, and, if such a word could be appropriate here, remorselessly. Then he had reached the edge of town, the rain coming with new fury, and turned up the side street off the front, leapt off the bike, feeling with surprise the sudden weakness in his legs, sprinted up the flight of stairs, threw open the front door and punched the off button on the circuit breaker box. She was in the kitchen, towels against the door, bailing frantically into the sink. The water had just reached two inches deep. He pushed past her onto the back balcony, reached down into the deep swirling water for the grate, pulled it out and threw it as far as he could. The sky was already clearing.

Time was passing, and if in her patient and dreamy way she might someday get around to painting the mountain, she still had already missed thousands of changes never again to be repeated. He couldn't stand it anymore, and rented a car and drove across the island to the one city and bought an expensive camera and a heavy surveyor's tripod. He was too busy to spend years studying art and training his hand to reproduce what his eyes saw. So why not get a machine, a piece of apparatus, that will do it at once, and more accurately than the hand could ever do? He felt in his pride of the machine the faintest contempt for the patient art of his wife. That was a bit mean, so he altered that to feel instead guilty that he was trespassing on her turf, or sorry that he would so easily and quickly accomplish what she was still only contemplating. The dreamers and the doers. Of course it was her idea. He wouldn't have thought of it. But that's always the way, the reason we need the dreamers on this planet.

Yet it was not guilt or sympathy he felt setting his camera up on its tripod and aiming it at the mountain. It was self-consciousness, because though she said nothing, and seemed outwardly to show only the most generous interest, he felt she would be judging him, judging his results by criteria he was not altogether sure of. He looked through the viewfinder, aware that he was repeating the process of holding the paper with the hole cut out at arm's distance in front of him. His was only a more sophisticated version. And though when she was doing it, it was all he could do to restrain himself from taking it out of her hands and looking himself and telling her just where to do it from, it seemed so obvious to him, here now that he was actually doing it from this spot rather than that, he felt the whole weight of her competency bearing down on him. He actually felt himself sweating with this new kind of labor. He began to understand her exasperation with him at times, and wanted to turn and say Let me do this my way!—when he noticed she was in the bathroom running a bath and singing to herself.

One angle of the mountain did seem to show it the way he most often thought of it, and he locked the tripod into place. He realized he had already learned something. What he wanted was not *the* mountain, but rather, the mountain as *he* thought of it. At any rate he thought that *the* mountain, and the mountain the way *he* thought of it, were pretty close. He took the light reading carefully—it was altering as he took it, clouds crossing, then leaving the sun—and pressed the cable release to take his first picture. Click. He had caught it. This time it hadn't got away.

Throughout the day, as he did other things, he watched the mountain out of the corner of his eye, and as it altered, he snapped it. She was at the table painting a tiny white autumn flower. The last picture on the roll was a several-second-long exposure of the sunset, which this evening was like a gorgeous swirling bruise. He felt it would definitely be the most spectacular. He had made a few notes with each exposure, describing the state of the mountain in a few concise words. He had a feeling after all that if he approached it systematically he would find that the seemingly endless changes would reduce themselves to a manageable few that repeated themselves. Perhaps a relatively small number of pictures, say a hundred, would tell the whole story of the mountain. In the morning he took the film to a shop that promised 24 hour service.

In the end it was three full days before he got them back. He had been in the shop a dozen times, his temper beginning to fray. But he smiled openly like a child when the shopkeeper, equally relieved, held up the packet as he entered. One satisfaction was that in all this time his wife had only managed to paint two petals on her flower. He ripped open the package as he was leaving the shop and could hardly believe what he saw. The giant mountain that had dominated his imagination for nearly two months came out in his pictures like a tiny pimple. Not only that, the colors were all wrong, much too blue at times, much too red at others, and everything he had seen as sharp and crisp was pale and washed out. The sunset was particularly flat and uninteresting. There was going to be more to this than he thought, and he set his jaw grimly, and went back into the shop and bought a big book on photography.

He read it straight through, and returned to the pertinent pages several times. He rented the car again and went back to the city and this time bought some filters to cut out haze and to correct color, and a longer focal length lens to bring the mountain forward to give it the magnitude he saw with his eye.

In the meantime she had completed her small perfect painting. The flower itself was blown and dry and unrecognizable, having faded in two days.

If things won't give in to your first rush, then you must be persistent and systematic. With an uneasy feeling that he was backing off slightly from his first resolve to record Big Dog in all its moods, he decided, for an initial objective, he would record it perfectly in *one* of its moods. He was so eager to begin he was up before dawn setting up the tripod. The sun, rising behind his back, illuminated the mountain before anything else, in a delicate faded pink, almost white, and it seemed like a fragile cone of infolded petals, until the sun was fully disengaged from the earth, when it took on the harsh black shadows and the glaring rocky face of its true substance. That's what he was waiting for, and he photographed it with his long lens to bring it up tall in the sky, crowding over the tops of the closer mountains, and he tried it with each filter, with every combination of aperture and duration, carefully noting down in his notebook which combinations he had used. It took the pictures a week this time to come back from the 24-hour place, but they were terrific. There was the overbearing face, the metallic sky, the strong relief shadows. He showed them to her, and she said Yes, that's it, that's really good, and the child-like smile was on his face. She had found a tiny winter flower in bloom, and brought a blossom and a bit of leaf back, and set it in a jar to paint. But the old couple across the way needed her. She had been doing their shopping for them—the old man's pension check was so meager, and food was so expensive, she had been secretly augmenting it when she bought their food—and doing a few other chores. She had started out with gestures, but had word by word picked up the local dialect from them until now they conversed quite well. But the man was ill, growing worse. His wife needed all her time to care for him, so she had been doing everything else, cooking, washing. After she and the wife got the old man through a particularly bad spell, she found her winter flower had dried out past the point of her being able to recreate it in paints.

For a few days he was complacent, but then he went back and looked at his pictures more critically. With the blush of newness off them, they seemed less good, compared less favorably with the actual mountain. Further, he could see now how sloppily they had been developed, stains, dust spots, small patches where the color was the wrong tone. He rented the car, and went back to the city and this time returned with an enlarger and darkroom equipment. He took more pictures, then blacked out the bathroom and went in and developed his first roll. He liked the instant service. The waiting had killed him. And he was absolutely careful about dust, and keeping the temperature right, and of course had made sure all his chemicals were fresh. He started with a roll of black and white, figuring after he got the hang of it, he would return to color. But when he showed her the results she said, "Do you know what? It's better in black and white than it was in color." "How can that be?" he said, but he was only arguing from logic, because now that she had said it, he could see it too.

He caught the mountain in a few more moods, and was at least moderately pleased with the results. He thought he was learning better to make the camera record what he saw. But there were calls on his time as well. He was becoming quite proficient with the language, and was now helping the budding language school—it had been started by talented and ambitious young students with not much money or expertise. Rather than using textbooks based on some professor's notion of the most used words and grammatical constructions, they had adopted his technique of taping actual speech in the shops and on the streets, and using that—the language really used every day—as the basis of each lesson. The school, as the tourists began returning in the spring, began operating profitably and gained a reputation, and they got a publisher interested in the textbook they were putting together based on their new method. He showed them how to set up records and keep books, drafted the English parts of the textbook, and even went with them to take their petition to the provincial government to be licensed as a corporation. So that very often the camera sat pointing at the mountain through its various moods, but no one was there to press the cable release. And when he did complete a roll of film, it sat for weeks before he had a chance to develop it.

He had not lost any of his 60 extra pounds, but nevertheless bought some running shoes and started running. "I don't know why you bother to get advice from people if you're not going to follow it," she said. "I probably know my strengths and weaknesses better than a doctor who's only seen me a couple of times," he said. "You don't have any sense at all of your weaknesses. That's why you worked too hard and had to see the doctor in the first place." "It was just nerves, nothing physical." "He said that your heart—" "My heart's okay." "Your problem is you don't respect anyone or anything except yourself. You'd think after you got that head injury in college you would have realized you're not immortal." "You'll notice it's my head I've gone on to make my living with. Your problem is you respect everything and everybody *except* yourself. You have no concept of how strong you are in your own way. And how good. You're like an angel come back to earth sometimes. People think *I'm* good, just because I'm connected to you."

There was certainly no way she could respond to that, and he took off downstairs running.

* * *

Spring was progressing, the weather clearing. The mountain, which had often been obscured behind clouds and mist, was not visible again, but the camera and tripod, in the way of everything she wanted to do in the front room, was seldom used, though he often paused meditatively to look through the view finder. They were still trying to get the school officially licensed but the red tape was incredible. She noticed he was beginning to eat more, a bad sign. He kept up with his running faithfully, each day running as far up the mountain as the road went and back. Most days now this sweaty shaggy bear of a man, looking even more ludicrous, brought back in his big hand a tiny new spring flower for her to paint. She was deluged by the bounty. Twenty flowers withered and died while she struggled to paint one. It might take her all day to paint one petal—and that was when she had all day to work on it. The old man was better, but the wife was ill, and this was worse than the other way around, because she had to nurse his wife as well as shop and clean, plus trying to keep the old man from sinking into depression. Then the woman was well, and both of them had come through another winter, the time when old people die if they are going to, and they were fiercely proud to have survived again. She had part of the day to herself again, and sat down to her paints and a tiny flower. He had taken a day off too, and set off running right after breakfast. She finished doing the breakfast dishes and came out to look at the mountain. The morning had started clear and warm without a leaf moving. But as she looked she saw a huge thunderhead rising up directly out of the summit of the mountain. She looked with her binoculars and saw it seething and pumping. There was not a sound. She tried to go to her painting, but in a few minutes was back looking at the mountain. The cloud rose ten thousand feet straight above it in the still air, solid as an iceberg. While she looked she saw a flicker of light through it. Trees only grew to about the 3000 foot line, so for the last few miles he would be above them, and would himself be the highest point on the exposed road. She wrung her hands helplessly. Two thick bolts of lightning struck the mountain in quick succession, jarring into it like fists. She set her jaw grimly, and went down to the garage two blocks from them, the one he always went to, and rented a car. "I know I'm just being stupid," she said to herself, but she drove like the wind. She came out above the trees and saw the lone runner near the end of the road several switchbacks ahead of her. The sky was black but there was complete stillness in the air. She downshifted and spun around the switchbacks, sending up a skein of gravel against the safety railings. From 100 yards distance she could see the hair was standing straight up around his head like an eerie aurora. He ran on, totally absorbed in what he was doing.

He reached the top of the road, the turn-around point, shrugging the stopwatch out of his pocket and raising it up to look at his elapsed time. With the other hand he was trying abstractedly to smooth down his hair. *Heart-attack, goodbye*

She didn't hear the stupendous crack of thunder either, she was too intent on getting the car stopped and getting out beside him, which she did in seconds, smoke still rising from the charred pieces remaining of his sneakers, a black after-image dividing her vision. She rolled him onto his back and put the side of her head to his vast sinewed ribcage. He was not breathing, nor could she detect a heartbeat. This was one process she did know something about. Because of the time she spent with old people, she had made herself take an advanced first aid course. She thumped at the huge chest, the defunct bellows, with her tiny fists, but knew that was not enough, and stood up on his chest and bounced her whole weight on it at one second intervals, and the heart, like a well-tuned engine, caught at the first try. Then she jutted out the sand-papery lower jaw, to open the wind pipe, and covered his mouth with hers, and blew in her child's breath as hard as she could, and again he took the spark of life from her, and was breathing. She has no idea how she got him into the car, only knows that the next day all the muscles down her side were pulled and were never quite right again.

In the hospital they told her she had plainly saved his life by being there at that second and knowing just what to do. It was a miracle, they kept saying. She began to find that a bit insulting. They found he had lost 60 pounds at the moment he was struck, body fluids simply vaporized, and every muscle in his body was shredded, and his calves and feet severely burned. He was already fully conscious and discussing with the doctor what steps he would need to take in his recovery, and how soon he could think about starting up his running again. He looked up at her, grinning. "You've got your nerve, following me around and thinking you know better than I do."

Everyone except him was amazed at the speed of his recovery. In less time than can be imagined he was back at the apartment, getting around a little bit on crutches. She gave him all her time, but he was very undemanding, a surprisingly good, obedient patient. Also he was obsessed again. This time, of all things, with photographing a plain drinking glass not quite full of water. Oh, he continued to photograph the whole mountain, and he continued, by telephone, doing some of the business of the language school, but maybe he had been just a bit chastened, and wanted to cover his bets by also trying to come at the whole by looking closely at one of its parts.

"You can't believe how challenging this is," he told her. "I must have taken fifty pictures of this thing and I still am just learning what to see in it."

She for her part continued her exacting painting of the single leaf, the single flower, but at moments during the day she let her point of focus come out a bit. She picked up her sheet of platted-out outlines of the mountain. None of the paintings took her more than two or three minutes to do. She filled sheet after sheet, her confidence and speed growing. She had been to that mountain, and felt she knew something about it. He had arrived at one position, one angle of light, that he thought was perfect, and he thought he was beginning to learn exactly how he wanted to develop the negative. By then however their time was up and they left the island.

LADY OF SPAIN

ROBERT TAYLOR, JR.

Robert Taylor, Jr., grew up in Oklahoma City, attended the University of Oklahoma, and now lives in Lewisburg, Pennsylvania. His outlaw book, *Loving Belle Starr,* was published in 1984, and a novel, *Fiddle and Bow,* appeared in 1985 (both from Algonquin Books).

When the Lady of Spain revealed herself to me, I was fourteen years old, the owner of an Allstate motorscooter and a large and shining Polina accordion. The accordion lessons had begun several years earlier with a tiny rented instrument and were held in the Sunday school room of the Britton Baptist Church. My teacher, a red-cheeked, dark-haired woman named Lorena Harris, wore little makeup and pinned her soft dark hair atop her head in a circle capped by a delicate net. I thought her the member of a strict religious sect, perhaps a Nazarene. The Nazarenes, my father once told me, had founded the town of Bethany, then a few miles away from Oklahoma City instead of surrounded by it, and to this day Bethany permitted neither the sale of tobacco nor the showing of movies. I also had the notion that the Nazarenes had no musical instruments in their church—that they only sang their hymns, and therefore would surely scorn Miss Harris' beautiful accordion, so lavishly trimmed in chrome and pearl. I entertained the idea that she might keep it a secret from them, lead two lives or more, like the spies on television who, throughout that innocent decade, kept track of communists, and this was a pleasant notion that bore much embellishment. Late at night when I grew bored with the radio broadcasts of the latest humiliation of the Oklahoma City Indians, I saw her take her accordion from its plush velvet case, strap it effortlessly to her chest, and begin to play, somewhere in smokeless, movieless Bethany, secret melodies, intricate versions of "Lady of Spain," "Dark Eyes," "La Golondrina." I always imagined her alone, by herself in a room, a version of myself, doomed to solitude but redeemed by strong feeling.

Closed up in my room with bunk beds, an old desk of my father's, and plastic model airplanes dangling above me from the ceiling, I played my accordion for Lorena Harris and for my mother. For Miss Harris I played "Blue Moon," "Sentimental Journey," "Are You Lonesome Tonight"; for my mother, "Whispering Hope," "Nearer My God to Thee," "Sweet Hour of Prayer." The accordion was costly, paid for in large part by money that my mother had managed to put aside from her grocery allowance. It had ten shifts on the treble, so that a single note might be made to sound at one moment rich and deep like an organ and in the next shrill and high like a piccolo. Three shifts lined the bass, and a marvelous black and white zig-zag design decorated the front of the bellows. Its weight alone bespoke a vast and intricate interior, a secret realm of lever and wheel. What made the sound? A system of trembling reeds, Miss Harris told me. In my mind the word *reed* was highly significant. It was Biblical. I remembered that among the reeds of the Nile the baby Moses had been hidden from the Pharaoh.

My father had to travel days at a time from one end of Oklahoma to the other, selling class rings and diplomas and band uniforms to reluctant school districts. I had heard stories of his tribulations. It was all politics, he said. His competitors were expert at politicking a superintendent. They did not permit their products to stand on merit. They sold their souls and robbed him of his rightful customers. I imagined smooth-talking, pallid men, plump in pinstriped suits and black and white wing-tipped oxfords. They drove big somber Buicks and their daughters were cheerleaders, their sons quarterbacks.

Such children I had nothing to do with. Anyway, they did not seek me out. My best friend Steve, who had only recently given up his accordion lessons in order to devote more time to baseball, was a quiet, nice church-going boy like myself. I knew he had betrayed something important when he quit his accordion lessons. His mother, I remember, attended all his lessons and had a small beginners' accordion of her own that she practiced on, using Steve's music. I heard her play on several occasions, late afternoons when, out of a need for companionship, I played catch with Steve. The songs floated forth from her bedroom as if from a phonograph record, distant and dreamy. Even the bright polkas sounded plaintive and sweet. Several years older than my mother, Steve's mother wore dresses rich with eyelets and lace. Her husband scowled a lot, though he was cheerful enough when spoken to. He was a U. S. Marshal. Once I saw his picture in the *Daily Oklahoman.* He was handcuffed to the notorious murderer of entire families, Billy Cook, and although considerably shorter than the killer he looked like he meant business.

My father was surely cut out for better things than measuring the breadth of the fingers of high school juniors for their class rings, the length of their legs for band uniforms. I knew that given the opportunity he would do nothing at all, or else be an artist. A high school teacher of his had urged him to pursue a career in commercial art, but he had graduated from high school in 1932 and had to take what he could get. Selling, he once told me, was the backbone of the country. But there was no conviction in his voice.

During this time his was a quiet presence in the house. He enjoyed a cigar with his evening paper. Then he went out to the office that he had built a few summers ago adjoining our garage, where he worked evenings and sometimes well into the night on his designs for class rings. I liked going out there and was always pleased when asked to deliver a telephone message from a customer, usually some superintendent or principal cancelling an appointment. After relaying the message, I sat on a small sofa just behind the desk, lingering amidst an amazing clutter of papers—what could they have been—orders, bills, magazines, unfinished designs. I remember liking to find copies of the newsletter put out by the company that he worked for, Star Engraving Company of Houston, Texas, a mimeographed pamphlet really, printed on a dozen or so pastel sheets stapled together, its chief function to report on the volume of business done by the sales force, ranking the top salesmen in various categories (rings, caps and gowns, diplomas, invitations, and the like). Finding my father's name most often near the top of each list, I was proud. Sometimes there were notes written by the sales manager or even the president of the company congratulating selected men, the week's leaders.

My father worked diligently at his broad desk, a cigar gone out in the ashtray, a crooked-neck fluorescent lamp glowing and humming softly above his head. Frequently he used a magnifying glass, holding it steady a few inches from the sketch, which might have been a representation of a lion's head or the entrance-way to a high school, an Indian's profile or a crouching tiger, or a coiled rattler. Once he had drawn (not for a ring design, of course) a picture of my mother, a pencil sketch of her head in profile, a good likeness and life-size, her long hair upswept in front and cascading into tiny curls on the side and in the back. It was done, I had been told by her, when she was pregnant with me. She looked stern, even a little angry, but a certain serenity also came through. The picture hung in a white frame above their bed and I thought it a very romantic thing to have drawn and wished that I had such a gift.

What do you think of this, he said, pausing to show me what he worked on. Pretty good, eh. There's nothing in McDowell's line to compete with this.

I believed him an excellent artist, but except for these moments of pride in a new design he spoke disparagingly of his talent. It had been compromised, he said, spoiled before it could properly be developed.

The Allstate motorscooter was the cheapest offered by Sears, its engine only slightly larger than the one on my father's power mower. It had a foot brake and tires the diameter of hubcaps. On it I was nonetheless enabled to crisscross Oklahoma City, circle it, ride out Western Avenue until on either side of me the plains stretched endless, the trees disappeared, and the strong wind in my face smelled of hay and occasionally of cattle or horses. Back in town, I paid visits to girls and took them for rides. They had to ride behind me on the tractor-style seat, their legs straddling my hips, their arms wrapped tightly around my chest. Often I could feel their hair brush against the back of my neck, and I shivered and wished, as we crept up a slight rise, the throttle wide open, for more speed, more power.

That summer I worked as a carhop at the Orange Julius stand on May Avenue, near the Lakewood and Lakeside Shopping Centers. Sometimes carloads of teenaged girls came in. These girls, mightily rouged and perfumed, their dark mascaraed eyes flashing, hinted in no uncertain terms of the wonderful pleasures one might have in the back seat of their father's Pontiac or Olds 88. I flirted mercilessly and cultivated a swagger, a nonchalant wink, a rakish grin. They told me I was cute, oh so much cuter than the boys their own age, and I began to fancy that I would always have a taste for older women. It did not surprise me that the girls seldom left a tip. Wasn't the feeling that we had so briefly shared beyond the realm of appetite and commerce?

Steve, who also worked at the Orange Julius stand, said that if he ever had the chance, he would be in that back seat in a jiffy. I feared for his soul, but suspected that he wasn't as likely as I was to be put to the test. My attraction, I believed, was somehow connected to playing the accordion, and Steve had left his accordion playing to his mother.

What would you do, I asked him, if you were in the back seat of one of those cars with girls in them.

We were picking up trash on the lot during a lull in customers, stabbing at paper cups and wadded napkins with our spears, as we called the broomsticks with nails in the end.

I would know, Steve said. I'd know what to do all right.

What.

It all depends.

If they let you kiss them then, what would you do?

It still all depends.

On what.

It was not the ethics of the situation that concerned me. I was after reliable information, and suspected that Steve might have known something that I didn't. I knew precious little, it seemed to me. My two sisters were younger than I was and no help. My curiosity was not just academic. Having kissed a girl before, I was keen on repeating the experience. Was it as pleasant for the girl though? That's what I couldn't imagine. A memory that I cherished was of a party given by my cousin and a few of her girlfriends at which kissing was the object of several games. These girls were a year older than I was, dazzling in their promise, with such smooth red lips and soft warm cheeks, the air surrounding them thick with the scent of a variety of perfumes. A boy was mysteriously chosen and led into a darkened room where one of the girls awaited him, kissed him before he could properly see her, and then he was sent back out to the lighted room, to be greeted by giggles and jeers. I wanted to stay in that darkened room. Let them laugh—in there I wouldn't hear a thing.

That night on the lot of the Orange Julius stand, Steve seemed annoyed by my question, but at last said that what you did after a girl let you kiss her depended on whether she let you kiss her on the cheek or on the mouth.

On the mouth, I said.

Then you just keep kissing her until she says quit it.

What if she doesn't say quit.

They always say quit.

A car came in then—my customer. The girl in this car sat very close to her date, and her hand rested on his thigh. I was the one she looked at—there was no mistaking it—and in that look I suddenly seemed to see all I needed to know. I vowed to memorize her eyes, and also the shape of that hand resting securely on her date's thigh. It was a small hand, the fingernails long and red. Her scent, I told myself, was like fresh almonds, her voice like a love song. She said, I could drink a pint. And her date said, Two pints, thick, no straws. When I picked up their tray after they were finished, she winked at me. Her boyfriend, a big guy in a letter jacket, left no tip. He sprayed gravel getting out of the lot and laid down rubber on May Avenue. Wherever he was taking her, he was in a big hurry. Too big a hurry, I concluded. I knew now that I would treat her different. I'd take my time.

This was the summer that my accordion teacher got married. I saw the man briefly one day as I was leaving my lesson. Leaning against the fender of her car, he smoked a cigarette and seemed on the verge of sleep. Tall and lanky, long-necked and tightly jeaned, he had a head shaped like the grill of an Edsel, with hair congealing into dark ribbon-like strands that curved over his head and curled at the upper reaches of his neck. I could not imagine him with a regular job, or even with one such as my father had. He would stand around like that all day, smoking, contemplating the trees, leaning on some fender. The money from my lessons—I saw it in a flash—would make possible his squalid languor.

Have a good lesson? my mother asked.

It was okay, I said, keeping my eye on the new husband as Mother pulled the car onto Britton Road.

I hope you did, she said. I certainly hope you had a good lesson. It means a lot to have a good lesson.

That was Mr. Cox back there, wasn't it.

Mr. Cox?

Miss Harris' husband.

I didn't see anyone.

He was right there. Leaning against her car.

I must not have noticed.

I'm sure it was him.

Well, maybe it was.

It was him all right.

Maybe it was. I wouldn't know the man if I saw him. I've got other things on my mind.

What could she see in a man like that.

I said I didn't see him.

Where are we going.

Home.

We don't usually go this way.

We had passed Western Avenue and now were in Britton, which was like a small town, though really part of Oklahoma City, on the very edge of it. There was a Main Street with a T. G. & Y. store, a C. R. Anthony Department Store, a Western Auto, and a drugstore that had a good soda fountain. Western Avenue connected it to the city, to supermarkets and shopping centers and subdivisions such as Nichols Hills, where we lived. I rode here often on my motorscooter and liked to imagine that I had come to a town far away from Oklahoma City, perhaps in Texas or New Mexico. In the drugstore I purchased cherry cokes and then examined the rack of paperback books near the cash register to see if there were any new titles among the westerns and detective thrillers and to read the covers avidly. I picked up a copy of *Playboy*, then a bold new magazine, and discreetly flipped to the centerfold photograph, careful not to linger too long on it before putting it down and then feigning interest in *Field and Stream* or, even duller, *Sports Illustrated.*

At the drugstore my mother pulled into a parking space.

You drive, she said.

Since I had never driven a car before—aside from backing and pulling forward on the driveway—this command came as a surprise.

You've got to learn sometime, she said. She took a deep breath and opened the door. I realized that I was to trade places with her, and I managed to do as she did, get out and cross to the other side, the driver's side.

Have I said that my mother was a beautiful woman? She was. I found this somewhat of an embarrassment, another instance of how my family was not right. Mothers were supposed to be plump and gray, slightly younger versions of grandmothers, but mine was trim and dark, with auburn hair and hazel eyes that flashed brilliantly. Around the house during the summer she wore shorts and high-heeled wedge sandals, usually with a halter top. When she picked me up at my accordion lesson she was on her way home from the volunteer work that she did every Thursday at the big Veterans' Hospital on N. E. 13th Street, and so she always wore what she called her gray lady uniform, in fact a gray dress rather like a nurse's uniform except for the gray color. But on this Thursday she wore a scoop-necked blouse, white with bright red and green trim around the neckline, and a flowing full skirt, also white, trimmed with the same bright colors as the blouse. So preoccupied with scorn of my music teacher's husband, I had not even noticed this bold departure from her usual Thursday style of dress until, seated at the wheel of her DeSoto, I watched her get in beside me, the engine running smoothly, air conditioner humming.

Push the lever to *R*, she said. You know how to back up. Just watch where you're going.

Where are we going?

I don't know. For God's sake, I don't know. Nowhere. Anywhere. Will you just go, please.

But I had been struck by two unnerving realizations: first, that I was scared to death to back into the traffic that was steadily coursing through Britton, and, second, that my mother was upset. Tears were in her eyes, and she began to rummage through her purse, at last pulling forth a crumpled tissue. It did not seem the right time for a driving lesson. The car loomed large and lethal, but at the same time was dangerously vulnerable. I kicked at the brake pedal and pretended to have trouble finding *R* on the gear-shift column.

I don't know, I said. Maybe there's too much traffic.

You just have to watch where you're going, she said, wiping at her eyes with the tattered, lipstick-stained tissue. It will be all right. Just go.

And so I backed the big DeSoto out onto Britton Road ever so slowly, looking from one side to the other. Sure enough, a car had to stop in order to allow me onto the street. Mortified, I pressed the accelerator. The immediate surge forward took my breath away. I gripped the wheel firmly and vowed to remain calm. One only had to concentrate, watch the road ahead, glance now and then into the rearview mirror. Would I have to stop? No, I had traveled this route often on my motorscooter and knew that there was no stoplight or sign between us and the open highway. Once outside Britton—a matter of only several blocks—traffic would fall off, the wide flat prairie land on either side of us, the highway stretching straight ahead as far as the eye could see. The knowledge of this ahead was comforting, and as we crept past the last of the storefronts, and then at last the frame houses on their small treeless lawns gave way to the full breadth of the sky and the land leveled out into immensity, I was certain that I could drive this DeSoto to the end of the continent if need be.

My mother began to sob, softly at first, so that I could easily enough pretend not to notice, and in fact I succeeded quite well in not noticing, such fun it was to see the highway ahead, to feel the power of the big engine, a hundred times greater than that of my motorscooter, that strange sense of limitlessness, as if this were my life itself opening up before me, a straight line to eternity.

I glanced at the speedometer. We were going sixty-five miles per hour, yet scarcely seemed to move, so vast was the land that we moved across. The sobbing had grown louder, and, in the quickest of glances, I saw that she covered her face in her hands. The crumpled tissue had fallen to her lap.

It's no good, she said. Everything's all wrong. Every time you think things are getting better, they only get worse.

I didn't know what to say. Really she didn't seem to be addressing me, but rather talking to herself. Perhaps she didn't mean for me to have heard. The road was smooth. Soon we would come to the Edmond turnoff. A few distant trees bent to the strong wind and now and then a red sworl of dust whipped across the highway. The sky was pale blue, cloudless. I was absolutely confident.

Keep going, my mother said. I can't go back yet. I don't care if we end up in Tulsa. I'll tell you when to stop.

I drove and drove. We skirted the city, staying always on the edge of it, away from the traffic, making an almost complete circle by the end. It is one of the most dreamlike memories that I have, those dizzying plains all around, the red soil badly eroded, the tufts of sharply pointed weeds bordering the highway, now and then the skyline of the city appearing, those twin bank buildings rising like grand gray monuments tall and eternal from the sealike vastness, now to the west, now to the north, at last again to the south, and then windmills in the middle of nowhere or oil derricks thumping steadily into the depths of a land that looked as dry as the dust ever blowing across it. The car rolled along, heavy and smooth and quiet. My mother's tears subsided. She told me about the sorrow of her life, and her voice might have been the very sound of the landscape. I cannot imagine that place, that straight highway, those gullies and the red flat land, without hearing again her voice as it came to me across the car, the grief in it as pure as any I have ever known.

The reason for my mother's not wearing her gray lady uniform on that particular afternoon was that there had been a special party on the ward. The veterans had seemed to languish of late, and the women who gave their own time to cheer up the men had agreed that something extraordinary had to be done. Thus the party. It was to be, my mother said, a *real* party. Everyone was to dress up for the occasion in his best clothes. There was to be music, dancing, entertainment, refreshments, the ward decorated with bright-colored streamers and balloons. The

balloons would contain messages and the veterans were to be encour-
aged to puncture those balloons and find the messages, which would be
cheerful, optimistic phrases from *The Prophet* and *The Power of Positive
Thinking*. My mother did not care for this last idea. It was treating
them like children, she argued, when what they needed was to be
treated as responsible adults. How else were they to regain their pride
and dignity. She was overruled. The men of the ward were *not* like
other men. In many ways they were like little boys—boys who had been
asked to assume the responsibilities of manhood before they were ready.
They needed to find their lost childhoods. My mother saw that there
was no arguing with the other women. At least they had accepted her
suggestion that uniforms be put aside in favor of nicer clothes, even
though one of them said quite vehemently that to do so was to invite
trouble. Wasn't that silly, my mother said to me, and of course I agreed,
having no idea what such trouble would mean.

I was never to find out exactly what did happen at that Thursday's
party to make her so unhappy, though she talked to me often of her
work with the veterans, of how much that work meant to her and at last
of the one veteran that she took a very special interest in. Sometimes we
went for long drives similar to that first one, drives that she spoke of to
my sisters and my father as instruction, but increasingly that instruction occurred late at night in my room, when I lay in the top bunk of
my bed only half awake. Sometimes she actually slept in the bottom
bunk—other times she returned to her own bed before dawn. I confess
that sometimes, tired from a particularly busy night carhopping at the
Orange Julius stand, I fell asleep as she talked. Nonetheless, I remember
with absolute clarity the underlying sorrow, the sense of lamentation
and attendant relief, the strange feeling of shared grief, the notion that I
had become for her a confidante, as much sister as son.

I constructed in my own mind a version of the Thursday party,
seemed at last to see it as though I had been there. I put this version
together as I rode out the highways that crossed wheat fields and
prairies, rutted soil and pasture, the same territory we covered in the
DeSoto for my instruction. The special veteran would have been waiting for her. He was a lot like me, she had told me, not in looks of
course, but in temperament. *Sensitive* was the word she used. Shy. Kept

to himself and thought a lot. Liked to read, and read everything he could get his hands on. She brought him books, paperbacks that she purchased at Rector's downtown, and he received them eagerly, gratefully.

He never had a chance, she said. His father mistreated him and then he was drafted and sent to Korea. Something bad happened to him over there. Maybe something bad happens to them all, but some can't forget it. Some are haunted by what they had to go through. Can you imagine? It's hard for us to imagine.

I could imagine.

She would have had a book for him on that Thursday, a mystery novel with a lurid cover, carried in her large straw handbag. He would stand to one side of a group of talkative men, somewhat taller than most of them, his face in shadow. Music comes from a portable record player, one similar to my sisters', the size of one of my father's suitcases, with the speaker across the front. It is lively music, music to jitterbug to, to rhumba or samba to. Xavier Cugat, Tommy Dorsey, Bing Crosby. Occasionally a ballad sung by Jo Stafford or Margaret Whiting, a love song, not too sad. Records the women would have brought from home, records such as my parents had, in book-like albums, six big 78's per album, each in its own slot within. Some of the men bat at the balloons. Others dance—this part was harder to imagine. I was no dancer myself, and I concluded that neither would her veteran be. But the others—I had little to go on, junior high school formals, to which the girls wore stiff gauzy dresses.

She would encourage him to dance, for she was a good dancer herself. I had heard my father say so, and even remember seeing him dance with her in our living room. They reminded me of Fred Astaire and Ginger Rogers, whose movies my sisters loved to watch on television, my father spinning her and twirling her, drawing her close, dancing cheek-to-cheek, twirling again so that her full skirt fanned outward and she began to laugh, saying, That's enough now. You'll knock something over. This room is too small, the way you dance! Oh, my father said, you always spoil the fun. Just like your mother! Come on. Let's show the kids what real dancing is like.

But she had had enough, and so the best I could do was picture something like that, incomplete but lovely while it lasted. For the others though, not for my mother and the veteran whom she wished to help. Off to the side the two of them stand. She looks pretty in her white dress, so pretty that the other women are envious.

You should dance, she says. Dancing is good for you.

No, he says, I don't feel like dancing.

Well, would you like a cup of punch then?

No, thanks.

I've brought you a book.

I'm tired of reading.

And with that he turns and leaves her, making his way across the crowded dance floor, through the crepe paper streamers and the floating balloons and at last down a long narrow hallway and into the tiny room where she would not be permitted to follow him. The room would have bunk beds—made of black metal though, not varnished maple like mine —and a single curtainless window with bars on the outside. He would throw himself upon the bottom bunk and glower at the mattress springs above him, his jaw clenched tightly. Then his terrible memories overcome him and he closes his eyes, sinks into the nightmare of war, bombs flashing and exploding all around him, friends shrieking and dying everywhere.

My mother makes her apologies to the other women.

I have to take my son to his music lesson, she says. He can't carry that heavy accordion on his motorscooter.

She sought understanding from me. While I pretended to understand, much in fact escaped me. I believe I learned to become a good listener, and perhaps, after all, that is a kind of understanding. Coming home late from the Orange Julius stand, my lungs filled with the sweet night air, I sat on the living room floor of the silent house and counted my earnings, then went to bed and awaited my mother's arrival in the bunk beneath me. Sometimes I heard a sound from my parents' bedroom first, the raised voice of my father, and then their door opening, shutting, and her soft footsteps in the hall. I imagine her pausing to look into my sisters' bedroom, seeing them deep in their own dreams, motionless in their twin beds. Why had she not chosen one of them to confide in? One was too young surely, only seven at this time, but the other was just a year younger than I was. This one, however, Carolyn, the elder of the two, was considerably more spirited than I, even scrappy, and often argued long and hard with her mother over issues that I would have let pass as trivial. She seemed to me in fact to go out of her way to pick a fight, and both girls got along better with their daddy, though even he could become the focus of their tempers. There is something with mothers and daughters, finally and significantly, that does not exist with mothers and sons: fundamental antagonism, no doubt a rivalry. Whatever, I was chosen and not one of my sisters.

She came to my doorway and I heard her breathing, even now hear it, and smell again the scent of her perfume, a smell in memory more carnal than floral. Are you asleep, she asks. I know that an answer is not required. She enters my room, and I hear her pull back the bedspread, the sheets, and then feel the bedframe move slightly as she eases herself into the bunk beneath mine. Are you awake, she asks. This time I say yes.

Once she said this: I knew nothing about men, not the first thing about love. My mother told me nothing. I was married to another man before your father. I was too young and though I cared deeply for him and he loved me that marriage failed. I thought that I would never marry again.

All my life, she said another time, has been a sacrifice for others. I didn't finish high school because my father needed me to bring in an extra paycheck to help support the family. I was the oldest, and happy to help. I know that he was grateful. I worked in Baker's Shoe Store downtown, selling hosiery, and then at the jewelry counter of John A. Brown's. That's where I met your father, and when we were married another long sacrifice began. I learned what it meant to be a mother as well as a wife, to be responsible for a home. Please understand. I don't resent what I've been given. I love my children, all of you. But I have to ask—do you understand this—when my own time will come, when I can begin to live for myself. Is that so much to ask for, a life of my own?

I said no, that it certainly was not, but I really had no idea what it would mean for her to lead a life of her own. I responded on an abstract level, guided only by a sense of fairness. Life was short, she said, and was one's own. You could kill the life within you if you neglected it. The life within—that's what mattered, that's what must not be allowed to die. It had to be kept alive.

From their hidden homes in the big elm outside my window, the crickets whirred, and above the branches that I loved so much to climb upon in the daytime, the stars no doubt held their own in the broad night sky. Everywhere an eloquence that would not—no matter how much it insist—be comprehended.

I did not practice my accordion often in the summer, but some mornings before the heat grew deadly I strapped the heavy instrument to my chest and labored mightily to perfect "Claire de Lune" or "Santa Lucia" or *"The Washington Post* March." My own favorite was something called "Sweet Sugar," a fox-trot in the key, if I remember correctly, of B-flat. Dutifully, to please Lorena Harris (now Mrs. Cox), I worked on chromatic scales, on arpeggios, on bass runs. In the afternoons I rode my motorscooter or had my instruction in the DeSoto.

Before I knew it, August came. In that month heat was general, day and night. My father purchased a small air conditioner, still somewhat of a novelty in those days, and had it installed in a living room window. This room, shut off from the others in order to keep the chilled air effective, became a cool refuge. When the air conditioner was turned on in mid-morning, we all sat around it, watching "Queen for a Day" or reruns of "My Little Margie" or the old movie musicals that my sisters were so fond of. Summer was my father's off-season, since the high schools that he called on were not in session, and so he often sat there in his big green chair, sometimes with a *Daily Oklahoman,* the cigar smoke puffing out from behind it. Mother kept busy in the kitchen or in the back of the house, claiming that the heat did not bother her, though frequently joining us by mid-afternoon—the heat of the day, as she called this time. On milder mornings she might be found stretched out on a towel in the backyard, tanning her legs.

In our talks she came to speak less of her youth—of her overly stern mother and sweetly indulgent father—and more of her dissatisfaction with my father. They argued fiercely all during those years. This had become simply a fact of our family life. Why don't they get divorced,

Carolyn wondered. How can two people live together and fight all the time. It made no sense to me either, but mine was not an inquiring mind in those days—if it *ever* has been! Maybe they still love each other, I said to Carolyn. In my heart I knew that this could not be true. Hadn't I heard her say as much.

She began to urge me to visit the ward with her.

I've told the men about you, she said. It would mean so much if you came to visit them.

She wanted me to play my accordion for them. "Lady of Spain," she kept saying. Wouldn't I play "Lady of Spain" for the men on the ward.

It was the last thing I would have chosen to do to end the summer, but there was no resisting her. She wanted "Lady of Spain." She would have it. I thought that she might have wanted "Whispering Hope" or perhaps my last recital piece, a complicated arrangement of "The Stars and Stripes Forever" that she had praised fervently, even though I'd made several mistakes and left out an entire section. But it made no difference to me. I'd played "Lady of Spain" almost from the start of my lessons—in increasingly difficult arrangements—and was fond enough of its quick pace and rollicking rhythm. In the sixth grade I'd played it for my girlfriend, who did a dance to it with castanets, on a program for the entire school. Perhaps it was that triumph that my mother remembered. Or perhaps the melody was a favorite of one of the men. Whatever, she had got it into her head that I would play "Lady of Spain."

All right, I said. When?

Thursday, she said.

This gave me five days to prepare myself. Once I had agreed, and the date was set, I began to feel intensely nervous, the way I always felt before those yearly recitals in the Baptist churches that Lorena Harris found for her students to perform in. The more recitals I played in, the more nervous I became beforehand. What got me through was the thought that it would soon be over.

The dynamics of "Lady of Spain" were crucial. So Lorena Harris had taught me, and as I took out the accordion and slid my shoulders into its cushioned straps I seemed to see her clearly before me. She wore a sky blue blouse of thin gauzy material and a tiered skirt that made a soft swish when she crossed her legs. A strand of her dark hair had come loose from her hair net and the top button of her blouse was undone. Soft here, she says, raising a finger to her lips. Now *crescendo!*

Sometimes the student who had his lesson after me did not come, and my lesson continued overtime. We were surrounded by tiny folding chairs and back of us hung a large bulletin board filled with color pictures of Jesus at the important stages of his life, from manger to cross. On a desk to one side of Lorena Harris the Sunday school lesson books were stacked in three even ranks. A banner across one wall displayed in large black letters John 3:16, For God so loved the world that he gave his only begotten son. . . .

My mother would be waiting in the car of course, but so would the new husband of Lorena Harris. It was pleasant to think that he was kept waiting. I imagined it while unsnapping the bellows of the accordion, saw him as I listened to the air flow through the mysterious corridors of that strange instrument. He wore pink-soled suede shoes and leaned on the fender of her little Plymouth, his palms pressed against the clean and shining metal. He would have to wait. "Lady of Spain," I played. *Lady of Spain I adore you.* And when I was finished, I played it again.

I practiced hard for the men. As I have said, I was scared to death. There was an edge to this fright that made it worse by far than the usual recital nervousness. Who, after all, were these men that were so eager to hear me play? What did a veteran look like? They have feelings, my mother had told me, just the same as you and me, only they've never been given a chance. But what would they look like?

At the Orange Julius stand the lights that encircled the lot bobbed back and forth in the strong wind, and I fancied them eyes, the eyes of the veterans. With the girls who drove up in their fathers' big cars, I flirted as usual, but my heart was not in it.

I asked my father if sometime in the fall I might go along with him on one of his sales trips. I must have been feeling guilty for having agreed to play on the ward. Unlike those veterans, he had never been to war. When the Japanese bombed Pearl Harbor, he had gone down to enlist, but was turned away because he had recently become a father—I was the child, of course.

Yes, he would take me along with him sometime. He did not look up from the book he was reading—I think it must have been Sandburg's *Young Abe Lincoln*—and did not remove the cigar from his mouth. The floor lamp shone brightly on his head, through his thinning hair and onto his pink scalp. When my mother and I left for the Veterans' Hospital, he was not home. I thought it just as well. He prided himself on her not having to work outside of the house and did not even approve of her volunteer work. Perhaps also he was suspicious, a little jealous. He had good reason to be. Years later, when my mother at last went through with her divorce, she told him she planned to marry one of these veterans. And she did. I could not have foretold such an event, but I sensed the reason in my father's fear of her work.

I hope you know how much this means to me, she said to me in the car.

I assured her I did.

It did not matter how well I played, she said. It was the gesture itself that counted.

I told her I understood.

I did not. Otherwise why would I be shaking so? When at last it came time to strap on the instrument, I felt faint. The great black thing was impossibly heavy.

The men milled about, tall and short, young and old. Some wore blue pajamas with white trim at the sleeve and pants-cuff. Others dressed as if for a formal ball, white shirts and bow ties, gleaming black shoes. Still others wore tee shirts and blue jeans. I thought there were hundreds of them, but surely there could not have been more than thirty. The room itself was small. Couches and chairs had been pushed back against the walls, and some of the older men, their mouths hanging open and eyelids half shut, slumped in the big cushions, clutched the arms of the chairs as if they expected sudden movement. Through the high oblong windows above the seated men, the glass so thick it was almost opaque, I saw the bars that I had imagined.

Gray ladies circulated among the men, carrying trays of paper cups and paper napkins. One of the women I had met before—she had come to our house on several occasions—but the others, perhaps there were six of them altogether, I had never seen. Yet they looked familiar. The gray dresses, of course, were identical, the same stiff uniform my mother wore. They smiled pleasantly, handing out the punch with ease. They might have been, I realized, the mothers of my friends.

My mother led me from group to group. *This is my son.* I shook innumerable hands, gripping firmly as my father had taught me. No, they invariably said, you couldn't have a son this big! They were all well-mannered, soft-spoken, polite. One man kissed my mother's hand.

I must have been brought there to meet the man my mother would later marry, though I remember no such meeting. The man I've come to know as my stepfather must have been one of the inconspicuous ones. He would have preferred watching me from a distance. My mother has explained to me that he cannot work because he refuses to be bossed around. They live on a government pension in an apartment complex near Will Rogers Field. Fearing robbery, they seldom go out. It is not an unfounded fear. Apartments all around them have been hit. He recently screwed shut their windows and during my last visit sat up all one night, his recliner turned to face the window, watching to be sure that no mischief was done to my poor, shabby car.

My father remarried—twice, but the first marriage was brief. She was a schoolteacher, a widow, and must have known right away that she had made a mistake. By then he had become a little wild, spending a lot of time in singles bars and not keeping track of where the money went. He lost his job—also more than once. Took to representing several companies, no longer handling profitable class rings and diplomas but textbooks, which he lugged around to the adopting school districts all over Oklahoma and the Texas panhandle. He no longer worked on his designs for class rings, of course. The house where he'd had his office was sold when he went into bankruptcy, not long after I started college. In the end he achieved a degree of stability. His last marriage lasted four years, until his death by heart failure quite suddenly last year. He was sixty-nine. He had begun to draw and paint again and was tolerably solvent.

That afternoon in the ward I played "Lady of Spain," and as I played, my fear passed away. In its place came a strange elation. The men listened, and their listening was of a different order from what I felt at recitals. They too might have played the tune, the sentimental quality of it giving way to a passion that went into the depths of all music and included my mother in it, drew her into it. *Lady of Spain!* When I saw her, that gray lady, that dark-eyed Nazarene atremble in the shadows of shades of men, it was as if I saw all the women I would love. This was music, this was the life within, this was the love I would sell my soul to possess. The air that set the reeds to quaver, God help me, might have been my own breath.

THE SINGING WELL

HELEN NORRIS

Helen Norris lives in Alabama. Her third novel and a collection of
short fiction, *The Christmas Wife,* which was nominated for the PEN/
Faulkner Award, were both published in the fall of 1985.

She was Emilu, named for two dead aunts, their names rammed together head-on like trains. And she thought as she lay on her back in
the corn, racing her feet a toe at a time up the head-high stalks, letting
one foot, then the other win: How you gonna handle these things that
come up? Get around these grown-ups pushin' you into some kinda way
you never wanted to be? But if you grew up so you could outsmart 'em,
then you did what they wanted. You got yourself grown and no turnin'
back. And maybe you couldn't stand it that way and waited around and
hoped you would die, with cancer even, just to get it over. The way it
seemed to her a lot of them did.

She was past eleven going on twelve and out of the torment of school
for a while. The days of summer were long at first and then ran away
like a rabbit flushed out of a blackberry bush. It scared her some, not
just to be looking down the barrel of school. Eleven years old and going
on twelve, she was staring right now both ways at once. She had got her
feet planted plumb in the ground to keep from getting any older at all.
But all the time she needed to get there. She had to know more, just to
stay the same.

She knew that she was smarter than Melissa, her sister who grew up
enough to get married. And smarter than Jo-Jo, who was off at their
Uncle Joe's for the summer. But it wasn't sufficient. This thing coming
at her was as big as a barn. Plowing her up into something else. Some-

times it was a freight train running her down. Sometimes she felt she was in there swimming and going under for the final time.

And then her grandfather came in July and she grabbed ahold of him to keep afloat.

How can you grow up when you have a grandfather like a Santa Claus with his beard cut off and he calls you little daughter and feeds you peanuts one at a time?

When he got out of the truck with her father, bigger almost than she had remembered, her mother said, "Emilu, run carry that box he's got in his hand. Lord knows what's in it." Emilu ran and dropped it hard coming up the steps. It flew apart, with an old uniform falling into the nandinas. And her mother said, "Well, I might've known. Well, bring it on in."

He was in his room when she got it together. The door was ajar. She waited in the hall. When she heard silence she edged in slowly with the box in her arms. He was sitting on the brass bed all hunched over, his chin down into the front of his shirt. His chest caved in and his face was like he was sorry he came.

She said to him then, "I folded it good." They looked at one another across the years between. Her mother had said he was seventy-seven. "It's got real pretty buttons sewed on."

He must have been, easy, six foot tall and big around. Like a football player with everything on, and shoulders big and round like a bear's. He had a great head of wavy white hair that curled around and under his ears. A sunned kind of face without many lines and blue-fire eyes that were almost hidden by the shelf of his brow and the white eyebrows that went so wild they must have been raked in the wrong direction. His hands were huge and brown from the sun, with white hairs matting on the backs of his fingers. His glance wavered, then returned to her. There was something in it different this visit from last.

"Are you Melissa?" he asked.

She was surprised and even shocked at his words. "No, Grandpa, I'm Emmy." He had called her that.

"Emmy?" He looked at the mirror above the green-painted dresser. "Not Melissa?"

"No, sir. . . Melissa got married and lives in Lafayette."

His glance swept her with such a lost look that she told him again, "I'm Emmy, sir."

He was very strange. But his blue eyes beheld her without a rejection. "Emmy. . . Emmy. . ." He moved a little inside his great frame and rubbed his arm. "I'll tell you how it is."

She waited for him to tell her but he seemed to have forgotten or thought better of it. "What, Grandpa?"

His eyes circled the room. "Is this the same room I stayed in before?"

"Sure, Grandpa."

"Same mirror and all?"

"Sure it is. . . You don't remember?"

He looked at her hard. "I'll tell you how it is: I don't recall you."

She was really amazed, but she tried not to show it. "We played euchre and all. You taught me, remember? Slapjack. Every day."

He shook his head slowly. "No. No, I don't recall." He spoke so sadly that she wanted to run away. "But it seems like whoever you are. . . it seems like a good thing, you standin' here now." He smiled at her almost. "We was good friends, you say?"

"We played euchre every day."

"What did I call you?"

"Emmy. You called me Emmy, like everybody does exceptin' Mama."

"You feel right. Somehow. How old would you be?"

"Eleven last month. I was nine before."

She couldn't wait to tell her mother.

"We shouldn't have him this summer. I said so to your father. He looks healthy. I will say that. I can't deny he's a downright specimen of health." Then she flattened her lips. "But his mind. . ."

"What's wrong with it?" said Emilu.

"Well, it's gone, that's all."

Emilu was defensive. "He talks all right."

"Talks!" her mother said and turned away to run water on the beans. "Just stay out of his way."

"Why?"

Her mother flung a sideways look at her. "Folks like that get full of notions." And she left the room with the water still on.

Emilu sucked the knuckle of her finger. Her mother never came right out and answered a question. You thought you had her on the track and then she ducked into a side road.

Emilu ran out the back and circled the house. She could look through his window and see him on the bed. He hadn't moved. He seemed just the way he was two years ago. They stared at each other the way she had looked at a deer she met once that Jo-Jo had trapped and he looked at her knowing she wasn't the one did it but there he was in the fix he was in. She came in the front door and down the hall to him again.

He seemed glad she was there. She sat down at length on the chair by his bed. Then he opened his suitcase and rumpled around and came up with a bag of peanuts. He sat back on the bed and gave one to her and one to himself. They were very still while they looked at one another across their chewing.

That night before she went off to sleep she could hear him moving in the room across the hall, then a scraping sound, a sour wail of furniture being dragged across the floor. It went on for some time. She could hear her mother in the room next to hers. "My God, what's he doin'? I can't stand it, Ray." She heard her father's muffled voice. . .

And then it was daylight. The wind outside was rattling the shutters. She woke up thinking it was still the furniture being dragged around, then knowing it wasn't.

When she went to his room she saw the dresser standing slap across the corner. And now a square of dust marked the place it had been. He was sitting on the bed looking out of the window at the waving trees.

She was full of the morning. "How come you moved the dresser around in the night?"

He looked at her with haunted eyes.

"Grandpa. . . how come?"

He shook his head. "It ain't the same room," he said at last.

She started to tell him that it really was, but she stopped herself. She could hear the geese being chased by the dog. She could hear the bus passing, rounding the curve, and then taking the hill. She sat on the bed and swung her feet. "You wanta play euchre?"

He shook his head. "I don't recall it none."

"You taught me, Grandpa. I could teach you how. I remember it real good."

"Wouldn't serve. I'd fergit."

She said with pride, "I never forgot nothin' I ever knew."

He shook his head in wonder. "It goes," he said. "I can't figger where it goes, but it goes all right. . . I think when it all goes what'll I be then? What'll I be just a settin' somewhere? Sometimes it scares the livin' hell outa me."

She swung her feet. "I know ever dadblasted thing ever happen to me."

"You think so, little daughter. But there is things gittin' away from you in the night when you fergit to hold on."

She shook her head. "Not me. I got it all somewhere. In my head, I reckon."

"Course you ain't live long. There just ain't that much."

"There's a plenty, I guarantee. There is plenty done happen."

"Well, hold onto it, little daughter."

"I'm a holdin' on."

She got up and walked to the square of dust where the dresser had been. With her toe she scraped a circle and a zigzag line. "Slapjack is nothin' to it. How long you figger you can hold onto somethin'?"

"No way a tellin'. Hard to say, little daughter."

She swallowed twice. "You called me that before. . . when you were here before. You called me little daughter."

"Did I, now? I musta liked you mighty well."

"Oh, you did. You did. Better than the others. Sometimes we sung songs. On the porch. In the dark. We sung 'Old Black Joe' and 'Oh! Susannah, don't you cry for me. . .'" She was pleading now.

"I don't recall," he said.

A feeling of hopelessness swept over her. The two of them sat there locked in mourning.

"We got to start over," he told her gently. "You willin', little daughter?"

She was sad in a way she had never been before. He patted her hair. "You willin', little daughter?"

But she did not reply.

"Was you wearin' your hair a little different?" he said.

"Just the same," she said faintly and shook her brown mane. "Chopped off straight. I just can't stand it no other way."

"You willin', little daughter? It's hard," he acknowledged. "I know it ain't fair. . ."

Her voice was uncertain. "But it seems like you don't want to start over, Grandpa. I could help but it seems like you don't want to try."

He was silent for a while. "I got somethin' on my mind, little daughter, to 'tend to. . . I can't think a nothin' else. It's on me night and day."

"What is it?" she said.

"It's a misty thing now. But what's so strong is how good it was. Good. Good. If I could remember it. If I could get it back once and then tell somebody who wouldn't let go. . ."

He looked at her with something like a plea in his eyes. "That's where maybe you could come in."

"Where, Grandpa?"

"You gonna come in two ways, little mother. You gonna help me remember and then you take it from me and you don't let it go."

"So I can tell you again in case you forget?"

"No. . . no. I wouldn't need it again. Just need you to have it. Just to not let it go. Now, I'm gonna die. Someday not far away. Who cares?"

"I care, Grandpa." Then she said, disbelieving, "But someday I'm gonna die."

"Don't you think it. You gonna live forever. And if you felt yourself slippin' you could tell somebody. . . You could tell the best person you happen to know. . . like I'm tellin' you. . . when I git it back."

"Am I the best person you know?"

"You are the one best person left with any walkin'-about sense."

She swung her feet. "That ain't the general opinion around here."

"It's mine," he said.

"What about Grandma?"

"Best woman I ever knew. But she's gone, you know."

He stared out the window. "There was a thing that happen to me once. Best thing ever happen. I never told nobody, it was that good."

"You gonna tell me?"

"I'm gonna tell you if I can recall it. *If* I can recall it. If. . . if."

"If it was that good, how come you forgot it?" She was sorry she'd said it, for his face clouded over.

"I ain't entirely done that, little daughter. There's somethin' still there. But it don't come together. I hold onto one thing and somethin' else goes. . . It's gotta be the right kinda weather for holdin'. Today is no good. There's a wind a blowin'. We could work on it maybe we could tomorrow."

She listened to the sucking of wind in the eaves and beyond it the murmur of wind in the corn.

"When it blows I can't recollect one damn thing."

He did not seem to want to talk anymore. She studied a stain on the papered ceiling and decided it looked like a crow or a buzzard. After a while she got up. His eyes had gone into the cave of his brows.

"Grandpa," she said, "you gonna recollect it. I double-dog guarantee it you will."

She went outside and raced up the bank that surrounded the yard. The house was built in a wooded hollow that held a fall of rain like a bowl. She walked barefoot through the rim of corn her father had planted to hold the bank. The silk was bronzed and hung from the ears in tassels that seemed to beckon the wind. She pulled away some and stuffed it into her own two ears. She closed her eyes and between the rows wandered deaf and blind, groping for stalks, plunging, weaving one row with another. But still she could hear a bird mournfully chirping. She followed its cry. "I hear you, little bird. . . I'm comin', little bird. . . You need me, little bird." She stepped on a rock and opened her eyes. Standing on one foot, she spat on her toe and rubbed it up and down and sideways.

His door, when she passed it again, was still open and she looked inside. He was sitting in the chair. The box for the uniform was in his lap. He looked at her as if she had never left the room. "I see a well. . . But it's blowin' too hard. Too hard to tell."

At last she said, "Grandpa? What happened had a well?"

He moved his head slowly from side to side. "Hold onto it," he said. That night before she slept she seemed to hear him singing in his room across the hall. It was a strange kind of tune. But not a tune at all, as if the notes got lost and he had to start again.

Her mother was a woman who put up food. When she was settled down into it somebody seemed to have started a war, and Emilu said the next bus that came she was climbing on. Each day was closer to the end of the world till it felt like a yell coming out of her chest. You better clear out or you'd get yourself sliced and chopped and crushed and scorched and stirred, boiled over and mopped from the stove and the floor. Her mother pink-faced, with pale hair loose and hanging in strings that had got in the jam or the succotash. "Emilu, will you hand me the mop?" And her daddy saying, "Mavis, when are we eatin'?" "Well, Ray, you see me. I can't let go. Well, fix yourself somethin'. Emilu, fix your father somethin' to eat." And Emilu saying under her breath, "This family is nuts," and thinking that for a grown-up man her father was as helpless as Barrelhead, who had to have something dumped in his dish. How come you could call yourself fully growed-up, enough to have half of your hair done gone, and couldn't slide a piece of cheese into some bread?

"I ain't gonna never get married," she said. "I double-dog guarantee it I won't."

"Suit yourself," said her mother.

"I double-dog guarantee if I did I wouldn't put nothin' up in jars. It like to ruin ever summer there is."

"Watch your tongue, Emmy," her father said.

What with living through all the fury of canning, half the time she would go what somebody present would call too far and get sent from the table before dessert. Now that her grandfather was here for the summer, her mother cut her eyes to him as Emilu rose. "I hate to have your grandfather see you like this."

"He'll have to get used to it," Emilu said. "Ever'thing around here ends up I did it."

She went to her room and lay on her bed with her feet against the headboard. Without turning over she could reach underneath and ease out the box that held her secret things. On the lid she had written

"Keep out or die." She opened it on her stomach and went through all its contents. A large dead June bug, a stick of teaberry gum, and a valentine that pictured a fluffy iced cake and was inscribed underneath: "You are the icing on my cake." On the back was printed "I could devour you" and below, "Guess who" with a series of question marks. She had thought it came from Alma, but Alma said no, it was probably a boy. She reviewed the possibility with horror and delight. She tore the gum in half and chewed out the sweet of it to make up for dessert.

Later on, she heard her grandfather moving the dresser around in his room. She got up and went to him. He had pushed it back into the place where it belonged.

He looked at her from where he stood by the window. "That woman muddies up my mind."

"You mean Mama?" she asked.

"I don't recall her," he said. "Was she here before?"

Emilu nodded.

"Well, she muddies my mind. Some women clear things. Your grandma. . . she did."

"What about me, Grandpa?"

"You clear things, little woman."

Her throat filled with pride.

"I been tryin' to get it straight."

She thought at first he meant who everyone was. But then she saw he meant the thing that had happened once. She heard her mother coming down the hall and slammed the door. She went and sat on the bed. "We gotta think about it harder."

He watched her in a kind of rich despair.

"Today is good," she said, coaxing him. "No rain. The sun is shinin'. The wind ain't blowin'."

He dropped into the chair before her. He hunched his head deep into the cave of his shoulders.

She sat and willed him to remember, holding her breath in as long as she could, plunging from one breathful into another.

"Little daughter. . ."

She sat stone-still and waited.

"There's a kinda mist. . . but I see a well. . ."

Still she waited. Then she said softly, as if she stroked a bird, "You already saw that, Grandpa." She waited again. "I got it for you."

He turned to look at her deeply. "You got it locked up tight? You won't fergit?"

She shook her head. "I got it."

She slung the hair from her eyes to see the things in his face. "Was it a real long time ago?"

"I reckon. It gits so it don't hardly matter when. It gits in your head and it don't hardly matter when it was. It's like it was in your blood," he said. "It's like it was always there."

There was pain in her chest from slowing her breath.

He began at last, "There comes a singin' in and outa my mind."

"I heard you singin' some in the night."

"It gits lost somewhere."

She smoothed his spread with a freckled hand. "It don't have to get lost with me to listen. I remember ever tune I ever heard, I guarantee. Words too." She waited for him. "Is it got some words to it, Grandpa?"

"I can't hardly say. I hear the tune, the way it went. . ."

She swung her feet and then she made them stop. "Maybe if you was to shut your eyes like it was dark."

He stared at her fiercely from under his wild brows. She could see in his eyes how it was he sailed his mind like a kite on a string and the two of them watched it soar above the house. He was seeing her now as if she was the string that he wouldn't let go. "I hear a kinda beat like a heartbeat in the ground. I hear it but I feel it."

"What is it?" she said.

"It was turnin' red."

"And singin'?" she said.

His mind caught in the branches of the sycamore behind him.

"And singin', Grandpa?"

He was caught. He was lost.

She was waiting and wishing the tree frogs would shut up their racket for once. Barrelhead the dog began to bark at the squirrels. The bus in the distance had almost made the hill. At last she said, "Grandpa?"

His eyes had never left her face.

"Do you think you might of dreamed it?"

"No! No! It happened. Don't never say that again. . . Just hold onto what I give you. Are you doin' that, Mother?"

"I got it ever bit."

Sometimes he seemed to think that she was her grandmother whom she had never known. Sometimes she seemed to be his daughter, Aunt Lou, her father's sister whose name was part of her own. She was afraid to ask. She wanted him to have her whichever way he would.

Slowly, very slowly, his eyes lost light and seemed to recede beneath the crag of his brow. A dark, baffled look came over his face. "I lost it," he said.

They sat together, grieving, hearing the guineas gone to roost in the tree.

"I lost it," he said. Over the hill the train hit the bridge with a mournful cry and beat along the trestle and echoed in the hollow.

She went out and crossed the road and climbed the hill. If a bus came by beneath she liked to practice her aim and pitch a rock at its roof. There was no bus in sight. It was maybe too late. She slithered down the hill to the tracks and walked a rail. It was cold as winter ice. She had learned how to skip along the rail and never fall. She skipped to a killdeer sitting on the track and flipped a rock to make him fly. She used to put nails where the train would make them flat. Her father said it was illegal. Now she felt a mingling of yearning and defiance. In the failing light she found a lid from a snuff can tossed between the ties. She laid it on the rail and willed the train to change it into something shining that had never been before.

After supper was over she went to her room. She lay on her back with her head at the foot to keep from going to sleep, legs perfectly straight, staring into the dark. She listened to the silence in her grandfather's room. She probed her own mind for the memory he sought, thrusting to the darkness and beyond to where it lay. Then the night opened like a hole in a gunnysack and covered her head. In a moment she slept. . .

But she woke in the dark to the sound of his song. She lay still and listened. It was almost her dream. She got up and tiptoed to his door.

His singing was strange. It was not any song she had ever heard before. It had no words, just his voice, a little cracked, humming, call-

ing the notes, as if he were lulling her back into sleep. She rubbed her
eyes awake and listened intently with her ear to the door. She hummed
beneath her breath until the tune was in her head. Then she slipped
back to bed and sang it to herself till she had it for good. She sang it to
the train and it answered her back as it skimmed the rails, making
something shining for her in the dark.

The next day after lunch her mother called her to the kitchen to pick
up the clean clothes and put them away.

"Emilu, I wish you'd stay away from those tracks. I knew a woman
caught her foot in them once, and along came the train."

"What happened?"

"What happened! She got killed, that's what."

"Did she get it caught where the rails got hitched or under the rail or
under the tie?"

"Now, how would I know? She didn't live to tell us."

"I bet she was wearin' shoes. . . I wouldn't have on shoes."

Her mother left the room with the towels. Emilu called out, "Was she
kin to us?"

"No, she wasn't kin. Nobody kin to us would do a crazy thing like
that."

"If she wasn't kin to us I bet it never happened. Somebody made it up
to scare people off a trains."

Her mother appeared in the doorway. "Emilu, it's time you grew up
to your age."

"I ain't got the slightest idea what that means." She looked at her
toes and the bottoms of her feet.

She went out to the barn and stared a hen in the eye and shooed the
red one off her nest. She took one of the three tan-colored eggs and put
it in her pocket and whistled from the doorway. After a while she
walked behind the sycamore tree and pulled a leaf and laid it on the
ground and broke the egg into it neatly. She knelt and touched the
sulfur half-moon with the tip of her tongue. Then she called to Barrelhead to come and get it.

She went looking for her grandfather and found him asleep beneath
the sugarberry tree. She sat down beside him.

She watched him sleep, his white hair stirring in the breeze. Crickets were jumping from the grass to brush his great brown hand that hung from the arm of the wicker chair. He was the oldest person she had ever known, and at the same time he was like a little baby that needed a mother. Nobody but herself would pay him any mind. Her mother seemed to think he was too much trouble just to have at the table, and now she let Emilu take his breakfast to his room. And her father never talked to him hardly at all. They talked around him at the table like he wasn't there. . . . She began to sing softly the song she had heard him making in the night. She sang it over and over again till after a while it seemed to be her song for singing him asleep. He woke up and listened with his eyes half closed. Then he shut them again and she thought he'd drifted off. But in a moment he said, "It was a woman done the singin'. It was like I was dreamin'. But when I come to she was singin' for real."

She listened in wonder. "Was it Grandma done the singin'?"

"No. . . no. But the moon was the brightest I ever seen."

He went to sleep again.

Her mother came to look at him and shake her head. "If it starts to rain I want that wicker chair inside."

"Mama," said Emilu, "can't you see he's asleep!"

"Well, I see that, Emilu. I don't need to be told. But if he's here for the summer we'll have to have things understood."

"I ain't got the slightest idea what that means."

"Never mind what it means. But I wish you wouldn't hang around him all the time."

"First it's the tracks and now it's Grandpa. There is more things around that I ain't got permission than there is I can do."

"Watch your tongue, Emilu."

Emilu stuck out her tongue and crossed her eyes to see it.

She had her supper and just before dark, while they sat around the table, she climbed the hill. The dark rails were now almost the color of the ground. They were like velvet ribbons you could hardly see. She skipped along one till she came to the shining round disc that caught light from the sky. The lid from the snuff can was like silver money and thin as thin. She picked it up and kissed it again and again.

She heard a mewing sound and turned to see that Barrelhead had followed her. He could sound like a cat enough to fool a kitten. "Go back," she commanded. "Barrelhead, go back." He sat down at once, blinking his eyes into the risen moon. Finally he turned and slunk away up the hill. "And don't you go blabbin' on me," she called.

Then she was walking the rail in moonlight, treading its silver. To make her free, in her mouth she held the silver disc with its faint snuff taste of honey and spice. Free of growing up. . . whatever it was.

She heard in the distance the song of the train. It was calling to her like the bird in the corn. She was nearing the trestle. Deep in the iron her bare feet knew the yielding and tremor. The hollow below her was faintly in bloom. She walked straight on as she stepped to the bridge and boarded the trestle. The rails sang out. Around the curve toward her the great beast hurtled; she saw the trees ashen in its aureole of light. It sprang to the trestle. The white rails stammered. The churning of wheels. And then the glory of the shining rails.

Sucked into thunder, she turned and ran. Buried in thunder, running in terror, reaching the end, dropping to the gulley to dwell forever in the house of thunder. She was rolling over, naked to the storm. Her heart was drowned, her life dissolving in the roar of the wheels.

She came to rest at the bottom of the gulley. She floated over the world like foam. The frogs came back, tremulous, halting, then mounting a tenor of sad betrayal, then screaming as they remembered their song. She lay very still, and after a while she pitched her trembling voice to theirs. She could not tell if she made a sound. But beneath the moon she heard the singing in the well. She herself was in the well and heard the voice spilling down. For a moment she thought that she was dead, stone-cold train-dead.

The cry rose inside her: If I got myself killed nobody could help. I'm the onliest one there is knows about the well. Not even Grandpa remembers it now.

She got up slowly and clawed her way through vines and frogs. At the top she found the silver round still clamped in her teeth. She took it out and buried it beneath a rock. . .

Her father saw her in the hall. "What happened to you?"

"I fell down."

He looked her over and sighed. "You all right?"

"Sure."

He opened his bedroom door and went in.

She stopped outside her grandfather's room and listened for a time to his gentle snore. And through the door she whispered to him: "Grandpa, I outraced a train."

Then she undressed and lay down to sleep. And the thunder shook her and shook her bed. She lay on her back and crushed the pillow to her face and choked and sobbed. I almost died, God. You 'most let me die. And God said, What got into you, Emilu? And Emilu said, I wish I knew.

In the night a rising wind was raking the leaves, and she covered her head to shut it out. She knew that tomorrow he would be caved in with everything in him slipped off somewhere.

In the morning he was desolate, hollow-eyed.

She became after that a watcher of weather. Fearful, she would sniff the damp in the air. When the wind hunkered down in the hollow flinging the leaves, drumbeating the panes with fingers of rain, in another year she would have dashed through the trees, clarion with joy until they called her to shelter. Now she despaired, prowling in the hallway outside his room, gliding in to coax, "Don't worry, Grandpa. It won't last long."

But the rain ran down through the fissures in the bank to fill the bowl, and the house was a boat aground in the shallows. The pale moon floated its face in the yard for half the night. The geese honked curses from their dry retreat in a hollow oak. The watchdog guineas, gray and drenched, sat high on the branches above her window and warned of the wind in querulous tones. Below them, the tree frogs screeched their dominion of the sodden world—till daylight came.

She stole in softly with his plate of breakfast. He lay in bed. "Eat it hot, Grandpa. It will help you remember."

She sat brooding over him, warm with her tenderness, smoothing his cover. "Grandpa, there is a whole heap a little things I got locked in my mind. About the well and the singin' and the lady and all." She let her eyes stroke his bulky form. "Some other things too. All we got to do is get it together."

"I don't recollect a damn thing today."

"I could sing you the song."

"Give me the box, little woman." He pointed to it in the corner of the room.

She brought the box and took off the lid. He sat up and propped the pillow behind him. Then he drew from the box his uniform jacket and inched one arm into a sleeve. It was too small to cover more than half his chest.

"Did it shrink?" she asked.

He shook his head.

"You musta had it a long time ago."

He thought of it, frowning, with some surprise. "I don't recall."

"It's got real nice pretty buttons sewed on." Then she fed him some of the cereal. He ate it thoughtfully from her spoon.

"Little daughter," he said, "you got pretty ways."

"That ain't the general opinion around here."

"It's mine," he said.

He drank a little milk. "I think that woman out there wants me to leave."

"You mean Mama?"

"I don't recall her," he said.

"She ain't got such a crush on me neither, I guarantee."

They brooded together. He pulled the jacket a little more across his chest.

She swallowed on the words. "If you was to leave I wouldn't have nobody here."

He thought of it, his blue eyes circling the room. "You gonna help me, little mother. You gonna help me git it back."

She got up and closed the door and sat down again. She began to sing him softly the song of the well. He listened intently, then he hummed it to himself, breaking into a croon, his voice rising and sinking. His voice seemed to listen. And she listened with it, falling into its dream.

One day she brought his breakfast and he wasn't in his room. She put it down and waited. When he didn't return she tried the bathroom down the hall. The door was standing open. He was not inside. Her heart was in her throat. She closed the door to his room so her mother wouldn't see his breakfast on the tray. She searched for him among the trees in the hollow, with Barrelhead before her yipping at the squirrels. She looked into the corn and the wagon shed. She found him at last in the field beyond the corn on the bank of a ditch looking into the stream. He was still in his brown cotton flannel robe, with the box for the uniform beneath his arm. His white hair was like something silver in the sun. She was so glad to find him that she almost cried.

He looked up bewildered when he saw her beside him. His face was flushed in the sun. "It ain't the well," he said.

It was not an easy thing to get him back inside the house when no one was around.

After that she knew she had to think of something more than just remembering what he gave her. He hadn't told her anything new for some time. She felt him growing empty, like he was hollowed out or something. She felt her mother just about to say he was crazy and maybe couldn't stay. And she felt herself sometimes like to break in two with holding off her mother and holding onto him.

Sometimes she almost got to wishing she was older, but then it scared her to look back and see how she was different at the first of the summer. Just with minding your own business, just treading water, things got dumped on you that you maybe couldn't handle any way but growing up. She thought it was enough to make you cuss out loud. And as soon as this was over she was backing up. But it was taking all she had and then some more to help him now. She had to get him what he wanted and then he could come back every summer of her life. Or they could live somewhere else, just the two of them together.

So she lay on her bed with her feet against the wallpaper, adding to the smudge she had already made. "I hate them rotten yellow roses," she said and stomped one with her heel.

She climbed the hill and dropped down to the rock where she had buried the snuff lid the train had flattened thin. She sat on the rock and crossed her freckled legs and held the lid in her mouth. She thought she would maybe chop her hair off at the roots and give her mother a fit. And then she was crying and she didn't know why.

It was almost noon. She was getting hungry but she wouldn't go home. She sucked the lid in her mouth and thought of dipping snuff and spitting in a can, the way a black woman down the road would do, who took her spitting can with her wherever she went. . . Emilu spit into the weeds and cried.

And finally it came to her she knew about a well that used to be in a field a long way down the road. She had been there once when her daddy had bought a hound for himself. She had a drink from it then and the water had tasted like a mouth of ditch water with scum thrown in. Her father had said not to worry, it was good to drink. But Emilu had thought, You coulda sure fooled me.

And now it seemed to her a last desperate hope. She could find the place. She could head straight back to any place she'd ever been. Like a cat, her father said. "We could put Emilu in a sack and dump her off down the road. She'd turn up the next day. Melissa you can turn around once and she's lost. Not Emilu."

I got to use everything I got, which ain't all that much. She wiped her eyes on her shirt and hid the snuff lid again.

It was hard work telling him about the well. He didn't seem to listen to what she said. She seemed to be telling it all to herself. When she had finished he sat leaning over with his head in his hands.

"Grandpa, I guarantee it wouldn't hurt none to look."

He got up and went to the corner for the box and put it under his arm. "I'm ready, little daughter."

At first she was too surprised to speak. Then she said, "We gotta take that bus and we ain't got time to make it today. We gotta wait till tomorrow."

Tears sprang to his eyes.

She went to him and pulled him down into the chair. She smoothed and patted his hair like silk. "Grandpa, you got real pretty hair. It's real, real pretty, I'm tellin' you. It ain't no time at all till tomorrow gets here. . . Don't go mentionin' the bus. There is some folks around like to mess up your plans."

She found his peanuts on the dresser and they ate some together.

She had a little money for the bus. There was her grandmother on her mother's side who sent her a five-dollar bill every birthday came

around. That way you could get it figured into your affairs. It had come
in June and she hadn't busted into it yet. It would be enough for one
way but not for coming back too. She slipped into her father's drawer
and got some from the box in the corner at the back. She knew it would
be the whole thing come down upon her if he found it out. Like she had
robbed a train.

The bus would come by a little after two, but she got him ready early
after lunch was over. She brushed and combed his hair and aimed his
eyebrows in the right direction. He wanted to take along the box with
his uniform, but she brought him around to taking just the jacket instead.

She put on her black leather sandals and her Easter dress that had the
jacket with the braid. She thought to pack corn muffins left from lunch
and stuff them into the pockets of her dress. And when her father left in
the truck and her mother was sitting out in back in the swing the way
she did after lunch, she took his hand and led him out to the road. She
walked him down around the bend so that no one looking out could see
them from the porch, and she pushed him into the shadow of an oak.

The air was empty, the way it is on summer afternoons when it's
making up its mind if it intends to rain. It seemed to her the bus was a
long time in coming. Then she heard it struggling with the hill. It was
bearing down upon them. She stepped out to hail it and it came to a
stop. She coaxed him up the steps. She had her money ready. She would
not look around for fear of seeing someone who would know her. But
when they were seated just behind the driver she did look down the
aisle. The bus was almost empty. Three blacks, a woman and two men,
were sitting in the rear. A white man halfway down appeared to be
asleep.

She patted her grandfather's arm and smiled at him. His eyes were
grave and trusting. She hooked her Sunday sandals on the driver's seat
and stared at the back of his head and ears and tried to tell if he was
kind and if he would stop where she said to stop.

He stopped the bus exactly where she pointed and never asked her a
thing. But she saw him looking hard at the uniform.

There was a haze on the fields. She took her grandfather's hand and
led him down a little dirt road between some burdock trees. Then the

road ended and they were out in the open. She climbed through a fence and held the wire up for him. But he just stepped over with no trouble at all. There were cows ahead, mostly Jerseys. But a Guernsey bull raised his head as they passed and looked at her hard. She looked back hard and kept on going, though she was scared inside. Insects were chirring like crazy in the heat.

She found a spot beneath a tree and made him sit down. She folded his uniform and put it beside him. "I gotta find it, Grandpa. It might take a minute." She took off running.

She explored every hollow and behind every hillock. She almost panicked. She had been so sure it was there in the field. . . And then through a section of broken fence she found it. She went running back for him and coaxed him to it.

There it was in the weeds, a square of old boards greened over with moss. She tried to lift it. "It's under there, Grandpa. You lift it up. It's too heavy for me."

He stood looking down at it with deep concentration. His eyes were blue pinpoints back under his brows.

She wasn't sure that he understood. "It's the well, Grandpa. I found it. See. You take off the top and look down inside. . ." She scanned the sky for him. "It's a real good day. No wind or rainin'. It's a real good day for rememberin' things. I can remember even bein' a teeny baby. I can remember the farthest back I ever done."

He stood without moving.

Now she was pleading. "Take off the top, Grandpa. It'll be just fine." She knelt in the weeds and patted the boards.

Slowly he approached and stood looking down at her moving hands. "Lift it up, Grandpa."

He stopped and grasped the edge of one board and threw the lid back with a crash. She fell over backward into the weeds. Then she got to her knees and peered into the well. A smell of decaying vegetation rose. She looked up at his face in the sky above her. He seemed bewildered. "Sit down with me, Grandpa."

He stared out across the field and stirred and half turned. She thought he would leave. She stood up and took his hand and pulled him down beside her. She was praying to herself: God, you gotta help me get it goin'. The hardest thing there is is to get somethin' goin' that ain't started yet.

She picked up a stone and dropped it into the well and heard it strike the ground. She turned to him a stricken face. "It used to be fulla water. I had a drink out it once. . . It's done dried up, I reckon. . . And it's got fulla dirt."

But his face was changing. She could not tell what it meant. He said to her, "Little daughter. . . you gonna give me what you got saved up. You hear?"

"It's a dried-up well."

"It don't matter about the water." He was impatient now. "Give me what all you got."

She held on to the muffins in each pocket of her dress. "I got a lady singin' and a well and a beatin' in the ground and somethin' red. I got the moon." She began to sing the well song but her voice was crying. She didn't want to cry, but her voice came out crying and she had to stop. "I got you said it was the best thing ever happen. . ."

"Not at first," he said.

"How come you told me it was?"

"Not at first," he said, shaking his head from side to side. Suddenly he grabbed the jacket and threw it on his back and drew it close around his throat. "It was some kinda. . . it musta been that war. . ."

"What war was it, Grandpa?" She tried to think of the wars she had heard about in school but they all ran together and she couldn't help. He stroked his head.

"What was they fightin' about, Grandpa?" She had to keep him talking. The worst was when he stopped. "I wouldn't a fought 'less they give me a reason."

"They give one," he said. "I fergit what it was."

He pulled the uniform around his throat and put it to his lips and smelled of it.

"They was runnin' through trees and outa trees. I heard shootin' in the trees. I heard Jake gittin' hit, and I turn and saw blood comin' outa his throat. Like he was tryin' to tell me somethin', 'stead a words it was blood. Me and him kep' runnin' and then he warn't there. And then I fell down and I seen I had Jake's blood all over my side. . . It warn't his, it was mine. But I didn't know it. I thought it was his. I run on further and I fell again. I fell into somethin' was a hole. . . was a well."

She heard thunder in the hills. He lifted his head. He heard it too. Now, she thought, he's gonna dry up like the well is done dried. But the words were still there. "I hear runnin'. I hear runnin'. Feet poundin' the ground. Like a heartbeat in the ground. And like all at once the sky goes away. . ."

He stopped.

"What was it, Grandpa? Did you pass clean out?"

He put the jacket to his lips. "No. . . no. It was the top for the well." He reached out and stroked it with his fingers. "She covered me up."

"Who did, Grandpa?"

He shook his head.

"Who did it, Grandpa? You gotta think real hard."

"You recollect your mother used to cover you up? 'Fore you was good asleep?"

"It wasn't Grandma. It wasn't her. It was back in that war."

"She used to sing you asleep."

She stared at him in despair. "Not Grandma. . ." She lay back on the ground.

"That woman. . . in that war."

She heard him from where she lay and was afraid to move.

"Feet was poundin' all around me." He began to moan and tore the uniform away and threw it onto the ground. "I could hear the shoutin'. And she was settin' on top a me. On top a the well. Right on top a the well. And she was singin'. It was a song. I never heard nothin' like it." He began to sing the song, at first a whisper, then loud. She could hear it way down in the pit of her stomach. And she heard how the cows were listening to it in the field.

"Then she stopped," he said. He began to cry softly.

I'm a willin' to grow up some, God, if it takes it. . .

He grew calm and wiped his eyes on the back of his hand. "They was askin' did she see me. They was talkin' foreign words, but I knew what they said. . . When you is settin' hunched up underground in the dark. . . in the wet. . . in the blood. . . and they is huntin' you down like a rabbit. . . it don't matter what kinda words. I am sayin' it don't matter what kinda words."

Then she saw him lean across the well and fall in. But not fall. He climbed inside.

She got to her knees and looked down upon him where he sat with his head against the sides and his white hair all speckled with sticks and fern. She thought it might be that he was going to die. She had never seen somebody die before, and she was aching all over with wanting him to live.

She heard him saying, "She was singin' in the dark. I never heard nothin' like it. They come back a dozen times. They was huntin' me down. But she was singin' on the well and they never look inside."

She heard his voice growing into a song. "I was young to be dyin'. I ain't grew up, and I wanted it like a drink a cold water when your tongue is dry. I seen how it was I been wastin' the world. I ain't half look at things in the field or the road or sky. I ain't half smell the hay in the rain. . . I ain't love a woman. I seen 'em in doorways and walkin' pretty, but I ain't love one. I wanted a woman and the chil'ren she give. Lyin' with her at night, gittin' up at day. . . I wanted gittin' old."

She heard the cows lowing, coming close with their lowing. Bees sang in the trees.

Wanted getting old?

But it wasn't over. For he turned his face upward and into her own. His eyes were seeking something beyond her face, beyond her help. "Long time in the dark 'fore she open me up. I thought it was sun. It was moon shinin' on me the brightest I seen. It was like her face was up in the moon lookin' down at me. It was like I been given it all right there, the rest a my life poured into that hole in the ground where I was. . . I couldn't hardly bring myself to come up then, 'cause I had it all there. I reckon I was 'fraid if I lived it out it might not be that good."

"Was it?" she said, not knowing what he meant or what she asked or why.

But it seemed to be gone. All she could see was his head sunk down and the sticks and fern and the leaves in his hair.

He stirred. "Did you git it?" he cried.

She swallowed and nodded down into the well. "I got it, Grandpa."

"It's slippin', a'ready slippin'. You got it, little daughter?"

"I got it, Grandpa." Inside she was crying, not knowing what she had.

"That's good," he said. "It's yours. You keep it."

Keep what? Keep what?

Going back was hard. The sky was changing, going gray at the edges, then gray on top. By the time they were back at the road it was raining. She got him to sit on the side in the grass. She took off her jacket and put it over his head. The uniform she buttoned inside his shirt, but he didn't seem to care about it anymore. She felt it was raining down inside of her. Counting on her fingers, she guessed it would be a good five hours before the bus would return.

But long before that, her father's car lights picked them out through the mist.

"Emilu," said her mother in the front seat, turning, "I would expect from you a little more judgment."

"Shut up!" she cried, coming out of the rain. "I was helpin' Grandpa. I'll never tell what it was. Not if all my teeth rot out! Not if you lock me up forever!"

But he was the one they locked away. . .

Whatever it was he found in the well, sometimes she wished she could lock it up in the box she kept beneath her bed. A thing you have to keep in your mind, it gets shrunk up, or else it grows the way you do and blurs like a lantern held too close till, like it or not, you look away. But after a dozen summers were gone, it must have been when her child was born, she heard the cry of the thing they had found. She heard the singing inside of her.

MIDRASH ON HAPPINESS

GRACE PALEY

Grace Paley lives in New York City with her husband, writer Robert Nichols. She is the author of three collections of stories, *The Little Disturbances of Man, Enormous Changes at the Last Minute,* and *Later the Same Day,* and a volume of poetry, *Leaning Forward.*

What she meant by happiness, she said, was the following: she meant having (or having had) (or continuing to have) everything. By everything, she meant, first, the children, then a dear person to live with, preferably a man (by *live with,* she meant for a long time but not necessarily). Along with and not in preferential order, she required three or four best women friends to whom she could tell every personal fact and then discuss on the widest deepest and most hopeless level, the economy, the constant, unbeatable, cruel war economy, the slavery of the American worker to the idea of that economy, the complicity of male people in the whole structure, the dumbness of men (including her preferred man) on this subject. By dumbness, she meant everything dumbness has always meant: silence and stupidity. By silence she meant refusal to speak; by stupidity she meant refusal to hear. For happiness she required women to walk with. To walk in the city arm in arm with a woman friend (as her mother had with aunts and cousins so many years ago) was just plain essential. Oh! those long walks and intimate talks, better than standing alone on the most admirable mountain or in the handsomest forest or hay-blown field (all of which were certainly splendid occupations for the wind-starved soul). More important even (though maybe less sweet because of age) than the old walks with boys she'd walked with as a girl, that nice bunch of worried left-wing boys who flew (always slightly handicapped by that idealistic wing) into a dream of paid-up mortgages with a small room for opinion and solitude in the corner of home. Oh do you remember those fellows, Ruthy?

Remember? Well, I'm married to one.

Not exactly.

O.K. So it's a union co-op.

But she had, Faith continued, democratically *tried* walking in the beloved city with a man, but the effort had failed since from about that age—twenty-seven or eight—he had felt an obligation, if a young woman passed, to turn abstractedly away, in the middle of the most personal conversation or even to say confidentially, wasn't she something?—or clasping his plaid shirt, at the heart's level, oh my god! The purpose of this: perhaps to work a nice quiet appreciation into thunderous heartbeat as he had been taught on pain of sexual death. For happiness, she also required work to do in this world and bread on the table. By work to do she included the important work of raising children righteously up. By righteously she meant that along with being useful and speaking truth to the community, they must do no harm. By harm she meant not only personal injury to the friend the lover the coworker the parent (the city the nation) but also the stranger; she meant particularly the stranger in all her or his difference, who, because we were strangers in Egypt, deserves special goodness for life or at least until the end of strangeness. By bread on the table, she meant no metaphor but truly bread as her father had ended every single meal with a hunk of bread. By hunk, she was describing one of the attributes of good bread.

Suddenly she felt she had left out a couple of things: Love. Oh yes, she said, for she was talking, talking all this time, to patient Ruth and they were walking for some reason in a neighborhood where she didn't know the children, the pizza places or the vegetable markets. It was early evening and she could see lovers walking along Riverside Park with their arms around one another, turning away from the sun which now sets among the new apartment houses of New Jersey, to kiss. Oh I forgot, she said, now that I notice, Ruthy I think I would die without love. By love she probably meant she would die without being *in* love. By *in* love she meant the acuteness of the heart at the sudden sight of a particular person or the way over a couple of years of interested friendship one is suddenly stunned by the lungs' longing for more and more breath in the presence of that friend, or nearly drowned to the knees by the salty spring that seems to beat for years on our vaginal shores. Not to omit all sorts of imaginings which assure great spiritual energy for months and when luck follows truth, years.

Oh sure, love. I think so too, sometimes, said Ruth, willing to hear Faith out since she had been watching the kissers too, but I'm really not so sure. Nowadays it seems like pride, I mean overweening pride, when you look at the children and think we don't have time to do much (by time Ruth meant both her personal time and the planet's time). When I read the papers and hear all this boom boom bellicosity, the guys outdaring each other, I see we have to change it all—the world—without killing it absolutely—without killing it, that'll be the trick the kids'll have to figure out. Until that begins, I don't understand happiness—what you mean by it.

Then Faith was ashamed to have wanted so much and so little all at the same time—to be so easily and personally satisfied in this terrible place, when everywhere vast public suffering rose in reeling waves from the round earth's nation-states—hung in the satellite-watched air and settled in no time at all into TV sets and newsrooms. It was all there. Look up and the news of halfway round the planet is falling on us all. So for all these conscientious and technical reasons, Faith was ashamed. It was clear that happiness could not be worthwhile, with so much conversation and so little revolutionary change. Of course, Faith said, I know all that. I do, but sometimes walking with a friend I forget the world.

TAKING CARE

LEWIS HORNE

Lewis Horne was born and raised in Mesa, Arizona. He attended
Arizona State and received his M.A. and Ph.D. from the University of
Michigan. His stories have appeared in such journals as *Ascent, Chari-
ton Review, Ontario Review,* and *Canadian Fiction Magazine.* He lives
with his family in Saskatoon, where he is a member of the English
Department at the University of Saskatchewan.

—came to mind during love, carried perhaps by the breeze that feath-
ered his ankle. Came close to the edge of awareness, centered on the
peak he had achieved, and hovered as he sank to stillness. To tenderness
he registered with a wistful kiss and then closed eyes as warm hands
settled on his back. The breeze entered as though fanned by the
branches of the tall spruce outside the second-floor bedroom window,
cooling damp skin, and out of the past came the lovely odor. The voice.

"Don't that smell good!"

The sound came to his mind, drowsy and unfocused, of a car motor.
Legs lifted from his. A jeep. The air came through the open doors of the
vehicle, the rear flap billowing where Anson had failed to fasten it as
tightly as he should. The headlights opened up the darkness. The hands
moved from his back, and in the darkness, as he lifted himself, he
smiled and kissed his wife once more, Lynette's lips touching his cheek.
He settled near the edge of the bed, uncovered, the breeze drying chest
and belly.

"Don't that smell good!"

"It's Sycamore Creek, isn't it, Von?" asked Anson of their father
from the back seat.

In the breeze the recollection set on a specific trip, though one of the
best parts anytime was arriving at Sycamore Creek after climbing from

the Valley and crossing the low desert hills. Few streams ran in the Valley, only irrigation ditches. So the smell of damp earth and the odor of the trees thick in the air, signaled that the desert, so hot in the summer, was left behind and they would soon begin climbing into pine country. As usual they had to finish milking before leaving home, so they arrived in darkness, unsure when the air would suddenly cool and the ripe odor of the creek where the road touched it would sharpen the breeze, an enriched surprise—a blessing.

Usually, Anson as the older had the front seat, able to stretch out his turn by wily strategems, until Big Von—late in the know—would finally tell him to switch.

"Your turn now, Travis."

But on this trip—recalling in his bed which one it was—Travis got more preference. As well, Anson, 15 years old and a sophomore in high school, had new interests that dulled the competitive flame between them.

Had Shirl come, he'd be crowded in back with Anson and the suitcase and their boxes alongside Big Von's gas can. But Anson lay sprawled, his long legs stretched so his bare feet bobbed behind his father's head with the bumps in the dirt road.

Big Von wasn't that big physically. Anson had grown as tall now, though thinner and lither, and would grow taller. Travis, once he got his growth, would likely stretch higher than either. But their father's name came from their view of him when they were small. They never heard the word "Dad" around him, no mother to use it or school them. Shirl tried later when she became Big Von's girl—"What you kids mean? He's your dad. Why don't you call him that?"—but the habit was too strong, and their father, sensitive to upsets they might feel, the motherless kids they were, cautioned. Shirl—as good-natured and adaptable as she was tough and loud—shrugged. "Well, he is big, isn't he? In his way. Big Von. I like that."

He seemed big in those years, rising above them high and strong. And he was big in other ways that hadn't to do with his average height, when their own growth brought them into direct view of his features. Of the close curly hair, pale with dirt when he drove tractor, black as a buzzard when washed. Of the too-large teeth with an overbite that drove inward the dimple-notched chin. Of the crinkled eyes, snappy and friendly, and the loose skin, weathered and lined like an old man's though it never made Big Von look old. "Him old?" said tangle-haired Shirl, strutting around their kitchen in her dirty Levis and boots and man's shirt. "Let me tell you, boys, 32 ain't old." And she grabbed him by the ears, smacking him on the lips with her mouth.

This was after Shirl went to the mountains the first time. Anson must have been nine so Travis was not yet six. Yet he had understood as well as Anson, for after lunch Anson wanted to follow them when the two walked away from the Adams' log house. He told Travis to come along.

"Don't make no noise."

The Adams napped after lunch. Big Von liked to spread a blanket over the pine needles. The sound of the cool wind high in the branches was like organ music in the days when they went to church. But this was Shirl's first time, and she and Von walked away from the log house instead of lying on the pine needles near the small stream the Adams dipped drinking water from.

"I know what they're going to do," said Anson.

So did Travis, though he couldn't have said. After that trip, Shirl began spending weekends at their farm. He had been neither surprised nor upset to see the two of them naked as jaybirds on the blanket, Big Von's white buttocks clanging between Shirl's knees. They lay so near the creek they couldn't have heard anything but themselves and the noisy water.

Thinking back now, he—Travis—figured that was the first time for Shirl and Big Von, that Von had been trying to tug her into bed for some months, that her going to the mountains was a way she could give in to his pull without saying yes outright. Hence, Big Von's lusty she-nanigans as they eased their way down the slope, the rolled blanket under his arm.

As the jeep climbed from Sycamore Creek, Big Von asked Anson to pass his Levi jacket to him. The older boy's long hair blew into his eyes as he leaned forward. Travis had curly hair like Big Von, matted close to his head. But Anson's was long and straight, and Travis envied him. Not only did his older brother have memories of their mother but he had hair like her, too—her long thin face and her hair as straight and black as an Indian's that she wore tied back. But not Travis. "The spitting image of his dad," people said of Travis. "But quiet like his mother," said others. He didn't want to come out, Big Von said, Travis didn't. She tried for 36 hours in the hospital before they cut into her. She never woke from the ether.

It was sometime after that, he figured, that Big Von earned the name his sons gave him and did the things that made the name so easy to give. Travis scarcely knew what a mother was until he saw that other beings had them—and his friends, too. Though as Shirl had said of him recently, "That boy don't have any close friends." Big Von with a broom, Big Von at the stove, Anson noisy at the table laughing at some antic Big Von had pulled while Travis sat in a highchair. Big Von running clothes through the wringer washing machine to hang them on the clothesline strung from the milking corral to the garden. Big Von on the tractor disking the citrus trees and talking and laughing with the pickers that the shed sent out to strip the oranges off. Big Von riding the school bus with him his first day—Anson embarrassed—so he'd know what to do and where to go. Big Von beside him at the trash pile, staring under the board he'd lifted at two yellow scorpions, pincers linked as they moved backward and forward across the damp ground and the bits of white sickly grass. "They're mating," he said. Then with a rock, he killed them. "I hate the goddam things." And why not? Didn't Anson and he have to shake out shoes and Levis every morning in case scorpions hid in them.

No one laughed at Big Von's name.

II

"That boy don't have any close friends, Von. And those quiet ones. You know how they say. Still water runs deep."

But Darrell Meacham had not been a close friend. They sat across the aisle from each other at school and clubbed with three or four more for chats and chortles at recess and lunch hour. Darrell didn't ride the school bus since he lived close enough to walk. He could be a little sly, too, like the day he slipped an eraser off Miss Chester's desk and into his pocket, an act that worried Travis.

Yet it was a prank, he came to realize. He could remember the boy's blond hair, straight and slicked down with water when he came to school in the morning and when he returned after lunch. His face was tanned, cheekbones freckled, and Big Von, knowing the Meacham family, was pleased to see him a friend of Travis. But not the kind of close friend Shirl's remark implied. He didn't know what she meant by "close friend." Darrell and he might sit with others and talk about girls, about the Japanese who bombed Pearl Harbor. Occasionally, Travis went home with him, and they swam in the irrigation ditch or played commando among the mesquites by the dry riverbed. They might see each other at church, but by then Shirl was staying weekends. Big Von was what the Mormons call "inactive," and then when he started loving Shirl he stopped going to church altogether. The ward teachers still visited, calling first because they didn't want to stumble in when Shirl was around, and Big Von was friends with the bishop. Now and then Travis would go to Primary on Tuesdays after school. There, too, he was in Darrell's class, and the boy was an eager student because he was anxious to become a Boy Scout. "Don't tell anybody about the eraser," he said to Travis. "Okay? I was kind of crazy." Staring into the eyes above the freckled cheekbones, Travis promised, for the frown of regret was earnest. He remembered so well how Darrell looked, he figured, because the boy was the first dead person he ever saw.

Big Von told Anson and him when they came in one Saturday morning from milking the four cows. "Know how I tell you always to shake your shoes and pants?" His overbite looked like a cliff. "Well, Darrell Meacham—he died last night from a scorpion stinging him. On his peter. For kids, some bites are poisonous."

Shirl was quiet that day. Travis thought of the two scorpions, shuttling backward and forward, mating, and Big Von with the rock. *I hate the goddam things.* He heard Big Von tell Shirl, "I'm going to see the family. They was good—they give me a big hand when Mona died." Big Von ran his fingers over Travis's head, ruffling his hair, and he squeezed Anson's shoulder, tilted as high as his own.

The three of them went to the funeral. Shirl stayed at her place since she wasn't a Mormon and didn't know the family. Travis wondered if he would see the dead boy. He was curious about how someone looked whose soul had left him. At the same time, he was afraid to look at Darrell Meacham whose dying was no more yet than his father saying it had happened. Never to see him again? No longer on earth? Anson and he each wore a bow tie with a white shirt Big Von had ironed. As hot a day as it was, Big Von dug out his suit and wore the coat all the way to church until he saw other men climbing the steps in their shirt sleeves. He left his coat in the jeep, his shirt soppy under his arms.

A scorpion sting wasn't supposed to kill—except for some kids. At school, classmates said big scorpions didn't kill you, it was the little ones. So maybe a little one crawled into Darrell's shorts and hurled its stinger over its back and into his peter. They put ice on it, said Big Von, and floorboarded him to the hospital in town, lying in the back seat clutching and crying. Travis had never seen him cry. He had never seen him asleep as he appeared to be—in a peculiar way—in the coffin. He had never seen anyone so pink among all the bright flowers from the florist shops and the organ playing softly when the church members filed by.

But what caused Shirl to exclaim about his few friends and what sent him with Anson and Big Von to the Adams' place in the mountains happened the next weekend, three or four days after the funeral. Coming back from town, he asked Big Von to show him where the body was buried because he thought of the boy as "body" after seeing the spiky knees and elbows stilled in the coffin and the skin of the face as polished as some of the flower petals. The name on the gray marker was more real than what lay under the fresh sod. DARRELL LEON MEACHAM. "Let's see mama's grave." MONA MARIE KIPPER. They had to cut her open to get him out. "You didn't want to come out," Big Von had said when he talked about it. How did they know? Maybe the want was there, as real as a root under the ground, but something kept the want from pushing through. Struck his mother, Mona Marie Kipper. Struck in his shorts Darrell Leon Meacham.

Later that sunny afternoon, he stood beside the woodpile where he'd seen the scorpions in their mating dance. He thought Big Von and Shirl relaxed in the cool of the house's adobe walls. Anson could be anywhere. The leaves on the citrus trees stood as stiff as the boards at his feet.

He stared under the first, lifting it away. Horrified, he raised another. One more. Under each scrambled hosts of little ones, pale scorpions crawling over each other. Large ones lay dead, half decomposed. He saw one or two ticking in the white grass, backs laden with babies, miniature beetles in shape. *I hate the goddam things.* He stamped his bare feet. His ankles prickled, his legs. His peter and balls shrank. He looked for a rock. Too many of them. Hundreds, thousands. Like the stars overturned, mean and nasty, on to the earth.

He ran to the kitchen, stamping his feet on the cool linoleum to stop the feel of their legs crawling. Inside, too, something squirmed. He grabbed the box of matches from the cupboard, two or three newspapers from the shelf on the back porch.

I hate the goddam things.

They kept him from coming out, he thought. So his mother had to be cut open. When he got back, the scorpions had swollen off the dark ground across a rotting 2-by-12, over a redwood fencepost lying on top, through the scraps. He wadded the paper, lighted it, and threw it on the scurry of them. The flame heated the air he breathed. He threw more, piece by piece. Splinters caught. Boards. The whole box of matches.

"I hate the goddam things."

The words came from his own mouth. The whole pile of wood flamed and its fierce heat backed him toward the corral.

"I hate the goddam things." Again, again. Until finally it came out, "I hate God."

Once and once only.

For Big Von hung from the back door, squinting with puzzled face, one hand gripping the door frame. And Shirl stepped from the corral just behind him. Why she was there he didn't know. Only that she stood two or three feet from him, saying, "Travis, Travis." And Big Von was loping barefoot toward them past the blaze.

III

As the road twisted upward in the dark, he knew that great chasms fell away outside the headlights, sometimes on Big Von's side of the road, sometimes on his own.

"Getting cold?" Big Von asked.

He shook his head because he knew Anson would jump to take his place unless, sprawled back there, he'd fallen asleep. When they drove down Payson's one street, the small town lay dark and quiet, a light burning over the locked door of the service station with its two gas pumps, a few windows lighted in the houses. Von used farm gas because of the rationing and carried a can in the jeep. "Highway patrol catch us," he said, "and we're goners, men."

Anson leaned forward as they left the town, his long hair flapping. "Twenty-one more miles. Sure as hell wish you was staying, Von." He'd taken to using cuss words in front of his father recently. Since he didn't get scolded for it, he was shoving them in like fenceposts, using more with Big Von than with Travis and his own friends.

"Can't leave Shirl to do a whole week's work. Wouldn't be right. And by the way," he said, "you watch your language with the Adams. They're civilized people."

"I won't shame you, Big Von."

After they'd gone 20 miles, they found the sign with two others nailed to a pine tree. ADAMS—hand-lettered and faded. Big Von put the jeep into 4-wheel drive as they eased over eruptions of roots and rocks, trees so close Travis could have reached out and touched them.

Big Von had met the Adamses as a young man when he went back to finish high school. Lloyd taught music in the schools, and he was in the National Guard that Big Von had joined half a dozen years before the war because money and jobs were so scarce in the Depression. He met Leona while he drove the school bus, himself an older student, and she was nurse for all the public schools. Some of Travis's early vaccinations had come from her needle.

But he—Travis—remembered them as he lay in his own dark bedroom beside Lynette as the couple were in middle age. Lloyd was a tall man with heavy limbs and a square face under graying hair, refined features loosened by a startled expression, mouth tipped with an open smile as though he'd just been questioned, answering, Yes? Yes? His chin lifted as though he'd heard something in the distance, standing on stiff legs made undependable by an early and mysterious stroke. Leona was a small marching woman with tiny hands. She pulled her iron gray hair back into a bun during the day, eyes behind the wire frame glasses observant, quick, and slightly Oriental-looking. He thought of them always as a pair, never singly. Perhaps because he associated their log house with their dual life. Because he remembered the walks and naps they took together every afternoon. Because together they lived frugally on Lloyd's disability pension, waiting for the day she would receive Social Security. Because they were as dependent upon each other as Big Von and Shirl seemed to have become, Big Von cussing the Iranians and how they held American citizens hostage, cussing Carter, muttering at Reagan. As dependent as Von and Shirl were now in their own retirement, well-being knocked sideways by a stroke Shirl had received —worse than Lloyd's in its impact—while Big Von looked smaller, the skin of his dark face rubbery with the wrinkles that finally showed his age. Yet both still raucous, living at Shirl's place, while Anson managed both Shirl's acres by the river and the Kipper farm they'd grown up on. In the old days, if he wanted to rile her, goose her into chasing him with broom or pitchfork, cussing his laughter around the yard and into the trees, Big Von had only to call her Shirley. "How you doing, Shir-ley? How you doing, old girl?" Rubbing his hands, adopting a mock bandy-legged walk. Now he would do the same, but he dodged about the kitchen table while she cussed him with slurred tongue, trying to guide the broom she'd clumsily snatched, and the sun poured in across the riverbed.

The Adamses had quieter games. Their house, when the jeep broke into the clearing that night, was dark.

"Shit, they're in bed," said Anson.

Big Von shushed him as they stretched their legs. The brook by the house, no wider than a foot or two, rushed noisily. The pines made tall shadows against the stars.

In the dark, Big Von dipped himself a drink with the tin cup hanging by the brook. As he finished, Leona stepped out on the small porch in her nightgown, brushing the faces of each in turn with the flashlight she carried.

"Come in, come in. We've been expecting you."

By the time she had the kerosene lantern on the kitchen table lit, Lloyd had shuffled in from the back room, dressed in day clothes. He gripped the door frame, his gray hair rumpled, his chin lifted. Yes? Yes? Leona's hair hung loose, let down for the night. Big Von apologized for waking them.

They slept in the attic under a sloping roof with the log beams showing in the lamplight, Big Von in one bed, Anson and he in the other.

"We ought to sleep good tonight, men," Big Von said. "Don't it smell good."

IV

At the time, he didn't remember much about the visit that distinguished it from others. Von drove back the next day, leaving them for the week, and returned after dark the following Friday. Before he left, the three of them hiked up the creek to where rocks dammed enough water for an icy swim. On the way, they passed the spot where Von and Shirl had made love. If Von remembered, he didn't show it, though once when Shirl was along, the two of them got into a scuffle, each trying to shoulder the other into the stream.

Travis knew he was supposed to feel better by the time he went home. Just why he felt bad, he couldn't say. He couldn't explain the fire. Like Darrell Meacham when he took the eraser, he didn't know why. He was being crazy, that was all. He didn't hate God either. He knew that. He worried because if he knew why he felt bad he could do more about feeling good.

Big Von had been so worried at the sight of him by the noisy fire that he'd loped across the yard right through the sticker beds so that standing beside him he scraped the bottom of first one foot and then the other against his Levis. The hand he rested on Travis's shoulder for comfort and concern worked as much for balance. "What's the matter here?"—glancing across at Shirl who leaned forward, hands on her hips, to see into his face.

Smoke rose in ripples you could see the corral and orchard through, cut by skinny black ribbons.

Shirl pulled him farther from the fire, Big Von teetering as he picked off a last sticker.

"Ain't no scorpion going to survive in that fire," said Shirl.

"Scorpion?" said Von. "What do you mean—? Hey, Travis, old buddy—"

Anson came out the back door.

"—Darrell Meacham, poor kid, but buddy—"

And his mother, he wanted to say, when he didn't want to come out. In the cemetery.

"Trying to burn out the scorpions?" said Anson beside the crackle of the fire. "Man, that's crazy."

The four of them.

In the darkness Travis wondered if he should pull the sheet over Lynette who lay closer to the screened window and the breeze than he did. But her smooth back rose and fell so evenly that he hated to disturb. Instead, he went to the bathroom. Though he didn't turn on the light, he could make out his shape in the dark mirror—taller than Big Von, shaggy-headed and bearded, shaggy-chested, the wrinkles settling into his features as they had Big Von's in his early thirties. He was glad he'd made the trip back from his home in New England last year with his wife and his own two sons. Anson, grown and married, was kept busy with the farm and with Shirl's old place. His wife was a city girl who liked the country but was not the help Shirl had been, and Anson's five girls were farmer's daughters in fact but not performance.

Shirl's husband had walked out on her before he and Anson ever knew her: he had walked out or she had booted him out, the story was never clear. She heard nothing of him until the War Department told her he'd been killed during a kamikaze attack on a carrier in the Pacific. Her place was tucked away to the northeast, next to the canal and the riverbed. Big Von scarcely knew where it was, though they'd seen Shirl drive by on her way to town, until Shirl wheeled in one day to ask Big

Von if she could pay him to disk her trees. "Damn tractor's broke down, there's no parts to be had, and the weeds is about to swallow me up." Big Von agreed, and he and Shirl hit it off beside the creek at the Adamses. These days it was Anson, the husband and father, who kept Shirl's place clean. Von mowed the lawn that he'd planted when he moved over, vacating the home place for Anson and family. He cleaned up the yard. "What do you think of it, Shir-ley? What do you think, old girl?" For she'd been satisfied all those years with bare dirt for a yard and the worn-out machinery rusting in back.

During his return, Travis asked about the Adamses. How were they? "Damned if I know," said Von. "And I should."

So the three of them—Travis, Anson, and Big Von—drove to Payson on the new paved highway that took three hours off the drive and opened up the town to new business and the traffic of tourists fleeing the heat of the Valley. They found an old-timer drinking a McDonald's milkshake. "Lloyd—he died four or five years ago. His health was never very good, not very good. Don't know what he'd of done without Leona. Course, soon as he kicked off, Leona slipped. Couldn't do without each other, not without each other they couldn't. She's in the rest home outside town."

They recognized her, though she had shrunk, her march brought to a hobble. Hollow-cheeked, white-haired, she smiled, pleased to have visitors.

"If I'd thought, Leona," said Big Von, "I'd of brought you some flowers."

"Oh." She gestured with a lift of her hands, smaller than ever, heavily veined. "And you were—which one? Travis?"

"No, I'm Von."

"I thought Travis was the father's name, and Von the little one. He seemed so perplexed and lonely. But maybe I've got you all confused with someone else. You'll have to forgive me. My memory won't work no matter what the effort. I'm sure you're who you say you are. My memory is at fault. Not you. I'm glad you stopped by."

What did happen to change Travis's feelings after the fire was something he didn't realize at the time. He could understand it better now.

He returned to bed, sliding his leg until his knee touched Lynette's foot as she lay curled.

A couple of evenings Lloyd pulled out his cello and tuned it. He'd once played in a small symphony orchestra, but as he played for them now, he played without music. "Home on the Range," "Abide with Me," and other such pieces. Only as Travis was tiring did he ask Leona for some music from the piano bench she sat on. He propped it on the rocking chair and adjusted the kerosene lantern. The music sounded more difficult—suites, sonatas, concertos. His vibrato was uneven, and his long flat fingers tangled in the rapid passages, dark shadows hovering across the pine walls from the lamplight. Yet Travis and Anson were impressed, and Leona said, "Why, darling, that isn't bad. It isn't bad at all."

She sat with her back straight, her hands folded in her lap. The dark Oriental eyes glowed. "Play some more."

The corners of the room were dark. Half of it was kitchen with the cupboard shelves on the walls, the woodburning stove, the table with a yellow oilcloth cover; the other half living room with the two rockers, the braided rug between them, and an old upright piano, brightly polished. Beside it, a wooden bookcase, an Encyclopedia Britannica and Book-of-the-Month Club selections on its shelves. White sheer gathered over the windows. Bedroom in the back.

What Travis remembered more than the music happened the next day when Lloyd went to the back room for his afternoon nap while Leona wiped out the dishpan, lunch dishes finished, preparing to join him. A step down led into the room they used for sleeping and storage, and somehow Lloyd stumbled, falling full length to the floor.

"Oh, darling, are you hurt?" She was beside him, immediately, the dish towel left damp in the pan. That was one thing that impressed him, her quick and spontaneous movement. The other was the way she said "darling," what Travis had heard in love scenes in movies and on the radio but never from any person, not with the concern that colored Leona's question. "Are you all right?"

"Yes, yes. I'm fine. Don't worry." He laughed his nervous laugh. "Just my old clumsiness."

Travis heard the bedsprings as Lloyd settled himself.

"You sure take good care of me."

"Have your nap. I'll be with you soon as I'm done."

"—take good care of me."

V

Lynette stirred as though cold, murmured in her mock pouty way, and reached behind her. He rolled over, slipping one arm under her head, the other around to cosy her breasts, skin warming to hers.

Big Von and Shirl always napped these days. Shirl had become a Mormon, and they had married, but Big Von was still "inactive." So was Anson, though his wife and girls were religious. With Lynette and the two boys, though, he—Travis—was kept busy. Not yet a bishop, but busy in church. He didn't want to come out and his mother, MONA MARIE KIPPER, had given her life trying. He'd lit no bonfires since he burned the scorpions, but those old flames had burned vividly again— he'd felt the searing heat—only a few days ago.

He'd received from Anson the newspaper clipping about Leona Adams' death and burial. *Von feels bad about missing the funeral,* Anson's note said. *I'd have gone if I'd known. Some people just get forgotten. Hell of a thing. But Von did get it in the newspaper. You wouldn't be reading about it now if it wasn't for Big Von. I'm glad I didn't know they were driving to town the way his eyesight is, big as the town has got.* Big Von had steadied Shirl across the lawn to the pickup and steered out the driveway along the dry river, Shirl steadying herself with her good right hand on the window frame, head of tangled hair rocking.

"Got to find us a reporter, Shirl," he said, squinting at the road.

Squinting harder as they got into town, not at the traffic but at the signs on the buildings. "What'd they do, move the goddam place? It used to be on Third. Did they change the name of this street, too?" Shirl said something. "What's that?" he asked. She spoke louder. "That's right, old girl," he said, "I knew they moved it."

Parking. Fumbling and swearing for change for the meter. Somehow as Shirl was climbing out of the pickup and he was calling, "Goddam it,

Shirl, just stay put till I get there," he recognized local affairs reporter, an elderly man, as he came out of the *Tribune* office.

"Leona Adams? Who was she?"

"Who was she?" cried Big Von. "She give my boys their first vaccinations. She drove my oldest home from school once way the hell to the country and stayed with him because there wasn't nobody home, stayed there till I got home because my wife was dead and I had me two little ones to care for."

The article was surprisingly long, amazingly prominent, with a picture of the woman drawn from a 1930 high-school yearbook. It told Travis things he'd not known. In the newspaper was the face of the young marcher, the trim smile weighted with seriousness, the head tilted slightly, eyes rimmed by wire frames. Straight hair slanted back over the ears. She was buried in the local cemetery beside Lloyd.

"Oh, darling, are you hurt?"

The headline to the article read: FEW MOURN AT GRAVESIDE AS PIONEER SCHOOL NURSE'S DEATH GOES UNNOTICED. She became nurse in the late 1920's because of "a quite severe smallpox epidemic," the article said. Finding that hardly any schoolchild had been vaccinated, she started "a vaccination program for schoolchildren." She had no car allowance to visit the schools in the area, but she was able to buy gasoline from the school garage for ten cents a gallon. In those days, the article went on, "vision tests were done with an unlighted Snellen chart and hearing tests were done using a whisper or watch ticking." Because dental health was such a problem in the early 1930's, she showed schoolchildren how to brush their teeth. "Some of the smaller children had very badly decayed teeth. The school was able to buy good but very inexpensive toothbrushes, which we sold to some and gave to others who weren't able to buy even a six cent toothbrush."

Gave him, Travis thought, a toothbrush.

In the bedroom next to theirs, he heard Mike, his younger son, speak out. "Don't forget the . . . ."—and his voice slurred back into sleep. Travis Von, junior, the oldest boy, waked for nothing. Leona lay under the sod with Lloyd. MONA MARIE KIPPER. He hadn't wanted to come out. Darrell Meacham. Trying to burn out the scorpions? Man, that's crazy.

But what held most strongly in his mind for this drowsy moment was the clatter and heavy roll of Lloyd Adams' stumble. Oh, darling, are you hurt? That question he heard—out of that past, what came with the breeze through the screened window. Come and lie down.

("How you doing, Shirl-ley? How you doing, old girl?")

You sure take good care of me.

The best we can do.

The least.

UP HOME

WARREN WALLACE

Warren Wallace was born in Port Austin, Michigan. He is an independent producer of documentary films for television, among them *Superfluous People, Men in Cages,* and *To Hell with New York.* He now lives in that city.

I often think of my grandmother, now that we are running out of things. She was never surprised at news of the world suffering. It only confirmed her conviction that man is a waster and needs to be punished.

> "If he was riding, had his horse and buggy, you know, going to town, and someone was walking, he wouldn't give them a ride. And if he was walking, he wouldn't take a ride. My grandfather was that independent. He said if he owed a penny, he'd walk ten miles to pay it; and if you owed him one, he'd almost do the same to get it."

Mrs. McFarland said that to me on camera. She might have been describing my grandmother. Sarah Wallace never walked ten miles for a penny, so far as I know, but she could have.

I am hanging over the cold leather back of the big black rocking chair in the front parlor, watching for her. This tall, gaunt woman walks toward me. She is wearing a long-skirted blue wool dress, and a short black coat. The wind off Lake Huron tosses wisps of white hair that surround her black straw hat. It also tosses the pale leaves of the high poplars, their branches bending and shimmering along Shore Road. Shifting, dappled sunlight blends with the whispering throb of surf to create a sense of imminent event. Something is going to happen, but what? Nothing. Still there remains a potential, it may be of danger, that heightens each day of my childhood.

The chair is not black, but orange, and the fabric against my cheek is cotton, not leather. It belongs to the people who bought the house after my grandmother died. They are away. They left me a key. Nothing much has changed, except for the furniture being different and the wood stove gone from the dining room. I am in town alone, shooting preliminary sequences for a documentary film about my childhood. I am also writing a treatment for a television program about the future, under the title "Nothing Works." My motel room has its own little kitchen. Some days are for writing, and some days are for shooting. The theme of looking backward keeps getting tangled up with the theme of looking forward in my mind. The visit to my grandmother's house kept getting postponed. Today I thought it was time to take a look. The feeling of danger returns.

She is holding her heavy brown handbag firmly. She has been to the bank, doing undefined things with her money. Money is a flitting, uneven presence, like wind. We are in the First Depression, but somehow our small-town bank has survived the general closing. People in this part of Michigan point to it as a sign that the New Deal may be working, though we are most of us Republicans by birth. Secretly I am proud, because I hear my father ran that bank, long ago. By the time the Second Depression comes, and the place gets boarded up, my grandmother will be ready for death. So she will make her exit without having to witness the prosperity brought on by war, and all that followed.

I have been keeping pretty much to myself. My excuse is worry over the treatment about nothing working very well any more. To stay in business, an independent has to leapfrog this way, shooting the one film while hustling the next. I don't feel I'm making much progress with either. The future is obscure, and the past seems very far away. Tom Hagan, a man my own age, heard about my being here and came with his wife to pull me away from my typewriter and take me to their home. They were plump and jolly. After dinner, we sat on the porch looking at the lake and talking about the old days. The lake was quiet the way it gets sometimes, with a regular "woof," followed by a protracted "ahh," like a person inhaling and exhaling emphatically, as the waves punctuated our conversation. Mostly I listened. Lots of their stories were funny. Like the one about Crazy Hans, the veteran of Kaiser Wilhelm's army, who used to do yard work to pay for his drinks. "It's Armistice Day," Tom says. "There's the parade getting ready, the flags, the band of the American Legion. Hans turns up in his German uniform—even the steel helmet! They call a meeting on the spot, and let him march in the parade! After all, it was the same war!" Laughter is building a fondness between us. I am remembering the delirium of Armistice Day, or the Fourth of July, that feeling of something being up everywhere, of everyone drawing closer for a moment.

Tom remembers us as being friends when we were young. The fact is, we always fought. My grandmother didn't want me to have anything to do with him because his people were Irish Catholic. I wanted to keep clear because the fighting bothered me. There was no pain that I can recall. Just a terrible inner turbulence over the web of truce being broken. Should I now with my camera try to recapture the circling and punching, the dry throat, the pounding heart, the reverberations that lasted for days? No, it would take too much staging. I'll leave it out. So I shall be lying by omission, and the film will be flawed. But then, cinema is not a truth-telling medium. It does something else: perhaps it builds dreams. Tom and his wife are smiling at me expectantly. I realize I've lost track of what is being discussed. "The truth is," he says, leaning forward and employing a soft emphasis that alarms me, "the truth is, your father always paid his debts."

I have always found half-truth preferable. Or, to be more accurate, have found that truth contains wild ambiguities. In truth, Tom and I fought as children. But would it be accurate to say we were enemies? We certainly were aware of each other. We had a serious, continuing relationship. I remember him better than any other kid. Now we seem to be friends.

Also take the matter of his religion. Would it be accurate to say that his family being Catholic scared me, what with the Pope planning to take over everything? There may have been a bit of fear. How could anyone confess? But there was also a kind of envy. Being different didn't lower them. They were mysterious and special. Perhaps they were on to something. The half-truth is that my grandmother's discourse made all organized religion sound like a strangely attractive form of self-indulgence. No, the best thing to do would be to leave the fighting out of the film:

> My father died when I was small, my mother was busy working, and my grandmother took on the job of looking after my soul. She was a very religious lady—so profound a student of the Bible that she could never agree with any preacher for very long. So my grandmother and I stayed away from church, and she instructed me. Unfortunately, she was sowing her seed on barren ground, because I never listened.

My relief at seeing her walking toward me under the poplars is mixed with a familiar sense of disquiet at her power. She is usually upset when she has been downtown. While there is time, I must run off to Kimball's Point, to watch the waves hitting the sandstone bluffs. It's too rough today for fishing, but the white surge and green retreat of water over huge broken rocks can keep me mesmerized for hours. I had to wait here until she got back, because the thought of the house standing empty would have spoiled my pleasure.

She has always stood in my mind as being against pleasure. This is not fair. She was forever active, and must have taken satisfaction from the tasks in house and garden that were part of every day. She loved to meet and talk with her sisters. She delighted in discussing Scripture, expounding her views in what ranked as exaltation. But her visions entailed an endless fight against dark forces, so that striving tended to win out over fun.

I recall her telling me once, while enlarging on human frailty, of an accident that happened when she was a girl. On a dare, she was walking the top of a tall fence. She slipped and fell, her legs straddling the boards. "Because of that," she confided, "I was never able to take any satisfaction in men." I was about nine years old when this information was proffered, so its full implications were hazy. However, I did see images of her two sons and three daughters floating toward me, conceived without pleasure, none of them ever wholly satisfactory to her. Behind them was the figure of a young girl who lay bleeding and weeping beside a fence, rejecting all comfort. I put the whole matter at the back of my mind.

During the periods we lived together and had extended conversations, there was much of what she said that had to be filed away without examination. The back of my mind was where I kept stories about Jesus. I really disliked that man. He was so harsh in his judgments of people, it was clear I had no chance of redemption. Nor did I really want to join the company of the elect. My grandmother sermonized incessantly. So half-listening became a habit, which persists to this day.

There was sneaky heroism in this, and it left me sympathetic to all movements of resistance. Ironically, it also made me into a smaller version of herself. My detractors say I always have an air of thinking about things other than what's going on, and certainly that was the case with her. I too prefer solitude. Both of us hurt people gratuitously, casually. In charity, I must acknowledge that neither of us ever managed to get a very clear grasp of our effect on others. But not knowing is a double affront. Most kids thought I was stuck-up, and I suppose I was. Still, this was out of shyness mainly. She was stuck-up on moral grounds.

I can see a great cluster of family at the big round table in the dining room, chattering happily, but all of them aware of her presence. Cooking for feasts like this always comes from my Great Aunt Annie, my grandmother's sister, who is better than anyone else at preparing boiled chicken and dumplings. Memory deceives, for the picture contains more people than were ever together here at the same time. Aunt Annie has been joined by the other great aunts, Biney and Maria. My mother sits with her sisters Eva and Belle, and her brothers Ed and Henry. All these people have the same attitude toward Sarah Wallace that I do. They love her, but she makes them nervous. I am minding my own business, which is to stuff myself on Aunt Annie's cooking. They are talking about Walt, my mother's favorite brother, who died young from consumption. It is ordinary, familiar conversation, comfortable to all. My grandmother has the lead. She is reciting how Walt, around 1900, conceived the idea of what he called "limber rails," a device like the tank tracks of a later day, to take vehicles through mud. There is a pause. "If he had lived . . . ," my mother says sadly. I happen to be watching my grandmother, and see her eyes narrow. "Do you question the ways of God?" she asks. The temperature changes. Now we are in for it.

I too have been accused of having an alarming presence. My first wife once cried out after a party, "It's not what you say! It's what I think you might say!" Mind you, I have never been known to mention the Bible. But I do have my own hobbyhorses, and the pattern remains the same. On that particular evening, certain of our guests had been going on about the spread of nuclear weapons and the approaching holocaust. This topic always triggers in me an explosion of oratory concerning the miracles of modern medicine. "If you'd been around at the time of the Black Death," I shouted, *"then* you'd have had something to grouse about!" At this point my wife and I locked eyes. She knew the next step in the monologue. I was about to take up the subject of human nature, which in my view had not improved much since the time of Caligula. I smiled at her dreamily, and fell silent.

The light would be just right for shooting on Kimball's Point. I had arranged to meet some small boys there and film them climbing about on the rocks the way I used to do. On my way out of the house, I stopped to peer through the dining room window at the property next door. Someone has torn down the house, cut most of the trees and turned the place into a miniature golf course, with metal traps and plastic loop-the-loops. There used to be a grove of pines out there, and in here by the window a ladder-back rocking chair. When I was of a size to fit on her lap, my grandmother used to rock me in the evening and sing hymns. The setting sun would strike through the pines, giving an amber glow and imparting a sense of things ending. I hated the hymns, but listening to them was the price I had to pay for the lap, which I liked. Out where the pines had stood, there was a man in orange speckled tweeds repeatedly hitting a ball and missing the hole, while he and the lady with him laughed and laughed. In my mind, the view dissolved into what it once had been: a long white house, with a porch at the front ranging along the whole side, framed by trees, topped by a blue sky and underlined by a flower garden. They told me I was born in that house, which belonged to my father's brother Lee. If Lee were in his garden today, my grandmother might take it into her head to holler across the fence at him about obscure iniquities. I did not want to be on hand for that, so I hurried out the back door.

I had waited too long. She rounded the corner of the house as I went down the back steps. Here was a woman whose dimensions changed in various perspectives. At a distance, she was tall and stately. Approaching, she seemed shorter, perhaps frail and thin. But close-up, the strong bones of the face, the penetrating dark eyes, and the mane of white hair made her grow again. "I want you to hang up that sign," she said. I said, "All right." She handed me a letter, stepped by, mounted the porch steps and went into the kitchen, banging the door. I recognized my mother's handwriting on the envelope, and tucked it into my pocket. There was no doubt a dollar inside. I did not glance at the upper glass panel of the kitchen door, for fear of losing my unconcerned air.

The pines next door bent and sighed in the wind. The flower beds were bright and empty in the sun. Spring roses nodded beside our woodshed. Inside there was that smell of chicken droppings that dated from the time we kept hens. The sign saying "ROOMS" was propped against the wall next to the door. Beside it lay a hammer and one large nail. The woodshed windows that face the house were a long, low line of double panes, and even at this age I had to stoop to look through them. I peered angrily at the house, seeing no one but feeling myself seen. The letter crinkled in my pocket, pressing against my thigh.

My anger came from the issue of the sign, from what was going to happen about the dollar, and from my own stupidity at not having beaten my grandmother to the post office. It was the custom to go down and watch the mail being sorted. Lots of people did it, grown-ups mostly. The town kids seldom came, perhaps having no expectations. My not living here the year round made me one of the summer people, and I presumed that was why the younger generation didn't have much time for me. In the post office, there was a big glass plate covering the boxes into which letters were tucked from the sorting area behind, and everybody knew which box was theirs. We all stood watching. It was good to see something slide in, a confirmation of one's existence. Nobody asked for their mail until the sorting was complete. We would sneak glances at the pictures on the wall of men wanted for terrible crimes. On the days when I went there, I could pocket letters that came from my mother without my grandmother knowing and getting riled. But today, there had been an argument at breakfast about the "ROOMS" sign, so I had moped about the house instead of going downtown.

The big oak tree between the newly-paved road and the sidewalk would do for the sign. When the W.P.A. men came to put a narrow concrete ribbon of road through the town, there had been talk of the trees going. That contingency, coupled with loss of the familiar dirt road, imparted my first open thought about the possibility that life might contain permanent change for the worse. The earlier death of my father was a closed thought. I did not remember it. It was a nonevent; and since nobody spoke of him, his absence stayed at the back of my mind.

Looking back, I am not surprised I was content at knowing so little. One main problem with the modern world may be that there is too much information. We have trouble living up to the sound of bells tolling far and wide; and this is bad for our character.

Most of us enjoy being well deceived. I have always felt there are occurrences that may some day be pulled back and lived again, perhaps on better terms. That day I looked at the trees and thought for the first time in a long while about my father. I had given up hope on these oaks, yet they had been spared after all. There seemed no possibility that my father would come back, though surely he was somewhere. He was dead, and nowhere. I didn't even remember what he looked like. Yet now I was thinking about him thinking about me. Or wishing he could. There swelled up in me an unspecific bad opinion of myself.

I hate myself for having mixed feelings, which occurs a lot. I had mixed feelings about renting rooms to tourists. Sometimes it seemed nice to have people about, making sounds in the house. Other times it seemed demeaning, an invasion of a safer privacy where the clock ticked and the wood settled in the stove and nothing much happened. It always meant more work.

For one thing, the laundry increased in volume when we had guests. I would prop open the two slanting doors that led to the basement. The next step was to go to the very dank back of the cellar, in order to draw fresh water from the cistern. It was like going into a cave. The room with the faucet had a natural stone floor that rippled, and a dark smell I associated with death. It took a couple dozen trips to fill the boiler and the two sinks. The sinks were stone, but the boiler was tin, and it sat on a kerosene stove. Soap had to be stirred in as the water came to a boil.

Then I'd go get my grandmother, and we'd carry down the big wicker basket containing the wash. The stirrer was a chopped-off broomstick grown white from years of use. She would push the sheets and towels and clothing around in the boiler with it, and then lift them piece by piece, to be dumped in the first sink and scrubbed against the metal ridges of the washboard. The exercise always put her in a special mood, for she would talk about her own childhood, matching the rhythms of speech to the motions of hands. To this day, whenever I pass a laundromat in Manhattan and pick up the smell of soap and steam, I get the echo of her phrases, "Early in the schoolyard . . . dancing in a circle . . . all the girls together . . . necklaces of flowers."

The job took a whole day. I handled the rinsing and wringing. When I got stuck, she would help me by loosening the rollers. I liked working with her. On the other hand, the green world outside forever beckoned through the high basement windows. I'd get restless, and fall to wondering if we really had to be doing all this. She said we needed the money, but I never thought this was so. It was just one of those things she did sometimes to show her strength, and also to call witness she was neglected by her own.

I reached as high as I could, and nailed the sign saying "ROOMS" to the oak tree. Stepping back to look at the result, I saw my father's brother Lee coming along the sidewalk from downtown. We never spoke to each other. He couldn't read the sign from where he was, but no doubt knew what it said. He glanced toward it, and our eyes met. As he looked away and passed on, the front screen door of our house screeched. There was going to be hollering. I tossed the hammer under a rose bush and turned to head for the lake. My grandmother's voice reached after me: "You're going the wrong way! The shops are that way!"

She was alluding to the hypothetical dollar in my mother's letter. I regularly received such funds, and as regularly spent them on soda pop, candy and pulp fiction. My grandmother resented the whole transaction, on the ground that it enforced my basic inability to hold on to money. She was not all that wrong. Still, the whole issue did not seem to me to be worth the noise. It did prove one thing, though: what women didn't know didn't hurt them.

Behind me I heard the screen door squeak as she went back into the house. Empty houses bothered me in those days. I felt free now that she was inside. Houses seemed to know more than people. They contained all the lives of their inmates, back to the beginning. There were certain ones in town I hated to go by. I knew they were staring at me, possessing information which concerned me but eluded me. On the way to the Point, it was necessary to pass the old Kimball place, deserted many years and reputed to be haunted. There were two maneuvers essential to getting by safely. First, glance casually at the house, but on no account lock eyes with any of the windows. Second, maintain an unconcerned air—revealing tension or caution gives victory to the house. At the point of closest proximity, the spell snaps, and the house loses its power. The rooms have now rejoined the past, taking with them their many inhabitants.

Today, the haunted house has been torn down, to be replaced by a stone bungalow with picture windows. I stare at it; it stares at me. Nothing. I miss my ghosts. Three small boys are coming down the path toward me. They are the ones who are going to help me recapture my past. I start to explain what I'd like them to do, but they keep eyeing my camera and tripod nervously. The rig entails a big, black box with a long lens poking out and a high magazine towering at the top, plus a fat, rotating tripod head and long legs underneath, so it must seem a very grown-up instrument.

The adult world, in itself, frightened me. Everyone seemed so knowing, so loud in their proclamation of purpose.

The barber shop was one grown-up place where I had to go periodi-
cally. It was scary, but attractive. Full of emblems of expert knowledge, masculinity.

"Do you remember cutting my hair?"

"Yes. I remember you coming in here. And that's the same board
over there that you sat on."

"To get high enough for you."

"That's right. As I remember you, you were a very quiet sort of a
boy."

"Shy."

"Well, you didn't . . . you didn't stick your neck out at all."

I was careful. The booming cynicism of barbershop talk deepened my suspicion that adults were creators of bad tidings. They kept company with death. Childhood, for all its perils and hobgoblins, was a safe time. Growing up was a necessary evil. Such insights have stood to strengthen me against predictions of holocaust. The truth is, this whole enterprise has got to be terminal. Our days always end, and we shall inevitably evolve by one means or another into extinction, as spaceship Earth sooner or later runs down.

To start the boys thinking creatively, I explained how the camera works, opening the side panel to show the way film flows through. Then I had them look at the shot through the viewfinder. They quickly learned how to put image into focus and manipulate the zoom lens. They had to be lifted up for this, and they felt surprisingly light and fragile. There were two tow-headed brothers, and a dark-haired, skinny boy who seemed the leader.

We plotted a progression for them to make along the bluffs, with action to be repeated over and over in order to let me change camera position and get material to capture a flow of movement in the final cutting. They threaded along the same route I used to take long ago, often grabbing hold of bushes to swing out over the edge where the sandstone had fallen away. Below, the surf pounded. A couple of times, they were hit by high shafts of spray. In about an hour, I was getting the last shot of them. They sat on the very tip of the Point, looking out, with the skinny boy pointing to the lighthouse.

I would need a shot of this from their point of view, but the work of shifting camera and tripod about had been tiring, so I decided to rest a bit before setting up for that. I shook hands, offering thanks and saying how well they had done. It had been fun, and would make a good sequence of at least thirty seconds. They wandered off toward town. I felt unaccountably sad. Why? Perhaps it was that I had, with their help, begun to succeed at entering the past. I sensed its waves flowing over me. I felt raw. I felt open. I was lying here, on this sun-warmed rock, under some sort of scrutiny.

> This was my church. I came here to commune with what was real. I
> worshipped the woods and the fields and the water with an intensity

that has not abated to this day. It never occurred to me that I was cut in the same mold as my grandmother. She studied the Good Book: she caught the eye of Christ. I studied the sky and the trees and the lake; and I knew with no effort of faith at all that Nature was personally aware of me.

The lighthouse itself looks like a church. On a large squat base are mounted towers for the lights, grouped a bit off-center and narrowing to a sharp point like a steeple. It is only five miles out, but appears to be on the horizon. I never got out there. Lake Huron is reputed to be fierce and treacherous as any ocean, and it may very well be so, since it is so big you can't see across it. My grandmother told me that when her husband took his fishing boat out, she often thought he wouldn't come back. I never quite believed this. For one thing, it sounded like one of those utterances women make to disparage men as reckless and irresponsible. For another, it worked to enforce her standing order that I was never to have a boat. I seldom felt reckless, I never felt irresponsible, and I truly respected the lake. The water was itself conscious of my presence. I would not have risked its anger. Still, I never got a chance to prove that. I never got a chance to compare notes with my grandfather, either, since he died, in bed, fourteen years before I was born.

In the end, I came to feel glad I never got to the lighthouse, since I love it right where it is. Wanting things to stay where they are has long been a failing of mine. It makes for sedentary habits. Anything that forced a change in the life pattern, the arrival of relatives from Detroit, roomers who responded to the sign on the tree, even casual visitors from the country, would make me realize the extent to which my grandmother and I were set in our ways. My mother's brother Ed drove up some weekends, and he would try straight away to get us out of our rut. Uncle Ed was a short, energetic man, stooped from long hours on the assembly line at Hudson Motors. "Get your fish pole!" he would shout. Or, "Time for a picnic!" Or simply, "Let's go for a drive!" When he made the last suggestion, I'd get garden tools and gloves to put in the back of the car, because we always ended up at the graveyard. This was a family ceremony that I enjoyed. Other ventures were less special: I could picnic or fish by myself, and often did. But cemeteries had to have people. My grandmother usually would bring petunias or sweet William to plant in her family plot. While she did that, the rest of us would settle down and trim the grass around the graves and headstones. They always talked about the folk lying there. I liked hearing about those who had gone before. It gave me a feeling of being blessed with a structured and luminous past. There was spontaneous love in the sadness. And there was the whisper of another world existing somewhere. Not the nonsense about heaven, but something.

> Small towns have long memories. People die, go away, but in a sense they stay, a lingering presence in the minds and talk of those who are left. My grandmother, Sarah Wallace, lies here. She is not here . . . but somewhere. Her hold on the present persists. I never believed in the soul, in the idea of personal immortality. In fact, the very notion was abhorrent to me. But I liked going to the graveyard. I liked the rituals of respect. And there hovered an abiding sense of continuity that carried no images. Of people having been, being, to be in the future.

Suppose, in the end, we're left with nothing but sentiment, that frail, subjective thing. There have been altars erected more profane. At some point while they were pruning and planting and chatting, I'd drift away and go to the far side of the graveyard where my father was buried, to look at his headstone for a while. I never brought flowers.

Uncle Ed had offered to rent a boat and take me to the lighthouse on the day of the last, terrible quarrel between my mother and my grandmother. To my own astonishment that morning, I found myself telling him I didn't want to go. Something bad was brewing, and my presence seemed necessary to protect the house. I was loafing over breakfast in the kitchen. Uncle Ed stared at me for a moment, then shrugged and turned to the wall cupboard beside the big wood range. He kept a bottle of rye whisky there on his visits, stopping to tap it occasionally during the day. I never saw any signs of drink on him, though my grandmother was fond of saying that when he was young, the horse knew the way back to the farm better than he did. He poured himself a nip, and nursed it while we looked at each other and listened. Mixed with the sigh of the wind in the pines next door was a noise that was rising from somewhere in the front part of our house. The two women were shouting at each other. Uncle Ed smiled at me and returned his glass to the cupboard. "I'd better get back," he said. As he passed through the door, I heard my mother shouting, "I have been your servant for thirty years!" My grandmother's voice rang louder: *"You cashed those bonds!"* I put my cereal bowl in the sink, pumped water into it, and turned to slide outside through the back door. Uncle Ed was booming, "You can't want to send your own daughter to jail!"

There was a tall twin oak at the bottom of the garden. To facilitate the start of climbing, I had nailed sticks across where the two trunks parted at the base, forming a primitive ladder. I chose the oak that stood slightly taller than the other, and mounted up and up until the tree trunk was as thin as a branch and plunged and swayed in the wind. Over the houses and the trees, I could see where the light blue bowl of the sky met the dark gray horizon of the lake. Closer to shore, there were streaks of white surf. Everything tossed as the tree whipped back and forth. Down below, Uncle Ed's car squatted in the yard. As I looked, he and my mother came out of the house and stood by the car. She had her spring coat over her arm. Probably they were calling me, but I couldn't hear. My mother got in the car. Uncle Ed went back to the porch and picked up a suitcase that had been standing behind the rails. My mother was going. I called and called, but there was no lull in the wind, and my cries were lost. By the time I got down, they had driven off. My hands hurt from descending so fast. I went down to the lake to watch the waves.

Uncle Ed's car was there when I got back around supper time. He was sitting on the back steps. "I put your mother on the bus to Detroit," he said. "She left you this note." I took it up to my room in the attic to read. She didn't say much, just that I should come back to the city at the end of the summer to go to school.

Nobody ever said much. As I was helping set the table, my grandmother asked, "How could she?" I didn't say anything. Once in a while during the remaining years, she would ask the same question, "How could she?" I didn't understand, so I never replied. Beyond that there was nothing. Summer here, winter there, silence. It was like being shared by honorably divorced parents, neither of whom would discuss the other.

Uncle Ed took me down to the drug store that evening to have a

Boston Cooler. He told me there were two sides to most things, a proposition I was prepared to accept. On the one side, my mother always was a fool about money, and part of the quarrel had been over that. But the base of their anger was darker and deeper. On the other side, serving as my grandmother's companion all those years couldn't have been much fun. Unwanted visitors did not stay long in the house, and this would have given short span to suitors. Uncle Ed set me to chopping kindling in the light of the back porch for the breakfast stove, and as I worked at that I wondered how my father had stayed around long enough to father me.

I positioned the camera close to the end of the Point, bracing the tripod against the wind for a last shot of the lighthouse. This was a slow zoom in, until the building filled the whole frame of film. It completed the final action sequence. Now the time had come to call in a full film crew, so I could be free to do on-camera narration and interviews, as a final step toward recapturing the past. Settling down again out of the wind, I reflected it was also time to pack away the typewriter, and give up for a while on my treatment about the future.

> We are possessed by the feeling that nothing works the way it used to, or the way it ought to, and that things are getting worse instead of better. Each person has his own set of gripes; and listing them is a standard feature of any conversation. Often the achievements of technology appear to produce more irritation than satisfaction. It is the same with social institutions: we complain about law enforcement agencies that do not enforce the law, schools that do not teach, welfare services that perpetuate misery. In an era of big government, we distrust government. There is a sense of life itself decaying, of man being bombarded by an increasing clutter of private and public mishaps. Nor do we know where to turn, for this general sense of uneasiness is fostering very few suggestions for improvement.

The network would think this too gloomy, and ask for "balance," but there didn't seem to be much of that around just now. I thought the immediate future would turn into a shouting match between patriotic optimists and subversive pessimists. It would be hard to explain why it is I get greater hope and comfort from the latter posture. Such ruminations were carrying me into my grandmother's belief that man is close to a bad end. If self-restraint is put in balance against self-immolation, the optimist will get no help from history. Still when the drums begin to roll, he must have his say.

My grandmother was dead right about one thing: that dollar did burn a hole in my pocket. I had opened my mother's letter after passing the haunted house on the way to Kimball's Point, and sure enough, the lovely green bill was there. I slid into a crevice out of the wind to read the letter. She wrote a long, Spencerian hand, which I found hard to read, so after I'd deciphered news about her going to a concert with the girls from the office, my attention began to wander. Back east, beyond sandstone bluffs, the beach curved out and out into the lake, to the point where sand and pine trees met at the horizon in a peninsula pointed at the lighthouse. That was Pointe aux Barques, where the rich families had houses. They were the real summer people. I was in between. I was restless. This was the ideal spot for a floating reverie I used to practice, where nature seemed to advance and retreat in a pulselike dialogue; but today my heart wasn't in it. The dollar was bothering me. The fuss my grandmother had raised made me want to get rid of it. An irresistable urge to spend arose in me. I climbed down to where the beach began, and headed back toward the dock and the road that led up to the stores.

Having money and spending it have always carried a mystical satisfaction for me. This has nothing to do with acquiring things. I've never acquired much. When I'm broke, I always say it's just bad luck, but I don't mean that. In my heart I know it is a judgment against me, and one that is deserved. Poor people—and there were plenty of those around in the Depression—always attracted and repelled me in a frightening way. It was as if they had invented a new, obscure form of sin. The odor of poverty was stronger in my nostrils than that of sanctity.

> The level factory was the only industry in town. It kept going, through thick and thin, turning out levels for carpenters and mechanics. Everyone who had jobs worked hard, including the boss. Having a job, any job, was an honorable condition. Mr. Upthegrove is boss now. He works hard all the time.
>
> "You were a child here during the depression. Did you have a happy childhood?"

"Well, I was an only child, but I guess I had a happy childhood. As happy as anyone could have. We always had something to eat: I guess that was the main thing."

"Do you remember it as being a time when people were afraid?"

"Oh, yes. Very definitely. You couldn't buy a job, I remember that. My father was supervisor for several years. People used to come that were really hard up. And he had Red Cross flour here, and salt pork, that he was supposed to give to people. If they really needed it. He'd always ask people how they got to town. And if they said they drove their car, he said, 'If you got money to buy license plates and gasoline, you got money to buy food.' But if a neighbor brought them in, or if they walked in, why that was the way he determined whether the people really needed it or not. People today, if you told them that people didn't have anything to eat, I don't think they'd believe it."

"Yeah. It's easy to forget that."

"But I guess I'm fortunate that I was in on the tail end of it—old enough to remember it, anyway. Maybe that's one of the things that's kind of haunted me all my life."

We are haunted by so many things that it's often hard to separate the ghosts who help us from the ones who do us harm. For myself, the image of authority has always been a useful spook. I am never at ease in its presence, viewing it both with respect and with what I hope is appropriate distrust. At that time, the air was so clouded with promises unfulfilled, with hopes drawn thin, as to bring human competence into question. So being fond of one's fellow man was all right, but it was a good idea to be suspicious of him as well. Somehow government itself seemed insubstantial, a kind of self-indulgence.

I project conditions where the gravy train of promises will grind to a halt, and where leaders will have to admit that some or many must do without. When that occurs, politics takes on a slightly different flavor. It begins to seem like something of a luxury. Politics is based on promises, which are based on expansion. Limit expansion, and hope begins to look like envy. Then politicians begin to look like people who not only fail to keep their promises, but also feed off the unhappiness of others.

As I was going past my Uncle Sam Wallace's big store on my way to spend that dollar, the main door opened, and he came out. We had to stop face-to-face to avoid bumping into each other. He was another of my father's brothers, and this was as close as we'd ever been. We stared. He was a stout man, with iron-gray hair. He looked dead. I started to move around him, but he reached out to stop me. His eyes traveled down to where his hand rested on my shoulder. "Wait," he said. We looked at each other. "Wait," he said again. "Come on in." He stepped back and opened the door. I followed. I had never been inside. It was a general store that had everything. It smelled good, in a very complicated way, of herbs, and grain, and bread, and kerosene. He stopped and looked back, waving his hands toward the glass cases. "Take anything you want," he said. I didn't know what to do. It seemed so unnatural for us to be acknowledging each other's existence in this way. "Go ahead," he said. "Take anything." There were groceries, suits of clothes, hunting and fishing equipment, bicycles, tools, rolls of cloth, bags of seed. The cases and racks glittered back into darkness. I stared about desperately, looking for something I wouldn't have to explain to my grandmother. Then I remembered the beautiful fishing lure for pike that had been sitting in an outside display window for years, ranking as one of those things that would be sure to change my life if I had it. I moved over and stood on my toes to reach beyond the rail and point. "That all you want?" he asked. I nodded.

There memory stops. I don't recall leaving the store. I can't remember if I thanked him. After that day we would return to our practice of not exchanging greetings on the street. Possession of the lure did have an effect, though perhaps different from the one expected. I just felt certain that something in my life had changed; and that was all. I never caught any fish with it. In fact, I never used it. The beautiful, long, slim, gray-green plug stayed in my fishing box and traveled about with me from place to place, until one day I noticed it was gone. Someone else had liked the look of it. I was glad it had passed from me in the same state it had come to me. Using it would have been wrong. I didn't understand this, or even think about it; I just knew it was true, and that something valuable was permanently preserved.

I may have learned about taking care of things from watching my cousin Will tend bees. He was thirty years older than I, and we never talked about anything theoretical in those days. But I loved to follow him around and watch him build his hives and take care of them. At the time I thought this was because bees were scary: they could sting, yet they delivered golden honey. Also the blended smell of fresh wood, wax, and sugar in his shop made me giddy. I now know it was also because Will is one of those people who know what's right and wrong without a lot of inner debate, and I wanted to be like that. He showed this quality when he talked to me on camera:

> "Once years ago when I was about twenty years old, why, they put a bounty on hawks. And they used to be a flight come along the shore here when they migrated. And I wanted a repeating shotgun. They'd just come out at that time. They had this twenty-five cent bounty on hawks. I could have shot enough of them to have bought me a new gun, but . . . couldn't do it. 'Cause I don't believe in that. I didn't believe that was right."
>
> "Where did you get these beliefs?"
>
> "I don't know. It seems like they were natural. They were always with you one way or another."

The truth is, we are all spoiling everything now. We know, but we don't want to let on. This is the cause of the inner conflict so many people complain about, and also of our flashes of fundamental anger. We know there is not enough space any more; we know that plants and animals are dying irretrievably. We know we are committing a human sin when we ravage the earth, building surplus amidst starvation. We know we have come to fear and distrust knowledge itself, since it prevents our pushing inconsistencies into the back of our minds. We know that self-deceit has become a modern art form. We know this means we are even spoiling ourselves.

Cousin Will was a light boned, quick moving man, with penetrating blue eyes. He played the fiddle beautifully. One evening, we had a gathering in the front parlor, and Cousin Phoebe played the piano while Will lilted into reels and jigs and country songs. It was magic. My voice hadn't changed yet, but even at that stage I knew I was born to be listener rather than lark. For a long time I tapped my feet and bathed in the joy of the group. Then gradually the feeling grew on me of being outside. My grandmother, my aunts and cousins seemed to recede, to stand enormous at a great distance, their sounds and gestures meaningless. I ran from the room. As I lay on my bed, the sounds gradually began to come back. Except something was missing. The fiddle was not there. Now there was someone with me in the dark, sitting on the bed. A hand began to stroke my head gently. After a bit, Will's voice said, "You better go back."

Going back is not easy. We want to distort the past so it will justify our present. Learning something is another thing entirely. I had this in mind when I talked to Will with the camera turning:

> "I wonder, when I'm thinking about my grandmother, or your parents whom I knew, and all the other people who were our family here, whether they were people that were basically different than we are. Whether they had something different about them."
>
> "Well, I think that—see, of course, I can only speak for country people and farmers—and I know what the early people, the pioneers, they had in mind was that they wanted to build a home. They wasn't trying to make money. They had to make some money, of course, to do the things that was necessary. But everything was for a home. And they, most all around where I lived here, they had beautiful gardens, and orchards of all kinds—and, they just, the whole thing really was of beauty. Takin' it all in all. And now, why, you see plenty of farms or houses that don't hardly have a shade tree at all. Seems to be just hard-boiled cash deal every day. Money you see is the thing. If there's money in it, do 'er. Get 'er done. Well, I don't believe in that."

"You pick me up coming around the corner," I said to the cameraman. "Pan and follow focus until I get to here, then continue the pan and start zooming so you end up with a medium close-up of that thing in the window." The film crew and I were outside Uncle Sam's store, and I was directing the cameraman on a shot. The store had changed hands several times, dropping drygoods and groceries in order to specialize now in sporting equipment. What stood dominant in the window today was a huge, adult-size tricycle. That was to be target for the zoom. I didn't know why I wanted the shot, but there it was. The cameraman wanted the tricycle. He had been nagging me to buy it for him. It would be a perfect vehicle for travel shots, he argued; although we both knew he just wanted to get on it and ride around town. I didn't want to debate this. I just wanted to get the shot and move along. I was looking at the tricycle and seeing the pike lure that had lain in that spot for years before it was given to me.

Supper was ready when I got home: hamburgers and creamed potatoes. Being stopped by Uncle Sam had cut down my urge to spend, so I
hadn't stuffed myself on candy. I was able to eat, though without enjoy-
ment. My grandmother was good at most things she did, except for
cooking. I waited for harsh words, but none came. We talked about
shifting some rose bushes, and where best to plant potatoes for a summer crop. When we'd finished eating, I heated some water on the range
and did the dishes. Then we sat at the round table in the dining room.
That was the best place to spend spring evenings when the temperature
dropped. She read the Bible, and I fed the big-bellied wood stove, and
worked at tidying my fishing kit box. I had mixed the new plug in with
the other lures, so it wouldn't be noticed. Now I picked it out and
studied it. It was a wonderful thing. Finally, I put it back and snapped
the box shut. Outside on the highway, a car went by. I listened and
identified it as the old Chevy belonging to Mr. Pittwood, the druggist. I
went to the closet, got out a back copy of *War Aces,* and sat next to my
grandmother at the round table. The stories in these magazines were of
two categories, the heroic and the comic. I preferred the latter, reason-
ing that since all fighter pilots had to be brave, it was best to be crazy as
well. War was the worst big thing that had ever happened, and the signs
were it would happen again. It would come as a bitter part of one's
education, as it had for the generation before. That's the way it felt,
anyway. I had read this magazine a couple of times, and my eyes began
to wander toward the patterns of flame flickering through the isinglass
windows of the stove. I snapped back, because if my grandmother noticed my availability, she was likely to start reading aloud from the
Bible, a book that upset me a great deal more than *War Aces* did.

It seemed hard luck that the gate had to be straight and narrow the
way which leadeth into life. Still, by all accounts this was so. What got
through to me in fragments of Bible quotation was a lot of it frightening. People were forever failing some vital test. As it turned out, not
peace but a sword did arrive, and brother did indeed deliver up
brother to death, and the father the child. But at the time, the approaching war was a matter for the front pages of the newspapers,
which never got read. I stuck to the comics inside, in my search for
the required personal heroism. Sunday was always a quiet day. I used
to like to sit on the front porch, and watch the cars go by. There

weren't many of them. It was about this time of day that the church bells began to ring—and for some reason, all the churches began to ring simultaneously. It made a beautiful pattern of sound. I never went to church, but the timing of the bells always signaled to me that it was time to start looking down the street for the newsboy. Ever since that time, when I hear church bells, I think about Moon Mullins, and Smilin' Jack, and Skeezix, and all the other heroes of my youth.

My grandmother closed the Bible. I looked up and our eyes met. We smiled. I reached into my pocket and pulled out the dollar, placing it on the table between us, but closer to her. She took my hand, placed it over the dollar and squeezed it shut. "It's for you," she said. "I know," I said. "I mean, it's for your own good." "I know." I felt terribly sad, not scolded sad or defeated sad, just sad. She must have seen this, because she opened her arms to me. I went to her, and bent down so we could embrace without her having to stand. She smelled old-fashioned. Her shoulders were bony. I felt great love for her, though I knew I couldn't help her much. She said, "Now that we have the sign up, we'll have to air the sheets." I said, "Yes. Then we can plant the potatoes."

I was leaning on the fence by his barn with old Mr. Petovsky, the farmer. We were looking at the pigs, and they from time to time glanced at us. The film crew were at the other end of the barnyard by our wagon, busy with reloading camera and sound between sessions of interview. I was having an open thought in the front of my mind, about what Mr. Petovsky had been saying in the last take before we ran out of film. It sounded as if he were describing a permanent change for the worse:

"People lived happier than they do today. Happier. We used to trash, you know. Grain. Trash grain. You'd go and visit a neighbor, you know. When we trashed grain there was eighteen, twenty farmers. You had to go to help pitch that grain out of the barn. You had to work your time back. Help the neighbors. Lived happy. Lived happy. Yeah. But today, why you don't know the next neighbor hardly. I don't know what's gonna happen. I wish I could live long enough, another five years, and see what's. . . . There might be a lot of different. There might be a lot of different. But I don't think it's gonna end up good. I don't think it. No, I don't think it'll end up good."

So here we are, and nothing seems to work the way it should. Did it ever? Hard to say. I was looking at Mr. Petovsky talking, but not hearing what he said. Instead, I was thinking about all those of mine who had gone before. Long, long I had wished there was some act of contrition I could perform, to induce them to forgive me. For what? Hard to say. Myself. Now the thought came flooding into my mind that it was the other way round. I had to forgive them. Once I did that, they could forgive me. Perhaps it was happening.

Mr. Petovsky caught my attention by leaning forward to address me confidentially.

"Maybe I shouldn't say this," he said.

"What?"

"Maybe I shouldn't say this."

"No. Go ahead. Say what?"

"Well, the Wallaces, your family, went bad."

"No! Sam, the merchant?"

"No, not him."

"Not Lee!"

"No, not him."

"Not the one who drank? That one? Frank?"

"No, it was John."

"Yes?"

"Head of the family. Banker. And, you see, his bookkeeper, half his age, first cousin, all that—why, she had a baby."

"Mr. Petovsky," I said, leaning toward him, "I am that baby."

When he had done laughing, he seized both my hands in his and declared, "I've got a dozen rooms in that house there. If you ever come to this town and don't stay with me, I'll never forgive you!"

He will, though. Forgiving is easy once you start doing it.

Sarah Wallace took a long time dying. I don't know what it was. In those days people died of age. She was seventy-two. I was fourteen. She lay and looked at me. "You are not my boy any more," she said, and turned away. The next time I saw her she was lying in her coffin in the front parlor next to the big black leather chair. They asked me if I wanted to kiss her. I am glad for her sake and for mine that I had the courage to say no.

ANCIENT AIRS, VOICES

JOYCE CAROL OATES

Joyce Carol Oates is the author of a number of works of fiction, poetry, and criticism, most recently *Raven's Wing,* stories (Dutton), and *On Boxing* (Doubleday). Her forthcoming novel is *You Must Remember This* (Dutton). She was the 1986 recipient of the O. Henry Award for Continuing Achievement, and her stories have been included in several previous O. Henry volumes.

TIMESPEEDEDUP: NOVEMBER 22, 1983

Eighteen years & five months will be a matter of (as the coroner afterward estimates) forty minutes' erasure. There is beauty in such economy. There is nobility of a sort. There is also, as Mikey had not dared to anticipate, a leisurely pace to the procedure because the heart's frightened pumping grows progressively weaker (and less frightened) as the pressure of the blood decreases.

A mathematical equation, an inverse ratio of some sort?—Mikey settles himself into the tepid bathwater, eyes closed, to think about it.

SUPERSTITION

When Mikey's mother Helen was much younger than he is at the time of his death, when she was in fact a slightly precocious eleven or twelve, she played at scaring herself and her girl friends with: *What is the worst thing that can happen?*

Whatever they said, whatever horror (usually personal and domestic) they came up with, Helen would say: But isn't there something worse?

Yes, okay, but isn't there something worse?

Yes, but—

But—

She saw that it was more powerful to be in control of questions, not answers. *What is the worst thing that can happen?*

When she was twenty-four years old and pregnant with her unknown yet-to-be-named baby, when her sharp angles and jumpy nerves were plumped out in a ripe rosy bloodwarm well-being that couldn't be hers yet *was*—when she thought secretly of herself as swollen with love (love *for,* love *of,* both her husband and the yet-to-be-named baby)—it occurred to her one day, crossing Harvard Square at an imprudent angle and at an ill-calculated moment (cautionary yellow about to change to red), precisely what the worst thing would be.

She told Neil about it that night in bed, whispering. She expected him to comfort her though it was late, past midnight, and he had a moot court session the next morning at eight. (He so often comforted her these days. These weeks. He was, as both his parents commented, not quite approvingly, "growing up fast.") But he responded impatiently, rubbing his forearm against his face, snorting with exasperation, as if Helen brought up such morbid things all the time now, and he'd had enough. That's superstition, he said angrily. You don't know it but that's superstition: trying to define the very worst so that it can't happen because if you define it, it *can't* happen as you have defined it.

That isn't true, Helen said, drawing away from him.

What isn't true?—that it's superstition, or that, if you define something to yourself, it can't happen? Neil asked.

She fashioned a little cocoon for herself of the bedclothes, at the very edge of the bed. She doubled the pillow up uncomfortably beneath her head. She was waiting to cry—tears had their own authority now—but nothing happened. When she and Neil quarreled a curious sort of flame-like rage shot up between them, instantaneous and heart-stopping in its virulence. Yet it meant nothing, they loved each other, they were in fact—were to be for five, six more years—crazy in love with each other.

DESIRE

These are the classic years of romance, of adulterous romance, when to think of desire is immediately to experience desire; and to think of (nobly, contemptuously) resisting desire is immediately to experience desire. Though Neil and his friend Garrett's wife are not conscious, at the time, of their good fortune.

These are the years of romance, bittersweet in memory; and of desire so potent it plucks at the roots of one's being. But these are not, in retrospect, years of love. (Neil is waiting, he tells himself, for desire to shade into love. Desire *must* shade into love. But he waits impatiently, resentfully. At times he fantasizes dying with Yvette—by accident—only by accident—driving on the Turnpike, for instance, crashing into a retaining wall.)

Neil is thirty-seven when the affair begins, Yvette is thirty-one, Neil's son Mikey is ten years old. Yvette's daughter Sonya is seven. Guilty, flushed with pride, the lovers talk about their children often: each pretends a genuine interest in the other's child. Mikey is the brightest boy in his fifth-grade class, Sonya is a sweetheart, so pretty. Mikey doesn't seem to make friends easily; Sonya is so *spoiled.* Does Mikey sense that something is . . . strained between his parents? Sonya, fortunately, cheerful, chattering Sonya, notices nothing.

They agree that they love their children, they love their children more than, well, their own lives. Neil grows vehement on the subject, Yvette frequently cries. Sweet, bittersweet, agitated, *poignant.* . . .

THE UNFORGIVABLE

You aren't thinking, God damn you, Neil whispers, so that Helen, who is sobbing, cannot quite hear. It is one of their "minor" quarrels, no one will be slapped, pummeled, thrown shrieking across a bed, banged against a closet door—no one will pull books or records off a shelf, or smash china in the kitchen, in a trance of hysteria. Indeed, the quarrel is so minor, it will soon be forgotten; except, perhaps, by the Schuelers' son.

Again, whispering, panting, Neil says: *You're thinking with your— womb.*

These are the frantic, jumbled months of 1975, the era of unforgivable insults that are not quite said out loud; and not quite heard.

(Except, perhaps, little Michael hears. Dark-eyed spiky-haired little Michael, Mikey as his grandmother calls him, who soon becomes an expert in things said and not said, heard and not heard. Michael who gets uniformly high grades in school—*very* high grades in arithmetic, then math—with an aristocratic sort of contempt for the mere act of performing, competing, *earning*. Mikey of whom both his parents appear to be nervously proud; of course they *are* proud, excitedly informed by one of the boy's teachers that his I.Q. has been measured at 183; and his "creative potential" is in the very highest percentile.)

Of course the guilty lovers insult each other as well, say unforgivable things calculated to do great injury—to lacerate, pierce, demolish. Simply by accusing Neil of not loving her, Yvette has the power of rendering him frantic; simply by walking out, slamming a door (not by design, that's the frightening thing, but furiously, helplessly), Neil (Neil Schueler the congenial, the entirely *reliable* husbandfathersonbrothercolleaguecitizen) has the power to reduce Yvette Held to an anguish so physical that she imagines her bodily gravity has increased tenfold. (What to do on such days but crawl into bed, hide away her misery, allow Garrett to console her without knowing why he is consoling her . . . without knowing whom, precisely, he consoles. What's wrong Yvette, what's wrong please tell me are you sick Yvette should I call a doctor Yvette please tell me what's *wrong*—the lament of many a kindly husband, in the year of romance 1975. While across town at the Schuelers' Helen discerns but cannot bring herself to name the love-abscess working in her husband's gut; and one evening it is Mikey, cautious little Mikey, who plays suddenly at being a much younger child and huddles in his pajamas in his Daddy's lap, burrowing into Daddy's chest, begging, giggling, You aren't going to go away are you Daddy. . . . ? You *aren't* going to go away *are* you Daddy . . . ?

Guilt, improvisation, despairing delight, oh delightful bowel-wrenching despair. The usual. Yet it's the first time, such fancies: telephone calls hot and breathless as bouts of love made from, for instance, a forgotten hotel in a forgotten Midwestern city, when Neil, sick with love, anxious to "finally get things straight," excuses himself in the awkward midst of a luncheon meeting, an important luncheon meeting, to rush away to his room on the forty-ninth floor and dial the Held residence back home—to speak with Yvette, with whom he'd spoken (and quarreled) that very morning. Yet another instance: Yvette, feverish, sleepless, slips away from her sleeping husband, walks barefoot past the door (always slightly ajar, to accommodate her nighttime fears) of her sleeping daughter, descends into the darkened kitchen to dial the number, *that* number, of her presumably sleeping lover some three or four miles away . . . and the phone is answered on the first ring . . . by Neil? or by Helen? or little Mikey?

NOVEMBER 1973

In Cunningham's Drugs beneath the too-bright fluorescent lighting she stands tall and splendid in a camel's-hair coat, her blonde hair glittering as if with chips of mica, lightly scolding her pouting little girl (such a beautiful child!—Neil feels an actual pang of loss, why hadn't he and Helen had another child, a girl, to balance Mikey), unaware of Neil Schueler a few yards away. Yes, she's the one, that woman, *her,* though he knows himself invisible and harmless, her husband's friend Neil, married to pretty dark Helen whom he loves and whom he would no more think of betraying than . . . than he would betray the confidence of the prestigious law firm for which he works.

Parties, dinners, accidental meetings in other people's homes, occasional (increasingly frequent) sightings in town, the public library, the dry cleaners, the Village Market, and always he's invisible, supremely innocent; he isn't spying on Yvette Held *(he* isn't that sort of man, happily married, thoroughly content with his life) . . . and she isn't aware of him. Except, perhaps, obliquely.

A wintry November afternoon, pitch dark at five-thirty, and again Neil happens to see her by accident, at the Texaco station, again in the camel's-hair coat, a sporty striped scarf wound around her throat. She's upset, she's arguing with one of the mechanics; he had promised her car for five o'clock but now he tells her it won't be ready for another hour, maybe an hour and a half, and she doesn't know what to do, it's so trivial and demeaning a thing, but what should she *do:* sit in the freezing waiting room and wait for her car, or call Garrett, have him pick her up, get the car in the morning. . . .

Neil offers to drive her home. Of course.

It's so trivial and demeaning, says Yvette, wiping angrily at her nose, and Neil says gravely, happily: I don't think it is.

THE WIVES

. . . are not friends though they might be said to have been, at one time, "friendly acquaintances."

Helen is nearly forty-four when the master of Mikey's residential college at Yale telephones with the news (two days before Thanksgiving of 1983); Yvette is thirty-nine. Both women are invariably "young for their age"; the remark (generally made by a man) is of course meant to be flattering.

Helen, who thinks of herself as numb, hollow, emptied out, as if (for instance) she'd had a massive gynecological operation, is a very attractive woman: small-boned, olive-skinned, with damp dark eyes and a delicate high-bridged nose, a small mouth. She becomes starkly visible to her husband only when something in the household goes wrong *and someone is to blame.* Otherwise, she is invisible to him and he loves her. He loves her well enough. No—he doesn't love her at all (why lie about it?) but he is responsible for her, a little frightened of her (her drinking, her spasms of cruel silent laughter, her *eyes),* worried about her effect (her "neurotic" behavior) upon their son.

Yvette, the beloved, the Object of Desire, is tall, rangy, blonde, with a wide oval face and strong cheekbones, gray-green eyes, a fleshy mouth. She mugs, she jokes, she makes faces, her gestures are loose and casual, her confidence in herself (her beauty, her power) is absolute: is it possible she has never grown up? She dresses with a stylish silly chic, Chinese woollen jackets, suede trousers and vests, high-heeled boots, fur-lined caps, white silk dresses, pale hair in tiny braids coiled prettily about her head. Her secret is a terrifying craving for forbidden foods (Planters peanuts devoured in fistfuls, M&Ms by the bag, French fries lurid with salty grease) which she combats by going on impromptu fasts, once or twice a month, losing so much weight (what exhilaration, to starve herself!—it's better than sex) her pelvis bones begin to show through her tightest pair of jeans and her cagey eyes are all shadow. At such times she exults in feeling light-headed, transparent, angelic. She exults in the fact that two highly attractive men—her husband and her lover—watch anxiously over her.

Even before Helen learned specifically of the affair, she bravely asked Neil whether he wanted a divorce; whether he wanted a trial separation; whether he might be "happier" without her. (Don't be ridiculous, Neil said at once, frightened, excited—you don't know what you're talking about.) Helen has a master's degree in biology, Helen plans to return to graduate school soon; she is fully capable (as she says, often) of living her own independent life.

As for Yvette: she intimidates Garrett simply by *hinting* . . . if he isn't entirely happy (with her moods, her treatment of Sonya, her circle of youngish friends) . . . he has the "option" of moving out.

Yvette is *loved,* Helen is *not-loved,* and is there any logical reason? There is not. There is not. As Neil would be the first to admit.

(Indeed, he sometimes imagines closing his fingers, hard, around Yvette's throat. The squirming eel-like body, the magnificent muscled legs, all that *blondeness* . . . erased forever. This is the woman who deserves humiliation, rejection, pain, and not poor Helen who is so . . . undeserving.)

The wives, the wives. Yet they are not interchangeable parts, that's the problem. As Neil would be the first to admit.

THE SEVEN BRIDGES OF KÖNIGSBERG

She is awake, walking about the house in the dark. Mikey knows she is touching things, groping, trying to keep her balance; he feels the tension, tightening, in her head. She has become a blind woman, prowling downstairs in the dark, sometimes her eyes *are* shut tight; does he dare to approach her?—touch her?—take her cold limp hand in his?

Mother I hate you. Mother please die.

But no: Mother I love you, *Mother please don't die.*

Michael Schueler's father is away: a conference in Brussels, a meeting in Frankfurt, confidential business in Tokyo. He telephones home dutifully, talking five minutes to Helen, five minutes to Mikey. He's a good father, he calls home. (It's true that he "moved out" for a while—a few weeks when Mikey was fourteen—but that's ancient history now, that's long forgotten.) There are Occasions: Thanksgiving, Christmas, the usual birthdays, Easter Sunday, Grandma's funeral, Mikey's First Prize at the State Science Fair. There are comradely fatherson Saturday mornings in the car, doing errands, taking Mikey to the dentist, stopping by the public library, that sort of thing, afterward raking leaves (in season), shoveling snow (in season), digging up the flowerbeds (in season) for Mother to plant her wax begonias and impatiens. Mikey calmly notes the *routine,* the *logic,* the *normality.* The Schuelers are (are *almost)* a television family, they strike the observing eye as so routine and so normal, and clearly they're an attractive threesome: mother and son dark and ferret-faced, father tall sandy-haired embarrassed scowling smiling, the skin crinkling heartily about his eyes. Hey Dad!

Mikey listens hard, but no longer hears the quarrels.

Were they a fiction of his boyhood?—his childhood?

Had he imagined everything?

Little Michael Schueler who isn't precisely popular at school—so taciturn, so solemn, yet with that sarcastic look, as if he knows the answer to the question (he knows the answers to *all* the questions) but won't condescend to raise his hand. His teachers pretend to be fond of him, his classmates make no pretense. (A shy kid. Scared. Weird. Has a temper. A nice enough kid but, well, maybe a little . . . unbalanced? One day another boy flicked water into Mikey's face at the drinking fountain and Mikey went crazy—hitting, kicking, screaming, *swearing* —every sort of foul word you can imagine. He bloodied the other boy's nose, had to be half-carried to the principal's office, sobbing, hysterical, *I'll kill anyone who touches me, I'll kill anyone who touches me.* A small kid but, God, really strong.)

But he doesn't know all the answers, he doesn't even know all the questions. He's frightened of what he doesn't know. *And there is so much.* At the age of twelve he investigates analytical geometry and calculus, at the age of thirteen he invents (not very successfully) his own geometry, at the age of fourteen he broods over the Möbius strip with its *single edge* and *single side,* a logical impossibility. (Or, as he tells his mother, an illogical possibility.) At the age of fifteen he amuses himself by making a model of the famous Seven Bridges of Königsberg to tape on his bedroom wall, with the intention (he's joking of course) of solving the problem within a year.

He won't solve it because, as the Swiss mathematician Euler demonstrated centuries ago, *it is insoluble,* yet, still, he's having fun, he likes to lie propped up on his elbows on the bed, staring, blinking, thinking hard, thinking very very hard, until his forehead is covered with an itchy film of perspiration and his eyes burn. Don't make yourself ill, Mother cautions, brushing his damp hair out of his face—don't make me worry about you, all right?

It's a hoary old puzzle, an ancient conundrum, a bit of Infinity to tape to the wall, and simple enough: Can you cross each bridge in turn *in one unbroken path* without crossing any of the bridges twice?

Yes. Sure. *He* (secretly) thinks so. Just give him time.

(A front-page story in the *New York Times,* which Daddy and all of Daddy's friends read: Fifteen-Year-Old Mathematical Genius Solves Classic Problem.)

So Mikey dreams of the Seven Bridges of Königsberg, he squints, shuts his eyes hard, opens them again, stares at the sheet of construction paper on the wall, feels his heartbeat accelerate with the . . . certainty . . . that he is going to succeed where hundreds, thousands, of mathematicians failed. Oh yes he's going to solve it! Maybe by accident, intuition, the way he beats his father at chess if he can get his father to play (Mikey beats him nine games out of ten though he hasn't any chess strategy *per se);* the way he guesses what his mother is thinking though she stands with her back to him, calm and rigid, unaware of his presence. Oh yes he's going to solve it, just give him time.

One bridge and then another and then another. A clockwise then a counterclockwise motion. And now he doubles back shrewdly on himself to travel on land. And now he twists about, in a surprising maneuver. And now. . . . No, he's been on this bridge already . . . or has he? . . .

THE LOVERS, PAST & PRESENT

The baby was born, there were no complications or ugly surprises, they named him Michael after Neil's father's father; they saw that he was a beautiful baby, a perfect baby, mother's and father's flesh mysteriously conjoined. A gasping fish's mouth, tiny fingers that clutch, eyes clear with hunger, then cloudy with the need to sleep: so sweet, so funny, hot with life: theirs. One of the stories Neil told for years was that he'd been communicating with his boy before the birth, oh as many as eight weeks before the actual birth, one of the stories Helen told, which she will begin to tell again after Mikey's suicide, was that she couldn't . . . quite . . . bring together the fact of being pregnant with the fact of having, being in the possession of, being responsible for, this particular baby. Not that she didn't, doesn't, love him; not at all. She loves him, or loved him, the way you love . . . your own flesh? . . . no, your own self. No. It is, yet it isn't, *you:* actually you love it better than you love yourself. Especially, says Helen with her breathless near-inaudible laugh—if you don't love yourself.

One of the stories Neil tells Yvette is that he and Helen "had very little to say to each other," that they were each lonely, a little angry, baffled; she spent a good deal of time by herself, by herself or with Mikey, sometimes she'd take a nap when he took his, Neil would find the two of them together, upstairs, lying beneath an afghan, sleeping or not quite sleeping, drowsing, dreamy-peaceful, the boy sucking a corner of the afghan in his sleep, Helen's eyes snapping open as Neil—the husband after all, *the* man—entered the room in the twilight, wondering, well, how long Helen had *been* there, comatose with a year-old child.

Helen dislikes lovemaking, Helen has become obsessed with lovemaking, Helen lies tight and clenched and inaccessible, Helen clutches at her alarmed husband with a need so ravenous, so enormous, no one (so he tells himself angrily) could satisfy it. But he complains to Yvette of his wife's . . . indifference; the cold sluggish feel of her flesh; the fact that, for more than a year after Mikey's birth, she refused to make love with him and stiffened in response even to his wayward casual affectionate questioning harmless touch. It was all Baby, Neil says, his voice lightly mocking, puzzled—it was Baby this, Baby that, all *Baby.*

(He does not tell Yvette—of course he does not tell Yvette, or anyone —that the new violence of his wife's passion, the rawness of her sexual need, has become disgusting to him. These past few years. These past months especially. It is repulsive, sickening, that concentrated self-absorbed thrusting . . . insisting . . . demanding . . . the smell, the sweat, the anguish . . . the willfulness of flesh. Why should I service *you,* Neil thinks, mean and gloating and frightened, why should I perform this task with *you,* I don't even know who *you* are.)

Whereas Yvette: the rather wild rather flamboyant rather outsized passion she displays (or in fact actually feels) excites him enormously. Enormously. At any time, at any hour, in her presence or apart. Oh enormously. *Isn't this what life is all about?*

The baby *was* born, the young father *did* communicate with it (in a poetical manner of speaking) before the birth, yes it was all a miracle, it is miraculous still, but Neil feels a natural masculine resentment at being expected to contemplate a miracle for the rest of his life.

Neil Schueler, in love, is angry much of the time though he would call it happy. In Yvette Held's presence he is a *lover,* elsewhere he is, it might be said—though who but Neil could say it?—a *hater.*

His breath comes short and quick, he walks heavily, aggressively, bangs into chairs, the corners of tables, an ugly bruise on his left knee, shaving cuts on his chin, head slightly lowered, eyes narrowed. He opens his mail impatiently, rips the envelopes more than they require being ripped, draws out letters to scan in mid-air as if it's a task he resents, applying his energy and attention and good will to something so inconsequential. But then isn't everything not Yvette inconsequential? The lover's dilemma, the lover's delight.

It's clear that he resents, generally, his hours in this house, the company of his wife, his frightened, adoring problem-son, clear that he yearns to be elsewhere, but where?—no one dares inquire. Are you angry with me, Helen asks, Why are you angry with me, Helen sometimes asks, please *answer* me, and Neil turns his distracted gaze upon her as if he has never seen her before. Though the questions are preposterous—though it is absurd for Helen to take herself this seriously—Neil manages, most of the time, a civil reply. No.

No, of course not, certainly not, he says, absently, kindly, sometimes stroking her thin shoulder, her arm—Of course not Honey, a soft consoling drawl, gaze already retreating.

(One afternoon he tells Yvette a story they both find sad, pitiable: Helen did not accuse him of being in love with another woman, Helen very carefully *declared* that he was in love with another woman, and if he wanted a divorce, if he wanted a trial separation, she would agree, she wouldn't cause legal or domestic difficulties, she wasn't, isn't, that kind of woman. Yvette, listening closely, wipes at her eyes, laughs nervously, says with a strained smile—I guess *I'm* that kind of woman.)

Should they get married is a story adulterous lovers tell.

A long exotic convoluted story. With variations, modulations.

Yes, he says, but I don't think so she says, not right now. Or, *yes* he says and *yes* she says too, but do they dare hurt so many people? He worries, she is stung. You don't care about hurting me, do you, she says, surprising him with her emotion. Plans are made, vague, like words written in steam on bathroom mirrors, the other wife is this, the other husband is that, in another month one lover will be, and Yvette is planning to (planning to spend a few weeks with her ailing mother in Sarasota, Florida, as she tells Neil, though in truth, as she can't bring herself to tell him, she is going to be operated on for a cyst, yes surely it will prove to be a harmless cyst, in her uterus, she simply can't *tell* him because she fears his fear and she fears his, well, disgust, she doesn't entirely trust him), and it's a difficult time right now, the stock market, interest rates so high, by the end of the year as Garrett predicts the rates are sure to start downward, it will make a considerable difference. Then perhaps they shouldn't indulge themselves in making plans except Neil is one afternoon so wounded, so furious, he leaves her without even making love to her, though in truth (as he isn't about to tell her) he's so upset he surely could not make love to her, not in his customary manly robust supremely triumphant way, and another afternoon Yvette begins to sob uncontrollably, Yvette hides her contorted face from her lover, Yvette is ashamed, ashamed . . . but of what? All these lying little maneuvers, all these games. Or, conversely, the fact that nothing means anything to her except Neil.

The story has to do with Garrett, good-natured sweet-tempered Garrett, Garrett of whom everyone is fond, and whom Neil dreads injuring, wounding in his pride (since Neil knows how he would feel, losing his wife to another man—and the other man a *friend*); the story has to do, yet more painfully, with Helen, poor Helen . . . who tells Neil that he should move out if he wishes then begs Neil not to pay attention to her, she loves him, she loves him so much, she and Mikey love him so much, doesn't he know? . . . of course he knows. Helen who has begun to see "some sort of analyst" in a nearby city, another woman (Neil says almost dismissively, not knowing how he sounds to Yvette), the two of them spending five hours a week (at $100 a session) poking about in the frayed inconsequential memories of her childhood, as if *her* childhood matters in the slightest to anyone. Helen, poor Helen, of whom Yvette has grown obliquely fond, in fact Yvette is one of the few women in their circle who still likes, or can tolerate, Helen Schueler: that brittle sardonic woman with the bruised eyes, the twisty little mouth, Neil Schueler's wife who has developed a truly bizarre mannerism of laughing silently, her eyes shut tight, and laying a meek little weighty little hand on her listener's arm . . . as if to beg sympathy, solicitude, she's actually in *pain* this is all so funny, aren't those tears running down her cheeks? . . . and then there's the problem of her coughing spells, her smoker's breath, her slightly weaving just perceptibly *floating* air after she's had, maybe, a single glass of dry white wine, and her big accusing eyes are black with pupil. She reports to Neil that she and her analyst sometimes discuss *his* childhood, but Neil hasn't any idea what they discuss since, after turning forty, he can barely remember having been an actual child, in the sense in which, more recently, his own son has been a child.

But the story they tell each other has most to do with children because of course they *genuinely love their own children, wouldn't hurt them for the world, they're innocent victims after all, they must come first.* Neil's son, Yvette's daughter. The precocious sixteen-year-old, the rather silly thirteen-year-old. One is obsessed with mathematical puzzles and games, and working with his computer; the other is obsessed with friends, telephone calls, clothes, whether she is pretty enough, whether she is pretty at all . . . whether she is *popular*. (She doesn't give a damn about her father and me, Yvette says sullenly—she doesn't know we exist.) Mikey is childish, demanding, emotional, unpredictable, a tough little shit as Neil calls him, a troubled boy as his mother calls him, who boasts of having no friends, boasts of being hated even by his teachers, locks himself away in his room for hours at a time, for complete Saturdays, Christ knows what he is doing apart from the computer, the math . . . the thinking. Neil has long given up trying to make sense of his son's preoccupations (what the hell *is* Infinity after all, isn't it just a pretentious word?—and what *is* Space/Time if you can't experience it?), he finds himself growing agitated, annoyed, if he's forced to listen to the boy's whining, self-absorbed, subtly reproachful voice. Well it's a sad story. It's a hell of a sad story. Spoiled by his mother and grandmother, made to think he's the center of the goddam universe, too smart for his own good, a born show-off, no wonder he hasn't any friends, no wonder he's never invited to anyone's house . . . and always his sly little air of reproach, reproach.

Still (as the story continues, month following month) both Neil and Yvette are acquainted with parents who have troubled adolescents, suicidal adolescents, kids who bring their friends home when their families are away and very nearly wreck the house . . . yes it's rage, raw aggression . . . yes some of these domestic situations are really tragic.

In which context it might be said (though who but Neil might say it?) that Mikey Schueler's problems are not so *very* serious.

Yes but should they get married, the lovers ask.

Yes but when. But how.

At what cost.

And isn't there a deadly risk in bringing the story to an end . . . ?

THE BITTER WOMAN

. . . Actually it is wonderful to be alive like this, says Helen's mother softly, actually it is . . . enough of a miracle . . . to be able to breathe deeply . . . to sit here in the sunshine and watch the birds at the feeder.

Yes says Helen, alert, attentive, staring out the window: two cardinals, several chickadees, a small cheery flock of juncos. God's in His

Heaven and all is right with the world, she isn't bitter, she isn't sick with hatred, she *is* grateful that her mother has been recovering steadily from the operation, hasn't she been smiling since her arrival?

Smiling for three weeks, smiling dry-eyed, empty as a drum.

Poor Helen Schueler: she's the last, isn't she, to know.

. . . Vowed I would never be one of those people, says Helen's mother bravely, her fingers clasping Helen's, one of those older people, like your grandmother, you know, your poor grandmother . . . vowed I would *not* . . . be filled with self-pity . . . recriminations . . . talk of health, operations, who has died and who is going to die. . . . No indeed, I am happy to be alive. Like this. Oh dear God just like this.

The warm dry bony hand, the thin thin old-woman hand, delicate as a sparrow's skeleton.

Helen is in White Plains taking care of her mother, Helen is trying not to think of Neil and his love affair (she's fairly certain by now, in September 1978, that the woman is Yvette Held—who else could it be?) and of Mikey, cruel impatient Mikey, who has told her she is "neurotic," "an old bore." Mikey who knows about his father, who has perhaps known for years. The shame, the disgust. The *shame*.

What shall I do, Mother, Helen wants to ask, holding her mother's hand hard, hard, feeling her throat constrict with the terrible need to cry—what shall I do, I love you but my love isn't enough to save you, to keep you forever, I love Mikey but it won't be enough to save *him*.

LYRIC

Neil, partly undressed, turns to see Yvette sprawled gracelessly across the bed, her hair in a tangle and her eyelashes matted, that coarse fleshy lovely mouth distended by a yawn, something kicks inside him, it has all been worth it, he thinks, both women, all of it, *all* of it, he'd do it over again, right now he'd like to tear the hot bitch open with his teeth and have done with all this ceremony.

THE EXPERIMENT

It's only a Thought Experiment, it isn't "real."

Mikey's computer is programmed to emit signals *into the past.*

Mikey's computer is equipped with a self-detonating device.

Mikey's computer is instructed to blow itself up at, say, 9 A.M., the signal having gone out at, say, 11 A.M. *Will the instruction be obeyed?*

"THOSE BOTTICELLI EYES"

Methodically, cruelly, she fasts; she is triumphing these days in the disciplining of the "animal appetites"; proud and secretly gloating at the delicate pulsing of a blue vein in her forehead, the new intensity of her gray-green eyes. A cup of bitter black coffee trembles in her hand, she zips up an old pair of her daughter's jeans (too tight now for Sonya), she hears the telephone ringing but declines to answer (for what if it is Neil's crazy wife—she *won't* answer), she's already on her way out: a white-hot energy compels her, *is* her. She feels weightless, near-bodiless, innocent.

She fasts, it is her pleasure to fast, preparing herself, rehearsing, for a final—*final*—conversation with her lover (at this moment flying home from Atlanta, their plan is to meet at the new Hyatt Regency fifteen miles away, or is it at the new Hilton, so splendidly tacky, by the Turnpike?—there have been so many), though in fact they seem to have had this conversation before. But now she is in the ascendancy, now she is suffused with power, *now* she can make the necessary break.

And they will, or won't they?—make love a final time.

A ceremony of sorts. Romantic ritual.

Pots of strong black coffee, the telephone that must not be answered (though there's the risk that it is Garrett who is calling, or even Neil with a modification of their plans), the sudden revelation in one of the household mirrors (though not a mirror Yvette customarily looks into) that her ash-blonde hair has been turning gray, silvery-gray, in secret, especially near the nape of her neck: that this is a fact about her others have observed in silence.

Yvette makes the observation with a wry shrug of her shoulders, tells herself she doesn't give a damn, she isn't after all the sort of woman who cares to deny her age, fight feebly against whatever age she *is*—she thinks too well of herself for that. (Also, she is still in her mid-thirties, six years younger than her lover and nine years younger than her husband. She may even be under the unexamined impression that this is middle age and she has already conquered it by an act of will.)

To think of herself is to think well of herself, for how could it reasonably be otherwise?—Yvette in one of her skinny translucent phases, looking anemic, fragile, something hot and tremulous about her mouth. (Beautiful, her lover says, has been saying for so long—beautiful he claims, a litany she takes for granted, worship of a sort, familiar and consoling—a beautiful woman. As if it were an accomplishment of his own, to claim her.) The story she tells herself is in itself consoling, though largely improvised, fantastic. The story she tells herself is that, one day, years ago, she was introduced to an attractive young couple, a very attractive young couple—husband sandy-haired, smiling, funny, wife quick and bright and dark and *sweet,* a female sort of flirtation: shall we—*can* we—be friends?—and she simply thought, even while shaking hands, exchanging pleasantries, joking with her husband, she thought: Him. It will be him. Whenever we are both ready.

She will, or will not, recover readily from the break with Neil; she will, or will not, know herself the victor (for, all sentimentality aside, all this crap about romance aside, there *is* inevitably a victor in such affairs); she will, or will not, feel intense guilt a few years later, when the Schueler's son kills himself. She will in any case urge her husband to accept his company's remarkable offer, made to all its top attorneys this year, of a six-week trip to Europe: yes they will take the Orient Express, yes they will stay in the perfect hotel in Venice, certainly they will fly to Morocco for a few days. . . .

No, they won't take the daughter, Sonya and her mother don't get along very well these days, Sonya has her own circle of friends, a very tight circle of friends, Sonya wouldn't have any interest in touring Europe with Mother and Father. *Not on your life.*

MOTHERSON

Mikey denies it all, denies everything, shrugging his skinny shoulders, giggling his mirthless laugh, the usual mannerisms—picking at his blemished skin, rolling his eyes as if he's in the presence of idiots, going suddenly mute, stubborn, a catatonia of the will. No he did not threaten thus-and-such; yes his teacher is full of shit, *yes* the whole school is full of shit, or does he mean (a contemptuous flutter of his eyelashes) *shits:* he's had enough of them.

And they've had enough of you, says Mother.

Okay I've had enough of *them*—that's the point.

But the point is also that they've had enough of you, they don't want you back unless—

I'm not going back. I said, *I'm not going back.*

Your father and I think—

I said—

Your father and—

Mikey begins to hum, his head bowed, bobbing, a queer rhythmic motion, hearing and not-hearing. The school won't take him back unless he apologizes and promises, etc., but how can he apologize when he did *not* say those juvenile things (wiring the place with dynamite, setting it off by way of a computer hook-up, Christ!—he's beyond *that)* or "threaten" (why is the word *threaten* always used, so corny, banal) to kill himself in such a way as to bring adverse publicity upon the school, any asshole (and the school is filled with assholes) would know he was only joking . . . he does a lot of joking . . . to relieve the boredom.

Don't lie to me, Mother says.

I'm not lying to you, says Son.

Please don't lie to *me,* Mother says.

I said I'm not lying to you, says Son.

I think you're cruel to make me so miserable. . . . I think you're sick, you need help . . . you've been contaminated by your father.

"I think you're sick, you need help," says Son, singsong.

You need professional help. . . .

"You need professional help. . . ."

Stop! Stop that!

"Stop! Stop that!"

Mikey, please—

"Mikey, *please*—"

A giggling fit, a fit of hot enraged tears, Motherson pummeling each other, Mother slapping Son and Son shoving Mother, it looks like an embrace, an awkward dance step, and what of that frenzied giggling?— as Father enters the twilit room.

THE FORGIVING WIFE

The MotherGrandmotherMother-in-Law in White Plains dies at the age of seventy-six, Helen discovers herself dry-eyed (she *is* empty as a drum and damn glad of it) while Mikey moons about the house sniffling and dazed . . . but tractable, civilized, *courteous* for once. And even Neil is struck by the loss, mourning (had he thought *her* mother was obliged to live forever just because *his* died years ago), tender with Helen, and consoling, and so forth, as if Helen needs, now, consolation, *now*.

It's a relief that Helen's mother is dead, she thinks cynically, because it spares her from knowing . . . certain details Helen would not wish her to know . . . now that the affair is over (Yes I can say that it's really over, yes I can say that I love you and I'm ashamed, says the repentant husband, frightened by something in his wife's face, oh yes *sincerely* frightened there's no mistaking it) . . . now that certain truths, specific and general, are being revealed. Such as: Neil had not really loved Yvette, he'd been going through a (is the word crisis?— psychic maladjustment?)—a difficult period in his life, professional primarily, all that pressure, that insane *competition*, too many aging Harvard Law boys under one roof, perhaps even some neurotic jealousy of his wife and son, *their* closeness, and wouldn't any father (murmured with a faint faltering laugh, a crinkling of blood-threaded eyes) be uneasy about having a son who is so—bright? So mercilessly bright? So much the whiz-kid? So much the—not smart-aleck, but what is the word—a precocious intelligence, brain—ah yes: *Wunderkind.*

Helen laughs, forgiving. All forgiveness.

Helen has it in her power to forgive, thus why not forgive? So she forgives.

(THE FORGIVING WIFE)

She forbids herself to think *what it must mean* that her mother has died despite the fact that she loved the woman so very much . . . so painfully childishly much . . . despite the fact that her mother loved *her.* (And who after all loves *her,* Baby is all growed up, or nearly.)

A lonely predicament here in the Void. Familiar but still lonely, not very comforting. She examines the Milky Way photographed and taped to Mikey's wall, yes these are lonely prospects, permanent-seeming though ostensibly "ephemeral" (how long *has* she been alive after all), and next year Mikey too will be gone, he'll make his escape, wait and see, already he flushes at the name Mikey saying Mother I *told* you my name is Michael, my name is *Mich*ael for Christ's sake *please.* A lonely predicament, wifeandhusband together at last.

She wants to cry for her mother but it's difficult, it isn't easy, this is a knotty convoluted "ephemeral" story she tells herself, raking her nails experimentally over her flesh to get a little . . . sensation: raw, throbbing, primitive, healthy. Her left forearm, her breasts, her soft flaccid belly. Numb for so long. Well why not be numb, dead inside, dead inside where it counts, not like Y. who luxuriates in lovemaking, laughs gasping for air, is drowning, dying amidst the smelly bed-clothes, greedy for what he has to give her, tireless, insatiable, those hips bucking, pelvis frantic, old tricks Helen deftly performed a life-time ago, Oh don't leave me don't stop don't leave me Oh Christ: *I love you.*

I love you, says Neil, only you, says Neil, and Helen says gently, her eyes turning in their sockets, I love *you.* It has always been you, says Neil, sobbing, huddling in her arms, you know it has always been you,

I'd be nothing without you, and Helen says, suppressing her laughter, I know, I know, I've always known.

THE SEVEN BRIDGES OF . . .

It is Infinity of a kind: you begin (for instance) with the bridge at the upper left, proceed to cross the island, cross the bridge at the lower left; you then turn to the left, proceed to cross the next bridge, cross the island, cross the *next* bridge. . . . You don't get very far, however, before the terrifying nature of the problem strikes you; and then it's too late. Then you must go back. Then you must go back and begin again, this time, perhaps, with the "horizontal" bridge leading to the island.

Mikey hasn't given a thought to the Königsberg puzzle for years, at least it seems like years, he has stopped thinking about many useless things, it is a function of "growing up." In fact he isn't Mikey now but Michael Schueler, respected if not greatly liked by his suitemates at Yale, admired in a way for his industry, seriousness, maturity . . . and for the astounding fact that, at mid-term, he has straight A's except for his course in algebraic topology in which he has an A +. But suddenly he's tired.

Among his parents' circle back home he is, he's been told, a model of sorts; an *exemplum;* living proof should such proof be desired that a brattish neurotic *Wunderkind* can make adjustments to ordinary life after all, laying aside certain childish obsessions forever, behaving normally, "pulling up his socks" and so forth, some stories have happy endings. Never too late in America. Never too late in the upper middle class. His high school teachers and his guidance counselor are after all the sort of people who ache to be proven wrong, to be surprised in their dreary predictions, they *want* to see a lost cause suddenly find himself: and then the father Neil Schueler is such a nice guy, and the mother, that poor nervous woman, actually she's an *attractive* woman if you can see past the God-awful mannerisms . . . she's said to have a Ph.D. or is it an M.A. in something like organic chemistry. . . .

Mikey Schueler the sombre whiz kid buckled down as the saying goes, applied himself diligently and tirelessly to his studies during his

senior year, did so well on his SAT tests he was accepted at each of the
four universities to which he applied: some stories *have* happy endings.
So he went away to New Haven. So he is in New Haven at this very
minute.

Feeling suddenly, unaccountably, very tired.

(Why aren't you applying to Harvard they asked him—teachers, Father—and he said something vague and flippant like: I was *born* there
after all why press my luck and go back?)

It's Thanksgiving recess and his suitemates have gone home, in fact
the college is nearly deserted, the silence is luxurious, why not stay
another day or two?—Yale has an entire week off. He is scheduled to
take the train home on Tuesday afternoon at two-fifteen but suddenly
he's tired, exhausted really, there is bliss in his empty suite and in a
bathroom solely his; he *is* tired from working so hard: four A's and an
A+ but he'll be embarrassed if Mother and Father make a fuss over
him because (as he has been admitting to himself for weeks) the grades
didn't come easily . . . no, they didn't come easily . . . and he isn't
certain that he wants to live it all again . . . yes he's pretty certain he
doesn't want to live it all again. His record is so very perfect, why press
his luck and keep going?

In any case he can't go back home. Not to that house.

No, he *can't* go home, that's his first premise.

A perfectionist to the end Mikey knows how to skillfully sever (not
merely slash at) the arteries in his left arm: a strong unflinching grip on
the razor with the fingers of his right hand, the blade drawn lengthwise,
deep and pitiless, exhilarated at the feat that can't be done (as Spinoza
teaches all things desire to persist in their being) yet is being done, only
observe. If this is dying it feels after a few minutes like goofing off as
Mikey rarely allows himself, hiding under the shower in steaming hot
water, or in this case hiding in the tub, the water splashing in as water
drains out, cleverly timed, he has everything cleverly timed, he isn't
going to be found until early evening when everything will be over. The

door is locked, the steam is consoling, he's sprawled out ungainly
(nearly six feet tall, only one hundred thirty-five pounds) but curiously
relaxed in the tub, as if he has done this before, oh many times before, it
isn't at all difficult once you've stated your first premise. Too cowardly
or too shrewd to open his eyes for a while, he wonders whether there
will be sinewy cords of blood, skeins that won't blend in with the water,
or whether it is all a pale tepid washed-out pinkish-red, and then, suddenly, he isn't interested, he can't be bothered to check, he notes the
peaceful unexcited heartbeat that feels like wisdom; suddenly he is
crossing one of the Königsberg bridges, he's simultaneously in the tub
amidst the noisy water and on the bridge above *that* water, he sees
himself crossing the first of the bridges . . . and then the island . . .
and then the second bridge . . . and this time he'll try something un-
expected, how about proceeding at once to the horizontal bridge . . .
and proceeding onward.

THE HAPPY ENDING

This is the final story they tell, this is *the* story, surprising and placating
them both; one mild Saturday morning in early September 1983 when by
accident Neil Schueler and Yvette Held meet in the Village Market, not
having spoken together since approximately June of 1982: a story with a
happy ending.

. . . so absurd, so *extreme,* Yvette says in a lowered voice, there were
times I actually prayed for . . . well, *both* of us . . . you think such
crazy things . . . for instance once when you were driving on the
Turnpike I think and driving quite fast . . . and I had this little fantasy of pulling at the steering wheel . . . something, anything, you
know . . . to make an end of it.

Neil listens fascinated, believing and not-believing, staring at a
woman he no longer loves despite her Botticelli eyes (hadn't he once
called them that?) and her slender snaky body and something secret and
sly and at-the-edge-of-frenzy in her voice, Neil murmurs, God did you
really, God I'm glad you *didn't*. . . .

Well of course I *wouldn't,* it was just a fantasy, anything, you know, to make an *end*, Yvette says, smiling to show her good strong damp white teeth—you get in these extreme states of mind when you're in love or are convinced you're in love, it's something I have to remember now that Sonya has a boy friend, I mean a *steady* boy friend. . . .

Sonya must be how old now? Neil says, though he isn't interested: he wants to hear more about Yvette's crazy fantasy and maybe just maybe (well, maybe not) he'll tell her about *his* . . . strangling her with her hair . . . when she wore it long, long and loose, falling past her shoulders. Oh is she really that old, he says, slightly perplexed, I think of her as such a little. . . .

And Mikey's at Yale, someone said? says Yvette brightly.

And Mikey's at Yale, says Neil, grinning, swiping at his nose, thank *God.*

So they talk, chat. Laugh. A shock for them to meet after so long (and Neil isn't altogether certain how much Garrett knows) but after a few minutes it seems, well, quite casual, even ordinary, two friendly acquaintances meeting in the Market, lounging over their grocery carts, a familiar sight. Yvette is wearing something that resembles a burlap tunic cinched in rather severely at the waist, a belt with a big Navaho buckle, sandals, her hair is close-cropped, a mass of stylish frazzled curls, she's given to smiling a good deal, laughing huskily, not at all embarrassed or uneasy. Neil is wearing khaki shorts and a sweatshirt, he's sporty, tanned, unshaven, hopes Yvette won't inquire after Helen who is in one of her lethargic phases, staying at home day after day, unwashed hair, bathrobe, bare feet, grainy flaccid skin but she's *all right,* it's just a cyclical thing by now . . . hopes Yvette won't notice the soft roll of flesh at his waist . . . or the fact that his hair is thinning at the crown.

. . . working out for the best, after all, says Yvette.

Yes, says Neil, after all.

Those Botticelli eyes!—hadn't he once called them that, in absolute dazed sincerity, framing the woman's face with his hands: and now he sees the fine white lines at the eyes' edges, now he sees the smudge of brown eyeliner on the lids, in any case he is immune, he certainly *is* immune, it's such an old hacked-over pondered-over story.

The thing is, Neil says carefully, his voice still lowered—that nobody was hurt. That's the important thing.

Oh I know, says Yvette at once.

That's the thing that matters most, says Neil, licking his lips, calculating when he should begin to edge his cart past hers—that's really it, you know, all the rest was—

Oh I know, says Yvette sadly, I *know*.

THE INTERPRETATION OF DREAMS
BY SIGMUND FREUD: A STORY

DANIEL STERN

Daniel Stern is a New Yorker and former professional cellist. He has
written nine novels, the latest being *An Urban Affair*. His earlier
novel, *The Suicide Academy,* has recently been reissued. "The Interpretation of Dreams by Sigmund Freud: A Story" will be included in
his new book, *Missing the Point,* a short story collection to be published in 1987.

"Always a threesome," she said. "Two men and a woman. Except that
one man, the one with previous rights in the matter, is always dead."

"I hate this nickel analysis," he said.

"I can't help it. When it gets neat is when it feels true. You don't have
to *do* anything about it. It's just that it's like a murder mystery with a
series of imaginary murders. If you marry two widows there are two
dead men in the background."

This is how it went after his second wife was bitten on the finger by a
squirrel. Dickstein had a feeling things would change, and not for the
better. It was a three-month situation: meeting, wooing, marrying and
up to New York for a new life. She was fourteen years younger than he
and nothing besides falling in love and marriage had been decided;
would she work at her music, at a job, have a baby, have two babies? In
the meantime, it was a muggy August and against his wishes—though
he hadn't examined them or actually expressed them—she had been
marking time taking a course at the N.Y.U. Summer School: *Dream,
Myth and Metaphor.*

The day had been warm and after class she'd lingered in a small
rainbow of sunlight and offered one of the peanuts she was shucking

and munching to a begging squirrel. She was a Georgia girl and the peanut habit died hard.

Fortunately, after the animal nipped her and drew blood a sharp Park attendant netted the squirrel. The rabies test was negative but they put the little bastard to sleep anyway. Leaving Sharon in bed for a few days with shock and a bandaged hand.

"You're mad at me," she said to Dickstein.

"Surprised," he said. "What happened to your country girl smarts? You don't feed New York squirrels from your hand."

"Well, how would I learn that in Chapel Hill?"

He snapped a portable dinner tray in place and tried a laugh. "I always thought that course was dangerous."

"How so?"

He shut up fast. There was no decent way he could tell her how he'd felt the day she came back from the class with a paperback copy of Freud's *Interpretation of Dreams.* Tell her what? That if he'd wanted to marry somebody who could rattle off about latent and manifest content, who could play peekaboo with symbols and wish-fulfillment and repression he wouldn't have waited until he was thirty-nine to remarry. He could have tied up with any of the smart-ass, over-educated, under-serious women he'd spent most of his life with.

Sharon was wonderfully articulate without being glib. She had the Southern gift for language flow without the little chunks of undigested information—okay, call it knowledge—that was the conversation he'd grown up with and hated. He couldn't tell her any of this because it would come out upside down. The truth of it was in intangibles: the intelligence of her smile, the quick wit that sparkled questions the night he'd lectured to a dozen students who'd swallowed a snowstorm just to hear him compare Schubert and Keats.

"They both go from major to minor keys and back again very quickly," she'd said. Not a question or academic comment: a fragment of song. Just what he was in need of: idea-tossed, song-hungry. "I mean," he said, "that I expected you to start poking at yourself with the new tools of psychology."

"Instead," she said, "I'm poking at you."

"Can you have wine?" he asked. "I forgot what the doctor said."

Sharon shivered against her pillows. "He didn't say. I'll have a glass, thank you. Listen, you knew I was a widow, right off."

"You told me instantly. With all the appropriately Southern Gothic details."

"Gothic! It was a hunting accident. Everybody in our part of Georgia hunts. But you didn't tell me your first wife—Alma—was a widow until —for God's sake, last week!"

"It didn't seem important. It's all of three months, not our Golden Wedding anniversary. Both men died natural deaths—one, sickness, one a shooting accident—both men were considerably older than the women. Now you know what I know."

Dickstein filled the bowls with linguine and shared the wine.

"Two widows," she sighed.

"I'm damned if I know why I didn't tell you sooner. But you didn't notice anything odd until New York University and Sigmund Freud told you it was worthy of thinking about."

He set down an amazement of utensils, any which way on the trays. It was not like him and he noted it.

"It gave me the shivers," she began . . .

"What did?"

"Reading the dream book. I think you have to read things at the right moment for them to get to you. I must have read Freud at school. I took all the right courses. I graduated. I took a year of graduate school."

"You were doing music, not psychology."

"But reading this now in class it gave me the eerie feeling that everything is connected."

"Overdetermined . . ."

"Please don't be just clever," she said. "I'm wounded and I'm trying to track something down. I got shaky in class and that's why I wasn't careful in the park . . . It wasn't a change in the way I think—I wasn't born yesterday. It was a weird change in the way I *feel* about the way I think."

"Let me see; is that oozing?"

"Looks the same. I've been bitten before."

"Not in Washington Square Park. City animals are more dangerous."

She ate carefully with her left hand.

"I'm talking about the sensation of strangeness—just thinking that causes and connections run through everything like the bloodstream through the body."

"Did you think everything was random, till yesterday?"

She laughed. "I *felt* that way till yesterday. Then, sitting on the bench with the bag of peanuts I got distracted, the wet heat, I'm used to more hot and dry in August, and I began to think about you and Alma and me and Joshua and widows and husbands and fathers and wives and mothers, and it was more like a dream than *thinking* and I fed this squirrel and I must have done it in a funny way because I've fed them a million times before and nothing ever happened and he bit me."

Dickstein didn't know why the memory appeared for delivery at that moment. It was not a buried one, was right at hand. Rather, it showed up at that instant to help deal with Sharon who sounded shakier every minute.

"To give you a dose of strange," he told her, "you're not my second widow. You're my fourth. You're living with a regular Bluebeard in reverse."

And he told her of being puppy-young, meeting the war-widow with the long legs at a fund-raising chamber music evening, and about his family's terror.

His father, Doctor Dickstein, the Gynecologist/Philosopher and his Big Moment in Paternal Wisdom!

"A woman whose husband has died and who marries a younger man puts too much of a burden on the boy. And don't forget: she'll always be comparing you to him."

So he was shipped out to Stanford instead of finishing at Columbia and fell in love, for a time, with a California aerospace widow. Nothing glamorous like a test-pilot crash; just an equipment explosion.

"It's not funny," Sharon said; she was purplish from trying not to laugh. His intent was distraction and seemed to be succeeding. She was slipping into her country accent as she did when she felt easier. She wasn't a modern West Side of New York Sharon; her full name was Rose-a-Sharon. "I grieved so much," she said, "when Joshua died. I was mad, too, 'cause I hated hunting."

"We're not talking about how it feels when your husband dies. We're talking about how much more connective tissue there is here than even you thought of."

She wasn't laughing anymore. "Four," she murmured. "A daytime dream of *the* dream. The older man who possesses your woman, first, dies, but you didn't kill him. You just get to have *her*. Over and over again. My God. Doesn't that count as murder and possession of the spoils?"

What he couldn't bring himself to bring up was what would seem to be the underlying strategy. He saw all these men as brutal, himself as tender; they were heedless of their women, he was concerned; they took what they wanted, he asked or waited for the moment to ripen.

When Dickstein envisioned those hunting trips of Sharon's husband, Joshua, he imagined some kind of secret, violent sex mixed in with the country satisfactions of blood sport. He'd never asked her about such things and she'd not offered much beyond a black mustache, six-foot-three height and a paper mill business. Questions of fidelity were not included in the data. But when he recalled his father's caution, he welcomed the comparison. Not only were they dead and he alive: *he was molded to offer precisely what they lacked. That was his enterprise!*

But he wasn't going to bring up all that and reinforce this dreambook talk. Instead, he poured the wine more freely than usual and the astonishment turned festive. Sharon was pretty in what she called her sick-time-of-the-month robe, though only her finger bled. They laughed again at her fears of the 'uncanny' connections in the mind. (Freud, he told her, had written a famous letter in which he claimed an absence of any such 'uncanny' feelings; more about religion than psychology, though.) And she promised never to feed squirrels in the city, again—and she grew coy and sensual, drinking more and eating less, holding her injured hand out into the air as she caressed him with the other and it seemed like a nice idea to eat dinner in the bedroom at times and afterwards she asked him if she were the more precious of the prizes he'd won from the dream-murder of all those father/lovers; and he kissed her mouth as answer and evasion and she grew most Southern and promised to at least consider dropping the class since something about it bothered him, if he would take her to Turkey at Christmas-time. (He had absolutely no interest in things Turkish.)

She wondered aloud if they'd made a baby; and he wondered, silently, thinking he could be a husband and a father and could die, like all the others, leaving his lovely Rose-a-Sharon for . . . who?

Late that night he woke, his head frantic from too much wine. In the bathroom he stared at the mirror and thought of his father's face for the first time in many months: square-immigrant tough where Dickstein's was second-generation soft-nurtured; perfunctory and commanding with his sullen, witty wife, where Dickstein was the one who provided attentions and the occasions for laughter. He remembered the early childhood Saturday visits to Dr. Dickstein's office, the women waiting patiently, obediently, and the chrome and the stirrups . . . and remembered, too, years later, how amazed he was that the old man should be at the mercy of the pain and fears which came with final illness. He'd never seen his father at the mercy of anything, before.

Dickstein's eyes blazed in the bathroom mirror with the awful knowledge that there were no more of these imposing older men to die and leave him their women to take for his own. He would be forty in three months, he thought and listened to Sharon's regular hiss of breath. Now, he was at the top of the ladder: an uncomfortable, precarious position.

There she lay, the next widow, unsuspecting; in spite of her squirrel-wisdom, in spite of N.Y.U. and Freud. Because she was young and easy in her skin and had been bereaved only by a rifle, not by time and entropy.

"Peasant pleasures," his father would have said, with irony, about people who died in hunting accidents. He'd sent himself through college and sold insurance to help pay for Medical School. These successes entitled him to a loftiness towards those less educated and less successful. Including, on occasion, his wife and son. But now Dickstein, staring into the mirror, saw mirror-images hard to ignore. He, too, had become a Doctor Dickstein, though only a Ph.D. shadow of the real thing: no chrome, no stirrups, not even a white coat.

Like his father he always had at least three major activities. (The old man lectured, did the first television medical education series along with his regular practice. Dickstein taught English, lectured when asked and edited a journal.) The income and prestige were not comparable but the restless multiple activities had similar outlines.

He searched in the mirror for some of the older man's features he could recognize and endow with the qualities he admired. What he thought of as a Hungarian mouth, he saw, eloquent, romantic.

"The better for talking out of both sides at the same time," Doctor Dickstein had said, laughing his runaway laugh. Dickstein, too, laughed nonstop, large and loud. For years he'd felt his father's heavy laughter aimed at him. The truth was, he suspected, that it was aimed at everyone, the good doctor included.

But that was all gone. It was utterly quiet in the night. He sat on the closed commode and leaned his flushed face against the tile of the sink.

"The top of the ladder," he whispered. And now it was not some young woman waiting to greet him. It was his father, waiting where vanished fathers wait for sons.

The disturbing image mixed with the wine in his gut in a surprise of nausea. He vomited into the sink with an energetic heave. It lasted several minutes and then he fell asleep wedged against the sink, the water still running.

Sharon found him about ten minutes after dawn. He was slumped over the sink. When she touched his shoulder instead of jumping he woke gradually, her lovely cloud of yellow-reddish hair swimming into vague then focused view. Her eyes and cheeks looked slept-in, striated, rumpled.

She had to pee and he tottered to his feet and waited. When she finished she washed the sink and sat him down again and washed his face with her good hand. He had the convalescent's quiet gladness that she was present, that she had found him, that he had found her.

She would undoubtedly survive him. That was in the natural order of things. But, first, for as long as possible, they would survive together. He would be her loving husband, father, friend, teacher: wise, sensual, patient; knowing that, like all teachers, he was temporary.

And for himself, he would learn to ward off the inevitable, to slow down the dance of death. It was time to become his own father: forgiving, intelligent, always remembering that he had once been young and lost and now was found.

A new arrangement.

The bathroom smelled of vomit and Sharon sprayed something lilac into the air and gave him something mint to rinse his mouth with and kissed him and stumbled back to bed and sleep.

Dickstein sat there a moment. He had never felt so lucky in his life. It was like a dream.

I GET BY

MARY ROBISON

Mary Robison was born in Washington, D.C. Knopf has published
her books, *Days, Oh!* and *An Amateur's Guide to the Night,* all being
reprinted in paperback by Godine. A frequent contributor to *The New
Yorker,* she is presently finishing both a novel and a story collection to
be published by Knopf. She teaches at Harvard University.

Right after the windup of the memorial service, there in the hospital
chapel that evening in February, the principal of the elementary school
where my husband, Kit, had taught approached me. Enough of a crowd
had gathered and passed that I had to inch over and strain to hear him,
because the chapel doors had opened. From down the hall there were
metal bed and tray noises, buzzers and dings, and doctor-paging voices,
as my husband's mourners made their exit.

My mother-in-law, Rennie, still sat in the pew behind me, arm-rock-
ing the baby, who was sounding little pleas. The principal was talking to
me. "I think I've found a replacement for Kit," he said.

I had to let that remark hang there for a beat. He meant another
teacher. He was either too cruel or too vacant a person to have prefaced
it in some way. He said, "Her name's Andrea Dennis. Came down from
Danbury for interviews this afternoon. Knocked us sideways, actually.
You two might get in touch."

I said, "Isn't that nice."

My kids, Ben and Bibi, helped me up from the pew. The principal
mentioned he'd tried to call with his condolences. Possibly he had; I
had unplugged all three of our phones.

After we got home, Ben and Bibi lingered in the back yard. It was
snowing by now—a friendly snow, scurrying in the floodlights behind

the house. Rennie took over the couch. She had the baby and our whole stack of pastel sympathy cards. "Going to *read* these," she said, as though someone ought to do more than open the envelopes and nod, acknowledging the signatures.

I warmed a bottle of formula in hot tap water, and watched my children through the window over the sinks. Bibi had fitted into the tire swing somehow. She is broad-bottomed at eighteen. The swing's rope, knotted around a limb of the weeping willow tree, was stiff with ice.

Ben was only a few feet away, urinating onto a bump of snow. I had to look twice, to be sure. He was eleven, *almost* eleven, and peeing in view of his sister.

Bibi had just colored her hair, but I wasn't ready to accept her as a champagne blonde yet. She looks *familiar,* I'd think, whenever I happened onto her.

The Saturday morning we learned about Kit, the Old Hadham police visited. So did two station wagons from television news teams. I took a confirming call from the idiot aircraft-company people who'd rented Kit the light plane in which he died. After the call, I snapped the telephones out of their plastic jacks, and Bibi chain-locked the door of the upstairs bathroom and stripped away the hair color nature had given her.

I met Andrea Dennis. I was at the school, sorting through two decades' worth of teacher paraphernalia, looking for anything personal in classroom cupboards and in Kit's mammoth oakwood desk. I found a comb, his reading glasses, a Swiss Army knife, and a hardback copy of "Smiley's People," bookmarked halfway. This was on a school day, but after classes had adjourned. Andrea pushed open the heavy door and found me. She introduced herself in an inquiring way: "I'm Andrea?"

We talked some. We didn't say anything I thought to commit to memory. I spilled Elmer's Glue all over. The white glue moved thickly across the desk blotter. "I'd better take care of that," Andrea said. "Let me fetch a sponge or something, from the lounge."

I used to be entirely comfortable in the staff-and-faculty lounge.

Old Hadham Elementary had gone up in '64. Inside and out, the building was an architectural oddity. Kit's classroom (he'd had half of sixth grade), for instance, was in the shape of a semicircle. His huge desk and his roller chair faced out from the straight wall. The room had three rising rows of student chairs with attached laminated writing arms. The floor was covered with jewel-blue linoleum. The curved wall wore a band of pale corkboard.

In the couple of weeks Andrea Dennis had been teaching, she'd tacked up stuff for the lull between Valentine's Day and St. Patrick's Day. There were pen-and-ink drawings that looked like student self-portraits to me. Some printed quotes were pinned up—sayings of statesmen and explorers. There were two science charts: one explaining the pollination of a flower, the other an illustration of polar and equatorial weather movements. Left over from Kit's days here were the usual flags —Old Glory and the Connecticut state flag—and some empty hamster cages with empty water fonts and play wheels. I planned to leave all those behind, of course, as well as Kit's globe, showing the continents and oceans in their proper cloudy colors. Kit hated globes with countries done in pink or purple.

I had to admit Andrea Dennis was an appealing woman. She had clearly put a lot of clever thought and effort into presenting herself at her best. She had on a touch-me-please cashmere sweater and a soft wool-blend skirt with a lining that rustled. Her sheer nylons gleamed. She had hair long enough to toss.

I had noticed something about us. Whenever I mentioned Kit, I nodded at his desk. When Andrea referred to him once, she gestured north. Toward the forest where the plane fell?

I hung around for fifteen minutes. Andrea didn't return with the sponge. Anyway, the glue had hardened by now. I pictured her yakking away with young Mr. Mankiewicz or flirting with old Mr. Sonner.

I packed Kit's things into a blue nylon gym bag. I bundled up and walked home—a matter of a mile or so—in the road. My part of Connecticut has no proper sidewalks. I kept stumbling. Ever since the baby, and then especially after what happened to Kit, I had been sleeping sporadically and then only in short spurts. That was part of the reason I'd been so clumsy and had flubbed with the glue. My getup was pretty cockeyed, too. I had forgotten to wear socks, and yet the shoelaces on my Nikes were triple-bow-tied. Beneath my parka, my sweater was lumpy and had the smell of Johnson's baby products, as did the whole interior of our beautiful saltbox house when I got there—baby oil, baby powder, baby's softened-fabric bunting. Everywhere I looked was bright with baby things, baby artifacts.

I went into the kitchen, grateful for Rennie, who'd tidied up. Rennie had almost never stayed with us when Kit was alive. We'd seldom gone to see her. She lived alone on what had once been an apple orchard, near Darien. She cared for the big central house there, and there were two barns and two brown outbuildings on the land. Her husband had long ago put himself into a V.A. hospital. He was a troubled, haunted man. I had witnessed some behavior. He'd sit for long afternoons with his head in his hands. He would roam searchingly over the yards and meadows. He'd seem to hide beside the shadowy brown barns. Other times, he'd pitch and splatter hard apples furiously against the fallen-in stone walls around the borders of the orchard. Thinking of him, I made a bet with myself that I hoped I wouldn't win. I bet that Rennie connected Kit's accident with his father's illness. That would have been unfair.

March came. We'd get a couple more snowstorms in Old Hadham, I suspected. Spring wouldn't arrive in any decided way for weeks and weeks. But I was seeing new grass and there was dry pavement. April would be breathtaking along our road. There'd be arbutus, hepaticas, downy yellow violets. In the living room, Rennie had sections of the local evening newspaper strewn around. The baby was in the playpen, wadding and tearing a Super Duper coupon page.

"Where's the baby's dolly?" I asked Rennie.

She said, "Ask Ben."

"Ben? Ben has Susie Soft Sounds?" But I didn't call up to Ben. Every day, it seemed, there was more about him and Bibi that I didn't care to know.

They had identical rooms, across the hall from each other—identical except that Bibi's wallpaper showed jazz dancers against a mint-green background, whereas Ben's had ponies grazing in a field. The night before, I had happened past the rooms and heard Bibi say, from behind Ben's door, "I am safely buzzed." Next I heard the pop-tab open what I assumed was a beer can.

"That's your *third!*" Ben had whispered.

Another curious moment was when I noticed something in among Bibi's hand laundry; she had borrowed my pushup bra.

Bibi talked a lot about Andrea Dennis these days. Andrea, it turned out, sometimes snacked after school at the Nutmeg Tea and Sandwich Shop, where Bibi waited tables. It seemed as if Andrea was always with someone I knew well, or had known. I could never resist saying, "Really? What did she have on? Did she look tired? Who picked up the check? Did they have desserts or entrées? Did she have that fruit cup?"

I was driving home from the lawyers'. The airplane company's insurance people had investigated and decided to settle some money on me. I liked it about the money, but what I wanted just now was my bed, pillows, the electric blanket. For three days, a quiet sleet had been falling on Old Hadham.

The car's windshield wiper on my side suddenly locked taut on a diagonal. A film formed immediately on my part of the glass. I tried the squirters, but all I got was blue fluid congealing with the ice at the base of the windshield. I maneuvered down Willow, on Old Hadham's steepest hill—a plunger that had been only cursorily sanded. There was a car not far ahead, and a truck on my tail, no shoulder. I had to tip my head out the driver's window to see. Meanwhile, Rennie was smiling, half asleep. The baby said a noise very much like "Why?" I had something close to nausea suddenly: suddenly missing Kit.

The baby woke me. It was an April morning, pre-dawn. I was groggy, but I had a sweet dream still playing in my head—some of the dream's color and its melody—as I heated water for the formula and started coffee. "Here we come!" Rennie said, and drove the baby's castered crib into the kitchen. Rennie was oddly cheerful, giddy. Her taffeta robe was on inside out. She sat down and swayed the crib and sang some ballad about whaling boats and messmates, with a line about the lowland sea.

To distract the baby, Rennie had dropped a fat nest of pink excelsior into the crib—a leftover from Easter baskets. I was a little afraid the baby would eat the pink cellophane, so I intended to snatch it away. But for now the excelsior ball rolled back and forth with the crib's movement, and with Rennie's song and what rhythms there were of my lingering dream.

When the baby was asleep, we two sipped coffee. I figured Rennie would be stepping out onto the porch for sunrise, as she sometimes did, but instead she said she wanted to talk about her son, about Kit. I told her what I knew was true—that his character faults included overconfidence and impulsiveness. I said that he had received flying lessons and his license. But whatever his license signified, he hadn't been ready, not competent, to solo-pilot a plane.

A lot of Old Hadham showed up at Chicwategue Park for Memorial Day. Some people brought picnic dinners and thermoses or coolers of drinks. The high school's brass-and-drum corps was there to do shows. There were two burros roped to a post for the little kids to ride around a guided circle.

Chicwategue Park had ducks on a pond, and a pair of swans—the town favorites—who'd made it through the winter, and bronze statues of Revolutionary War generals, and, in the center, a white-painted, lacy-looking gazebo. On the soccer fields beyond the woods, there would be footraces and other competitions throughout the day. Rennie had given Ben a two-year-old boxer she'd purchased through a newspaper ad, and Ben had entered himself and Reebok in the Frisbee contest.

I set up camp on a faded quilt with the baby. Rennie took Bibi to gamble away some of her waitress tips from the Nutmeg at the bingo tables. Watching them go, I noticed Andrea Dennis over by the penny-toss place—sporty and pretty in spotless sky-blue sweats, with a balloon on a ribbon looped at her wrist. She and Bibi greeted each other like classmates, with a hug.

Bibi's appearance looked to me like a screaming-out-loud reaction to

Andrea Dennis. Bibi had whacked her fake-blond hair into bristles and points, and her face was dusted with chalky makeup. Her lips looked almost black, and the tank top and jeans she wore were black. Still, Andrea was giving Bibi approving looks and nods.

But if Bibi's getups scared people, at least her manner had improved. That morning at breakfast, I'd overheard her saying to Ben, "Relax and sit still. I'll fix you a fresh glass of orange juice."

Now Ben's name was called over the P.A. system. I carried the baby and trailed Ben and Reebok over to the starting stripe on the Frisbee-competition field. Ben had the dog's collar in one hand and his yellow Frisbee in the other. Ben was down on one knee and the dog was trembling with excitement as they waited for the judge's signal to begin their routine.

At the whistle, the dog bolted away down the field. Ben stood up and let fly. His first couple of tries were long, too fast throws, and the Frisbee sailed yards over Reebok's head. The dog wasn't paying attention anyhow. On their third and last turn, Reebok watched as he ran, then leaped, fishtailed, and chomped the disk, but only after it had ricocheted twice off the dirt. At the gazebo, the Frisbee judge held up a card, giving Ben and Reebok a "4" rating.

Andrea Dennis strolled over to us. She introduced herself to the baby and sort of shook hands with him. Ben and the dog came over. Ben's young face was bright, but I couldn't tell if it was from excitement or embarrassment.

Andrea said, "Man, you got robbed! Your dog flew six feet straight up. What do they *want?* They should've given you guys a special award."

Ben absorbed this. I knew that on the car ride home he would relive Reebok's last effort for Bibi and Rennie. He'd say he got robbed.

I asked him to watch the baby a minute—to make sure the kid didn't crawl away, go swimming after the swans, or filch anyone's barbecued spareribs.

I clapped a hand on the smooth blue sweatshirt material on Andrea's shoulder.

"What did I do?" Andrea said, and I said, "A lot."

We walked along together by the rows of blankets and the outdoor furniture that bordered the competition fields. We said hello to people—fellow-teachers of Andrea's, the families of some of her students, old friends of mine.

I was thinking how to tell her that she had been an important distraction for me—maybe even a necessary one. She'd been someone safe for me to focus on while the reality of having no Kit was so fierce. I realized I couldn't make my interest in her into anything polite or easy to explain. I said, "Generally, thanks, Andrea," and I told her how great she looked in her blue.

MAGAZINES CONSULTED

Agada, 2020 Essex Street, Berkeley, Calif. 94703

The Agni Review, P.O. Box 229, Cambridge, Mass. 02238

American Book Review, P.O. Box 188, Cooper Station, New York, N.Y. 10003

The American Voice, The Kentucky Foundation for Women, Inc., Heyburn Bldg., Suite 1215, Broadway at 4th Avenue, Louisville, Ky. 40202

Antaeus, Ecco Press, 1 West 30th Street, New York, N.Y. 10001

Antietam Review, 33 West Washington Street, Hagerstown, Md. 21740

The Antioch Review, P.O. Box 148, Yellow Springs, Ohio 45387

The Apalachee Quarterly, P.O. Box 20106, Tallahassee, Fla. 32304

Arizona Quarterly, University of Arizona, Tucson, Ariz. 85721

Ascent, Department of English, University of Illinois, Urbana, Ill. 61801

Asimov's Science Fiction Magazine, Davis Publications, 380 Lexington Avenue, New York, N.Y. 10017

The Atlantic, 8 Arlington Street, Boston, Mass. 02116

Aura, P.O. Box 76, University Center, Birmingham, Ala. 35294

Backbone, P.O. Box 95315, Seattle, Wash. 98145

Black Ice, 571 Howell Avenue, Cincinnati, Ohio 45220

The Black Warrior Review, P.O. Box 2936, University, Ala. 34586

The Bloomsbury Review, 2933 Wyandot Street, Denver, Colo. 80211

Boston Review, 991 Massachusetts Avenue, Cambridge, Mass. 02138

Buffalo Spree, 4511 Harlem Road, P.O. Box 38, Buffalo, N.Y. 14226

California Quarterly, 100 Sproul Hall, University of California, Davis, Calif. 95616

Canadian Fiction Magazine, P.O. Box 46422, Station G, Vancouver, B.C., Canada V6R 4G7

Carolina Quarterly, Greenlaw Hall 066-A, University of North Carolina, Chapel Hill, N.C. 27514

The Chariton Review, The Division of Language and Literature, Northeast Missouri State University, Kirksville, Mo. 63501

Chicago, WFMT, Inc. 3 Illinois Center, 303 E. Wacker Drive, Chicago, Ill. 60601

Chicago Review, 970 East 58th Street, Box C, University of Chicago, Chicago, Ill. 60637

Clockwatch Review, 737 Penbrook Way, Hartland, Wisc. 53021

Colorado Review, Department of English, Colorado State University, Fort Collins, Colo. 80523

Columbia, 404 Dodge Hall, Columbia University, New York, N.Y. 10027

Confrontation, Department of English, C. W. Post of Long Island University, Greenvale, N.Y. 11548

Cosmopolitan, 224 West 57th Street, New York, N.Y. 10019

Crosscurrents, 2200 Glastonbury Rd., Westlake, Calif. 92361

Cutbank, c/o Dept. of English, University of Montana, Missoula, Mont. 59812

Denver Quarterly, Department of English, University of Denver, Denver, Colo. 80210

Descant, Department of English, Texas Christian University, Fort Worth, Tex. 76129

Epoch, 254 Goldwyn Smith Hall, Cornell University, Ithaca, N.Y. 14853

Esquire, 2 Park Avenue, New York, N.Y. 10016

Fiction 84, Exile Press, P.O. Box 1768, Novato, Calif. 94948

Fiction International, Department of English, St. Lawrence University, Canton, N.Y. 13617

Fiction Network, P.O. Box 5651, San Francisco, Calif. 94101

The Fiddlehead, The Observatory, University of New Brunswick, P.O. Box 4400, Fredericton, N.B., Canada E3B 5A3

Five Fingers Review, 100 Valencia Street, Suite #303, San Francisco, Calif. 94103

Forum, Ball State University, Muncie, Ind. 47306

Four Quarters, La Salle College, Philadelphia, Pa. 19141

Frank, Mixed General Delivery, APO, New York, N.Y. 09777

FM. Five, P.O. Box 882108, San Francisco, Calif. 94188

Gargoyle, P.O. Box 3567, Washington, D.C. 20007

Gentlemen's Quarterly, 350 Madison Avenue, New York, N.Y. 10017

The Georgia Review, University of Georgia, Athens, Ga. 30602

Grain, Box 1154, Regina, Saskatchewan, Canada S4P 3B4

Grand Street, 50 Riverside Drive, New York, N.Y. 10024

Granta, 13 White Street, New York, N.Y. 10013

Gray's Sporting Journal, 205 Willow Street, P.O. Box 2549, South Hamilton, Mass. 01982

Great River Review, 211 West 7th, Wirona, Minn. 55987

The Greensboro Review, University of North Carolina, Greensboro, N.C. 27412

Hard Copies, Dept. of English and Foreign Languages, California State Polytechnic University, Pomona, Calif. 91768

Harper's Magazine, 2 Park Avenue, New York, N.Y. 10016

Hawaii Review, Hemenway Hall, University of Hawaii, Honolulu, Hawaii 96822

Hoboken Terminal, P.O. Box 841, Hoboken, N.J. 07030

The Hudson Review, 684 Park Avenue, New York, N.Y. 10021

Indiana Review, 316 North Jordan Avenue, Bloomington, Ind. 47405

Iowa Review, EPB 453, University of Iowa, Iowa City, Iowa 52240

Kansas Quarterly, Department of English, Kansas State University, Manhattan, Kans. 66506

The Kenyon Review, Kenyon College, Gambier, Ohio 43022

Ladies' Home Journal, 641 Lexington Avenue, New York, N.Y. 10022

The Literary Review, Fairleigh Dickinson University, Teaneck, N.J. 07666

Mademoiselle, 350 Madison Avenue, New York, N.Y. 10017

The Magazine of Fantasy and Science Fiction, Box 56, Cornwall, Conn. 06753

Magical Blend, P.O. Box 11303, San Francisco, Calif. 94010

Malahat Review, University of Victoria, Victoria, B.C., Canada V8W 2Y2

The Massachusetts Review, Memorial Hall, University of Massachusetts, Amherst, Mass. 01002

McCall's, 230 Park Avenue, New York, N.Y. 10017

Medical Heritage, Georgetown University Hospital, 3800 Reservoir Road, N.W., Washington, D.C. 20007

Memphis State Review, Department of English, Memphis State University, Memphis, Tenn. 38152

Michigan Quarterly Review, 3032 Rackham Building, University of Michigan, Ann Arbor, Mich. 48109

Mid-American Review, 106 Hanna Hall, Bowling Green State University, Bowling Green, Ohio 43403

Midstream, 515 Park Avenue, New York, N.Y. 10022

The Missouri Review, Department of English, 231 Arts and Sciences, University of Missouri, Columbia, Mo. 65211

Mother Jones, 1663 Mission Street, San Francisco, Calif. 94103

MSS, State University of New York at Binghamton, Binghamton, N.Y. 13901

The Nebraska Review, The Creative Writing Program, University of Nebraska–Omaha, Omaha, Neb. 68182–0324

New America, Dept. of English Language and Literature, Humanities Bldg. 217, Albuquerque, N.M. 87131

The New Black Mask, 2006 Sumter Street, Columbia, S.C. 29201

New Directions, 80 Eighth Avenue, New York, N.Y. 10011

New England Review and Breadloaf Quarterly, Box 179, Hanover, N.H. 03755

New Letters, University of Missouri–Kansas City, Kansas City, Mo. 64110

New Mexico Humanities Review, The Editors, Box A, New Mexico Tech., Socorro, N.M. 57801

The New Renaissance, 9 Heath Road, Arlington, Mass. 02174

The New Yorker, 25 West 43rd, New York, N.Y. 10036

The North American Review, University of Northern Iowa, 1222 West 27th Street, Cedar Falls, Iowa 50613

Northwest Review, 129 French Hall, University of Oregon, Eugene, Ore. 97403

Ohio Journal, The Ohio State University, Dept. of English, 164 W. 17th Ave., Columbus, Ohio 43210

The Ohio Review, Ellis Hall, Ohio University, Athens, Ohio 45701
Omni, 1965 Broadway, New York, N.Y. 10067
The Ontario Review, 9 Honey Brook Drive, Princeton, N.J. 08540
Orim, Box 1904A, Yale Station, New Haven, Conn. 06520
Other Voices, 820 Ridge Road, Highland Park, Ill. 60035
The Paris Review, 541 East 72nd Street, New York, N.Y. 10021
The Partisan Review, 128 Bay State Road, Boston, Mass. 02215/552 Fifth Avenue, New York, N.Y. 10036
Passages North, William Bonifas Fine Arts Center, 7th Street and 1st Avenue South, Escanaba, Mich. 49829
The Pennsylvania Review, University of Pittsburgh, Department of English, 526 C.L., Pittsburgh, Penn. 15260
Phylon, 223 Chestnut Street, S.W., Atlanta, Ga. 30314
Playboy, 919 North Michigan Avenue, Chicago, Ill. 60611
Playgirl, 3420 Ocean Park Boulevard, Suite 3000, Santa Monica, Calif. 90405
Ploughshares, Box 529, Cambridge, Mass. 02139
Prairie Schooner, Andrews Hall, University of Nebraska, Lincoln, Neb. 68588
Puerto Del Sol, English Dept., New Mexico State University, Box 3E, Las Cruces, N.M. 88003
Quarterly West, 312 Olpin Union, University of Utah, Salt Lake City, Utah 84112
Raritan, 165 College Avenue, New Brunswick, N.J. 08903
Reconstructionist, Church Road and Greenwood Avenue, Wyncote, Penn. 19095
Redbook, 230 Park Avenue, New York, N.Y. 10017
River City Review, P.O. Box 34275, Louisville, Ky. 40232
Salamagundi, Skidmore College, Saratoga Springs, N.Y. 12866
The Seneca Review, P.O. Box 115, Hobart and William Smith College, Geneva, N.Y. 14456
Sequoia, Storke Student Publications Building, Stanford, Calif. 94305
Seventeen, 850 Third Avenue, New York, N.Y. 10022
The Sewanee Review, University of the South, Sewanee, Tenn. 37375
Shenandoah: The Washington and Lee University Review, Box 722, Lexington, Va. 24450
Sinister Wisdom, P.O. Box 1023, Rockland, Maine 04841
Sojourner: The Women's Forum, 143 Albany Street, Cambridge, Mass. 02139
Sonora Review, Dept. of English, University of Arizona, Tucson, Ariz. 85721
The South Carolina Review, Department of English, Clemson University, Clemson, S.C. 29631
South Dakota Review, Box 111, University Exchange, Vermillion, S.D. 57069
Southern Humanities Review, Auburn University, Auburn, Ala. 36830
The Southern Review, Drawer D, University Station, Baton Rouge, La. 70803
Southwest Review, Southern Methodist University Press, Dallas, Tex. 75275
Stories, 14 Beacon Street, Boston, Mass. 02108

Story Quarterly, P.O. Box 1416, Northbrook, Ill. 60062

St. Andrews Review, St. Andrews Presbyterian College, Laurinburg, N.C. 28352

St. Anthony Messenger, 1615 Republic Street, Cincinnati, Ohio 45210-1298

The Texas Review, English Dept., Sam Houston University, Huntsville, Tex. 77341

This World, San Francisco Chronicle, 901 Mission Street, San Francisco, Calif. 94103

The Threepenny Review, P.O. Box 9131, Berkeley, Calif. 94709

Tikkun, Institute of Labor and Mental Health, 5100 Leona Street, Oakland, Calif. 94619

TriQuarterly, 1735 Benson Avenue, Evanston, Ill. 60201

Twilight Zone, 800 Second Avenue, New York, N.Y. 10017

Twin Cities, 7834 East Bush Lake Road, Minneapolis, Minn. 55435

University of Windsor Review, Department of English, University of Windsor, Windsor, Ont., Canada N9B 3P4

U.S. Catholic, 221 West Madison Street, Chicago, Ill. 60606

Vanity Fair, 350 Madison Avenue, New York, N.Y. 10017

The Virginia Quarterly Review, University of Virginia, 1 West Range, Charlottesville, Va. 22903

Vogue, 350 Madison Avenue, New York, N.Y. 10017

Washington Review, Box 50132, Washington, D.C. 20004

Webster Review, Webster College, Webster Groves, Mo. 63119

West Coast Review, Simon Fraser University, Burnaby, B.C., Canada V5A 1S6

Western Humanities Review, Building 41, University of Utah, Salt Lake City, Utah 84112

Wind, RFD Route 1, Box 809, Pikeville, Ky. 41501

Woman's Day, 1515 Broadway, New York, N.Y. 10036

Writer's Forum, University of Colorado, Colorado Springs, Colo. 80907

Yale Review, 250 Church Street, 1902A Yale Station, New Haven, Conn. 06520

Yankee, Dublin, N.H. 03444

Zyzzyva, 55 Sutter Street, Suite 400, San Francisco, Calif. 94104